SILVER BLOOD

THE BLOOD SERIES, BOOK TWO

TAMARA WHITE

CONTENTS

Silver Blood

The Blood Series, Book Two

Tamara White

This book is for all the readers out there who have showed me such an overwhelming support in continuing this series. I can only hope it lives up your expectations.
I also want to take the time to thank my editor, Rach. She's spent hours upon hours on this book, trying to get it to its best and she truly surpassed all my expectations. And despite the fact that the Google docs wanted to break us, we did it girl. Now onto the next one xx

Chapter One

CONSEQUENCES

EMERALD

*W*armth envelops me, and I smile at the feeling of peace that blossoms within me. I could get used to this.

"Come on, babe. Time to get up."

I ignore Talon, pretending I'm still fast asleep, desperate for just a few more minutes of rest before getting up. A hand touches my shoulder, nudging me insistently. "Em, I know you're awake," Talon says sternly. Despite his harsh tone, I can easily imagine the smile on his face as he looks down at me lying there with my eyes clamped shut to avoid getting out of bed.

Groaning, I snuggle in closer to the body at my back. "I don't wanna wake up. It's so warm and comfortable. I'm just going to stay here a little longer." I sigh contentedly, smiling when the arms around me squeeze me tighter.

"Yeah, go away, man. She wants to snuggle with me. Go do something productive," Dev murmurs into my hair, and I smile lazily. This is how life should be.

The sound of the bedroom door opening makes me want to take a quick peek, but I resist, at least until the bitter scent of coffee becomes so strong that I know it's right in front of me. My eyes snap open to see Nik smiling down at me, holding out a cup of coffee like a peace offering.

"I thought you might need this." He winks, placing the mug on the small table beside Dev's bed.

1

"Really? You'll open your eyes for coffee but not for me?" Talon mock glares down at me.

I poke my tongue out, unable to resist teasing him. "Yep. Maybe you should take notes. Note number one, do not wake me without some kind of offering, unless you want to be ignored."

Nik chuckles as I wiggle out of Dev's arms and into a sitting position. Dev lets me go with a groan and rolls away, beginning to drift off again almost immediately. Talon shakes his head and grabs Dev by the ankle, yanking him off the bed and sending him crashing to the floor with a thump.

"Dude, what the fuck?!" Dev gets to his feet, glaring at Talon, who just grins. I think he would have done the same to me, but knew the others would stop him before he could.

Dev turns away, and storms into the bathroom. I hear him mutter under his breath, "Dude needs to get laid," before slamming the door behind him.

I turn my attention back to Talon with a smirk on my face. "You know he's not gonna forget that, right?"

He shrugs his shoulders, smiling broadly. "I'm not afraid of his payback. Nik, however, is someone you have to watch out for. He likes to get even on a whole other level."

My gaze swings to Nik, who is sitting on his bed, watching the conversation with a look of amusement. He simply shrugs with a wicked grin, not disputing Talon's claim.

I shake my head at them, reaching for my coffee and inhaling it with a moan. "God, this smells amazing! What did you do to it?" I ask Nik before taking a sip. After I swallow the liquid, I understand. "You added your blood to this?"

"Yeah, does it taste okay? I wasn't sure if you would like it or not," he admits with a sheepish grin.

I take another sip, a soft moan crossing my lips. "Well, I think it's divine."

He smirks in triumph. A moment later, Talon joins him on the bed, taking a seat beside him. They wait in silence, letting me drink my coffee in peace. As I'm swallowing the last mouthful, Dev comes out of the bathroom, looking more alert but still irritated. "Okay, now why did you wake us up?"

Nik gets up from the bed and sits down at my feet. He gently grabs my left foot and picks it up, beginning to massage it slowly. I try not to moan, but a small whimper slips free as he applies pressure to the arch. It feels incredible, and I have to fight to keep my gaze on him when he speaks.

"We were summoned by the Queen." He applies a little pressure to the heel of my foot, and my eyes close unconsciously. "She has something to discuss with us, but we asked her if we could meet here to talk about it instead. That way you don't have to leave right now. We can't quite let you out of our sights just yet. Besides, I imagine you're still tired from everything that happened."

He moves onto my other foot while I think about what he said. You'd think after dying and coming back to life, there would be some kind of negative side effect, but there's been nothing. If anything, I feel rejuvenated and more powerful than ever.

Nik finishes massaging my right foot, and I wiggle my toes appreciatively.

"In ten minutes, everyone will be here. We thought it may be a good idea if you're dressed when they arrive."

I look down at my pajamas and frown. They're super comfy, and I don't particularly want to get changed if I don't have to.

"Can't I just wear these?" I pout up at Talon.

He smothers a smile before replying. "If you want to, but your parents will be there, as well as Britt and her husbands. Are you sure you want them to see you in your cute bunny pajamas?"

I sigh and put down my empty cup. "Fine, I'll get dressed. But don't think I'm happy about having to wear a bra."

All the guys share grins and Dev moves closer, his eyes hooded with lust. "You know, if bras really bother you so much, I'd be happy to help you remove it right after the meeting if you'd like."

He leans over the vacant side of the bed to hover closer to me. I'm keenly aware of Nik and Tal watching us to see how I respond.

I lick my lips in anticipation and move up to my knees. Dev's gaze flicks down to my pajamas where the top button is undone, allowing him to catch a glimpse of cleavage, before coming back up to meet my eyes in challenge.

I move an inch closer until I'm mere breaths away from his lips. I gently press my lips to his, enjoying the groan that escapes his lips. Echoing groans sound from nearby as Talon and Nik watch the whole show and I pull back with a teasing smirk.

Dev looks up at me with a look of confusion as I get up from the bed. I move to the bags that house what few belongings I brought with me, grabbing out a set of clothes and walking towards the bathroom. I pause at the door before turning back to the guys. "I'd better get dressed. You know, bra and all." I wink at them before stepping into the bathroom, shutting the door behind me.

I giggle to myself at the sound of Dev's loud groan, which is followed by the sound of what I think was a pillow smacking into his face.

I can hear Nik's voice, even through the door, and I have to fight not to laugh. "It's your own fault, Dev. What did you honestly think would happen when you teased her like that? That she'd just fall at your feet and say, 'Take me Dev. I'm at your mercy?'"

Dev remains silent, which only makes Talon and Nik burst out laughing. I smile and tune them out while I get dressed. When I walk back out of the bathroom, Talon is the only one waiting for me. He guides me out into the main area where everyone has gathered, sitting in various spots around the room, or in the case of Britt and her husbands, leaning against the wall.

Macy, along with my mother and father, are all squished together on one of the sofas, with Nik and Dev on the matching one opposite them. That leaves only the recliner, which Talon walks me over to, taking a seat and pulling me into his lap. I squirm a little at such a blatant sign of affection in front of so many.

My mother smiles over at me, which helps ease the discomfort, and I notice the small cup in her hand. I would absolutely kill for another coffee to go with this meeting. I go to move, but Talon tightens his hold on me. Before I can get upset, Nik jumps to his feet and hands me a steaming cup. "Already got you one, Em."

I inhale deeply, savoring the rich aroma, before greedily gulping it down to the sound of chuckles from all around me. I don't care what they say, coffee is life.

After I finish the cup, I hand it back to Nik with a grateful smile. He places the mug on the table in front of him and moves back to the couch, sitting close enough this time to reach out and take my hand in his. I smile at him fondly before turning my attention to my parents. "So, what's up? Why did you need to call a meeting?"

My mother gives a small smile, her gaze lingering on the spot where Nik is stroking his thumb over my hand. "Well technically, you weren't summoned. Only Talon, Nikoli, and Devin were. I think they just didn't want to leave you alone."

Dev leans back in his spot and turns to look at me, his eyes warming when they meet mine. "Can you really blame us, Sie?"

My mother smiles back at him and shakes her head. "No, I don't."

My father coughs, drawing our attention. He looks towards Talon and I with a grim smile. "You've been summoned by the local pack. They found the three wolves you killed. One survived, however, and is refusing to say anything other than the fact that a trio of vamps attacked him. The Alpha wants an explanation for your actions."

Talon shifts angrily, and if I weren't in his lap, I'm sure he would have stood to stare down at them defiantly. As it is, I can feel the anger radiating from him through our bond.

"What? Those rogues are wolves so it should have been taken care of before they got near Em. In fact how the hell did the Alpha not know they were in his territory? They nearly killed Em! And now they want to lay charges against us for something they should have been on top of?"

My mother sighs and clasps her hands in her lap. "Talon, you know the rules as well as we do. We should have informed them of the attack, but with all the drama that happened, we simply forgot. The treaty between our kind was implemented for a reason. If we deny them this, then we open ourselves to attack and run the risk of being removed from the treaty entirely. You'll just have to suck it up and go to the meeting. I doubt there will be any repercussions since the Alpha is one of the more progressive leaders of our time. If anything, I think he will just ask to be involved in any future executions."

That calms Talon down and he leans back in the seat, relaxing once more. He waits for them to speak again, but Britt interrupts. "Can someone make some more coffee? It's too early for this type of hardcore topic without caffeine."

Nik goes to stand, but I grip his hand, keeping him in place. "I'll do it."

I climb up from Talon's lap and let go of Nik's hand before walking over to the opposite side of the room to begin making coffee.

Britt joins me as I busy myself preparing a fresh pot. "So, you settling in okay?" she asks as I lean against the counter while waiting for the coffee beans to grind.

I shrug and look over at the others, who are all discussing something, but I choose to tune them out. "Yeah, I guess. I mean, sometimes it's still weird to think about the fact I'm some kind of cross between two species and that I have three soul-ties. I'm still plagued with questions. One being, if I have three soul-ties, do you think I might have a shifter mate out there as well?"

She considers it for a moment before responding. "I guess so. After all, Talon, Nik, and Dev are your soul-ties, but that's only one side of you. You could have a mate, or even mates out there for your wolf side too. Oh, do you think it could be the Alpha the guys have been summoned to meet with?" she asks, a dreamy look on her face.

Blaine approaches us, coming over to Britt's side and poking her in the ribs playfully. "B, we can all see you fantasizing over the Alpha. Maybe tone it down a little?" he suggests, before taking the first pot of coffee I made and returning to the group.

She sticks her tongue out at his back as he leaves, and turns back to me with a wicked gleam in her eyes. "Seriously, Mer, if the Alpha is your mate, I'm going to be super jealous."

I shake my head at her. "Well, you can have him then. I'm perfectly happy with the men I already have."

Once the second pot of coffee is ready, I take it to the table, hoping that the two pots will be enough. None of Britt's husbands touch the coffee and only Britt, my father, and I reach for refills. So, maybe I made too much. Oh well. There's no such thing as too much coffee.

I squeeze between Nik and Dev, sensing Talon needs a bit of space. Whatever they were talking about obviously hasn't improved his mood at all.

Talon leans forward in his chair and looks at my father, his voice intense as he speaks. "Have you talked to the council about bringing Em's old pack up on charges? I can look through our files for a suitable neutral territory to hold the meeting." His eyes are filled with an anger I haven't seen since the night I died.

My mother and father exchange glances and I know immediately Talon isn't going to like what they have to say. The way my father acts reminds me so much of my dad back home. The moment he straightened his back, I could tell it was bad news. The subtle shift of his knees as he moves into a more defensive position. The way he holds his hands beside himself to appear non-threatening, while at the same time being prepared to fight. It's very much the way an Alpha is supposed to act. Submissive when the situation calls for it, but able to do what's needed to keep the pack in line.

"Talon, we aren't pressing charges yet. We need everyone to think Emerald's dead right now. We don't know what kind of effect this new development will have on the community. She has three soul-ties and can come back from the dead. If people learn of this, then who knows how they'll react? We need to ease them into the news that she's still alive, so we can minimize the fallout."

He pauses, and my mother takes over. "Before you get your knickers in a twist, Talon, we are going to bring them up on charges. Don't think I will let what they did to my daughter go without serious repercussions. We just want to let Emerald settle into her new life first. Her pack isn't going anywhere, so it won't matter if we delay for a few days."

Before Talon has a chance to respond, a knock sounds at the door. Dev gets up to answer it, opening the door so a tall man can come in.

The stranger directs his gaze to my mother, bowing slightly while completely ignoring the rest of the room. "I'm sorry to interrupt, my Queen, but your interviews commence in thirty minutes. I took the liberty of gathering all the files you'll need to review beforehand."

She nods regally. "Thank you, Jasper. We'll be there in a moment."

With that, he nods and takes his leave, exiting the room without so much as a backward glance at any of us. *Rude much!*

I glance at my mom with a raised eyebrow, and she chuckles. "Jasper is very old school. He only speaks to those he deems are worthy of his time. It took three years before he would even look at Axel."

I smile and look down at my hands, knowing that it could be worse. I imagine a few of the vamp covens out there aren't going to be happy learn of my existence.

"Speaking of old school. Emerald, I would like to discuss the possibility of you attending lessons in order to learn what will be expected of you. As a Princess of our coven, you will be expected to know certain things, and being tutored in the matter is the only thing I could think of to quickly get you caught up on our society and its rules."

Oh shit. I'll actually have to do royal duties? That's going to be an epic suck fest.

My father gets to his feet, and everyone in the room follows suit, including me. He takes a step towards me, obviously intending to hug me, but then seems to think better of it. Instead, he claps a hand on my right shoulder, giving me a comforting squeeze. He lets go just as quickly, moving aside so my mother can pull me into a hug, squeezing me tightly.

Before she lets go, I ask, "Do you want to get lunch later? It might be a good time for us to talk about my lessons?" Seeing the hopeful light in my mother's eyes makes it all worth it.

"I would love that, darling!" The massive grin on her face makes her appear years younger than I know she is. I smile back at her as she and my father get up to leave. As she walks, she has a spring in her step. My father turns back to look at me, mouthing 'thank you.'

Macy leaves right after, giving us a small goodbye as she goes. She hurries to catch up to my mother, and they laugh as they stroll down the hall together. They are obviously good friends, and I'm glad my mother has someone she can talk to.

Britt comes over to me while her husbands are busy offering the guys words of support about the impending pack meeting.

She hugs me fiercely, and I return the embrace just as eagerly. I've missed her so much and every time she leaves, I wonder how long it will be until the next time I get to see her.

"I'll talk to you soon." She pulls away with a grin. "My men and I are going to eat some human food. You vamps and your schedules always throw me off. It makes me hungry," she says with a groan, and I roll my eyes.

"Britt, you're always hungry."

She shrugs shamelessly. "Meh. I need food. And who knows, maybe I can convince my husbands to feed me dessert." She winks at me.

I can't help the bark of laughter that escapes. "I'm sure you could convince them to do anything."

She turns when Torie summons her from where he's standing by the door. I shoo her away, shaking my head as she struts towards him. I can see Torie's eyes filling with lust as he watches her.

After the room has emptied, I shut the door and turn to see Talon leaning back in his chair, looking completely exhausted.

I walk over to him and press my hand to his forehead, noticing that his skin feels clammy. "When was the last time you fed?" I ask, concerned by the defeated look he gives me.

Nik joins me, looking down at Talon. "You should have fed already, man. Come on, I gotta check the security tapes. I'll drop you at the feeding room on the way," he says, pulling Talon to his feet.

Talon wobbles a bit, pushing away from Nik, clearly preferring to remain on his own two feet. I imagine he needs to maintain his tough image among the coven, especially as they're considered the guards of royalty. It wouldn't be good for them to be seen as weak when they protect such important people.

"What about Em? She still needs to be fed too," Talon points out.

Dev wraps an arm around my waist and pulls me close to smell my neck. "Don't worry, I can feed her. Can you bring me back some bags, though? I'm gonna need to replenish," he says, his voice filled with desire.

I roll my eyes, shaking my head at them. "Okay, while you three discuss what's happening, I'm going to have a shower. Whoever stays behind is welcome to join me."

I mimic Britt and strut into the bedroom. Once inside, I frantically try to calm my racing heart. What was I thinking challenging them like that?

Chapter Two

NEED

EMERALD

The water runs over me, and I relax under the hot spray. I hear the bathroom door open and smirk a moment later when I feel hands move to my hips, and a body pressing behind me. I lean my head back and meet Dev's hazel eyes.

He smiles before pressing his lips to mine, and I sink into his touch. He reaches for a sponge on the shelf, dousing it in the shower gel closest to him.

"May I?" he asks, his voice filled with desire.

I nod, unable to speak. He lathers the gel into foamy bubbles and begins to slowly move the sponge over my neck and collarbone. His moves are deliberate and painfully slow, inching along at a tortuous pace. He shifts to my breasts, avoiding my nipples as he focuses on the task at hand.

Meanwhile, I feel pressure building inside me, the need to be touched rising. As he moves over each delicate bit of my skin, the energy builds within me. I let him do what he wants, while reaching down to cup him in my hands, but he pulls away with a smirk. "No, Em, this is for you."

I groan and let him continue working his way down my body, setting my nerves alight as he goes. As he gets to my waist, he pauses to watch me before he moves lower. His thumb brushes against my clit, and I fight the urge to jerk in response.

He drops to his knees, moving my legs apart in order to thoroughly clean me, and I moan as he touches my most intimate parts. The care he exhibits has me panting with desire. I need him to touch me. Something, anything to relieve that pressure building inside me.

He moves on and I whimper, feeling the sudden loss of his touch where I need it most. He continues cleaning down my legs and reaches my toes before making me turn around. He works his way from my ankles back up again; the slowness with which he moves is driving me crazy. When he finishes washing my back, he presses his body against me. I bet he can hear the racing of my heart, but I'm powerless to stop my reaction to him.

"What's wrong, Em? Do you need something?" he purrs, moving his hands over my hips, reaching around to my front and slowly sliding over my clit. His touch is light, his thumb moving in circular motions before dipping down to tease my entrance. But all too soon, he's coming back up again and I'm left wanting.

"Please," I beg, as he deliberately avoids my entrance yet again. I feel him smirk against my shoulder as he places a delicate kiss in the crook of my neck.

"Tell me what you want," he murmurs, his voice easily heard over the sound of the water.

"I want you to touch me," I pant, my arousal building with each second we're apart. "I want your fingers inside me, bringing me to the edge of oblivion. I want you to turn me around, lift one of my legs up around you, and fuck me until I forget my own name. I want you, Dev."

I turn in his arms and see his eyes are filled with lust. "What's wrong, Dev? Not what you wanted to hear?"

He growls, pressing into my lips greedily. He continues to kiss me for a long moment, before moving gently to my collarbone. He pulls away with a groan. "I have to feed you."

I feel the bloodlust rising within me, and know my eyes have turned red at the mention of blood. He smirks, cocking his head to the side to give me the access I need.

I lick along his skin, relishing in the shudder that runs through him. He moves a hand between us to stroke my clit. As I bite into his skin and begin drinking my fill, he slips two fingers inside me. It takes all my willpower to keep from throwing my head back in ecstasy. Instead, I growl through my lips as I drink the blood he's freely giving me.

He keeps thrusting into me with his fingers, my orgasm quickly building between his touch and the taste of him, until it's like fireworks behind my eyes.

Once I'm satiated, I pull away from him, licking away the blood that trails down his neck. I smile and place a gentle kiss on his lips before washing off the fluids that are on me. I guess pleasing me must have been just as exciting for Dev, because he came when I did.

We get out of the shower and I try to grab the towel, but Dev takes it, holding it out of reach.

"Let me take care of you!" Dev says, sounding irritated.

I throw my hands up, my naked body on full display. "Dev, I can dry myself. Just give me the towel."

He gives me a pointed look and keeps it out of reach. I sigh, giving in. "Fine! But for the record, I let you dry me. You didn't win this."

He cocks his head with a smirk and begins to dry me, using the same amount of care as when he washed me in the shower.

After drying off, we move into the bedroom. I dig through the clothes I brought with me, finding a matching red lacy bra and underwear set, which I put on. I bend down to look through my bags for clothes to wear for the day when I hear a sharp gasp from behind me.

I spin around to see Talon in the doorway, taking in every exposed inch of my body with a hungry look. I cock my hip to the side. "See something you like?" I challenge.

He hands Dev the blood bags and stalks towards me.

Unconsciously, I take a step back as he gets closer, the feral gleam in his eyes making me nervous. He stops abruptly a few feet from me and inhales deeply.

"Damn. You just had to do it, didn't you?" he asks Dev, his voice laced with humor.

Dev just shrugs innocently. "Not my fault if feeding and sex emit the same pheromones. Besides, if you had taken care of yourself rather than acting like a whiny girl locking yourself in your room, then you could have been the one here to take care of Em's needs."

I look back and forth between them, not quite sure if I understand what they're going on about. It almost sounds as if Talon knows what happened in the shower.

A flashback of Dev's hands on me has me feeling flushed and Talon groans, moving away just as Nik walks into our room and freezes. He sniffs the air and groans just as Talon did, his lust-filled eyes zeroing in on me. I realize they can smell it on me and give an exasperated sigh. And here I thought living with wolves was bad.

Nik strides straight towards me, not stopping until his lips slam down on mine. I moan in anticipation of what's to come, only to realize we have an audience. I push away, panting. Each of them is watching me with the same intense hunger in their eyes.

"Okay, I'm going to take a cold shower. Alone!" I declare to the room. Without waiting for a response, I stomp back into the bathroom, remembering to take my clothes with me. I don't want another repeat of what just happened.

I turn the shower to cold and search for the strongest smelling body wash I can find, lathering it over myself. Hopefully, it will help mask the scent. I really don't want my mother or father to smell the arousal on me.

That's something no one wants.

JEREMY

THE SUN SETS OVER THE MOUNTAINS AS I WAIT FOR MY STUDENTS TO meet me.

I gave them one job. To rid us of the abomination that had been hiding under our noses the whole time.

Brent tried to appeal to the council, and while most of them remained neutral, I know the threat she poses. If interspecies breeding is possible, it's only a matter of time before they start allowing mixed-species relationships. And that's something I can't allow to happen.

When Xander told me of her bright red eyes, I thought he must have been mistaken, but that pup was terrified of what he'd seen so I decided to look into the matter myself. I thought I could deal with the problem before it ever reached the council, but our traitorous Alpha had been too soft on her, letting her run back to her parents.

He thought we would go easy on her because she's the rightful Alpha's daughter, but that doesn't mean she isn't still the child of a vampire.

He knew what she was the entire time. The only reason he's still Alpha is because his abomination didn't once hurt the pack. The council thinks that if he could control her all her life, then he can control her if she ever decides to come back. They think she could be the perfect weapon if a war between our species breaks out, but I know the truth. She will be the reason war unfolds on us in the first place. She will be our downfall not our savior.

I at least knew the truth and decided to act. I sent my two best fighters to dispatch the threat.

As if my thoughts summon them, I see the two of them loping up the hillside to my cabin, each of them appearing rejuvenated. Xander was well aware of my plan and while Brendan was more hesitant when I spoke of the mission, he still volunteered which cemented his loyalty to me.

They shift back to human, taking the clothes I offer them. Xander grins at me, his eyes filled with joy. That's one of the reasons I picked him for the mission He hates the abomination just as much as I do, so I knew he would not fail me.

"Well?" I wait for a debriefing, but Xander seems to defer to Brendan, waiting for him to speak.

Brendan's eyes show reluctance, and I fear he will tell me he failed, but why would Xander appear so overjoyed if that were the case?

Maybe Brendan is just suffering from a little guilty conscience. After all, he still believes the abomination is his sister.

"I hope you have good news for me?"

Brendan remains silent, his gaze fixed to the ground.

I turn my attention to Xander, who's still grinning ear from ear. "The bitch is dead. Brendan staked her when her back was turned. I got us out of there before they could retaliate. Her stupid guard was too distracted with her dying to do anything. It was sickening to watch."

The pure exuberance in his voice as he speaks make me proud to have chosen him. He's bloodthirsty, but knows what must be done.

A slow smile spreads across my lips, and I find myself unable to hide my relief. She is no longer a threat to our way of life.

"Very good," I praise, clapping him on the shoulder. Brendan refuses to meet my eyes, and I begin to wonder if I chose the wrong person to fulfil this mission. I need strong men at my side, but he seems to have a guilty conscience over what he's done. I need him to be willing to do what's needed in the days to come.

My phone rings in my pocket, and I nod to the boys. "Go back to the pack. Enjoy your success."

I answer the phone, and the voice comes out clear as if the person on the other end was standing right in front of me. "You failed."

My heart stops for a moment before I smirk.

"My boys told me the girl is dead. How is that a failure?" I ask, using the same neutral tone I did the first time we met.

"The girl lives. She has three soul-ties bound to her. Your pups failed."

The phone goes quiet letting me know my spy has hung up, and I grip it tighter, hearing the screen crack. She was staked. How the hell is she still alive?

I've heard rumors of some of our species having multiple mates, and I curse the fact I underestimated her.

I turn and punch a nearby tree, letting my wolf rip from my body. The need to hunt and kill grips me as I run through the woods, seeking out my prey. I pounce, ripping into the doe's throat, wishing it was the abomination being torn apart with my teeth.

Soon I'll make her pay. She shouldn't exist. I will right the mistake our Alpha made before war breaks out among us all. He should have killed her while she was a child. Because he was too soft to do what needed to be done, now I must find an ally, someone who can help me destroy an immortal.

Chapter Three

MOTHER

EMERALD

I can't help fidgeting in the clothes I'm wearing. I'm having a meeting with the Queen of the vampire coven, who is also my mother. I wasn't sure if I was supposed to dress casual or fancy. I don't think it would have mattered either way, but I still fretted over it.

I dressed in my nicest jeans and was lucky enough to find a pale green button-up top. It was the fanciest thing I had hiding in my bags. I didn't even have time to find an iron after my second shower, so I keep smoothing down the top with my hands when the nerves rise, which is fairly often.

I knock on the door to her suite, and just hope I look good enough.

The door opens and my father steps out into the hall with a grin. "Go on in, Emerald. She's waiting for you." He winks before walking down the hall the way I came.

I step inside and can't help the smile that crosses my face. My mother is rushing around, trying to tidy her quarters up. She's got a pitcher of lemonade sitting on the table and keeps fluffing up cushions, only to come back and fluff them again. I hover in the doorway, watching her go around the room doing various things such as straightening pictures, moving the plants, and rearranging the cushions five times before I make my presence known.

Seeing her nervous goes a long way to easing my own anxiety.

"Sierra?" I call out, stopping her in her tracks as she goes to move the picture frame again. As much as I want to call her 'Mom,' it feels too soon for that. Even calling her 'Sierra' felt off, but I can't think of a good alternative.

She spins around to face me, a grin plastered on her face. "Emerald, darling. Sorry, I guess I got a little carried away," she says nervously. She wrings her hands together, anxiously wiping her sweaty hands on her pants, and I hold back my urge to smile. Nice to know even vampire Queens can become nervous.

I take a step forward, feeling just as nervous as she looks. "If this is too soon for you, we can always reschedule?"

Her face softens and she steps closer. "Emerald, I would never dream of making you leave. I've waited your whole life to meet you. Any longer would be too long. I just want to spend time with you. I will admit, I'm nervous, but that's not your fault. That's all me. I fear that I won't live up to your expectations." She takes a deep breath before meeting my eyes with a look of fierce determination. "Come, sit. We'll order you some food."

We both sit down, and she pours me a glass of lemonade, pushing it across the table towards me. I take it gratefully as she goes to pour herself a glass as well. I watch, fascinated as she drinks it.

She puts the glass down with a grin. "I take it you didn't know we could drink liquids?"

I look down, letting my hair fall down over my face to hide my flush. "Sorry, I didn't mean to stare."

I guess not being a part of their coven, and with my pack hating vampires as much as they do, I never learned most of the things they could do. I just assumed they were like the vampires you read about in books. You know, the 'burn to flames in the sunlight, can't eat or drink, and no heartbeat' kind of vampires.

"It's natural for you to be curious about my kind. Our kind. If you have any questions, I will be happy to answer them," she offers with a soft smile.

I nod eagerly. "Yeah, that would be awesome. I know some things from the time I've spent with the guys, but it's hard to separate the myths from the facts. It would be nice to know exactly what is and isn't dangerous at the very least."

She leans over to the side table by her seat and grabs the cordless phone. "How about I order you some food first? What are you feeling? Pizza? There's an amazing restaurant down the street that delivers. They have this insanely good garlic bread from what I hear."

I snigger at the mention of garlic bread. "Won't that be lethal to you?" I ask, holding back a laugh.

She grins. "Ha! Only to your father! He hates garlic! Says the odor is too strong for his wolf senses."

"Sorry, I couldn't help it. But yes, pizza would be lovely," I respond with a smile.

I remain silent as she calls down for a pizza. She puts her hand over the mouthpiece. "What kind would you like?" she whispers, as if just realizing there's more than one type of pizza.

"Pepperoni," I reply with a broad grin.

With that, she goes back to placing her order with the person on the phone. When she hangs up, she turns to me with a smile. "The pizza will be here in about twenty minutes. In the meantime, why don't I fill you in on a few of our myths?"

I nod excitedly. "Okay, so I take it the garlic thing is a definite no then?"

She shakes her head with a look of amusement. "Nope, garlic is just a myth. It has a very strong scent, though, and as I'm sure you've noticed, vampires and wolves have an incredibly keen sense of smell. Personally, I think that's where the myth came from. Some idiotic vampire was probably just turned off feeding on a human after they ate too much garlic."

Interesting. I guess it makes sense, though. I actually don't mind garlic in my food, so at least I know I won't have to boycott it all together.

My mother continues listing off the facts and fiction of vampire kind. "Holy water is a myth, too. It may as well just be water. Then there's crosses. They do absolutely nothing to us."

I tick off everything in my mind, and suddenly a thought occurs.

"But what about a wooden stake? I died after being stabbed in the heart with a wooden stake, so that can't be myth."

Her face goes serious, and I immediately regret mentioning it, but before I can apologize, she explains. "Emerald, you died because you were stabbed through the heart. Anyone will die if they get stabbed through the heart, and vampires are no exception. A stake just happened to be their weapon of choice. Stakes have no other effect on us, other than being an ideal weapon to stab us through the heart with. The only other way a wolf, vampire, or witch can die is to be decapitated. It's a lot easier to carry around a stake than a sword."

I nod, deep in thought. So, my brother just happened to have a stake on his person when he called me to meet? That's just hard to believe. Maybe Xander had it, and Brendan took it from him? It's not much better, but at least then I can hold on to the hope that my own brother hadn't set out planning to kill me that night.

"As for silver, well that myth started very early on in our kind. According to our oldest histories, silver was believed to be pure and was said to contain mystical properties, so humans came up with the foolish idea it would protect them from us. Years ago, silver was used in mirrors, which was around the time the whole 'we don't have a reflection' nonsense started. It was just a few tricksters among our kind, moving too fast for the humans to see their reflections. Until one ended up smashing through the mirror, a piece of glass piercing his heart which solidified for the humans that silver could hurt us. It was all fun and games back then, but now, if humans met with one of our kind, the only thing they could do would be to stake us. We'd kill them before they could try anything else."

She pauses as if trying to think of any other myths pertaining to vampires. "Ah! Last, but definitely not least, coffins. We obviously don't sleep in them. We do, however, prefer to remain underground, though. Only because the light from the sun weakens us. We don't burst into flames, but it takes away from our powers. We are slower and easier to kill in the sunlight, so we prefer to remain hidden away where it's safe. I'm a little awed you've survived as well as you did living in the daylight."

She studies me, obviously intrigued, and I try not to squirm under her gaze. It's like she's trying to uncover and pick apart my every secret, but I don't have any answers. I have no idea why the sun doesn't weaken me.

After the quiet gets too much, I clear my throat and meet her eyes. "Can I ask you something? Something personal?"

Surprise shows on her face but her expression quickly softens into a smile that lights up her eyes. "Of course. You can ask me anything, Emerald."

I take a deep breath, unsure how to phrase the question delicately, so I just spit it out. "Why don't you have more children?"

She sucks in a shocked breath, but I plough on, not letting the guilt I feel stop me. "I mean, I'm an adult. You thought I was dead for twenty years, and you obviously healed after everything that happened. I guess I'm just curious why you didn't try for another child at some point."

I look down at my feet before finally meeting her eyes. The pain I see in their depths makes me regret asking, but she steels herself.

"Because you are my daughter. I didn't want to replace you with another child. Your father and I had discussed trying for another child after we had healed from your loss, but it just felt wrong. I wanted you, but I couldn't have you. In my mind, losing you was a sign from whatever gods there are that I wasn't meant to have children."

She smiles sadly and sniffs, obviously trying not to cry. "It didn't help that the community wasn't exactly torn up over your death. If the wolves reacted that way to your birth, I couldn't imagine what they would do if I had another child. I couldn't go through that pain again."

She pauses as a tear rolls down her cheek before she harshly wipes it away. "I am so sorry for everything, Emerald. Your father and I were so excited to find out we were pregnant that we didn't think about how everyone would react. We never comprehended everything you would have to go through and the judgment you would face. We didn't protect you like we should have." She lets out a shaky breath. "I've never been happier than I was when I found out that you were alive and raised with love. I don't even feel any ill will towards Brent for keeping you from us. He did what was necessary to keep you alive, and I'll be forever grateful for that. And now you're here, a strong young woman, ready to start your own family."

I blanch at the thought of children. "Ah... No offense, but children are not in my plans."

She looks at me like I'm naive. "Oh, don't worry, you'll have plenty of time for children, Emerald. I'm sure if Talon has anything to say about it, you'll be pregnant sometime within the next ten years."

She chuckles and pours more lemonade while I just sit there, frozen to the spot.

I'm stuck on the thought of Talon wanting me pregnant within ten years! He didn't strike me as the type of person eager to have children. Dev or Nik maybe, but Talon? He never struck me as the type of guy who would be interested in kids. Or if he was, he'd be the type to keep them locked away in a tower away from anything that could harm them, much like Rapunzel.

Ugh, why am I even thinking about this? I don't even want kids.

My mother leans back in her seat, cradling her glass of lemonade as she watches me. "Is there anything else you would like to ask?"

I think it over for a moment and smile. "How did you and my father meet? I imagine it wouldn't have been easy for a werewolf and vampire to find each other, fall in love, and then also become the rulers of a vampire coven."

She smiles fondly. "No, it wasn't easy. Some days, I wondered whether we were doing the right thing, but your father pushed through, telling me love is love. It didn't matter whether we were different species, we loved each other, and that's all that mattered. I would be lost without him."

A flutter of butterflies erupts in my belly, and I can just imagine how she's feeling. It's very much how I am starting to feel towards each of the guys.

A knock sounds on the door. My mother gets up to answer it, and the smell of pizza assaults my senses.

She closes the door after thanking whoever brought the pizza up to us. Then she brings it over, placing it on the table between us.

My mother walks into another room and returns with a whole pack of paper napkins, putting them on top of the box.

"Do you think that's enough napkins?" I ask wryly.

She tuts. "Your father goes through three times that amount. He hates using cutlery, insisting he can just use napkins. In all honesty, I think he just hates doing the dishes."

I press my lips together, fighting the urge to grin. My father and I have at least one thing in common it seems; we both hate doing dishes. At least napkins can be recycled. Plus, think of all that water I'm saving by not doing dishes.

"Help yourself to some food while I tell you how your father and I met."

I pull out a napkin and open the box, blushing when my stomach growls with hunger. My mother just smiles and waits for me to start eating. It's not until I finish my first slice that she starts speaking.

"Your father and I met while we were on patrol. He was visiting our local pack at the time, when a witch started attacking helpless humans. We were all in the first stages of the treaty so we were split into mixed teams of vampires, wolves and witches to hunt down the one responsible. Your father and I got separated from our groups and ended up stuck in a building together. The witch we were after was controlling dozens of zombies and had managed to surround the entire building. The only way to destroy so many reanimated corpses was with fire, and with no witch to help us, we were trapped.

"I remembered about a tunnel under the building that I had used many times as a teen to get out of the coven. I knew if we could just get to it, we could follow the sewer system. We were partway through it when the building exploded. I passed out in the explosion, and when I came to, your father was trying to dig us free."

She pauses, lost in the memory for a long moment before her eyes clear, and she comes back to the present. "The tunnel had collapsed in both directions, and no matter how many times we tried to dig our way out, it was no use. We knew we were going to die."

I take a sip of lemonade while reaching for another slice of pizza, completely entranced by the story.

"After three days trapped down there without having fed, I finally attacked him. The bloodlust had grown too strong to ignore, but instead of fighting me off, or killing me, which he should have, he used a sharp rock to slice into the side of his neck. He let me feed from him until he was near death. It was one of the few moments in my life I was truly scared. My hunger was so strong that I had no clue if I would be able to stop myself from killing him.

"After I fed, I was back to my normal strength, maybe even stronger. Your father was unconscious, however, and I resolved myself to get us out of there. I began to slowly dig, moving the rubble away from the tunnel entrance that led to the sewer. After about an hour, I heard the sound of people calling my name.

"Melanie had been looking for me since I went missing, using my magical signature to track me. She brought me blood, assuming I would be hungry, but I had her help your father first to make sure he would heal before I fed. I told Melanie what happened, how he practically allowed me to drain him, just so I was fed. She told me that the world worked in mystical ways, and maybe the whole situation was destiny's way of telling me I needed to get to know this wonderful man.

"I stayed with him in the coven infirmary until he woke up. When he finally did, I thanked him for what he had done and left, not wanting to cause a scene. At that point, my parents were already enraged I was showing so much attention to a wolf, so I knew I had to be careful. However, no matter how hard I tried to resist, I found myself drawn back to him. If I walked the halls aimlessly, I'd eventually find myself outside the infirmary door, feeling confused as to how I got there. So I finally gave in, and visited him as often as I could without drawing attention. When he checked out of the infirmary, he asked me on a date.

"For our first date, he took me hunting for deer. Right on the edge of the city, we ran together as humans until we found a deer, which we took down together. At the end of the night, he kissed me, and it was like fireworks erupting inside of me. That's when I knew who he was to me, and in that moment, we became everything to each other."

My mother takes a sip of lemonade as I listen in wonder. She knew within two weeks my father was it for her? That's so romantic.

I can't help but feel there was a lot of bad that came along with their romance, though. No one gets to live life that easily.

"Did everyone accept him?"

She laughs harshly. "No, he was not accepted. Within the first few years of us being together, he was almost killed eight times! When his parents made it clear he was no longer welcome among the wolves, my parents started seeing the good I saw in him. He moved into the coven, staying in one of the guest quarters to begin with. After a year of him being with us, they gave us our own suite and taught him what it would mean to lead a coven of vampires. He trained hard with us, learned our politics, and two years later, the coven leaders decided he was fit to lead us. Which was lucky because within a few months of being married we found out we were expecting you. There were still doubters among the coven that he could lead us. Even my parents, despite showing outward approval, tried to convince me to find a vampire to at least rule by my side and just be married to him, but your father proved them all wrong.

"When I was taken by his parents, he was the only one here. My parents were off visiting another coven, so he was the only choice our people had for a leader. He stepped up and assumed control, leading the search to find me. He almost killed himself in the days leading up to my unfortunate return. He went to multiple different packs, challenged many wolves for information on where I was and almost died. All of that led to the night I returned. He'd come back from yet another challenge, when he saw me on the front stairs."

I watch as the painful memories flash through her eyes, before she schools her expression. "Anyway, he proved himself to my parents and the coven. That's all that matters," she says, firmly ending that line of discussion.

Awkward silence encases us, and I begin to fidget. I look down at the empty pizza box, surprised to realize that at some point I had eaten it all. My mother sighs and leans forward in her chair in order to catch my gaze.

"What about you, Emerald? I missed your whole life and would love to know more about you. What you like, what you don't. Everything," she says eagerly.

I smile and adjust to get more comfortable. Then I tell her everything I can think of from my favorite movies to my favorite bands. I give her a rundown of pack life, including training and school, while glossing over the fact I was treated as the pack mutt.

I tell her about my love for my car, which makes her laugh and she informs me my father also has a passion for cars. It makes my heart melt a little, knowing I have something else in common with him apart from our reluctance to do dishes. It makes me feel more connected, I guess.

We sit for a few hours, just talking about random things. The conversation flows easily between us, and I can't help the little thrill of happiness that I feel realizing I may actually be accepted by my mother.

After years of thinking she was dead, not only have I met my mother, now I have the chance to get to know her. We may never get that bond we would have had if we had been together from the start, but at least now we are in each other's lives.

Chapter Four

DISAGREEMENTS

EMERALD

My mother and I are laughing when my father walks back through the door.

I had been helping my mother dispose of the used napkins and pizza box when she made a comment about needing to buy new air freshener so my father wouldn't pine over the scent of pizza. Then that got us talking about food-scented air freshener for vampires. We started by listing normal scents until those became ridiculous, then we just started naming random mixes of food. My mother's current suggestion of blood and garlic is the reason for our fit of giggles.

He freezes, seeing us with flushed faces and clutching our stomachs from laughter. Instead of questioning that, however, he asks, "Do I smell garlic?"

At that, the giggles start up again in full force, and my mother collapses into hysterics on the couch. I chuckle, trying to remain composed as he walks over to mock glare down at my mother. "Are you laughing at me?

The affection in his eyes is obvious, and I can tell he truly loves her heart and soul. She finally sobers enough to calm herself and sits up.

"Sorry, hun. I wasn't laughing at you, I swear." The innocent expression on her face doesn't match the mischievous look in her eyes, though. It's the look I'd give to someone if they were, indeed, the butt of the joke.

He frowns and looks to me, but I remain silent. He sighs and turns his gaze towards the pizza box where it was resting, on top of the garbage can. "Please tell me you saved me some pizza? I'm absolutely famished."

She narrows her eyes. "What did I say about you and eating takeout? We bought you a food fridge so you could have healthy food. Not so you could order takeout every day. Just because you're a werewolf doesn't mean you shouldn't take care of your body."

He rolls his eyes. "Oh, so it's okay for our daughter to eat pizza but not me?"

"She's allowed to eat pizza because she has two natures to satisfy. Until we know how to accurately maintain her diet, she can eat what she wants."

My father mutters something under his breath before leaning in to give my mother a quick, love-filled kiss. You can see in the way they both sigh in contentment that even though they were separated for just a short time, they still missed each other. It's sweet.

I get to my feet, wondering if I should leave when my mother turns to me. "Emerald, if you could stay a moment? Your father and I need to have a chat with you about your lessons."

I sit back down on the edge of the seat, feeling slightly nervous as my father sits down beside her. I've been dreading this conversation and had hoped to keep putting it off for as long as possible. I know, technically, I'm a Princess among the vampires, but I am so not Princess material.

My mother intertwines her hand with my father's, as if using him for courage before speaking. "I'm not sure if you know much about your duty to the coven, but at the end of the day, you're their Princess. As such, you need to know about our politics, our culture, and our history. What I'm trying to say is I want you to attend royalty training. One of our most loyal vampires has volunteered to teach you all you need to know, and I would like to talk to your soul-ties about explaining things, too. There is so much you need to know, and you're at a significant disadvantage until you've been brought up to speed. At any moment one of our own could use your lack of knowledge against you."

I nod in agreement when my father interrupts. "What about physical training? And patrols? Em has been training in the pack for years, and I imagine she would like to use her skills in the real world, rather than sit around drinking tea and reading history books."

My mood lifts, but my mother immediately shoots down that idea. "It's not all drinking tea and reading books, Axel. These are things that Emerald will need to know if she's ever sent on our behalf as an envoy. Would you really want her walking into another coven while being unaware of our customs? She would likely be punished or, worse, killed for her ignorance." She shakes her head adamantly. "No, I won't risk that. She will learn our traditions and cultures. Then, when I am convinced she knows all she needs to, she can assist with patrols."

I watch for a moment in fascination and the slight edge of fear creeps in as my parents bicker, each adamant that they're both right, before I interrupt.

"What if I do both?"

They both stop arguing and turn their attention to me, and I go on. "I can go to lessons when you need me to and still go on patrols with the guys. They can even teach me stuff while we're on patrol if that makes you happy, but I think both things are equally important. I need to learn how you patrol, and I also need to learn about my kind. This way it's a win-win."

A small grin appears on my mother's face, while my father outright smirks. "She's good," he whispers into my mother's ear.

They stare at me for a moment before they both nod. My father meets my gaze, and his face goes into serious mode. "Your mother and I agree with you. Both are important, so with that in mind, you will attend royalty lessons as well as go on patrols with the guys. If at any time we feel you are lacking in one area or another, we'll mention it to your tutor, so she can focus more on that subject. Does that sound acceptable?"

I smile, feeling relieved that we settled the issue pretty quickly. I hate being in the middle of conflict and their bickering over me going on patrol or attending lessons just remind me of the way my step-mom would yell at Dad for what I considered small things. "Yes, that's perfect. And I promise to grill the guys for information whenever I can."

A knock sounds on the door, and my heart picks up the pace. Based on my body's reaction, I'd bet everything one of my guys is standing right outside.

Sure enough, when my father gets up and opens the door, it's to reveal Nik standing in the hall with a sheepish grin on his face. "Hey, sorry to interrupt. I just wanted to see if Em wanted to go for a walk?" he asks. I jump to my feet, ready to go.

It's not that I don't like hanging out with my parents, but I hardly get any alone time with the guys, so I want to take the chance anytime I get.

"I would love that." I smile brightly, excited to spend some one-on-one time with him.

My mother and father each offer me a quick hug, and I'm surprised it doesn't feel off. I would have thought that kind of affection would still feel awkward, but spending time with my mother today has made me feel a bit closer to them.

As I reach Nik and take hold of his hand, my mother speaks. "I'll schedule your first lesson in two days' time. Someone will come to your door to escort you to your lesson and I will make sure Talon is informed of what days and times they fall on so he can plan your training and patrols."

Nik leads me out the door, and I can't help the sigh of relief I let out when we reach the other end of the hall. "Thank you so much. You saved me from being caught in the middle of a marital disagreement."

He chuckles as we step into the elevator. "I could feel your anxiety and thought I'd better check on you." He lets go of my hand and wraps an arm around my waist, pulling me closer. "Now how about I give you a tour? I know you haven't really had much chance to explore yet," he offers as he glances down at his watch.

Huh? He must have a meeting or something later. Better not keep him waiting. "Yeah, that would be awesome. Let's go."

The elevator stops on a floor I haven't yet been on, and we step out. This level is set up the same as other floors I've seen, the only difference being that this hallway leads to a massive kitchen.

"Each of these rooms are for guests. Since we never know whether we will have humans, wolves, or witches staying with us, it makes sense to keep them close to the kitchen since its stocked with everything our kinds need to remain well fed. It used to be an abandoned level, but when your father needed a more efficient kitchen, your mother had the whole floor upgraded. Britt would be in one of these rooms usually, but she demanded to be close to you, which is why she's on the same floor as us."

He opens a few of the doors in the hallway, showing me the rooms are all empty. They seem cozy enough for guest quarters.

When we reach the kitchen, I notice him glance at his watch again, the corner of his mouth lifting in a smirk. I start to wonder if he's late for some kind of meeting. Why else would he be watching the time so vigilantly? But then again, if he were late, wouldn't he act more concerned about it?

We walk through the kitchen, and he goes on to explain why there are two fridges. The stainless steel one with double doors contains human food for their wolf and witch visitors. Then there's the small white fridge, which contains blood bags for vampires.

At least now I know if I get hungry, I can take a quick walk down here to get a bite, rather than have to order food.

I open the fridge, curious as to its contents, and reach in to grab the lone can of soda on the top shelf. Nik snatches my hand back with a sheepish grin. "Ah, that belongs to one of the guards. He likes to mix it with his blood for extra flavor," he explains.

"Oh, sorry."

He shrugs and cocks his head to the side, as if hearing something. I listen and hear the distinct sound of footsteps approaching. Nik drags me back into the pantry, pulling the door shut behind us. He presses a hand to my mouth to stop me from speaking and moves me so I too, can see out the small crack into the well-lit kitchen.

"Watch," he breathes so low I barely pick it up, even with my sensitive hearing.

A tall man walks into the room, humming happily. He opens the white fridge and pulls out two blood bags, pouring them into a large mug on the counter. I watch as he throws the bags in the bin, still humming to himself as he does so. He moves to the silver fridge and pulls out the can of coke I tried to grab before. This must be the guy who likes to mix soda with his blood.

I watch as he walks back to his blood-filled mug and opens the tab of the soda.

Liquid explodes out of the top of the can, spraying over practically every surface in the room. The once white cabinets are all now spattered with brown drops, the roof has even more droplets covering it, and the floor is covered in the mess as well.

I feel Nik chuckling quietly against my back as we watch the guard take in the mess he just made. Shock is clear on his face, as if he can't believe what just happened, but I watch as his shock quickly morphs into anger. His eyes dart around as if looking for us, and I see his gaze shift to the pantry where we're concealed.

He takes a step in our direction when Talon's voice suddenly cuts through the room. "Tyler, what is all this? You know Queen Sierra hates any mess in her kitchen. Clean it up at once."

The feel of Nik's mouth against my shoulder as he smothers his laughter makes giggles well up. I almost suffocate against Nik's hand as he keeps me muted while the guard cleans up the mess that Nik somehow caused.

After Tyler finishes, Talon inspects every surface before allowing him to leave with his blood. Tyler leaves the room, muttering under his breath about payback against the ass who messed with his drink.

Talon cocks his head, listening as Tyler walks away before he turns to glare at the cupboard. "Nik, I know you're in there. Only you would be stupid enough to hang around and watch."

Nik lets out a laugh and removes his hand from my mouth before pushing me out of the small space.

Talon's eyes widen in surprise when he sees me, but then his gaze moves across to scowl at Nik who comes out after me. "Seriously? You had Em in here while you were provoking Tyler? Are you stupid?"

Nik leans against the counter and smirks. "She was fine. I am more than capable of protecting her against Tyler if need be. Besides, he didn't even know we were here."

I roll my eyes, feeling annoyed. "Guys, I'm right here. Can you please stop talking about me as if I'm some helpless little girl who can't defend herself? I'm more than capable of fighting off a vamp or two."

Both guys keep staring intensely at each other, not even acknowledging my words. I sigh and shake my head. Men. Never bother listening to what a girl has to say.

After a long moment, Nik breaks the stare down and moves to the door. "Come on, Em. I'll show you the rest of our coven."

I sigh and walk towards Nik, stopping to give Talon a quick kiss on the cheek before I go. I offer him a small smile as Nik and I leave. As we walk back the way we came, I start to wonder how I can prove to them I am more than capable of handling myself.

Sure, I died one time, and now they're holding it against me. I will find a way to make them understand I'm stronger than I appear.

Chapter Five

MARKETS

EMERALD

$\mathcal{W}$e end up on yet another floor I've never been on. When the elevator opens, I can't help but gasp at all the activity going on.

Large groups of people are milling about in a market-type setting, complete with everything from the cobblestones on the ground to the many tables holding various items. If I didn't know any better, I would assume we were out in the street. The lights in here shine down on the setting like the sun.

Vampires of varying ages walk around, and I get my first glimpse of what vampire children look like. They aren't that different from human children; the only real difference I can see is that they're paler. Their skin is almost translucent. I try not to stare, but I find myself fascinated. Was I that pale as a child?

Nik guides me past various stalls filled with all sorts of things such as candles, blood, gemstones, and other curious items, and I notice that there are signs by each table.

"What do those signs mean?"

Each table holds a sign, which appears to list various items to trade. The first sign seems to be asking for the following blood types: O-negative, B-negative, and AB-negative.

One of the other table's signs asks for tanzanite or cash. There are other signs, asking for things such as diamonds, gold, other blood types, and the like. There are even tables that asks for certain services in exchange for goods or other services.

"Oh, that's how our currency system works. We trade. The majority of our kind deals in human cash, but with having lived as long as we have, we all own many things others may find useful. Like take this table, for example." He moves closer to a booth that holds little vials of multi-colored liquids with a sign asking for blood in exchange.

"These are powerful potions made by witches. Sean here might have a source that supplies him with these which he then trades for items he needs. Blood, in this case."

The man behind the table gives us a little bow and speaks up. "Yes, what your soul-tie says is true. I have a friend in the local witch coven who I trade my services for. He uses my blood to make certain magical potions, and in exchange, he makes simple ones for me that I can use to trade for blood types that are more rare."

Sean reaches forth and picks up a green potion. "For example, Princess, this potion here gives you the ability to hide one's self from sight. While your soul-tie may not need that particular boost, some of the guards like to use them on patrols when they need to remain unseen. Then we have this one," he continues, putting the green potion down to pick up a bright red one. "It's an infatuation potion. It can't be used on someone who's got a soul-tie or mate, but it can be used on supernaturals. There are many vampires, werewolves, and witches out there who have lived alone for so long that they just want someone to love them back. This is the closest it can really get."

At my look of horror, he rushes to add, "Do not worry, Princess. The potion wears out after twenty-four hours unless they keep feeding it to the affected individual."

Somehow that doesn't comfort me as much as the man means it to. What if someone buys a lifetime supply of that stuff? Would that mean their victim would be forever infatuated with someone they didn't like? Seems very cruel to me. It makes me wonder if the witches police that kind of thing? Surely they must, otherwise everyone would be running around like lovesick fools.

More than ever, I'm glad that my guys are tied to me. I couldn't possibly imagine them infatuated with someone else. Honestly, I'd probably kill the person who tried to take them from me.

Nik thanks the man for his time and we continue on our way. We walk past each table, with Nik explaining each thing that I don't understand. All in all, their bartering system seems to be a pretty easy concept. One table steals my gaze and holds it, and I have no idea how to process what I'm seeing.

The table houses various weapons and other relics but two twin swords are where my gaze keeps being drawn to. I feel an overwhelming connection to them for some reason, as if they're mine somehow. Nik sees my gaze riveted on the various items and moves us closer while he explains. "Some of our kind are thousands of years old. That means most or all of the material things they had when they were alive are lost to them now. But with historical finds being made every day, some of those long lost items are being recovered by the humans or other covens."

Nik runs a hand over an old engraved pocket watch before speaking again. "These items are invaluable to those who have lost their treasures. Imagine being a vampire who was turned hundreds of years ago, but you had a child before you turned. We aren't exactly allowed to see our family after we turn, it's too dangerous. So take a family photo, for example. Some pictures of loved ones are sold for upwards of a million dollars."

Holy... That's unbelievable.

We move from the table, and I notice the way Nik glances back longingly at the pocket watch. "Do you know who that watch belonged to?" I ask, intrigued.

He casts one last lingering look at it. "It belonged to someone I knew, but he's dead now."

We continue to walk, my thoughts continuing to drift back to the twin swords as we explore the remaining tables. The longer we remain here though, the more people start to notice me. They begin to stare, whispering as we pass.

They all know who I am, and are curious as to what I'm doing here.

"Em, you okay?" Nik asks, noticing my anxiety rising.

He wraps an arm around my shoulders, and I try to keep myself from huddling into him. "Um, no. I mean, I'm okay. It's hard going from the shadows to being in the spotlight."

He nods in understanding and steers me down the hall to a large set of glass doors at the end. The moment we step through them, the scent of ammonia overwhelms me.

I grimace and try to stop the instinct to cover my nose, even as my eyes well with tears from how concentrated the scent is.

Nik notices and puts his wrist under my nose. The scent of him and fresh blood running in his veins overpowers the strong chemical smell. "Sorry, I should have warned you before we came in. They have to disinfect this room daily in order to prevent the scent of blood from overwhelming any newbies who come in."

I nod, moving Nik's hand away and using my own to cover my nose and mouth to soften the scent.

Nik pulls me towards a bright white desk in the middle of the room where a woman sits, wearing an all white suit. She couldn't wear even a little color? The white on white is a bit much for me. I find it a little disorienting, just as the smell is. Maybe they want to have that effect if new vampires are coming through here?

The woman smiles up over the desk at Nik, ignoring my presence completely. She flicks her auburn hair over her shoulder, revealing her neck where a set of bite marks sits in invitation. "Why hello, Nikoli. Do you have an appointment today or is this a pop in visit?" The flirty tone of voice has my beast on edge, and I long to dive across the desk and smack her across the face for flirting with my man. *He is mine!*

Nik chuckles, as if sensing my jealousy and kisses me on the temple, which draws the woman's gaze to me. "Don't worry, Dolores, I'm just showing the Princess around. Do you mind if we go through the back? The Princess hasn't been down here yet."

She nods, assessing me for a moment before returning her focus to Nik. "You're fine to go back." She winks, and I fight the urge to growl.

He starts to lead us through the door behind her desk, only to stop and turn back. "Are there any newbs back there?"

"No new ones today, Nikoli. I will alert you if any come in," she says with a polite smile. That smile quickly turns to a frown when Nik keeps me firmly by his side.

I try not to smile too smugly, but I doubt I repressed it well enough, because the moment Nik closes the door, he bends down and offers me a quick kiss. Before I have a chance to respond, he pulls back with a wink. "There's no need to be jealous, Em. I'm all yours."

I flush and meet his teasing gaze. "How'd you know?"

"Em, I felt your jealousy the moment she smiled at me. I gotta admit, it was pretty hot, and if Dolores wasn't on the other side of this door, I would have done a lot more than just kiss you," he murmurs, his eyes filled with lust.

I shiver with arousal before shaking out of it and shifting my focus to our surroundings. Getting aroused right now won't do any good. Not when there's nothing I can do about it. Later though, I promise myself.

Nik leads me down a white corridor lined with doors on either side. Each door has a window, so you can see inside and watch. I see some vamps clearly feeding from humans. Others are devouring bag after bag of blood, or are being handed bags of blood from a person dressed in white before putting them in cooler bags.

Nik explains as we walk. "We feed down here on human donors—those who are worse off in the world who choose to trade their blood for cash. We don't discriminate. Humans can donate to our blood bag supply and receive payment in exchange for their contribution. We allow members of the coven to take a weekly supply to their rooms, so they don't have to come down here often, but just like with any substance, some vampires suffer from an addiction to it. This can be dangerous, so we prefer those who suspect they have an addiction to feed down here. Then of course we have the others of our kind who know they're addicted and don't give a rat's ass and have to be dragged down here and locked away until their addiction is under control. Then they are given the choice to try and assimilate back into the coven or move to a special facility we have for those cases that can't be put back into the coven and out into the human world."

He leads me to another room's window, and my jaw drops at the sight before me. The whole room is made of what looks like solid metal.

"These rooms were designed for newly turned vampires. The metal makes it impossible for them to break their way out.

"We have locks on the inside that require both fingerprint and retina scans from one of the guards before it will let the vampire out. We try to make sure our facilities are as safe as possible for all of us. If we ever have an extreme crazy cross through here, we send them to a special facility that houses vampires for long-term care. If they don't snap out of the blood craze within five years, they are usually destroyed. Sometimes, they just don't accept cloned blood, and we can't exactly give them human blood when that is what caused the addiction in the first place."

"Cloned blood? Is that what's in the bags?"

He looks at me, clearly surprised by my question. "Yeah, didn't anyone tell you that?"

At the shake of my head, he frowns. "We have deliveries that come in from blood banks, the real human stuff that we pay for but the majority of our food source it is made by a pharmaceutical company. Some vampires were scientists before being turned and have spent years developing these. In the past twenty years, the formula has been perfected, so we've been gradually moving our kind off of human blood and onto the synthetic.

"We've even started to sell bags of it to the human hospitals. Your mother makes quite a profit from hiring out the scientists to create blood for the humans."

A blaring noise suddenly pierces the room, and Nik lifts the edge of his shirt where a pager-like device is attached to his waistband. He clicks a button on the side and holds it up to his head like a phone.

"Nikoli here."

He listens intently for a moment before sighing. "Yes, fine, I'll ask her. If she says yes, we'll meet you upstairs."

Without another word, he clicks his communication device off and puts it back on his waistband. "That was Dev and Tal. They would like to know if you want to go on a date? With the three of us? We all agree you've been pretty cooped up in here and thought you might like to get out for a bit and get some air."

I nod excitedly. "Yeah, that's sounds great. Do you mind if we take my car?"

He shakes his head sadly. "Maybe another time. The guys have something else in store today."

Chapter Six

DATE NIGHT

EMERALD

"Where are we going?" I ask as we meet Tal and Dev at the surface.

Talon holds out a coat for me, and I pull it on while wishing I had the chance to change into something else. My jeans and button-up shirt are not exactly what I envisioned for my first official date with the guys. It feels a bit too formal.

Dev gives me a soft kiss before pulling away. "We're not telling you yet. It's a surprise."

"But how will I know which direction to go in? I could get lost. So, it's better to tell me now to save yourselves the suffering you'll endure if I get lost." I pout and look at each of them while giving my best innocent look.

Talon shakes his head, and a chuckle escapes. "You are one impatient woman, Emerald. Just trust us that this is a surprise you will like."

Nik and Dev both grin, murmuring to themselves as they walk out the main doors, while Talon reaches out to intertwine our fingers, pulling me after them.

We walk the streets, the night feeling peaceful. People walk the streets but none stop to watch as we walk from the church and I find myself being drawn into the beautiful scenery. I look back at the church and still can't quite get over how abandoned and out of place it looks on this street. People walk right by it without a second glance

45

moving on to the shops, or to their cars that line the sidewalk. I push the thoughts of the church to the back of my mind as I look down the street at the lamps that are decorated with the beginnings of Christmas.

A hand slips into my free one, and Dev leans in to whisper, "What ya thinking about?"

I smile at him, staring into those hazel eyes that look down at me filled with desire. I look away, trying not to get lost in his gaze when I still have Talon holding my other hand. As if Talon senses my internal struggle, he strokes my hand, trying to draw my attention back to him. *Damn it all to hell.* How is a girl supposed to remain focused when she has a hot guy on either side of her?

"I'm just thinking about the city. It's so beautiful." I sigh happily.

The lamp posts are adorned with shining snowflakes, and the stores have all started to decorate in preparation for Christmas. Fake snow lines the inside of windows and soon, the Christmas trees will be up.

As we walk, snow starts to fall and I gasp.

"It feels magical," I explain, in awe of the surrounding sights. The sun has only just set, and the early evening carries the scent of snow in the air. The guys picked the perfect night for a date.

They smile at me as we walk along, but after a moment Dev pulls me to a stop and Talon lets go of my hand.

I look up and my mouth drops open in shock at the sight of the massive silver monument in front of us. I've read about this place. I always planned to visit if I ever left the pack. Something I had only ever told Britt. "Britt told you I wanted to visit the Gateway Arch, didn't she?" I ask wryly.

Dev bounces on his feet, his eyes filled with glee. "Yep. I had to grovel just to get an idea of what you may want to do. This is the only thing she mentioned, but I thought it would be perfect. You will also get to see the city at night from an unbelievable height while it's all lit up for the holidays. You'll see absolutely everything."

Oh, that's so sweet that he thought to ask Britt for advice. She could have made him do a lot worse than grovel, though. She could have given him the wrong information, which she actually kinda has. I mean, yes, I want to visit the top of the Gateway Arch, but I am absolutely terrified at the same time.

I don't fully understand why, though. Maybe it's the height or the idea of being stuck in such an enclosed space but I really don't want to find out for sure.

"Yo, Dev!"

A young guy with dreads comes walking out of the entry to the monument. Dev lets go of me and heads over to the stranger, preventing him from getting close to us. That's when his scent reaches me, and I realize he's human! Why is Dev mingling with humans? This guy must be the night operator of the archway.

I turn my attention to study the building, and notice how dark the entryway is. Then I see the huge sign proclaiming the building to be closed, and I breathe a sigh of relief, knowing I won't have to go in and pretend it doesn't scare me to death. I'd rather the guys not know I have such an irrational fear, especially when I'm some awesome immortal being. What kind of immortal is scared of anything?

Nik leans in to whisper in my ear while Dev is still occupied talking to his 'friend.' "You know, you don't have to go up. He'll understand."

I shake my head, confused by his statement. "It's closed, we can't go up anyway."

Talon barks out a laugh. "Nothing is closed to Devin. I'm sure he called ahead to convince this human to take a ridiculous amount of money in exchange for private use of the arch tonight. He's too conniving not to."

Sure enough, Dev comes back wearing a toothy grin and scoops me up over his shoulder, slapping me on the ass as he walks me through the entry doors.

I can't see where we're going, and my heart continues to pick up speed the longer we walk, until he stops and sets me back on my feet.

He grabs me by the shoulder and turns me around. I see Talon and Nik sitting in a tiny little pod-shaped room with massive grins on their faces as they wait for us.

Dev squeezes into the cramped space with them, and I can't help but chuckle. They look like three giants the way they're stuffed in there. It looks incredibly uncomfortable.

Why are they squeezed into such a small space? And what are they waiting for?

Dev frowns, obviously uncomfortable. "Emerald, we're waiting."

I blanch. "Ah, you guys go on up, I'll take the next one."

Dev goes to move, and I sigh, knowing he will just drag me in. "Fine, I'll come up. Just, stay there. I don't know if you'll be able to get back in again if you hop out."

I crouch down under the doorway and step inside, the space only just able to fit me. I wonder whether I'm supposed to stand the whole way up, since there aren't any more seats, but then Talon pulls me onto his lap. Though with how close we're squeezed together, I'm sitting half on Nik's lap too. I try to settle, but it's difficult when I'm painfully aware of how happy Talon and Nik are to have me in their laps.

The human guy takes a look inside to make sure we're ready and Dev gives him a nod. "We'll signal when we're ready to come down," he says. With that, the human leaves and the elevator door closes.

A moment later, the small pod starts to rise, and I can feel it swaying. Bile rises in my throat and my heartrate kicks up a notch. I'm sure it's loud enough for all three of them to hear.

Emerald, do not throw up on your soul-ties. For the love of all things holy, remain cool. You're a badass hybrid, not some weak girl who is afraid of heights. You can do this!

I mentally cheer myself on, but not one word of it sticks. The higher we get, the more wildly our pod begins to swing. My beast rattles around inside my mind, reacting to my fear.

Talon nuzzles his head into my neck, and I focus on his scent, the sweet smell of chocolate distracting me from what's happening around me.

Time goes by agonizingly slow, and I start to wonder if this is really only a four minute ride up. That's what all the tourist information said, but it feels more like a lifetime.

Dev remains oblivious to my fear, for which I'm glad. I don't want him to be upset, especially since he was just trying to do something nice in order to make me happy.

We're almost to the top when the pod sways, and I have to bite my tongue to stop from screaming.

I grab Nik's hand, my nails digging into his skin as I grip tightly, needing to feel grounded.

I can feel Dev's excitement build, and he starts bouncing in his seat as we get closer to the end of our ride.

Finally the pod stops, and I take a deep breath in order to keep myself calm. The doors open and Dev pushes out first before reaching back in with a hand to help me out.

I smile nervously and my legs shake as I step onto the firm floor. Dev notices, and his eyes go wide. "Shit! Em, what's wrong?"

I quickly plaster a smile on my face. He obviously loves this, and I don't want to ruin it for him. "I'm fine, just not used to this altitude I guess."

"You sure?"

I nod, beginning to feel steadier already now that we're not in a tight space that moves with the wind. "Yes, I'm good. Just excited to see the view," I lie.

Talon hides a chuckle with a cough, and I fight the urge to turn and glare at him.

With my hand in his, Dev leads me through the viewing room over to a window, his enthusiasm contagious. He lets go of me as I take a step towards the windows, and I'm unable to contain my gasp. "Holy shit!"

Arms wrap around me from behind, and Dev's unique scent envelops me as I stare down at the city below us. He rests his head on my shoulder, and we both gaze down at the beautiful city below us.

I can sense Talon and Nik standing behind us, but they hang back, letting us have this moment. I sigh and relax into Dev's embrace as we watch a light layer of snow fall from the sky onto the beautifully lit up city below.

The fear I had on the ride up seems to have completely disappeared now that I'm actually up here. It helps that I'm wrapped in the arms of a man who I know would never hurt me intentionally, and would protect me at all cost. If I had told him I was nervous, he would have never made me come up, that I'm sure of.

"Alright, you two. We came up here, you saw all the pretty lights. Can we go now?" Talon asks, his voice filled with boredom.

Dev heaves a sigh of disappointment. "Yeah. Sorry, Em, but we should get going. Steve has to delete our time up here from the tapes, and the longer we stay, the greater the chance his superiors will get suspicious of the time gap."

"That's okay. Thank you for bringing me up here." I turn in his arms and press a kiss to his lips.

He hesitates at first, but then deepens the kiss with a groan. I let him take control of the kiss, running my tongue over his fangs. It fascinates me that they sit there, only elongating in times of arousal or hunger.

I fight for breath as a wave of arousal rushes through me and know I have to stop this before things go too far.

I break the kiss, leaning away from Dev as his gaze darts down to my neck. "Come on, Dev. We don't want to give your friend on the ground a show." I wink playfully at him. He laughs, shaking his head at me as we walk towards the others, who are waiting patiently for us by the elevator door. They didn't seem to want to interrupt, and for that I'll be forever grateful.

It's hard enough for me to find the time for each of them separately without me feeling like it will cause jealousy, but to get time together as a group while also feeling like a date, makes this night all the more special.

Nik and Talon watch me closely as we pass, their eyes filled with desire. While I'm tempted to stop and offer them each their own kiss, I know the thin veil of control I have will fall to pieces if put in any more tempting situations.

Dev gets into the tram or elevator, I'm not too sure what it's called to be honest, and I perch myself on his lap.

Talon and Nik squeeze in on either side of us, but Dev keeps a tight grip on me in his lap, just to be safe.

The four minute ride back down is silent and filled with tension. Not the uneasy kind, but an anticipatory type of tension. My fear on the way down disappears into the background as I'm far more focused on the arousal that soaks my panties.

When we hit the ground again, I climb out first, followed by Talon and Nik. Dev is last, and when he leaves the pod, he grabs me by the hand and drags me outside into the shadows of the building, moving me until we're completely obscured from any people who may be walking past. My heart speeds up and I can see Talon and Nik standing just off to the side, with their backs to us as they keep watch.

I look up into Dev's eyes, surprised by the guarded look I see. Usually, I can read his eyes like an open book.

"Why didn't you tell me you were afraid of the ride up?"

Those words were the last thing I expected to come out of his mouth. I thought he wanted more of what happened on the viewing platform. Or maybe even more.

I stammer out a response. "I don't know. I just saw how happy you were, and I didn't want to upset you."

His eyes narrow for a moment before he sighs, resting his head against mine. "Emerald, please don't do that again. You pushed your fear away and hid it from me. I had no idea. If I hadn't felt the irritation coming from the guys, I wouldn't have focused on it enough to notice you were concealing your fear. I'm supposed to make you happy, not terrify you," he says, with obvious hurt in his voice.

Damn it. "Devin, I didn't think about that. I'm sorry. The next time we do anything that makes me feel like that, I'll be honest about it. Even if I'm shitting myself to the point I think I am going to throw up all over you."

He cringes at the visual I painted. "Ah, maybe don't go into that much detail. Just a simple 'this is making me uncomfortable' will do."

I shake my head with a smile. "Okay, I promise to tell you if I get uncomfortable. I am sorry, though."

"I know, and I'm sorry for not focusing enough on you to realize you were afraid. I should have felt it through our tie, but I was too excited and let myself get carried away. Now that we're all good, it's time for something fun. Let's go shopping!"

I groan as he leads me back to the others. "Are we really going shopping?"

Nik laughs at the dejected tone in my voice. "Don't worry, Em, we're just window shopping. Britt wants to pick up clothes for you, but knew you'd want to try some on first. So, we're going to explore the city and take photos of any clothes that you like, and then Britt can buy them. Just pretend you knew nothing of her plan."

I can't help the sly grin that crosses my face. I knew Britt would have demanded something in return for telling them about my desire to see the view from the Gateway Arch. "So basically, Britt demanded to be the one to buy me clothes in exchange for giving you information. I'm guessing she has some kind of horror story or embarrassing secret on each of you that you don't want me to know, and she threatened to tell me if you don't pay up, is that about right?"

Dev nods with a smirk. "Yep!"

"Okay, fine. Let's do some window shopping."

We walk the streets for a while until they lead me to a set of shops known as the Loop. I let them guide me into each shop to try on various articles of clothing, taking pictures of the ones that I like the most.

I'm getting tired of looking at clothes, so Nik leads us to a nightclub to have a drink. We're sitting at a high table and the music is pumping, but I feel a bit awkward since everyone else is dressed in club clothes, while I'm just sitting here in jeans and a shirt. It's a wonder they even let me in. I thought human clubs were strict on these things, but Talon knew the bouncer who just waved us right in.

Talon and Dev are sitting on either side of me, and I can tell they must have done this kind of thing before to feed. The way they watch the humans heightens my own desire to feed.

Nik disappeared a few minutes ago to grab us drinks, and when I see him making his way back to us, he's surrounded by half a dozen drunk chicks! *Oh, hell no!*

I slide out of my seat and make my way towards him. I push the girls out of my way, using more strength than I probably need to. Nik gives me a relieved smile and I guide him back to our table, with the girls unfortunately still following after him. I roll my eyes as they fawn all over my guys. Once Nik sets the drinks down, I grab his hand and lead him out onto the dance floor. He raises a brow in question when I start moving to the sultry beat, the song screaming of sex as I move. He watches as I run my hands through my hair, before trailing them down my neck. Slowly, I undo one of the buttons on my shirt, revealing my neck to him.

I can tell the moment he understands my intention from the way his blue eyes darken with lust and hunger. He moves behind me, pressing himself to my back, and I can feel just how excited he is to be there. We move to the beat of the music for a moment before he stops us, pointing in the direction of our table. I lift my head to see Talon and Dev watching us. The girls are still around them, trying to get their attention, but the guys are one hundred percent focused on me.

Nik moves my hair out of the way, and I arch my neck, eager for what is about to happen. I glue my eyes on the others as his fangs plunge into my neck. Talon and Dev both visibly jerk when his canines pierce into me. My moan is drowned out by the club music as my arousal quickly builds within me. Something about being fed on while the guys watch is making me hornier than ever.

Nik lets go of my neck just as Dev reaches us in a burst of vampire speed. He steps in front of me, and I tilt my head, giving him access to the other side.

He eagerly strikes, and I moan in ecstasy. The humans dance around us, oblivious of what's happening around them. After taking his fill, Nik steps back and I'm left staring into Talon's intense green eyes. He leans in, but instead of biting me, he whispers, "Let's go home."

The promise in his voice has me nodding, more than eager to continue this in a more private setting. We walk quickly through the club, my hand gripped firmly in his. We leave and start a hurried walk back to the coven.

We're about two blocks away when I freeze, my hand slipping from Talon's as he keeps walking with the guys, talking about some patrol shift they have for the wolves that live in the area.

I tune them out, looking down the street, trying to make sense of this feeling. My beast is telling me something isn't quite right. The guys seem to notice I've fallen behind and turn back to look for me.

"You ok, Em?" Dev asks, taking a few steps towards me while my gaze darts side to side, my beast sensing danger. All thoughts of my earlier arousal have been thrown out the window in the presence of a threat.

I ignore Dev's question, cocking my head to the side to listen carefully. The guys notice my change in mood and have only a split second to prepare before we're attacked.

Chapter Seven

ZOMBIES

EMERALD

*T*alon moves faster than I've ever seen, coming to stand in front of me protectively. "Em, stay behind me," he growls.

I roll my eyes and step out from behind him. "It's not like they can kill me," I scoff, gesturing to the small group of misshapen corpses that are stumbling towards us.

They look like something out of a low-budget horror movie. I wonder if I walked over to one and gave it a good hard shove, if it would just fall to the ground like a ton of bricks?

Nik and Dev move to cover my sides, flanking me.

"What could zombies even do to a vampire? They're just corpses."

There's no other word for what they are. Pasty-faced corpses in various stages of decomposition, still wearing the clothes they were buried in.

Dev looks around behind us before coming around to stand at my back, so we're defended on all sides. "Just because they can't kill us, doesn't meant their master can't."

Master? I look around for the master he speaks of, but see nobody other than the reanimated corpses.

Nik pulls a sword from somewhere with an irritated sigh. "I had hoped for once, the night would go uninterrupted, but I guess that was too much to ask."

Talon chuckles darkly. "What, Nikoli, you don't like a little action to build up the anticipation? Just imagine the adrenaline rush when we dispatch of the threat."

"Now is not the time for your dark humor, Tal. Let's just protect Emerald and find the idiot who thinks it's fun to play with the dead."

Dev sighs and rolls his shoulders. "I'll take the two on the right, Nik you've got the two on the left, while Talon protects Emerald. Everyone clear?" The guys nod their agreement. "Good."

Dev and Nik move faster than I could have expected, striking at the zombies. Energy hums within me, strange and powerful, demanding to be released, but Talon is holding me back.

His attention is focused on the guys as they hack at the zombies when my beast alerts me to a new threat. Someone's close by.

Ever so slowly, I back away from Talon, looking for the source of my unease, but not wanting him to notice my disappearance.

I breathe in deeply and follow the foreign scent to an alley across the street. The longer I stare at the shadows, the more I can see within their depths. The shape of a man hiding among the dark shadows catches my attention. His hands dance and jerk like he has marionettes attached to them.

I look back at Talon before sneaking across the street, while the man remains oblivious. I walk towards the entrance of the alleyway, acting like I'm just on a nightly walk. When I pass the spot where the stranger is hiding, I react, swinging my fist in the dark and aiming for his face.

He falls to the ground in a heap, and I grin down at his unconscious body. "Guys, I got him."

I look up in time to see Talon whip around towards me, and I smile smugly over at him. Who's in need of protecting now?

Just as I'm about to start boasting, Talon's eyes widen, and I'm sent flying. I hit the alley wall hard, my head smashing into it with a resounding crack.

Dev moves with his super speed, snapping the witch's neck before the man can even react. Talon and Nik appear above me and I sit up with a groan. Talon crouches down and scoops me into his arms. "Emerald, what were you doing?" he growls angrily.

Nik and Dev disappear for a moment, and when they return, they hold out their wrists to me. I can taste the blood in the air and know they went to feed on humans, to ensure they have enough to heal me.

Nik slices his wrist using the sword at his side. Blood wells, but it doesn't have time to even run down his hand before I latch on, inhaling as much as I can. After a minute, Talon pulls me off, and my beast takes over. Dev is the next to offer his wrist, and even after feeding from Nik, I still take almost twice as much from Dev. *Why am I so hungry?*

That's when I feel it. My head is no longer in agonizing pain; it's reduced to a dull, more manageable throb.

Talon sets me down on the ground and looks me over before holding out his wrist. "Take what you need." I press him against the wall and push his wrist to the side, rising on my tippy toes to get to his neck instead. He groans, allowing me the access I want. I nuzzle my face into his neck, breathing deeply before sinking my fangs right into the pulsing vein there.

Nik and Dev give us space and focus instead on cleaning up the mess in the street, hiding the zombie parts down this alley safe from human eyes.

Once I've finished feeding, I pull away and lick the blood off my lips. I see Nik take his communicator out, pressing it to his ear as someone answers on the other end. "This is Nikoli of the Princess' guard. We need a clean-up crew on Academy Avenue, just behind the blood blank. We encountered a witch who was controlling the dead. We took care of the problem, as well as the witch. Oh, and bring a few bags with you. We had no choice but to cut them up into pieces."

I look down at the body parts that litter the ground around us and feel absolutely nothing but relief that none of the guys were hurt.

When the clean-up crew arrives, I'm surprised to see that one of Britt's husbands, Blaine, is with them. He spots me and smiles, before coming straight towards me. "Hey, Emerald. Britt gave me strict instructions to come to you before I start the clean up and deliver a message. She threatened to put a hex on me if I don't, so here's the message. 'I'm coming by later so we can have some girl time. Be ready.'

And that's it... I think," he says with a look of contemplation and worry. For his sake, I really hope that was the entire message.

I nod, giving him a smirk. "Okay, you can tell her the message was received."

He smiles, looking relieved for a brief moment, before taking in my appearance. I imagine I don't look my best with blood stuck to my neck from where it has dripped from my head wound.

He reaches a hand out and places it on my cheek before closing his eyes in concentration. I feel a warm tingling sensation run through me and then his eyes snap open. He steps back with a sheepish smile. "Sorry, Britt heard through our connection that you looked hurt and demanded I check you over."

I laugh at the way he's standing there awkwardly, obviously trying not to upset my guys for having touched me. Surprisingly, none of the guys seem to be bothered by it, probably because they're too busy drinking their bags of blood that the clean-up crew brought with them to pay much attention.

Once everyone who needs to has fed, the guys start to walk me back to the coven, but instead of it being just us, we have four other guards accompanying us. When I try to complain, Blaine makes it clear that they won't deviate from their orders, which came directly from my mother.

The moment we're back in the coven, the guards lead us straight to our quarters. When we open the door, I see my parents are already inside, pacing back and forth.

I shrink back into the body behind me, but Nik pushes me forward into the room. "You're a grown woman, Emerald. You have to deal with the consequences of your actions."

At Nik's voice, my parents both turn and immediately abandon their nervous pacing to descend upon me.

My mother reaches me first, and I have to fight to hold still. The instinct to run is strong. Give me evil attacking zombies over concerned parents any day. At least I know how to handle the undead hordes. Worried parents? Not so much.

My mother grips me by the shoulders and looks me over carefully while my father stares daggers at Talon, Nik, and Dev.

"What happened?" he grits out. His eyes shift to amber, a sign of the difficulty he's having reining in his wolf.

Talon looks at me with narrowed eyes before speaking. "The witch was hiding off in the shadows when Emerald attacked him. He dropped to the ground and she began bragging about it. However, she didn't actually bother checking whether he was actually unconscious or not. Of course he was faking it, and when she was distracted, he got up and threw her against the wall. We heard her head crack, and we all reacted. Dev reached her first, and snapped the witch's neck."

Dev stands tall as if waiting for some kind of reprimand for his actions, and when it doesn't come, he relaxes. Instead, my father turns to look at me.

He sighs and joins me and my mother as she offers me comfort I don't actually need. My father gazes down at me intensely. "Please be careful out there, Emerald. You may be a hybrid, but that doesn't mean you're invincible. Even if some higher power says so, there's no telling whether you coming back to life was just a fluke or not." He runs a hand over my hair, gingerly as if I'm nothing more then delicate china. "I don't know what your mother and I would do if we lost you. We only just got you back."

I nod, heaving a sigh of relief. Then I pull my mother into a hug, reaching out with an arm to bring my father in closer. We stand huddled together for a long moment. This feeling of happiness wells up inside me, and I don't want it to end. Reluctantly, I sigh and pull away before it gets too awkward between us. My parents both wear serene smiles on their faces, which makes it all worth it.

Dev moves between us and wraps an arm around my shoulders. "Okay, now that we have that all cleared up, we're going to go to bed for a bit. I think we're all a little exhausted after our activities and could use the rest."

My father glares at him, and I shake my head at his boldness to intervene.

"Sorry, but I think Dev's right. I'm about ready to drop, and Britt's going to be popping by soon. I'd like to get some rest before she drags me out for whatever she has planned."

My mother smiles and nods in understanding. "Of course, sweetheart. Go get some rest, and we'll talk tomorrow."

With that, my parents make to leave the room, but before I head to our bedroom, my father runs back in, holding his hand out to me. In his palm is a small communicator device, much the same as Nik's. "Here, Nik and I thought it might be a good idea for you to have one of these. It has all of our numbers programmed into it. If you need us for anything, you'll be able to contact us. It'll give your mother and I a bit of peace of mind knowing you have a way to reach us."

He winks and pats me on the shoulder before hurrying back out of the room, closing the door behind him. I turn to Nik and smirk. "So, I should probably say thanks for the communicator, but you should know that you're gonna have to teach me how to use it. I'm not so good at technology." I flip it open and press a few buttons and a noise goes off at Talon's hip.

He sighs and looks at Nik. "Have fun teaching her how to use that. I wouldn't wish that on my worst enemy," he says with a chuckle.

I'm about to respond with something snarky when a yawn escapes me. Talon notices and scoops me up, walking me through the bedroom. "You are going to need a shower to wash that blood off your neck, and then you're going to get some much needed rest."

Talon gets into the shower with me and I rush through washing, far too exhausted to take advantage of our current situation. When I climb out, Nik is there to dry me off, and then Dev helps me get dressed in a loose tee and underwear.

Dev sits me on the edge of his bed and dries off my hair before running a brush through it. My eyes feel heavy, and I can feel myself slipping, falling sideways onto the bed. Dev cradles me and tucks me in under the blankets before climbing in behind me.

I let out a sigh of contentment as he encases me in his arms. My eyes close, feeling heavy with the need to sleep. I feel the bed dip as someone joins us and my eyes flutter open to see Talon crawling under the covers. Dev pulls me back a little to make room for him, and I settle in between the two of them, feeling completely safe and content.

Chapter Eight

HAPPINESS INTERRUPTED

EMERALD

I don't want to wake up. I'm so warm. Something is telling me I need to, though. I sigh softly and open my eyes a crack, smiling at what I see.

Talon is sleeping in front of me, and the color in his face has returned back to normal. Feeding has done wonders for his complexion. I'll need to make sure he doesn't neglect his needs again. I'm also going to have to find a way not to feed on them. They keep offering, and I keep caving. If I can't accept blood from the bag, maybe I should talk to my mother about other donors. I can't keep draining the guys whenever I need to feed.

I roll over to find Dev laying behind me, his eyes still closed in sleep. His eyes are shifting rapidly behind his lids as he dreams, and I notice a small scar over his left eye. I can't resist the sudden urge to reach out and run my fingers over it. I didn't realize vampires could even get scars. I wonder what happened to him? Did it happen while he was human or after he became a vampire? Having all these questions just goes to show how much I still don't know about each of them.

I withdraw my hand as my mind turns to thoughts of my mother. Does she carry the scars of my birth? I couldn't imagine the pain she must have felt if that were the case. They must have been horrible constant reminders of what she went through when she was taken, and of my supposed death.

She's an extremely strong woman, especially if she was able to live every day with a physical reminder of what happened to me, but still come out of it somewhat stable. I don't know if I could have that kind of internal strength, or if I could bear to go through anything like what she had.

I rub a hand over my chest, thankful that there doesn't seem to be a scar after my resurrection. I'm not vain, but the thought of a glaring reminder of my death makes me sick to the stomach. I still don't understand why Brendan staked me. I mean, I was no threat to him. Does he really think I'm the bad guy in this situation? Does he realize that what he's done could cause a domino effect that would affect all members in the supernatural community, possibly even resulting in war between the species?

Next I have to consider, if Brendan staked me once, will he come back to finish the job? I'm so hurt by his betrayal, but I'm still clinging to the hope that the younger brother I know and love is still somewhere inside that angry young man. I won't believe that all the good in him is gone. He's just been led astray. He thinks I'm the bad guy because he was so shocked when he found out what I am, that's all it is. There must still be a part of him that loves me.

I feel Talon's body shift, and I roll to face him. He frowns, reaching out a hand to wipe away a tear I didn't know had fallen. "Em? What's wrong?"

Dev stirs from behind me, and Nik sits up from where he was laying behind Talon, gazing down at me with a look of concern. "What's going on?" he asks, blinking rapidly as he tries to shake away the last remnants of sleep.

I sigh and turn to stare up at the ceiling, unable to meet their concerned eyes. "I'm just thinking about my brother. Wondering if he's going to come back for me when he finds out I'm alive."

At first, my concerns are met only with silence, but then Nik breaks it with an ominous chuckle. "I really hope he does come back. Then he'll find out just what happens when someone messes with my soul-tie."

Talon sits up and leans over me, obstructing my view of the ceiling so I have no choice but to look at him. "He won't hurt you again. We won't let him."

I nod because I know he means it, but that's part of what I'm afraid of. What if next time, Brendan really does just want to talk? Will they attack first, and ask questions later?

Dev groans and crawls out of bed. "Damn, Em, we need to come up with some kind of sleep schedule. It's too cramped with all of us sharing the same bed every night."

He walks around and stops at the end of the bed, stretching out his cramped muscles. I take a moment to admire his toned body, taking in the other scars that decorate his chest. I make a mental note to ask about them when we have some alone time.

Dev catches me watching him and grins wickedly. "Besides, if we were in my bed, maybe other things could have happened." He smirks, waggling his eyebrows playfully.

Talon throws a pillow at him, which he dodges with a laugh. Then Dev makes his way to the bathroom, boldly calling over his shoulder, "I'm going to take a shower, Em. Would you care to join me?"

I let out a small laugh, my heart lifting, which I'm sure was his goal all along. He always seems to know just what to do to lighten my mood. "Sorry, Dev. You're on your own this time."

He sighs dramatically and slumps his shoulders in mock defeat. "Okay, but don't say I didn't offer." He turns to Nik with a grin, his feigned sadness disappearing in an instant. "Nik, be a dear and make us some coffee, would you?"

Nik grumbles from Talon's other side and gets up from the bed. "Fine, I'll get the coffee ready. Dev, go take your shower. It'll be ready when you get out."

Dev gives a nod before closing the bathroom door, and Nik turns to us with a mischievous twinkle in his eyes. "Don't worry, I'll make sure no one interrupts." With that parting comment, he leaves, closing the bedroom door behind him, which makes me painfully aware that for the first time in a while, Talon and I are completely alone.

I avoid meeting his eyes, unsure if he feels the same burning desire I do. He lifts my chin and the moment our gazes meet, I suck in a breath. Talon's green eyes are blazing with desire. He doesn't give me a chance to speak, quickly claiming my lips in a frenzied kiss.

I respond eagerly, running my hands over his naked chest as he moves to hover over me, his hard length rubbing against me. I moan and arch my hips up to meet his encouragingly. He takes that as all the approval he needs and trails his lips down my collarbone.

I slip my hand down between us to grip him tightly through his boxers, drawing a moan from him as he peppers me with kisses.

I've wanted him since the moment I first laid eyes on him. When I couldn't have him, it drove my beast crazy. But now he's here, within my reach, and he wants me just as much as I do him. I can feel it.

I slide my hand over his boxers, undoing the buttons so I can free his cock. I run my hands over his shaft, making him growl against my chest. I can't help the smirk that crosses my face as he pulls away and looks down at me with such hunger in his gaze. "You like that, do you?" I purr, my own eyes hooded with lust.

I push him back so I can peel off the shirt I'm wearing and throw it across the room. His gaze locks on my left breast, clearly focusing on my faster than normal heartbeat. My whole body tingles with his appraisal, and I pull his head closer, offering what I know he's desperate for.

He clasps onto my nipple without hesitation, and I feel his fangs scrape against my breast as he teases me, bringing me closer to the edge of my climax.

He bites down at the same time a blaring noise rings throughout the room. I ignore the sound, too absorbed in the feel of Talon drinking from me. He slides his hands down over my ribs to move to my panties, sliding them off. After removing them, he throws them carelessly across the room. Then I hear Dev's voice shouting from behind the bathroom door, breaking the haze of lust we'd descended into.

"Is someone going to get that?"

Talon groans and presses his head to my stomach before rolling to the side. I grab the communicator, which is the source of the annoying noise, and press the little green button to answer.

"Hello?"

Britt's voice echoes through the communicator, and also from the outer room. "Bitch! Whatever the hell you're doing, hurry the fuck up. Nik won't let me in!"

As if to back up her point, I start to hear banging on the wall next to the bedroom door.

I laugh and let my head sink back into the pillow. I've got to give her an award for the most awful timing ever.

I sigh, knowing she won't leave, and that I should just get up. "Alright, give me a minute to get changed, and then I'll be out." I press the red button on the communicator and glance over at Talon with a sheepish grin. "Sorry, I forgot I was supposed to be meeting Britt. Do you mind taking a rain check?"

He smiles and pulls me close, offering me a chaste kiss. "We will finish this sooner or later, Emerald. You can count on that." His eyes darken, and I roll away, standing from the bed without caring that I am giving him a complete view of my naked body. If I stayed in that bed with him, I know I won't be leaving to talk to Britt anytime soon.

His eyes focus on the little trickles of blood that runs from the marks he left on my breast. He closes his eyes with a groan. "Go have fun with your friend." Then his eyes snap open, and he looks at me with concern. "Just please be careful. The coven knows of your existence, but some may not be too happy to have you here. The last thing we want is for you to get hurt."

I smile reassuringly before making my way over to my bags to pull out some clothes. "I'll be fine. I'll be with Britt. She has wicked magic and knows that you guys would hunt her down if anything happened to me."

He sighs, and I get dressed without looking at him, knowing if I turn back he's going to use those sinfully gorgeous eyes to lure me into staying, when I really could use a break.

I look down at my jeans and pale pink tee before running my fingers through my hair. Dev's still in the shower, so I go over and open the door, offering a quick goodbye. "Dev, I'm going out with Britt for a while. I'll see you when I get back, okay?"

67

"Sure thing, Em. I'll see you soon. Stay safe."

I smile and close the door behind me. I look over to see Talon is slowly getting dressed, and while I want to stay and watch, I know Britt will be growing more impatient by the minute.

Sure enough, when I open the bedroom door and take a step into the other room, it's to find Britt and Nik locked in an intense stare down. He looks ready to throw her out of the room, and she looks equally as likely to force him out, or cast a spell on him more likely.

"Okay, you two. Enough," I chide.

Britt relaxes the moment she sees me. "Oh, thank God. I thought you were gonna be hours."

I shake my head at her impatience and walk over to Nik, pressing a kiss to his cheek. "Sorry I took so long. You okay?"

He purses his lips. "Yeah I can handle Britt any day, but I think we need to get some kind of magical lock for our quarters. She keeps walking in as if she owns the place," he says, huffing in annoyance.

I chuckle at the way Britt stamps her foot at that like a scolded child, and give him a lingering kiss. He pushes me away with a growl. "If you don't go now, I may not let you leave at all."

"Fine, I'm going."

Britt walks over to the door, waiting for me. I begin to make my way towards her, but before I'm out of reach, Nik grabs my hand and pulls me back around. I see a hint of concern shining in his eyes. "You have your communicator?"

At my nod, he gives a relieved sigh. "Good. Use it if you get separated from Britt for any reason. We'd rather you not be alone right now."

"Okay, I promise."

"Oh, and Em?"

"Yeah?"

He smirks. "Have fun."

Before I have a chance to respond, Britt grabs hold of my hand and drags me from the room.

"Well, that was rude!" I exclaim, turning on her as we walk down the hall towards the elevator doors.

She scoffs, "Oh, I was the rude one? You two were flirting so much that I was about to be sick all over your floor."

"'Oh, and Em? Have fun,'" she mocks in a deeper voice than I would have thought possible.

I can't help but laugh. "Okay yes, there was some flirting, but what do you expect? I haven't exactly had much alone time with them. I keep getting interrupted." I narrow my eyes pointedly at her.

She stays silent, but the shit-eating grin on her face says it all." I think I'm going to invest in that magical lock after all, you little witch. I didn't even get to have my morning coffee because of you."

She rolls her eyes. "Where we're going, there will be plenty of coffee." The elevator doors open, and she pulls me in after her, before pressing the button for the ground-level garage. "Uh, Britt? Are we leaving the coven?"

She grins gleefully. "Yep! We deserve a little pampering, so I thought we'd go to this special place I know of. We can get mani-pedis, and the place next door makes the best coffee you could ever dream of."

I smile at the longing in her voice when she says the last part. We've both got it bad when it comes to coffee.

A thought occurs to me. Britt generally has pretty lavish tastes, and I didn't plan for a day out. "And just how exactly are we paying for this extravagant day out? I don't know about you, but I am bitch-ass broke."

Well, that's not entirely true. I still have cash that my dad gave me stashed away in my bag, but I didn't think to bring it because I assumed we would be staying within the coven.

She gives me a cheshire grin and reaches into her back pocket, pulling out a wad of bills. "Courtesy of your Prince," she gloats, waving them near her face like a fan.

I nod absently as we exit the elevator and walk towards the garage, but then what she said sinks in.

"Prince? Who's a Prince?" I ask, my shrill voice echoing in the empty halls.

Her grins grows. "Oh, Nikoli hasn't told you yet?"

At my blank look, she continues. "Your vampire is practically royalty, even though he never likes to acknowledge it. Even without being royalty, he has enough cash to buy himself a noble title if he was so inclined. He suspected I was taking you to the surface, so he gave me plenty of cash to pay for our trip. He wants you to let off some much needed steam with your bestie." She winks, rubbing her hands together in anticipation.

I shove her arm playfully. "Sure. He gave you a wad of cash just for me," I respond sarcastically.

I doubt he'd give her a bunch of cash just for us to have a day out. If he did, then we're going to be having words later. I can pay my own way and while its a sweet thing for him to offer, he didn't. He just bypassed me in the equation, giving my friend money like I'm some kind of burden.

"He did, I swear. I'm supposed to buy clothes later, and this is going to cover that as well. He didn't want me using my own money, spouting some gibberish about how soul-ties provide for their partner. I really don't know, but I won't look a gift horse in the mouth. Though, I'm pretty sure he wanted us to go lingerie shopping, too. Maybe that's why he gave me so much," she muses.

I roll my eyes at her.

"Whatever. Let's just go and have some fun. I'll have a chat with Nikoli later about the money."

I glance around in confusion, expecting a car to be waiting for us, but there isn't one. Why else would we have come to this level, though?

Britt laughs at my obvious confusion and reaches into her jacket pocket, pulling out a set of familiar keys. Keys that have my heart racing in excitement. "Are those what I think they are?"

A wicked smirk appears on her face. "Hell yeah, they are! I swiped them when you were out last night." She winks, throwing them to me.

I catch them one handed, and I grin happily. Oh, this is going to be a fun day out, indeed.

I race through the garage, not stopping until I get to her.

"Hey, baby. Did you miss me?" I coo, stroking the navy blue hood before unlocking the car for Britt.

I walk around my baby, making sure no one has scratched or dented her, and let out a sigh of relief when I see her unharmed.

I take my seat behind the wheel and breathe in the comforting smell, recognizing the lingering scent of the guys but also that of myself as well.

Britt is already in the passenger seat, and her giddiness is contagious. "I put a spell on the car, Emerald. Anyone who sees you going over the speed limit will forget within seconds. The only ones the spell won't affect are other supes."

"Excellent. Let's get out of here then," I say with a wicked grin.

I start the car, and the purr of the engine gives me chills. I smile broadly as I speed out of the garage and onto the road. Britt is happily bouncing in her seat, unable to contain her excitement, and I would do the same if I wasn't getting ready to push my baby to the limits. I slam my foot on the gas, enjoying the power of the engine vibrating through me as I speed off down the road.

The sun is still out, and I'm driving my baby in the city with my best friend. I don't think I've ever felt freer.

Chapter Nine

COFFEE DATE

EMERALD

We drive the streets aimlessly for a while before Britt gives me any directions. She knows how much peace driving gives me and lets me do my own thing for a bit, for which I'm grateful for. She's such an amazing friend.

"Turn here," Britt instructs after a bit. I take the corner sharply with a delighted laugh. Britt chuckles as I speed down the street.

"Okay, Em, slow down now. We're almost there."

I ease up on the gas pedal and bring my speed down to a more reasonable level. Britt directs me down a small side street that houses a few boutiques and a small parking lot. I park the car at the back of the lot, and we climb out with massive smiles on our faces.

Britt comes around to my side and leads me down a deserted alleyway lined with a few shops. "I've missed your driving, Mer. The guys are such wusses when I'm in the car. They think going fast is too dangerous and all that crap. I think they're just afraid of me hurting myself, even though they know I'm invincible. I mean, do they not get that we all have to die at the same time to really stay dead? It's like grow a pair."

Wow! Doesn't sound like things are going too well for Britt if she's got pent-up frustration over something as small as going fast in my car.

"I think it's different because I'm a pro at driving. When I get behind the wheel I know I have complete control over the car.

Whereas when you're in the driver's seat, all your husbands see is a lunatic behind the wheel. They want you safe and you driving like I do probably terrifies them. My advice, work them up to it. Find a deserted street or neighborhood where you can prove to them you are in complete control."

She sighs, wrapping an arm around my shoulder as she leads us down the street. "God, I missed you. Just hearing you say all that out loud comforts me, but if they say something like that, I get all angry. Why? Ugh!"

I chuckle. "Because when your friend tells you something, it's completely rational. When your partner does, we think they're just being arrogant idiots."

"True! Oh well, I guess you and I will just have to take the car out for a spin more often. I trust you implicitly behind the wheel, although maybe we should bring Kellan on a drive one day. He hates fast cars," she says with a laugh, and I can't help the giggle that slips free. She likes playing tricks on people as much as I do. I wonder if Nik would like to come with us too. I'm sure if he knew I was planning to trick one of the others, he'd be up for it.

She continues plotting as we walk. "Or Blaine. He likes to think he's a fast driver, but I swear he's slower than Aunt Macy."

I throw my head back, laughing at the sudden image I have of Blaine going pale as I speed around the corner, all while Britt's laughing her ass off.

"Oh, God! I can just imagine it. It would be the same if I took Talon out. He'd be a mixture of scared shitless and pissed beyond belief at how reckless I was being."

We both erupt into giggles at the image of Talon, terrified, but still lecturing me at the same time. Though, I imagine if we did take Talon out, he'd never let me drive again.

When we finally regain our composure, Britt leads me into a cute little coffee shop.

"This place is amazing! They use real cream in their coffee rather than plain old milk. You're gonna love it!"

I inhale the rich aroma, not even bothered that it's overwhelming my senses. The fragrance is mouth-watering.

We walk up the counter and place our orders before choosing a spot to sit. We manage to find two comfy seats tucked in the back of the shop, happily sinking into them while we wait for our orders.

I study the place, with its soft brown walls and brightly colored furniture. Even the mugs are done in cheery colors, so they stand out in the room.

After a few minutes, our coffees are placed in front of us, and Britt thanks the server before he leaves. She takes a sip and winces as it burns her tongue, but then she grins over at me. "I love this stuff. Even if it burns me every time, it's just too good to wait for it to cool."

I shake my head and take a sip of my hazelnut latte, sighing happily. She wasn't wrong. This has to be one of the most amazing coffees I've ever had.

"Wow, that's so good. I will definitely be coming back here, that's for sure."

"Right!" She puts her cup down a little more forcefully than I think she intended, causing it to rattle on the plate. "I stumbled by this place around the same time I first met the guys. I was having some trouble dealing, and this was the first coffee shop I found. Now I come here at least once a month to get my fix."

I take a small sip of my latte and find it's cooled down enough for me to really enjoy it. We sit in comfortable silence for a few minutes before Britt decides to get serious.

"So, how's the sex between you four?"

I choke on my coffee, almost spilling it all over myself in my hurry to put the mug down. Britt laughs and hands me a napkin so I can clean up the small bit coffee that has dribbled out of my mouth.

"Seriously, Britt? You couldn't wait until I swallowed before asking that?"

She grins, clearly unperturbed. "Where's the fun in that?"

I narrow my eyes at her.

"Oh, come on, Mer! Stop trying to avoid the question and give me all the juicy details."

I look around to make sure no one is watching us or listening in. Thankfully, though, everyone else seems to be distracted by their own things.

I fidget in my seat before responding. "Sex is... good."

She grimaces and leans forward in her seat. "Seriously? All you've got is good? Are they not giving you mind-blowing orgasms that make you forget your own name?" she asks, before getting a far off look in her eyes. After a moment, she shakes her head and focuses back on me. "If you can still remember your name after sex with any one of those delicious men, then I may have to get my guys to give them some tips." She smirks mischievously.

I squirm, unable to meet her gaze. "Uh, well..."

She leans back in the chair, her eyes going wide. "No!" she gasps. "No freaking way! You have got to be kidding me!"

The look of shock on her face makes me feel incredibly awkward. I mean it's not that big of a deal, is it?

"Emerald, I swear by all things that are holy in this world, if you haven't let at least one of those men pound you into every known surface imaginable to man, I may just have to slap you!"

At my continued silence, she slaps a hand against the table, drawing the attention of a few nearby customers. I blush furiously as she begins to laugh, drawing even more attention to us.

I beg her to quiet down. "Britt! Control yourself!"

She regains her composure, wiping a tear from her eyes. "Sorry, I just don't know whether to admire your extreme self-control or slap you upside the back of the head. You said Talon hadn't slept with anyone the entire time he was with Heather, so I assumed the moment you came back from the dead, he would have jumped your bones."

I narrow my eyes at her. "Well, maybe he would have, but the timing didn't exactly work out in our favor. Besides, we would have if you didn't keep interrupting us!"

"Wait! I've interrupted you? When?" she demands, staring me down intently.

"Well, earlier today for one. Why else do you think Nik wouldn't let you into the bedroom?"

Understanding crosses her eyes, and she chuckles. "Sorry, Mer. I'll try to be more tactful in the future. But, damn. I can't believe nothing has happened between you two yet. The chemistry between you and Talon can heat up a room." She sighs, fanning herself dramatically. "Please tell me you plan to get a piece of that man, and soon?"

I sigh dreamily. "Oh, yes. I definitely want some alone time with Talon. But with everything going on, in order to get that alone time, I think I'm going to have to pull a fire alarm or something."

"You know I could magic you some alone time if you really want," she offers, waggling her eyebrows suggestively.

"Thanks, but I'd prefer to find some alone time on my own. Otherwise, I'm sure I'd be thinking about the fact you knew why I needed the alone time in the first place." I shudder at that. I understand she can hear my thoughts occasionally, but for her to know exactly when I planned to do something with one of my soul-ties, nope! Just can't do it.

"Okay, time for a subject change. Tell me, Britt. How is married life for you and your four sexy men? Now I bet you're getting plenty of action." I wink, cradling my mug as I lean closer.

The mood between us goes from carefree to tense in an instant. When Britt finally meets my eyes, her blue ones are watering, and I watch in absolute shock as the first tear falls.

I rise from my seat, crouching down beside her as she wipes the tears away. "Britt, what is it? What'd I say?"

She shoos me back to my seat. I go begrudgingly, but I know she won't talk if I coddle her. It's just who she is. Instead, I move my chair a little closer to be able to reach out and just hold her hand. It's the small things that mean the most to her.

After a few moments of silent tears, she regains her composure. She lifts her head slowly and meets my eyes, hers filled with sadness. "The coven is threatening my husbands. The head witch is saying I'm hoarding power by not sharing them with the other females. There are far more female witches than there are males. Usually, one male is paired with multiple females, but lucky me, I fell in love with four men instead."

She sighs heavily and takes a sip of her coffee before continuing. "Anyway, the head of the coven says I have to share my men, or he'll unbind us. It just sucks. We had just started talking about having kids after a pretty scary situation, and now I just don't know what to do. If I want to have a child, we have to register with the coven. But if we do that, then the head of the coven will know I don't plan on sharing my men. I just don't know what to do. If I tell my husbands I want to hold off on having children, they'll be devastated, but I don't want to risk us being unbound either."

"Oh, honey, I'm so sorry. Is there anything you can do? Can you just go ahead and have a child without telling the coven?"

She shakes her head sadly. "No, there's nothing I can do. As for having children, I don't need their permission to have one, but if I got pregnant without registering it with them, the old laws state they have the right to take my newborn child from me and sever all ties with my partner, or in this case, partners."

I gasp in shock. "They would do that? Take a child away from its mother because of some stupid archaic law? I can't believe your coven would be that heartless."

She shrugs. "It all depends. They could also leave me with the child, but then take away my husbands. And if the coven decided to do that, they could bind our feelings, magically suppressing what we already felt for each other."

"They can do that?" I ask, thinking about my own ties. I hadn't ever planned to have children, but the thought of someone taking an unborn child from its mother enrages me nonetheless. It would be just like what happened to my own mother. I pity any fool that tries to take a child from my friend, because I guarantee a small army will rise up to get that child back, with me leading the charge.

She nods, looking completely defeated. "Yeah, they can. It has to be an unanimous vote, but most of the council doesn't exactly approve of us. It doesn't help that one of the council members has been after Torie for a while. She propositioned him before we got together and has been trying to get her hands on him, even after we got married."

She sighs and rubs a hand over her eyes. "Don't worry about your ties, though. Witches won't interfere in vampire soul-ties unless a coven Queen deems it's a suitable punishment for a crime that's been committed, and since your mother is the Queen, I doubt you could ever do any wrong in her eyes."

I frown, wondering if there's anything I can do to help Britt. Maybe if I bring it up to my mother, she could talk to the witches for me? There must be something we can do.

I can't imagine being torn from one of my guys because my kind lacked the number of males necessary to procreate. Not to mention my right to have a child being based solely on a bunch of witches deciding whether I deserved to or not; it must be hell in the coven.

Britt claps her hands together, startling me from my thoughts. "Enough doom and gloom. I promised you a fun time out, not some depressing day of problems." With that, she pushes away from the table and gets to her feet, a happy mask falling in place.

I can tell it's a mask because I know this bothers her far more than she'd care for others to see. Her husbands must have some kind of idea that this is eating at her, though. If not, maybe I should make them aware?

"Mer, you coming?"

"Yep, sorry just thinking too hard." I force a smile and follow her out the coffee shop. We head into the nail salon two doors down, and the workers rush us to a seat, greeting Britt by name. I take it she's been here a lot, too.

We spend the next two hours getting pampered in our massage chairs, all the while talking about what we missed out on in each other's lives in the last several years.

After we finish up and Britt is at the counter paying for the pamper day, an uneasy feeling sends a shiver through me. I freeze, having felt something watching me, and turn subtly to look out the shop windows.

I try to remain inconspicuous, pretending to leaf through pamphlets on appropriate nail care while taking a peek outside.

I swear I can see something shift in the shadows across the street, but it could just be a trick of the light. As we leave the shop and head back towards the car, I take another quick glance over, seeing nothing but an empty street. I must have imagined it.

I shake my head at my silliness. I'm just being overly paranoid. I can't think that something bad will happen every time I leave the safety of the coven, or I'll never be allowed to leave again. Besides, I'm not sure when I'll get the chance to spend time alone with Britt again and I don't want to ruin things by panicking over nothing.

Chapter Ten

SURPRISE TRAINING SESSION

EMERALD

I drove us back to the coven, and we rode in comfortable silence. We had a relaxing day out, but I could sense that Britt wasn't in the mood to talk.

Britt walks with me back to my room, but stops me before I can open the door. She wraps her arms around me in a massive bone-crushing hug. "Thank you for letting me take you out today, Mer. I didn't realize how much I, too, needed the break." She pulls away with a teary grin. "I really did miss you."

"I know, Britt. I missed you, too."

After a moment, she lets go and waves goodbye, before walking back down the hallway towards the elevator. I can tell her heart is heavy with sadness, and I vow to find out if there's anything I can do to make her life easier. My mother may know of a way we can intercede on her behalf, or at the very least, could ask Macy what exactly the big deal is and why her council is so against Britt having four husbands.

Still thinking about Britt, I go into our room and freeze at the sight before me. Talon, Nik, and Dev are all dressed in suits, but that's not the most shocking part. They're busy stashing weapons anywhere they can in the suits as if they were designed to have little hidey holes and secret pockets for just such a purpose.

"What's going on, guys?" I ask, closing the door behind me.

Nik and Dev avoid my gaze, instead seeking out Talon's. He

mutters, "Why do I always have to deliver the news that's gonna upset her?"

"Upset me? What's going to upset me?" I ask, feeling confused.

Dev chuckles. "You get to deliver the bad news because she's less likely to kill you than she is us."

Talon sighs and meets my eyes, determined. "We're meeting the local pack today, remember? We have to explain our reasoning for killing those three rogues and almost killing the fourth."

Oh, I'm just gonna pretend that I didn't totally forget about the pack meeting. "Oh, right. Hold on, give me two minutes, and I'll be ready to go." I smile at them and walk into our bedroom to get ready, with Talon following behind me. When I open the drawer, he speaks. "Em, you're not coming."

I freeze, turning as my eyes narrow dangerously. "What do you mean, I'm not coming?"

Dev sucks in an audible breath from the other room, and Nik's whispers can be heard even from here. "Should we leave him? She might kill him in a fit of rage."

"Both of you two idiots better get in here right now, or it will be you two that I'll kill in a fit of rage," I growl through clenched teeth.

They hurry into the bedroom but refuse to meet my eyes, all signs of their cheeky demeanor gone. I guess it's not as funny when you're actually faced with the woman who may very well put you in the direct line of fire of her rage.

"Explain! Why am I not coming? Do you even think you have the power to stop me?" I demand answers as I stand there with my hands on my hips, my anger quickly rising.

Talon takes a step towards me, but halts when I spear him with a glare. He shakes his head as if he's disappointed in me. "Emerald, you're not coming with us, and that's final."

"Final? Who do you think you're talking to, Talon? One of your little lackeys that you train? No, I am your goddamn soul-tie, and you will treat me like one! If you guys are in trouble, then so am I!" As I talk, my voice gets steadily louder. By the end, it's risen to a full shout, and my beast is pacing in my mind, demanding to be released.

Dev holds up his hands and approaches slowly. I imagine my eyes are blood red as my beast pushes to be free.

"Em, please, think about this logically. You died and came back to life. Everyone thinks you're dead. If you come with us, then they'll know you survived the attack, and it will paint an even bigger target on your back. They'll demand to know how you survived, and some of the unsavory members of the pack will tell their friends and so forth, until word gets back to more rogues, or even to your pack. Then what will you do? The whole world will be after you, hunting you because of your existence alone. We're protecting you by leaving you behind."

His words make sense, but the thought of them leaving me alone to go deal with the pack makes me... anxious. What if they get hurt because of their actions saving me? I should be there to defend them!

But after a few tense moments, I sigh, giving in. "You're right." I turn to Talon and take the few steps towards him until his arms envelop me. "I'm sorry I was acting like such a bitch. It's just that I only recently found you guys. If one of you got hurt because you saved me, I could never forgive myself."

I inhale Talon's scent and find myself relaxing against him. He runs a hand down my back and rests his head on top of mine. "Don't worry, Em. We'll be careful. And if it helps, I'll protect the two idiots," he murmurs, and I laugh against his chest.

"Oh, sure. I'm the one who convinced her to stay here, but I'm still classed as an idiot," Dev mutters indignantly.

I turn in Talon's arm and see Dev's pout from across the room.

"Come here, Dev," I coax and open my arms invitingly.

He approaches, walking into them willingly, and I end up sandwiched between the two of them. Nik watches us with an open fascination, and I smile at him.

After a moment of being sandwiched between the two of them, I squeeze myself out of their arms with a sigh. I move, so all three of them can see me clearly as I speak.

"While I'm not happy that I'm staying behind, I understand why I must. Maybe next time, though, we discuss it first, yeah?" I approach

Talon slowly, feeling seductive as I move my hips side to side, drawing his unwavering gaze. "Otherwise, I'm going to make sure it's me that interrupts us from going further next time," I purr, stepping up to press my lips against his. His mouth parts in a soft gasp, and I take advantage of the movement to grip his bottom lip between my teeth, pulling it lightly until he groans.

I let go of his lip, and step out of reach before he can grab me, a wicked grin on my face. I walk around the three of them and into the bathroom, my heart racing a mile a minute with the need to have him.

I close the bathroom door and sink to the floor, my body flushed with need. I definitely need a cold shower after that.

A few minutes later, and after my heart has calmed down enough that I trust myself on my feet, I go to take a quick shower, setting the water to cold until I know I'm no longer craving my soul-ties. Who am I kidding? I'll always crave them, but at least now I feel somewhat calmer. Slowly, I turn the water to warm while I think about what I'll do while the guys are gone. It's the first time since being here that I'll be alone and I'm not too sure how to feel about that.

I dry myself off, feeling a moment of regret for not bringing in a change of clothes, but there's nothing I can do about that now. I walk out of the bathroom, glad to find the guys have left the bedroom, so I can put my clothes on without my hormones getting fired up again.

Once dressed, I walk out into the outer room, and see the guys are all standing by the door, ready to go.

Nik smirks at me and pulls me in for a quick hug. "We have to go now, but I promise we'll be back before the night is over."

With that, I'm handed off to Talon. He inhales the scent coming off my hair, which is the new lily shampoo one of the guys put in the bathroom for me. "We figured you might get lonely without us, so we have someone coming by soon to keep you company."

"Who?" I ask, feeling intrigued.

Dev wags his finger at me with a mischievous grin. "Nuh uh, no telling. That would ruin the surprise." He bends down to give me a quick kiss before striding out the door, Nik following after him with a wave. Talon hesitates, his hand on the door knob. "Stay safe, Emerald. We'll be back before you know it."

With that, he closes the door behind him, leaving me to myself. I sigh heavily, before moving into the kitchen to make myself a cup of coffee. When it's done, I take my mug and go sit in front of the TV.

As I sit there, I find myself becoming increasingly anxious from the loneliness, but then a knock sounds at the door, distracting me from my thoughts. I'm curious who the guys invited over, but a bit nervous as well. I hope it's Britt, but I have a feeling it's not her.

I walk to door, inhaling deeply to determine if I recognize the visitor by their smell. I smile at the familiar scent and open the door with welcoming arms.

My father waits out in the hallway, his green eyes full of glee. "I hope you're ready to come for a run." He grins, bouncing on the balls of his feet.

A genuine smile splits my face, and I nod eagerly. "Yes! I'm dying to burn some energy!" I exclaim, excited to go for a run. I can't believe the guys invited my father over. I will definitely have to thank them for this.

I step out into the hall, closing the door behind me. My father smiles warmly. "After you, Emerald."

We walk side by side down the hall towards the elevator. When we get inside and the doors close, I almost burst with joy. "Where to?" I ask, unable to contain my excitement.

"We're going down to the forest to train." He beams, obviously just as happy as I am.

There's something about being with another wolf and running that has me bursting with happiness. Wolves need to burn off their energy daily, and I am still struggling to find the balance between my two natures. My beast is a mix of both races, but some days, she needs the physical burn of a hard workout, and on others, she just wants to sleep. I never noticed that when I was with the pack. I was so busy trying to fit in among the others that I kept myself physically exhausted and never had the time to notice just how weird my beast is compared to normal wolves.

Especially with feeding. I've been drinking the guys' blood and lots of coffee, of course, but the need for food is almost completely gone. Sure, when food is placed in front of me, I'll eat it, but the hunger, the craving for meat I felt as a wolf is disappearing, replaced with a lust for blood.

I close my eyes and shake my head to clear it. That's something I can think about at another time.

The elevator doors open, and we step out into the beautiful underground forest. My beast is practically vibrating inside me with her need to be released.

"Can I shift?"

He shakes his head sadly and directs us towards a well-worn path among the trees. "I thought we'd run as humans today. The guys would be able to sense if you shifted through the soul-tie, and the last thing we want is them killing the pack in their hurry to get back to you," he says with a roll of his eyes.

I laugh because I can see it playing out exactly like that. If I shifted, the pain and momentary fear I'd feel from it, followed by the excitement would confuse the hell out of the guys.

As much as the thought of not shifting disappoints my beast, I won't because I know he's right. I don't want the guys hunting me back down to the coven and causing an incident because of my desire to shift.

We take off at a slow-paced jog, which quickly speeds up and becomes a race between the two of us. I laugh as my father moves ahead of me on the trail. He thinks he can beat me, but I know different. Speed was one area I always excelled in.

I grin before picking up the pace. My legs burn at first, but the more I push myself, the faster I go. In no time, I pass him, laughing at the way he tries to keep pace with me.

My father's face reddens as he tries to catch up to me, but it's no use. I have both vampire and wolf speed on my side.

The clearing we started at is up ahead, so I push myself a little harder for the final stretch, laughing when I clear the tree line, my father a minute behind me.

I fist pump the air while my father bends over, putting his hands on his knees and taking deep breaths. When he's recovered enough, he smiles at me proudly. "You won that round, but I'd appreciate if we didn't tell your mother about this. She already hates me eating unhealthy food. If she finds out I was beaten by my own daughter, she may make me go on a crazy health cleanse or something." He shudders, a sliver of real fear in his eyes.

If there's one thing you don't do, it's take food from a wolf. He may just bite you out of starvation. I feel for him, I truly do.

I laugh. "Don't worry, Dad. I can train with you so you can get back to your normal wolf standards."

My father's face pales and I frown, wondering what I said to upset him. His eyes mist over, and he has to clear his throat a few times before he can speak. "You just called me Dad."

I think back over what I said and feel the blood drain from my face. I did call him Dad. "Oh."

I don't quite know what to say, so I just stay quiet and try to pretend it didn't happen, choosing instead to focus on stretching out my muscles.

My dad always used to stress the importance of stretching before and after training. Knowing I called my father 'Dad' makes me miss my dad even more and leaves me feeling more confused than ever.

What does it mean? I don't want to betray my dad, but the word just slipped out. I hadn't even realized I had called Axel 'Dad' until he mentioned it.

My father sits down beside me as I stretch. I keep my gaze focused on my task, even when he starts speaking to me. "Emerald, it's okay for you to call me Dad, too. I know it's hard, but I swear I don't want to replace Brent in your life. He raised you and is your dad, which I respect. Nothing will change that. I just want to build my own relationship with you. To bond the way we should have while you were growing up. If that's too hard for you though, just tell me, and I will understand completely."

I sigh and turn to meet his eyes. I can see the pain in them and feel shitty for being the source of that hurt. "I know you don't want to replace him. It's just my issues. I'm worried that the longer I'm away from him, the less I will remember him, or worse, that he'll forget about me. I mean, I'm not even his biological child. He has Brendan to lead the pack now that I'm gone, but I can't bear the thought of being replaced. Not to mention all the trouble Dad is in because of me. He may not even be Alpha anymore," I admit sadly. "It's hard for me, because I feel like if I talk about him, I'm hurting you and my mother more since I barely know the two of you. I don't even mention him to my soul-ties for fear that it will lead to anger at Brendan. It's just better for everyone if I stay quiet and pretend nothing is wrong and that none of this bothers me."

"Oh, Emerald, my sweet girl. You don't need to hide your feelings from us. We all understand how much you love Brent, and Brendan, despite what he did. You wouldn't be who you are if you didn't show at least some small ounce of compassion. It makes us love you more, knowing after everything you've been through, you still try to find the good in people. The only advice I can give you is to be careful. Some people truly want to be good, others don't care about right or wrong anymore, only power."

"As for your soul-ties, if you sit down with them and express your fears and concerns, I'm sure they will listen because as your soul-ties, it's their responsibility to look after you, both emotionally and physically."

With that, he gets to his feet, holding out a hand to me. "You ready to train against your old man?"

Chapter Eleven
King Vs Princess

EMERALD

I bounce around on my feet, and my father smirks. "Do you want to know more about your dad and I, Emerald? Maybe a little incentive for your training?" he suggests, his eyes full of light after our emotional talk.

I nod eagerly, not taking my eyes off him for a second. My father used to drill into me that once a fight has started, you never take your eyes off your enemy, unless they're dead or unconscious.

We start off slow, assessing each other. Then I lunge, trying to catch him by surprise.

He laughs and easily steps out of the way, using my momentum against me to send me scrambling in the dirt.

I get to my feet quickly before he can spring an attack on me, but he just stands there, his face filled with... cockiness?

"Brent obviously hasn't changed his training. That's the exact same move he used to use on me when we were children. He hated being the younger brother, you know? He knew that I would always be Alpha unless something happened to me, so he had to fight even harder to prove himself. Not that he really needed to, though. I always knew he was Alpha material, but archaic rules dictated the first born is typically chosen as Alpha."

"Huh? I thought my dad was older than you? Maybe I got confused?"

He smirks and shifts his body weight to the right before attacking me with two quick punches. I dodge the first, but the second grazes my right side along the ribs. It doesn't hurt much, and I'm sure I've already healed by the time I'm out of range.

"Your dad is most definitely younger than me. I watched him being born. Your grandmother made sure I was in the room because she thought it would teach me how to respect women." He shudders, obviously recalling the memory vividly, and I can't help but grimace in sympathy. No way would I make anyone watch me give birth, if I didn't have to. Sure, the father would be there, but I would never make a child watch something that gruesome. And I'm sure it was gruesome. Most shifter births are.

All pack members over the age of thirteen are taught how to deliver a pup, just in case our healers are not around at the time of labor, because if a woman gives birth without proper care, she may just die from it.

Usually, we need someone stronger than the wolf there to force the shift, so we can heal all injuries, but sometimes the wolf helping may not be dominant enough to force the shift. If that is the case, she will most likely bleed out from any injuries that occured while giving birth.

My father seems distracted by his thoughts, and I make another attempt at an attack, only for him to step to the side, avoiding me yet again. I somehow trip over my foot and am sent sprawling to the ground, my knees grazing on impact. I feel a small bit of blood run down my leg and my father's gaze tracks it.

He shakes his head with a sigh. "Your dad really hasn't changed his style of fighting at all, even after twenty years. Such a shame. Just means I have to teach you more than I thought."

I grin and feint to the left, laughing on the inside when he takes the bait. By doing so, he left himself open for me to swipe his legs out from under him. I leap away before he can get to his feet, a wide smile in place. "Did my dad ever use that trick?" I ask mockingly.

He narrows his eyes, but the glint in them tells me he finds me funny, rather than a threat. He circles me for a moment, but then his gaze shifts over my shoulder, focusing on something behind me. They widen in fear, and I whip around, ready to respond to the unknown threat, only to be tackled from behind. I'm pinned to the ground by my father, who is chuckling above me.

I groan and drop my head forward, feeling foolish for falling for such a trick. It's the oldest one in the book, after all. I let my senses be lulled into a false sense of security, so when I thought I was about to be attacked from behind, I responded without thinking. Such a foolish mistake to make.

He climbs off me, leaving me to scramble to my feet. "Use all of your senses, Emerald. You're not just a wolf. You're a vampire as well. All of your senses should be more advanced than that of a normal vampire or wolf. If an attacker really was approaching you from behind, you would have heard, smelled, or at least felt them before they got close enough to do anything. But, you responded to my cues rather than listening to your own instincts." He sighs with disappointment.

Screw it. If he's already disappointed, what's the harm in going all in then? Nothing. I lash out, attacking with all I have, using my full strength and hoping I can make some kind of impression. I want to prove I can handle myself against anything. I'm not some little girl that has to be left behind out of fear that I'll get hurt. Okay, there's a chance I'm still a little upset the guys left without me, even though I told them I understood.

We don't speak as we exchange blows. He blocks every punch, kick, and swipe of the legs, and I can only hope he'll tire soon. That's when I realize that while I may have beat him on the run, it was only because he let me win. There's no other explanation for the level of stamina he's showing me right now. How could he have been so tired then, yet be able to match me blow for blow now? Yep, he definitely let me win.

People start to trickle in, and begin preparing for their own training. While we're aware of them, my father and I continue to fight back and forth, neither of us allowing ourselves to get distracted. The more intense our blows get, the more people stop what they're doing to watch, eager to see a sparring match between their King and Princess.

When it becomes obvious we're evenly matched and neither of us is gaining any ground, my father backs off and starts to circle me again, looking for weaknesses in my defense. "Brent didn't just limit you to normal classes, did he?"

I laugh, but there's no joy in it. "Normal? You've got to be kidding me, right?" He doesn't respond, and he looks confused by my words, so I elaborate. "I was never normal in the pack. My trainer was Jeremy, and he was ruthless. The only reason I learned to defend myself properly was because Dad insisted I learn other techniques beyond what was covered in normal training. He was convinced only he could teach me properly, so we started training every day, morning and evening, until he was satisfied I was improving. But even with his extra training, I couldn't use those skills in normal classes. Jeremy would have beaten me within an inch of my life if I looked even remotely strong compared to the other pack members. He was so convinced I would never be Alpha of the pack and treated me in such a way that nobody else would respect me either."

My father frowns and moves slightly. My eyes track his movements carefully, but he's just distancing himself before speaking.

"Don't take this harshly, Emerald, but your pack doesn't respect you in part because you didn't stand up to Jeremy. Yes, he would have made your life even more of a living hell, but you took the easy way out. The pack would have respected you a lot more if you had stood up to him each and every day. I get in hindsight it's probably better that you didn't, because you may have revealed yourself by accident, but wolves respect strength above all else. Jeremy bullying you is just another show of strength, and it translates to the pack that if he can bully you, the future Alpha of the pack, then he can bully anyone and get away with it. Why would they offer to help you when in their eyes, you were too weak to lead them when you couldn't stand up to him on your own? That's what being Alpha is. You have to be strong enough for anything and sometimes, you have to accept that you will be the only one capable of making things change for the better."

I shake my head, outraged. "You have no idea what I went through. He made my own brother hate me. I guess cousin is the more accurate term really, but either way, he made Brendan hate me just because he was bitter. He hardly had any power left in the pack, all because my dad took his enforcer position away."

He cocks his head to the side. "And have you not yet realized that Brent trained you the way he would an enforcer, if not better? If you had to face Jeremy right now, you should be more than capable of defending yourself based on what I've seen. That's what Brent was training you for. To prove your worth among the pack.

"The only ones who undergo that rigorous level of training are pack members that want to become an enforcer or Alpha. He was grooming you to lead, whether you knew it or not."

The surprise must show on my face because he chuckles, while the gathered vamps mutter among themselves. "Yes, your father knew exactly what you would be capable of and has trained you well. And to think, you haven't even reached your full potential yet," he muses.

I sense a sudden tension in the air just before the wind shifts behind me, alerting me to an incoming threat. I dodge the attack from a vampire, and my father uses my distraction as an opportunity to lunge towards me, hoping to catch me off my guard.

I twist, reaching out to grab his arm before throwing him across the area we were training in. He lands in a heap next to a few vampires, but quickly gets back to his feet. His eyes are the amber of his wolf, which shows me how short his control is right now.

He runs at me, throwing punch after punch, and I block each blow. My beast responds to the wolf shining in his eyes, and I work my way closer, sneaking past his defenses and landing a punch straight to his jaw.

He's thrown back a few feet, and I see his eyes roll shut. After a moment passes with no movement, a few vamps gather around him, shaking him gently to see if he is okay.

I watch fascinated by the care they show, but refuse to go to his aid. The witch may have fooled me with the whole 'oh, you've knocked me unconscious trick,' but I won't fall for it again.

I guess it also helps that I can feel his elevated heartbeat through my shoes, reverberating in the ground. I don't know how I'm sure, but

I just know it's his, and I also know he's fully aware of everything around him.

I stand where I am, with my arms folded across my chest for a few more moments before I hear the sound of laughter coming from him. He sits up, cracking his neck with a groan and grins over at me. "I take it you've fallen for that one before."

I smirk back at him. "Yep. Besides even if you were unconscious, I knew you'd heal, eventually."

He chuckles and climbs to his feet, stretching out his body. I must have caused a little more pain than I thought.

My father addresses the vamps who are gathered around us. "Show's over, guys. Get back to your own training."

They disperse without needing to be told twice, giving me looks of appreciation as they move off to different areas, leaving us alone again. I try my best not to blush under their appraisal, but I can't help it. They look like they are actually impressed with me rather than hating on me, which I guess is better than at my pack. I hope I can prove myself worthy to them all.

My father makes his way over to me, wearing a massive grin. "You did amazing, Emerald. With a bit more time and practice, I reckon you could easily best Talon."

I can't help the dreamy smile that crosses my face. Now that will be the day. Talon is all kinds of powerful. Being able to beat him would mean I've learned something pretty epic. Or I cheated. Not going to lie, I have considered it. I think Nik and Dev would both help me out if it meant taking him down a peg or two.

He places an arm around my shoulder in a way that feels comfortable, like we've actually bonded. "I know your dad would be proud of you. Just as I am."

Chapter Twelve

FELICIA'S RETURN

EMERALD

*A*fter sitting with my father for a bit, he dismisses me from the underground forest.

"Sorry, Emerald. As much as I'd love for you to stay, I have to train these recruits. Besides, Talon and the others should be back by now."

I smile reassuringly. "Oh, that's okay. I was planning to head back anyway. I need another shower. I'm sure I'm stinking up the place after that workout."

He chuckles, wrinkling his nose in mock disgust. "Hmm, that's true. Better get back and shower before the whole coven catches whiff of your distinct odor."

I playfully shove his arm before waving goodbye and making my way towards the elevator, a smile on my face. For the first time since arriving, I feel relaxed in my position among the coven members.

While my father and I had been sitting to the side chatting, people would insert themselves into our conversation with random comments about my performance, making me feel accepted. None of them shied away from me like so many in the pack had. They actually accepted me.

As I take the elevator up to my room, I focus on the gnawing hunger that has been rising within me since my father and I finished our round together. I must have used way more energy than I thought. Hopefully, if the guys are back, one of them will offer to feed me, because I don't really know how to ask.

Lately, it feels like I'm just using them for their blood and I don't want them to get the wrong impression from it. I really need to figure out a new way to feed. It's not fair for them to have to drop everything just to feed me, but I fear that taking blood from a bag only to vomit it up again would be one, a waste of blood, and two, a waste of time.

I take the time to wonder what happened at the meeting. Surely, the guys didn't get in too much trouble. After all, those wolves attacked me! I merely defended myself! And the same was true of the guys. I would have died without their help. I wish I had the chance to tell the Alpha exactly what went down.

I still don't understand why those wolves attacked me in the first place. There was no real reason I could think of for them to barge into my hotel and attack me.

Another thing I can't figure out was how they knew where to find me. Did they just happen to see me as I explored the city and decided to follow me? Or did they actually know just where I was? That would mean that someone had told them I was coming, but who would do such a thing?

I guess those are all questions for another day.

The bell dings and I get out of the elevator onto my floor. I make it two steps down the hall before a door opens to one of the other rooms. I freeze as the scent of the person reaches my nose.

Sunlight and leather. The smell of someone who I thought had left the coven. Apparently not.

Sure enough, when I look up, I meet her shocked vibrant blue eyes. Nothing much has changed with her. Her long auburn locks flow behind her, and her pale freckled skin still has me as envious as ever.

Something is different, though. Her skin, while still pale, looks slightly sun-kissed. She must have been spray tanned or something, because no way would a vampire weaken themselves by going out in the sun just for a tan. Then again, she does strike me as the type of person to be vain enough do such a thing if anyone was.

Felicia stares at me, opening her mouth before closing it a few times until her face finally settles into a mask of determination.

"Emerald, I'm so glad I ran into you. I've been wanting to talk to you, but I didn't know when would be an appropriate time after everything you've been through."

I fight the urge to roll my eyes at her words. Her tone may come across as polite, but it feels forced. Instead of calling her out on it though, I remain silent, letting her say what she needs to. I can be the bigger person and listen to whatever she has to say.

"I just want you to know how sorry I am for the way things happened. Heather said some things to make me believe you were just out to hurt us, but I should have known better. A soul-tie between two people is treasured among our people, but with the way she used to talk about you and your soul-ties, she made me believe you were faking the whole thing."

Her gaze darts down to look at the cursive script on the right side on my collarbone where Nikoli's name is forever burned into me before meeting my eyes again.

"After Heather left, I had some time to think over your words, and I realized you were right. Nik deserves someone who makes him happy, and while I tried my best to do that, it's not my job to make him happy, it's yours as his soul-tie."

She pauses to take a deep breath. I see the sheen of tears in her eyes, which leaves me a little shocked. She must be really torn up over Nik, or is just a really fucking good actor. I don't quite know which to believe right now.

"I know you two will be happy together, and I don't want to stand in the way of that, but I would love it if we could find a way to be friends. I know it may not happen right off the bat, but I would like to get to know you more and can help ease you into our way of life. There is so much I could teach you about our kind, and our women in particular. The past is behind us, and I believe we can move forward and look towards the future instead. We live too long to let that kind of drama to affect us. So, if you're open to it, then I would like for us to be friends," she finishes with a smile.

I frown, not sure how to respond, when she moves past me. "Don't worry, Emerald. I know it won't happen straight away, but I just wanted to offer my apologies and let you know I would like us to become friends. Unfortunately though, I have an appointment I have to get to now, but maybe we can talk soon?"

I nod mutely as she presses the button for the elevator, offering a friendly wave as the doors close shut behind her.

What the fuck just happened?

I continue down the hall to our room in a daze. When I get there, I open the door, relieved to find it unlocked because I couldn't remember whether I had locked it or not. Considering I don't have a key, I would have been out of luck if I had and the guys weren't back yet.

Thankfully though, they've returned and are all laughing at some joke between them when I walk in. The sound of the door closing draws their gaze. One look at my face, and they leap to their feet, surrounding me with concerned expressions.

Talon grips me by the shoulders. "Em, what happened? Are you hurt?" When I don't immediately respond, he shakes me firmly. I snap out of my daze just in time to hear him threaten anyone who dared to hurt me. "I swear if anyone so much as laid a finger on you, I will destroy them!"

I choke out a laugh. Talon, my amazing protective Talon who always assumes I'm hurt. I move away from the guys, distancing myself.

I decide to make a coffee, wanting to keep my hands busy while I digest all the information Felicia just piled onto me.

The guys leave me alone, letting me do what I need, backing off into the background until I'm ready to talk. When my coffee is ready, I cradle it in my hands and take a large sip before lifting my gaze to meet the guys'.

Talon's eyes, while blazing, also show understanding. Now that he's no longer worried I'm hurt, he seems to have calmed down. Dev's face is a blank mask, and I know he's waiting to react until he has all the info.

Last but not least, I see that Nik's eyes are filled with concern. I'm not sure how he will handle what I'm about to say, but he should be aware of the situation regardless.

I sigh and steel myself. "On the way back from training with my father, I ran into Felicia. She was leaving our floor and stopped me to apologize. She also offered to be my friend."

Nik frowns at that and refuses to meet my gaze, choosing to look down at the floor instead. Talon stands as if frozen, shocked into silence. I think that was the last thing either of them expected to come from my mouth.

Dev, however, takes charge of the situation, straightening his back as he meets my gaze with hard eyes. "Tell us exactly what happened," he demands.

I nod and move over to the nearest couch, sitting down with my coffee. Then I relay everything that happened, almost word for word. When I get to the part about Felicia and how she talks about me being the one to make Nikoli happy, Nik goes and grabs a beer from the fridge, downing it in three gulps before pulling out a second. He starts to drink that one as well, but at a more reasonable pace.

When I finish recounting the conversation, I lean back in the chair to finish drinking my coffee, leaving the guys to their thoughts. I don't know how much time passes in complete silence, but I can't help glancing at each of them as I sit there. When my gaze reaches Nik, his eyes dart up and pierce me with a fierce expression. Some emotion is playing behind his eyes, and all I want to do is climb into his lap and erase whatever it is that is making him hurt so much.

"What are you going to do?" he asks, his voice sounding deeper than normal.

I scrutinize him, trying to figure out why he seems so bothered by this. Does he still have feelings for her? I know the relationship between Talon and Heather was built on lies rather than love, but I never stopped to think about what things had been like between Nik and Felicia.

Britt told me that Nik had been used by her in their relationship but he never actually said as much to me. Was I wrong to assume he was better off with me than he was with her?

But I don't ask any of the questions that are burning in my mind, knowing there's another time and place for such questions.

Instead, I merely shrug and focus on answering his question.

"I have no clue what to do honestly. I'm leaning towards ignoring her offer, but I just thought it was strange as hell she approached me. At first, I thought she was playing some game, but she cried real tears, Nik. I think she was actually being sincere. And if she was, do I not owe it to her to be the bigger person and try to be friends, or at the very least, be polite to her in passing?"

"Friends?" Nik spits out harshly. He forces a laugh and turns to face me with a hard expression.

"Be careful, Emerald. You may think all she wants is friendship, but then it will evolve into something more. She may start just by asking for a small favor, or for you to do something for her, and I guarantee she'll make you feel bad for her until you finally do it out of pity. That's when you're screwed. You won't ever be able to escape her at that point. Trust me, Felicia has perfected the art of crocodile tears, and if they can get her what she wants most, then she'll stop at nothing. Trust me, I know." He slams the empty beer bottle down on the bench, and I watch as it shatters to pieces, shards of glass scattering across the floor. Then he storms off without another word, leaving a mess behind him.

I swing my gaze to Talon and Dev, hoping for some kind of explanation for what Nik just said, but they remain immobile, both with drawn expressions.

I let out a breath of air, feeling exasperated by their lack of information. If they won't tell me, I guess I'll just have to find out for myself.

Shaking my head in irritation, I get to my feet, stepping around the pile of shattered glass to go set my empty cup gently on the counter. As I walk towards the bedroom, I call back over my shoulder. "That mess better be cleaned up by the time I come back out here."

Chapter Thirteen

MOVIE NIGHT

EMERALD

I'm standing behind the closed bedroom door, feeling confused beyond belief. Nik is nowhere to be found. Maybe he went to take a shower? I look inside the bathroom, but it's quiet, and there's no sign of him having used the shower recently.

I brush my hair out of my face and look at myself in the mirror. How on earth did Nik just disappear? That's when it occurs to me.

That son of a bitch! I stomp from the bathroom in a rage, my hair whipping behind me in my hurry.

I march straight over to his bed, my anger controlling me as I glare down at the thick gray comforter. It's the only explanation I can think of.

"Nik! I swear to all things holy, if you don't reveal yourself right now, I'm going to start throwing shit around the room until I find you. Then I'm going to strangle you for using your powers to hide from me!" I threaten, waiting with my hands on my hips. His comforter shimmers, and then he appears, plain as day, lying on his bed with his hands behind his head.

I try not let myself show how impressed I am by the use of his powers. I never thought he could make himself completely invisible. I thought it was more like a camouflage kind of effect. That's a pretty cool ability to have, to be honest.

While I'm busy marveling at his power, Nik is staring up at the ceiling, his eyes conveying a level of sadness which makes all my questions about his power disappear.

I sigh and move around to the side of the bed, taking a seat next to his hip. Leaning against him, I wait until he meets my eyes.

When he does, there's so much pain in their depths that it takes my breath away. "Hey, what's wrong? Please talk to me."

He moves over so I can lie beside him, and rolls onto his side to look at me. I stare back and discover an emotion in his eyes that I wasn't expecting: fear.

He leans forward, pressing his lips to mine, gently at first, but then the kiss becomes filled with desperation. I groan, letting the kiss continue, knowing he needs this closeness right now.

When he pulls away, I reach out and run my hand over his smooth cheek. "You don't have to talk if it bothers you, Nikoli. I'm sorry I tried to push you," I soothe, trying to convey my sincerity.

His eyes, while now filled with lust, still also shine with the fear I saw before the kiss. He sighs heavily. "You don't have to be sorry, Emerald. I'm just worried about you. At the end of the day, I can't tell you who to be friends with. However, I want you to know, if you choose to accept Felicia's offer of forgiveness and become her friend, I don't want any part of it. That's not to say I would leave you, but I won't spend time in the same room with her. I'm sorry if this sounds like an ultimatum; it's honestly not. I just... can't go through this again. I won't let myself be manipulated again."

He takes a deep breath and blows it out, making a strand of hair fall back down in front of my eyes. I push it out of the way as Nik continues. "While her offer seems sincere, and I love that you are the type of person that is kind enough to consider it, even after everything that happened, I just know how she is. She'll become your friend and act all sweet, then she'll turn around and use everything you tell her against you. She'll start doing things to undermine you or manipulate you. Then she'll flirt with you, and before you know it, you're in a relationship you have no way to escape from," he says with a shudder.

I chuckle at his words. I think he got a little too lost in his thoughts to realize exactly what he said.

"Uh, Nik? Felicia's okay looking, but she's definitely not my type.

For one thing, I am one hundred percent interested in men. A certain three to be more specific. It just so happens one of them is lying directly opposite me." I grin over at him teasingly.

He flushes before returning my grin with one of his own. "You know what I meant."

I roll my eyes at him and sigh. "Yes, I know what you meant. And I want you to know, if you don't want me to try to be friends with Felicia, I won't. How you guys feel matters to me. We need to communicate to make this relationship work. We're tied together for the rest of our lives. We can't be selfish. So, I will steer far from Felicia unless we all agree on giving her a second chance. Okay?"

He nods, looking relieved. "You're right. I should have trusted you to make the right decision and talk to us first, rather than just assume you would act in a similar way to how Felicia would. I'm sorry, Emerald. I guess there are still a few issues I need to resolve."

I roll out of the bed and lean down to give him a gentle kiss. "You aren't the only one who has relationship issues, Nikoli. I have them, I'm sure Talon does too, and who knows what issues Dev's hiding? Regardless of the problems we all have, though, there's all the time in the world to build the trust between us and work on all of our issues."

I hold out a hand to help him to his feet. He takes it, sliding across the bed until he's sitting on the edge, directly in front of me. "How did we get so lucky to have such a compassionate soul-tie, who happens to be completely badass as well? I swear, it's like you were made for us."

I smirk and lower myself onto his lap, relishing the feel of his hands as he grips onto my hips firmly. "I *was* made for you. I can promise you that," I murmur before pressing my lips to his gently.

After our lips part, I climb off his lap before things get too heated between us. "Come on, let's go tell the guys you haven't killed me in a fit of rage."

His face goes immediately blank, and he freezes in his position on the edge of the bed. "Em, you know I'd never hurt you, right?"

I cock my head, feeling confused. He didn't really believe I thought he would actually kill me in a fit of rage, did he? "Of course I know you wouldn't hurt me. Why would you ask that?"

He shakes his head with a soft smile. "Sorry, it doesn't matter. I'm just projecting my issues."

I let the matter go, refusing to let anything else ruin our night. He'll tell me when he's ready, so I won't try to force it anymore. We have all the time in the world to learn about each other. I don't need to know everything all in one go. Besides, it wouldn't leave much mystery in our relationship if I knew every little detail about them within just a month of meeting them. We could have hundreds, maybe thousands of years ahead of us. That's a long time to get to know each other.

Hand in hand, we head out into the main room where Talon and Dev are both on the couch conversing quietly. As we walk past the kitchen, I look around to make sure the shattered glass has been cleaned up. I smile when I notice the floor looks even cleaner than it had before the bottle broke. I guess they took my instructions seriously.

Nik and I take a seat on the sofa opposite Talon and Dev. Once I'm comfortable and all eyes are on me, I start in on my questions. "So? How did the meeting go?"

Dev smiles over at me, but it doesn't quite reach his eyes. "It went fine. Just like we told you it would." He relaxes back into the cushion, throwing his arms up to rest along the back of the couch. "They just wanted to grill us about why we didn't report the rogues and their attack on you. We had to explain that after the attack, we were all so focused on getting you back to the coven to deal with all the drama that none of us really stopped to consider proper procedure for when rogues attacked. As it is, they still have absolutely no idea who the fourth wolf is because he refuses to speak, so they've arranged for him to be sent to another pack. One that's known for getting rogues to talk. Anyhow, we should have more info in about a week, maybe two," he says with a shrug.

I make a surprised sound in my throat. I thought for sure there would have some kind of reprimand for not contacting the pack after the attack. "Really? That's all? No punishment at all?" I ask skeptically, sure they must be messing with me.

Talon clears his throat, a frown on his face." Well, not a punishment exactly, but the Alpha did have a request. And seeing as we screwed up by not calling them in the first place, we couldn't exactly say no."

"As much as we wanted to," Nik mutters under his breath, but I catch the words anyway.

"Okay... what does he want?" I ask apprehensively.

"You."

Nik squeezes my hand as what Talon said sinks in. I look between each of the guys, waiting for one of them to start laughing and say 'gotcha,' because it's got to be a joke, right? Why would the Alpha of a pack I've never even visited want me?

Nik takes pity on me and pulls me closer. I can rest my head on his chest as he starts explaining. "He doesn't want you exactly, but he does want to meet you. For some reason, he finds it intriguing that you're a hybrid that has three soul-ties, but no wolf mate. We believe he thinks he's your mate for some reason."

I feel the color drain from my face, and I sit up straight. I knew it was only a matter of time before someone else came to the realization that I could have a wolf mate out there. I'm not sure how I feel about it being the Alpha of a pack thinking that, though, let alone it being someone I haven't even met yet. Wolves need to meet for them to know they're true mates. Unless he concealed his identity when he visited my pack at some point, there's no way for him to know that. I guess it is possible, though, because some Alphas do hide themselves to keep from being attacked.

Hold the fucking phone! "Wait, he knows I'm still alive? Meaning the bullshit you fed me about keeping me here so nobody found out was nothing but lies! You motherfucking sons of bitches! I can't believe you lied to me!"

Talon chuckles at my outburst, and Dev has a massive grin on his face, both confirming my suspicions. When my gaze swings around to Nik accusingly, he holds his hands up in surrender. "Hey! Don't blame me for the lies! I was outvoted! I wanted you to come with us, but those two," he vehemently points at Talon and Dev with narrowed eyes, "they voted against me."

Talon rolls his eyes. "We have more important things to discuss than one little white lie that could have saved your life if something had gone wrong. Emerald, do you think there's even a slight chance he's your mate?"

I push the argument to the back of my mind, but it is definitely not forgotten. I'll show him a little white lie. "To be honest, it's doubtful. We have to have met our mate to know if they are ours or not. There's a connection, not like soul-ties. It's more animalistic from what I've heard. Our wolves react to each other and make our human side more drawn to that person than they would be otherwise. What do you think? Do you think I might have a wolf mate out there, in addition to my soul-ties with you guys?" I ask, throwing the question back at him.

Talon shrugs and leans forward, his eyes locked on mine. "Honestly, it hadn't crossed any of our minds that you may have a werewolf mate out there. I guess we'll just have to cross that bridge when we come to it. But even if you do have a mate out there, even if it's the Alpha of the pack, it won't change what we have between us. You understand that, right?"

I nod, feeling so relieved to hear him say that. It may seem stupid to be put at ease by such a thing as them being willing to accept me with a mate, but it means the world to me. I've been stressing for days since the thought first occured to me and knowing it isn't a deal breaker is a big relief. All I fear now is that if I do have a mate, my soul-ties will no longer consider me worthy of their tie.

"So, uh, what are we doing tonight?" I ask awkwardly, trying to distract myself from my morbid thoughts.

The guys all glance around at each other, as if hoping the other would have an idea. Obviously, no one had any plans. An awkward silence settles over us for a moment before Dev claps his hands together, making me jump. He gets to his feet and walks behind the couch Nik and I are seated on.

I watch as he reaches down, his hands gripping something under the bottom of the couch, and gives a hard pull.

I had expected him to pull something out from underneath us, not pull the whole couch back, which is why a girly squeak leaves my lips. Nik grins and wraps an arm around me, helping me remain sitting until Dev has finished moving the couch.

"Dev! What on earth are you doing?" I demand as he straightens with a grin.

He shrugs, moving over to the other couch. Talon has the good sense to stand up, and watches with amusement as Dev drags it back a few feet. "Since no one else had any ideas of what to do tonight, I thought we could watch a movie. Unless you have another suggestion?"

I shake my head with a smile, happy to give in to his decision. Besides, he's right; none of us had come up with any other alternatives. "No, a movie sounds good, but what are you doing with the couches?"

He grins wickedly. "You'll see. Now be a good girl, and go grab our pillows from the bedroom. Oh, and maybe a comforter, too," he adds as I make my way to our room.

I poke my tongue out at him over my shoulder, but go to do as he asks, grabbing us each our pillows and a blanket. My only thought is that maybe he is positioning the rug so we can all lay down on it. It's shaggy enough to be comfortable, at least for a few hours.

When I come back, all the couches and chairs have been stripped of their cushions. It looks like he's used the rug as a guide for placement and built a makeshift bed of cushions angled towards the wall-mounted TV. He bounces on the balls of his feet with excitement as I take in the sight before me.

"Ta-da!" he shouts with unrestrained enthusiasm. "I made us a giant bed, so we can all watch a movie together without having to move the TV into the bedroom."

He looks so proud of his achievement that I smile and give him a quick peck on the cheek. Then, I drop the pillows I'm carrying on top of the makeshift bed of cushions, before going back for a comforter.

"Okay, one of you can pick the movie. I want to see what kind of taste you guys have." I smirk and lay down on the bed, getting comfortable.

I wiggle around as Nik and Dev settle in on either side of me, leaving Talon to peruse the movies from a hidden shelf that appears at the press of a button, built into the wall directly under the TV.

Talon finally makes a selection, putting it into the DVD player before coming to lay down on the opposite side of Nik, settling in as the movie starts to play.

As the credits start to roll, I can't help the laughter that bursts free. "Oh my god, Talon! You're a closet acapella lover. Please, please, tell me you sing, too." I rise up onto my elbow to look over at him.

His face is pinched tightly, and he refuses to meet my eyes.

Nik's expression remains stoic as ever, but I see the slight twitch of his lips as he fights the urge to smile. Dev, meanwhile, tries to hold back, but after one look at my face, he's curled into the fetal position, laughing his ass off. Talon props himself on his elbows and glares over at Dev, before shifting his gaze to me. "I put it on for you."

I nod, trying to restrain myself when all I want is to laugh, but I feel that will make the situation worse. Dev, however, has no trouble adding fuel to the fire. "So, you never once tried to play 'cups' in the kitchen?" He snorts, unable to contain his laughter any longer. "Tell us, Tal, how long ago did you buy the DVD?"

At that question, Talon seems to realize he has no choice but to fess up. He looks away before muttering, "I bought it a year ago."

I chuckle. "So, long before you met me, then?"

Dev starts cackling again, and this time Nik joins in. Talon, however, picks up a pillow and throws it at me. "Just shut up and watch the movie," he says as the pillow smacks into my laughing face.

I pull the pillow towards me and hug it as a girl on the screen gets serenaded on a college campus by some creep in a cab. The image of Talon as the guy in the cab pops into my mind, and the laughter comes bubbling back up.

He smiles over at me, and I'm glad to see he doesn't take the ribbing too seriously. I'm also happy we're getting some down time together. Who knows when we'll get a chance to relax like this again?

Chapter Fourteen

ONE AND ONLY LESSON

EMERALD

Waking up on a bed of cushions wasn't exactly what I expected. I thought for sure the makeshift bed would have fallen apart at some point, and I'd end up sleeping on the rug, but that hadn't happened. Instead, I opened my eyes to a pair of bright hazel eyes watching me.

"Why are you watching me sleep, Devin?" I murmur, closing my eyes again and shifting to rest my head against his chest. Somehow, I ended up laying half across Dev's chest and half on the cushion bed. Not that I'm complaining.

I feel extremely well rested, considering we slept on the floor. Hands stroke down my strawberry-blonde hair, and I look back over my shoulder to see Nik watching me with hooded eyes.

"Morning, Emerald."

"Hey, Nik," I mutter sleepily. My eyes close again of their own accord, unable to keep them open while he's softly caressing my hair.

We stay like this for a while before I hear footsteps approach us, bringing with them the bitter sweet scent of freshly brewed coffee. I perk up immediately, my eyes zeroing in on the coffee mug in Talon's hand.

He grins down at me, holding the cup just out of reach. "Nope. No coffee for you until you've showered and dressed."

I glower at him, wishing he could see the gruesome death I'm envisioning for him after withholding my morning coffee. You do not keep a woman from her coffee. Especially not first thing when she wakes. That's how murderers are created.

He sighs heavily, clearly seeing his potential death reflected in my eyes. "Look, if you go and get showered and dressed, I'll sweeten the pot by adding a touch of my blood to it. How's that sound?"

At his offer, my mood brightens considerably. The coffee I'd tried that contained some of Nik's blood was surprisingly good, and apart from the coffee Britt and I had on our adventure out of the coven, it had been the best I'd ever had.

Talon's blood already has an edge of chocolate to the taste, so I can just imagine the taste of his blood in my coffee. It would be like a blood mocha.

My mouth is already drooling at the thought, and I hurry to climb out of the bed of cushions, making a mad dash for the bathroom to get ready.

In under five minutes, I'm showered, dressed, and ready to get my special treat. When Talon hands it over, I treat it like the Holy Grail it is.

Taking a sip, flavor explodes on my tongue, and I moan in ecstasy. This is the most amazing drink I've ever had. There's one catch, though. It doesn't taste like the blood mocha that I envisioned.

When I pull the cup away from my lips, an overwhelming loss rises within me and I frown unsure why.

I look up at Talon, feeling confused. "This isn't just your blood, is it?"

He chuckles and watches me take another sip; I'm unable to stop myself from inhaling the deliciousness that is this coffee.

"No, it's not just my blood. We added a little from each of us. Thought it might help you get you through your day of royalty training."

"Ugh, royalty training. I totally forgot about that. Has anyone come by yet?"

Dev chuckles. "Yep! Jasper is waiting outside the room for you. He agreed to let you have your coffee before escorting you to training."

I sigh and take another sip of my heavenly beverage. When the cup is empty, I go to rinse it in the kitchen sink, and set it to the side before turning to face the guys.

"I don't wanna go." It may be pathetic, but I just feel like it's not going to do much good. Sure, I may learn some things I don't know, but I'm just not the royal type. I don't like getting dressed up for meetings or dealing with political issues. Sorting out arguments and being all Princess-like, it's just not me. Why should I force myself through training if I won't use majority of it? Maybe I could convince my parents to limit the amount of subjects to things I don't know or will need to know in the future.

"You agreed to go, so now you have to. Just think though, we'll be training later. Then you can take your frustration out on me. Well, if you can hit me, that is." Talon grins over at me, and I can see the challenge in his eyes.

My resolve to stay here and just abandon my lesson flees from my mind at Talon's words. I did agree and my mother would be hurt if I didn't follow through on this. She asked me specifically to do this training, and if I back out now, she'd be devastated. I can't do that to her.

Talon sees each thought as it passes through my mind, and I bet he can tell the second I make my decision. "Okay, fine. I'll go to the lesson." I glare over at him. "But if it sucks, prepare to have your ass beat."

I offer each of the guys a quick kiss before leaving, but when I get to Nikoli, our kiss becomes a lot more heated than I expected. It leaves my heart racing and my body aching for more.

Jasper is waiting for me when I open the door, but doesn't say a word. He just turns and starts walking down the hall as if he expects me to follow him. I don't understand why he refuses to speak to me. Though, if what my mother said about earning his respect is true, then I probably still have a long way to go.

I imagine coming from a pack of wolves, especially the same pack who was responsible for my mother, his Queen, almost dying does nothing to inspire any trust in me. Oh well, I guess there's nothing to do but be patient and hope he'll trust me one day.

I'm led down three floors, using stairs I didn't even realize were in the coven, since I'd only ever used the elevator up until now. Though I guess if the coven caught fire, there would have to be some kind of alternate means of escape, so it makes sense.

We walk through the stairwell door and then down another hall. This floor isn't littered with rooms like the others I've seen. Instead, there are only a few doors, that are all floor to ceiling in height and are made of a deep burnished red pane with dark gold trim. We keep going down the hallway until we reach a double set of doors at the end.

Jasper knocks three times before turning to me with a stern expression. "She'll be here in a second. Do not move."

At that, he turns on his heel and takes off down the hall without another word, leaving me standing awkwardly as I wait for whoever will be teaching me these lessons.

I stand here for a full minute, shifting from foot to foot and picking at my nails as I wait.

Finally, I hear the sound of footsteps on the other side of the doors, so I straighten, projecting an 'I'm stronger than you' vibe. Then the doors swing open to reveal none other than my grandmother.

She stands there and looks me up and down, scrutinizing my clothing choices before pursing her lips. "At least you're dressed. I guess that's something."

My mouth drops open in shock, and I stand frozen in the doorway. My grandmother rolls her eyes and moves further into the room. When she reaches a large ornate desk, she turns to scowl at me. "Well? Are you coming in, or do you plan for me to teach you while you stand out in the hall like a fool?"

I shake my head, feeling a mix of shock and annoyance. *How dare she treat me like an idiot!* I walk into the room, closing the doors behind me. I pause and take a deep breath before facing my grandmother.

Her dark hair flows down her back, and she moves with such grace that I'm taken by complete surprise. Seeing her this close, I have time to appreciate her form and study her figure. Not only is she absolutely breathtakingly beautiful and the absolute picture of a dainty Princess from afar, but when you're faced with her, you can see the defined muscles in her arms and legs that are obviously from years and years of training, or even fighting.

My grandmother retrieves a large book from the desk, and I marvel at how someone can look so delicate, yet still so strong. Even her clothes. She's wearing a black pants suit that lends her a badass look, that also somehow projects innocence.

She takes the book and moves towards a dining table surrounded by six chairs. I follow her, taking the seat she directs me to at the head of the table. Once seated, she slams the book down in front of me; I have to fight not to flinch at the sudden move.

My grandmother grins and takes a seat at the opposite end of the table. "That book contains a detailed history of our kind. It has all our family trees, the vampires born and killed, as well as how they were killed. It also covers the treaty, when it was introduced, as well as its conditions and rules. There's also a comprehensive rundown on key members of our species, including those who were turned by idiotic vampires with some kind of sick fantasy of acquiring a great name under their belt."

My eyebrow raises at the way she speaks about said idiotic vampires. "I didn't actually know that. By great names, do you mean like famous people?"

"You'll find out when you read the book. For example, there was a Queen of France that was turned in the late sixteen hundreds that still rules the coven over there. She might be the best person to start with actually," she muses with a devious twinkle in her eyes.

I don't know why she seems so excited for me to read about this Queen chick, but I'll do it so I don't get on her bad side. I want her to like me, or at least act like she likes me. I'm sure my mother arranged for her to be my teacher because she wanted us to bond. As if that will happen. My grandmother seems to have taken an instant dislike to me, and I doubt there is much I can do to change her mind. But, for the sake of my mother, I will still try.

Now, we sit across from each other in silence. Her intense gaze makes me want to fidget in my seat, but I do my best to remain calm.

After a few moments, she leans forward with narrowed eyes. "My daughter wants me to teach you everything I can to help you lead a successful life as our Princess. How to behave around others, how to walk, talk, and whatnot." She leans back in her chair with a smirk. "I, however, don't think I should waste my time on you."

My eyes narrow. Is she being serious right now, or is she just messing with me? Why give me that stupid book if she doesn't think I'm worthy of her time? Enough of this crap!

"I don't know what your problem is, or why you think now is the time to play these games, but enough is enough!" I get to my feet, my chair sliding back and scraping across the hardwood floor. I lean forward, my palms splayed out on the table and glare at my grandmother.

"If you don't want to teach me what you know, fine! I can go to my soul-ties and ask for their guidance instead. I don't need you."

She bares her teeth at me, also rising to her feet, using her height to try to intimidate me as she moves closer. "Don't pretend with me, girl. I don't know who you are, or what you plan to achieve here, but I won't teach you a thing. Wolves raised you, and my guess is they sent you here to infiltrate our coven. I won't allow you to get any more information about us than you already have."

"You think I'm some kind of spy?" I laugh, unable to believe what I'm hearing. Even though she saw my blood turn white in the chalice, which proved my bloodline, she still thinks I'm here for some nefarious reason.

I sigh in defeat and decide to leave, taking the huge fucking book with me. I stop at the door and turn back, needing her to understand. My gaze finds hers; she watches me with arms crossed and a glower on her face.

"You judged me based on what I am. I understand why, but still. It's been made abundantly clear I'm not one of you, but... I'm not one of them either. I'm part wolf, but I'm also part vampire too, and there is absolutely nothing I can do about either of those," I say with a shrug before focusing a glare on her. "I came in here hoping to form some kind of relationship with you because I know it would make my mother happy, but it's not worth being made to feel like I'm some traitor. I didn't choose to be this random hybrid between species. Just like I didn't choose for my mother to be taken and for me to be ripped from her womb! I chose to come here in the hopes of maybe finding the family I never had. I can see now that was a mistake." I take a deep breath before adding one last comment. "You may have been the best person to teach me, but I think I will need to speak to my mother about finding someone who isn't a bitter old fool."

I take a step out the door before she calls out. "Wait! Come back in here, child."

"I'm not a child," I grit out through clenched teeth as I turn back around and face her.

"No, you're not. Come back inside and close the door."

I do as she requests, but only because that twinkle in her eyes is gone, replaced by a vulnerability that surprises me. My footsteps echo in the otherwise quiet room as I approach her.

She bows her head and sighs deeply before meeting my eyes. "I won't say I trust you completely, because I don't. But... you're right. My prejudice towards your kind comes from everything that was done to my child. When you have children of your own, you will understand the fear that comes from the thought of anything that could hurt them. I will teach you what I can today, but that will be all. The book in your hands contains everything you will need to know about our history, so there is little else for me to teach you. I will leave my door open for you, though, should you have any questions."

I nod as she speaks, happy to agree to pretty much anything. I know it may seem pathetic, but I've never met my father's parents, and it would be nice to try and form some kind of bond with her. Ugh, I'll have to try to remember to say uncle next time. It's all getting confusing in my head right now.

"Very well. If you're ready to learn, then let's begin." With that, she settles back into her seat. I return to my original seat, placing the book on the table beside me and waiting for my first and only lesson to begin.

Chapter Fifteen

JOAN OF ARC

EMERALD

"*P*ay attention!"

Ugh, I rub at my temples and look down at the notes on my page with a small smirk. All I've done is write 'sex,' 'blood,' and 'vampires' all over the page when I should have been taking notes on our currency system.

My grandmother walks over and looks at what's written on the page before I have a chance to conceal it, and she sighs in annoyance.

"I get this is not the most interesting thing you could be doing right now, but you really need to know this subject, Emerald. Our system of bartering and trading is complex. You can easily get swindled on the value of an item by not understanding the correct way to negotiate."

She's been going on and on about this currency system for what feels like ages, but it seems easy enough to me. That doesn't stop her from launching back in from the beginning, though.

"Blood has the highest trading value. As vampires we need blood to survive, and with the introduction of cloned blood over the past few decades, organic blood is becoming increasingly more valuable. Despite people being able to survive on cloned blood, we still crave blood that comes directly from the vein. But some sellers have their own soul-ties out there and so won't offer blood from the vein, which decreases its value. You need to remember this because there are going to be times when you will be forced to offer your blood and you need to be fully aware of its value. You may even resort to selling your blood to get certain items or offering to trade it for valuables you come across. Though, I would advise against selling or trading your blood to a witch because sometimes they'll use it for one of their spells."

"Yes, I know." I sigh and begin doodling on the paper in front of me.

She walks past me towards a glass display case that houses a huge broadsword. She pulls a chain from her neck, using the key at the end to unlock the case. She tucks the chain back beneath her pantsuit to dangle between her cleavage and pulls the sword out with reverence.

She brandishes it in front of her as she strides towards me, and I jump out of my chair, backing away with my hands raised.

As she gets closer, I realize she's not wielding it to hurt me, she's just showing me a priceless artifact. I get excited when I see five small crosses on the blade, and wonder if it's really the sword I'm thinking of. I absolutely adored the person who owned such a sword as this. She was strong, but also a champion for the people, and someone I had been fascinated with when I went through the human history books.

"This sword, while an absolutely remarkable artifact for most, is my most prized possession. The man who found it had no idea what it was worth and was selling it for only two bags of blood. After he handed it over, I revealed just who I was."

"Joan of Arc," I whisper, completely awed by the woman before me. I'd heard rumors that she was a vampire, but I never believed that I would actually get to meet her, let alone that she would be my own grandmother!

She's over six hundred years old!

"Yes, Emerald. I was known in my human life as Joan of Arc. But that was a long time ago. My name now is Jeannie."

She lets me stare at the sword a minute longer before taking it and locking it back in its case.

"As I was explaining, that sword of mine, while a useless trinket to many or an artifact to the humans, was absolutely priceless to me. The vampire who had it requested only the two bags of O-negative blood. I would have gladly paid every dime of my fortune, which totals almost ten million human dollars."

She looks pointedly at the empty notepad on the table, and I hurry back to my place to resume taking notes. No wonder my mother wanted her to teach me. If she's been alive for over six hundred years, there would be plenty of things she would know that could help me. At least, that's what I hope.

I jot down 'Joan of Arc–my grandmother' on a new page and add a few notes about her sword. I'd love to come back down here sometime when we're not in the middle of a lesson to study the sword in more detail.

"So while I would have given up my entire fortune to have such a memory from my human life, most other vampires would have only been willing to pay a small amount. I don't know if you've had the chance to visit our marketplace yet–"

"Yeah, I did. Nik took me down there. There were so many stalls and I couldn't believe the different things people were selling," I cut in, before closing my mouth when she purses her lips in annoyance.

She stares down at me, as if to see if there will be any further interruption before continuing. "As I was trying to say before you rudely interrupted me, the market has various different stalls, and their wares change from day to day. Some days, there will only be a few items, while on others, the booths will be close to overcrowding."

She pauses as I jot down a few notes. When I look back up, she resumes speaking. "Vampires will come from other covens, and wolves and witches do the same, traveling between the individual marketplaces we have set up."

I raise my hand with a roll of my eyes, hoping this is better than interrupting her. "What is it, Emerald?"

"Sorry, I think I'm confused. The way you're talking about the marketplace makes it sound like anyone can visit them? I thought wolves weren't allowed in the coven." Her wording suggested pretty much everyone could go to these things, but how the hell can they even get in the coven when Brittany alluded to the church being under the witches' protection?

My grandmother gives me a pleased smirk. "Very good, Emerald. You are quite right. It's true that anyone can visit the marketplace. There's a portal on the back of the church wall which allows any supernatural to pass through it. The witches of the local coven managed to tweak their protection spells so the whole market is available to everyone, but no one can enter the elevator unless they live here. Think of the church as a living entity that knows who comes in and out. No one is getting past the elevator that it doesn't want to, unless they use some extremely powerful magic which is rare enough to pass detection."

She paces along the wall, pulling out another book from the collection of hundreds that line the shelves. "As long as our kind has existed, we've used this bartering system as well as the traditional way humans tend to swap currency for possessions. We have markets all over the world, at various times. We also like to have a bigger one once a year, where people from all countries are invited to sell off various possessions they have gathered over the course of the year. Humans are also a part of that market, offering themself for donors or as slaves, but you'll see that in a few weeks."

"I will?"

"Yes, Sierra has sought out our council's advice in this dark time, and we decided to use the opportunity to introduce you to the entire supernatural world at once. We will reveal your nature and gauge the reactions of everyone present, thus determining who already knows and who is frightened by the news."

Oh great, just what I wanted to hear. Like life isn't hard enough already.

"Anyway, you can trade for pretty much anything you might need. All you have to do is offer. Wolves like to hire themselves out as security. Have you noticed how few children there are here? Well, wolves are often hired to ensure their protection. Basically, they're glorified babysitters. One woman in the French coven pays approximately two million US dollars every year to ensure the safety of her children. So yes, if you can think of it, there is probably someone there who does it."

I scribble down notes, trying to keep up, but I'm sure I'm going to need to ask the guys about all this soon, as there's just so much still to figure out. Especially as I don't have much cash to my name, and I don't really want to rely on my soul-ties if I need things.

"My suggestion, Emerald, would be to sit down with your mother or your soul-ties, and get them to help you make a chart of sorts. Something that helps you identify what kind of price you will be paying for the most common items. Until you have a handle on our values, I wouldn't advise going after items that you don't understand. Or at least take someone with you so you're not ripped off."

My grandmother checks her watch, her eyes widening as she gets to her feet. "I'm sorry, Emerald, but I have to cut this lesson short. If you would like to have another one later on, I would be open to it, but instead of a one-on-one, maybe we could have your mother join us?"

I nod, feeling a sense of relief that the lesson went well considering how it started. I go to grab the large volume she first gave me, and she hands me the second book she grabbed from the wall.

"Take this one, too. It will explain a few of the key items that have been traded throughout the many centuries of our existence. I'm glad we got the chance to clear the air, but I really do need to run."

I frown at her sudden change of attitude, and she grins wickedly. "Our lesson for today is done. You have training in the forest now."

My slow footsteps echo as I walk out into the hall, confused by the quick dismissal. I stand in the doorway, watching as my grandmother went around straightening the room up, not that it really needed it. The place was immaculate when I walked in, and we barely moved from the table.

When she notices me hovering in the doorway, she walks over and gives me a quick shove, pushing me out in the hall without a word, and slams the door shut in my face. Well, that was weird.

I sigh and make my way to the elevator, heading down to the forest level. I have no idea whether Talon is down there yet but I'm sure if he isn't, he won't take long to find me.

Chapter Sixteen

TRAINING WITH TALON

EMERALD

I saunter into the underground forest, heading straight to the open area I know is reserved for training. The path is littered with fallen leaves, and I watch as some of the trees with broken branches mend themselves before my very eyes. It's absolutely breathtaking to behold. I don't think even the grass has grown since I last came down here.

There's a clear worn path through the grass, though, which leaves me wondering just what magic they have on this place.

As I clear the trees, I see Talon in the middle of the open training arena, his shirt off as he stretches. He doesn't seem to sense my presence, so I stand there watching the slight bulge of muscles as he moves each limb precisely to where it needs to be, showing amazing control and flexibility. His movements remind me of the yoga videos my stepmother used to watch, and I admit it fascinates me. I can just imagine him using his lithe body for other, more promising exploits.

"Come here, Emerald."

I startle at his voice, slightly embarrassed to have been caught watching so intently, but still move towards him hoping he didn't pick up the whiff of arousal that surely seeped off me while he moved. He goes over to a duffle bag that's off to the side. He pulls out a set of workout clothes and hands them to me before pushing me to the changing cabin. Again as I walk, I take more notice of my surroundings, marveling at the way that the building housing the change area still looks natural in this forest, rather than standing out and appearing out of place in this serene. It blends into the wooded area, the colors on the outside a mix of greens and browns to better camouflage it into the background.

When I finish changing into the black sports bra and matching lycra pants Talon gave me, I head back out. I come to a stop directly in front of Talon, who is standing tall, raking me over with his heated gaze.

"If you were just planning to ogle me, we could have done that somewhere a little more private," I suggest teasingly, enjoying the way his eyes narrow.

He lifts his eyes to meet mine in challenge, smirking as he does so. "Oh, don't worry, Emerald, we are training today. I just thought what I originally had planned would be too easy, so I decided to make it a bit more of a challenge for myself." He lifts his hand, gesturing at me in my sparse clothing. "Seeing you like this, with my name scrawled on your neck for all to see, well that distracts me a bit. Here's hoping it distracts me enough to give you a chance." He grins cockily, obviously enjoying taunting me.

I roll my eyes and stretch my neck, enjoying the small pops I feel as I loosen up my muscles. I bounce around on the balls of my feet, my beast eager to burn off some steam after the mostly boring lesson I had with my grandmother.

Five hours locked away in a room is not good for any wolf, let alone me with my beast's quick tendency to anger.

We circle each other for a few moments, both grinning. Then he lunges, forcing me to throw myself to the side, landing hard on the ground to avoid his quick succession of blows. I stumble to my feet, my eyes blurring as my head spins. I'm feeling off, so much so that I don't even see his fist before it connects to my jaw.

I crumple to the ground, my legs no longer able to support my weight, and Talon freezes as he looks down at me, his wide with fear. "Holy shit, Emerald!" He drops to his knees beside me, and I rub my jaw, knowing it's already bruised. He's lucky he was pulling his punches or it would have broken my jaw.

"You okay, babe?" He lifts my head to look up at him but I find myself unable to focus on him. Talon sits in the dirt and pulls me into his lap facing him, with my head framed between his hands as he stares at me.

He frowns and growls through clenched teeth. "When was the last time you fed?"

My stomach sinks, and I close my eyes, feeling stupid. "Um, last night? Unless you count the blood in the coffee..." I trail off, feeling the anger vibrating off of Talon in waves.

"And food? When did you last eat human food?"

I blush when I realize what he's saying. I denied my human, wolf, and vampire natures. I'm lucky I'm still up walking around. From what I know of vampires, if they don't feed, they can become weak, or even go mad with bloodlust, feeding on everything in sight. Really not something I want to happen.

"I'm sorry I forgot to feed. It's just hard to remember because my body hasn't been giving me any warning signs. Usually I would eat the moment I felt hungry, but I guess the change in natures and habits has me a little off," I apologize and lean my head into his hand, feeling a bit lightheaded.

He sighs and lifts me into his lap to look into his eyes, my own just clear enough to see the sympathy they convey. "Em, I know this is hard for you, but with your dual nature you need to be more careful. Your beast usually holds back your vampire nature, but if you don't keep both sides of yourself fed, there's still every chance your vampire nature will overwhelm you, and you'll end up doing something you regret. Trust me, there are some things you can't be forgiven for."

The sadness in his voice has my heart hurting with the need to comfort him, but he doesn't give me the chance.

He shifts my position so I can wrap my legs around his back, then smirks at me. "If I had known you hadn't fed yet, I would have done this before we got started. I am surprised you only felt faint and didn't fall back on your natural instincts. Most do, and end up attacking the closest person to them."

He tilts his head to the side, offering me his neck. My hunger rises quickly, and I bite down on his neck, drawing a groan from him.

His grip is iron tight as he grabs my ass, and I try to tamp down my arousal. We're here for training, nothing else. Maybe after training, though...

The thought trails off when Talon suddenly thrusts up, grinding against me. I suck even harder and growl into his neck as he grips my hair, pulling firmly, just on the edge of being painful.

Talon groans, and I pull away, worried I took too much, but I see that his eyes are hooded with desire. He growls as he watches me lick the blood from my lips.

He pushes me back in the dirt with a predatory growl and claims my lips, his own fangs scraping my lip, making it bleed slightly, which just spurs him on even more.

"Damnnnnnn."

The long drawn out word from a male voice we don't recognize has us both freezing. I tilt my head to the side to see two vamps I haven't yet met, both looking down at the way Talon has me pinned to the ground.

I harden my eyes. "Do you mind?"

They both back away quickly, raising their hands raised in surrender. "So sorry. We'll, uh, just go train over there," the one on the right says, pointing in the opposite direction.

Talon rests his head in the crook of my shoulder, chuckling as they hurriedly retreat.

The moment they're on the other side of the room, I focus on the feel of Talon through our bond, sending soothing vibes to him because I can sense his frustration. He lifts his head from where it was nestled and rests it against my forehead, closing his eyes. "I swear the fates are out there laughing at me. Why else would people keep interrupting us at every turn?"

He groans before climbing to his feet, holding out a hand to help me up.

"Maybe it's just bad timing?" I suggest optimistically.

He shrugs and looks me over intently, his gaze trailing over his name on my neck. "Either way, I will claim you sooner or later. There's only so much a man can take before he feels tempted to just take you, regardless of who might be watching." The level of heat in his voice sends shivers through me, and I'm thrown straight into my imagination.

Me, lying on a bed as Talon eases himself inside me, with Nik and Dev watching from the doorway. Wow. I didn't realize I was into exhibitionism. Sure, it felt great when Dev and Nik both pleasured and fed me, but them watching as Talon fucks me? I shiver at the thought, my nipples hardening in the sports bra.

Being part vampire at least gives me a long, long time to figure out just what pleases me in the bedroom.

A slow smile curves my lips, and Talon shakes his head with an exasperated laugh, climbing to his feet and detaching me from my clinging position. He then sets me on my feet, moving back a few steps to create space between us.

"I don't need to know what you were just thinking, Em because it's clear on your face. But we need to cool down and do what we came here for."

I cock my head suggestively when a growl slips free from his chest as his eyes flash red, the first true sign that his vampire nature is just as eager for me as he is.

"Training," he grits out as if telling me but I sense he's really only saying it to remind himself.

I watch as he goes over and reveals a cooler he had hidden away in his bag. I stare as he pulls out a blood bag, ripping it open with his now descended fangs. I wait for myself to feel weird about it, but I'm still feeling needy after what happened between us, so I can't say I mind the view.

When he finishes the bag, he smirks at me, raising an eyebrow in challenge. "Don't even think about it."

I pout and stretch out, bending my legs forward, enjoying the way his gaze is drawn to my chest. "I wasn't going to do anything," I tease.

He chuckles and goes to dispose of the empty bag, before retrieving another and gulping it down greedily.

I straighten with a frown, worried I may have drained him more than I thought when I fed from him. "Did I take too much?"

He finishes feeding before replying with a small smile. "No, you didn't take too much. I just needed to make sure I'm fully fed for patrol later."

I step into his embrace, ignoring the blood bag still in his hand and wrap my arms around him gently. "I'm sorry I had to feed from you. Maybe we should start looking for alternate ways for me to feed?"

He sighs, leaning back far enough to look down into my eyes. "Emerald, as your soul-tie, it's my job to take care of you. If that means feeding you, then I will. If that means bathing you, I'll do that too. If that means carrying you through fire, I would in a heartbeat." The fierceness in his voice stuns me and his eyes blaze with an intensity I never thought I'd see from him.

"You are everything to me. To us. We would die to make you happy." I open my mouth to tell him they don't have to do that, but he halts my words by pressing a finger to my lips. "No, I know you're going to say something about you not wanting us to do those things, but we want to. We want to take care of you. Yes, there will be times when it's too much, and if that happens, you can just tell us to back off, which I'm sure you'll have no problem doing."

He moves his finger away, and I grin. "Damn right, I will."

Talon chuckles and steps away from me, raising his hands in a defensive position to protect his face. "Now, my little wolf, are you ready to train?"

"Little wolf?" I growl, baring my teeth in challenge. I know he's teasing me, but I feel like playing along.

"Yes, my little wolf. Let's see what you're made of," he mocks, right before lunging at me.

I duck, block, and throw punches at him over the next few hours, but to no avail. No matter what I do, I still end up on my ass with him looming over me, with that damn smirk on his face.

Chapter Seventeen

DIRTY SECRETS REVEALED

JEREMY

The man before me stares at me with disdain, and it takes everything in me not to wipe the smug smile off his face. And the more he speaks, the angrier I get.

"I don't see how this is my problem. You had the chance to kill her, but the young pup you sent failed in his mission. Why should I help you deal with your ineptitude?"

I keep my polite smile in place, only to be jostled to the side as the pup in question lunges for the witch.

Xander pulls him back at the last second, and I frown as he leads the pup back out the door, leaving the two of us alone.

The witch smiles smugly at me. "You'd better control your wolves if you expect to be taken seriously around here." He looks out past the door to where Brendan has disappeared to with Xander and in the snap of a finger, his expression sobers and he looks over me in disgust.

"Now, leave my house," the man demands. "I no longer consider the cross breed to be of any threat to our kind, and we don't kill just for the sake of killing."

His words infuriate me, but I hold back my anger, keeping my mind focused on the mission at hand. I need his help, which is the only reason I am putting up with his snobby attitude. "What if I could get you proof that she's a threat? Would you reconsider then?"

He tilts his head, as if considering my offer. My patience starts to wear thin, and he finally responds. "Very well. If you can prove that the cross breed is indeed a threat to our way of life, then I will assist you in your cause."

I nod my head, a thrill of satisfaction coursing through me. "Thank you, that's all I ask."

His hand comes up to grasp mine, and we shake, sealing the deal. My footsteps sound through the house as I walk out the door and to my car. I let out a sigh of relief that Xander had the forethought to get Brendan far from here.

On my way back to my cabin, I go over ideas of how we can get the evidence we need. If she dies again, and is resurrected, then maybe that will be enough to convince him of the threat?

I ponder my options as I pull onto the land that houses my cabin, seeing Xander and Brendan brawling in their human forms out front.

I sigh as I climb out of the car, knowing it's time I tell Brendan the truth. He's been conflicted about everything that's gone on since stabbing his sister, but maybe the truth will ease that burden.

Sophie and Joel are right there in the fray, trying to rip them off each other, not caring about the punches that ricochet off them in their hurry to get Brendan and Xander apart. When they see me coming, Sophie and Joel stop their efforts and take a step back, standing at attention.

My presence goes unnoticed by the brawling young men in front of me until I reach in and grab them both by the ears, twisting cruelly until they cry out in pain.

"Sophie, Joel, leave now."

They both depart without another glance, and I'm pleased to have chosen such loyal subjects to aid me in my mission. It will take them a while to get back to the pack on foot, not that anyone really cares these days.

The pack is too focused on Emerald and what they can do to bridge the gap between our kinds, because of the animosity between the vampires and wolves, but I know they're wrong about any kind of reconciliation.

That's why I chose to move out here. I was tired of being disrespected. Isolating myself seemed like the best move to make sure that one, they couldn't find out what I had planned, and two, so they would come to realize how integral I was to the inner workings of the pack.

I let my wolf rise to the surface as the boys stare up at me. They shrink back with small whimpers, and I growl down at them menacingly. "No fighting. If you two can't get along, then how do you expect the pack to follow you? Show some goddamn leadership!"

With that, I release them, and they rub their ears as they slowly get to their feet. "Xander, go back to the pack and resume your training. Brendan, I want you to stay behind. There's something we need to discuss."

The two boys before me exchange glances, and I pity them. One is filled with anger because he slept with something that is not one of our kind. He feels unclean and disloyal to his pack and has no way to deal with those emotions.

The other is struggling with the knowledge he failed to kill his sister. At first he was confused over how to feel when he thought he had killed her but now, the failure is eating him up. Xander takes off without another word and leaves Brendan standing before me, his eyes filled with confusion.

"Come on, Brendan. It's time we had a talk."

He follows me into the cabin, and I lock the door behind him, activating the silencing spell. The moment he learns the truth, he's going to want to run, and I can't let that happen. No, I need him to understand everything before he leaves here.

He takes a seat at my dining table, something which has become habit in the past few days since he found out what his father was hiding from him. I grab a bottle of whiskey down from the cabinet in the kitchen. May as well give him a little something to soften the blow.

He takes the glass, downing the whiskey in a single gulp before holding his glass out for a refill, and I smile proudly. Boy can handle his drink.

He leans back in his chair, meeting my gaze with a drawn expression. "Jer, I'm sorry about losing it. I just got so angry when he insinuated I was weak." He slams his glass down on the counter, hard enough for it to crack. "I killed her! I killed my sister! I know I hit her heart. I stayed behind and watched her die while everyone else was busy freaking out. I don't know how she survived, but it drives me absolutely insane every day to know that she's still alive!"

I choke back a second glass, slamming the empty glass on the counter. It shatters, sending fragments of glass into my palm, but I ignore my wounds as they start to heal. Enough is enough. He needs to know the truth.

"Never mind Emerald. That's not what I wanted to talk to you about. Well in a way, I guess it is."

I take a breath before hurrying through the next part. "You have to know something, Brendan. I know you have been told all your life that Brent is your father, but he's not. You share no genetics with Emerald at all."

"What?" he whispers, his eyes flashing dangerously.

"I know this probably comes as a shock, but I felt it was time you know the truth. Brent is going to lead us down the wrong path, and soon, you will need to step up and tell the pack he is not fit to lead us."

He shakes his head and stands abruptly, knocking the chair back and onto the floor. "No, my mother is his mate. You can't fake that."

I nod sympathetically. "Yes she is, but she had an affair in the first year after they moved back to the pack. I imagine your mother was having trouble dealing with all the lies and sought comfort in another."

"Does he know? Does my father know I'm not his biologically?"

"Yes."

Brendan starts to pace furiously. "Why are you telling me this now?"

"Because, I need you to get close to your father. You need to step up and show him how much of a threat Emerald is. He won't listen to reason but he might if you tell him."

I can see the wheels turning in his mind and then his eyes clear, a new resolve in place. "Okay, I'll do it, but on one condition."

I tilt my head, impressed by the shrewdness the boy is beginning to display. My smile threatens to break free when he speaks. "I want you to help me find out who my father is."

I look him straight in the eyes, trying to determine whether that's something he's ready for yet. Knowledge is power, but at times it can also become a weakness. What he does with the knowledge of his father could be either a strength or a weakness, depending on how he handles the news.

"I know who your father is, but I want a promise you will stay focused on the task at hand. The knowledge of your father won't cloud our mission?"

My eyes must resemble steel right now, but I won't budge until I know for sure he can handle this.

"I promise to stay on target and keep my emotions in check. Now who is he? Do I know him?"

"Yes, you know him," I smirk, watching the confusion on his face morph to a look of apprehension. "I'm your father, Brendan."

Chapter Eighteen

AN OFFICIAL DATE

EMERALD

My eyes open to the darkened room, and I frown, wondering what woke me. As I roll over, I notice the bed empty and shoot up in surprise. Someone always sleeps with me.

Talon dropped me off in our room after training, and I showered before climbing into bed. Nik and Dev came into the room just as I was drifting off to sleep, but no matter how hard I tried to stay awake, my body was exhausted. I fell asleep, comforted by the thought that they would both be in bed on either side of me, keeping me safe.

The scent of coffee slowly wafts into the bedroom, and I smile. They really know how to spoil a girl. I hurry out of the bedroom, so eager for coffee that I forget I'm only wearing a tank top and boy shorts. That fact, however, becomes glaringly obvious when my eyes meet Nik's from across the room.

My mouth drops open with a small gasp, and I can't help but stare at him, my heart racing.

He's wearing a suit similar to a tux but slightly less formal, with no tie. Why the hell is he so dressed up?

I stand here dumbfounded, unsure what to say. "Um, hi," I finally manage.

"What's wrong, Emerald? Cat got your tongue?"

I shake my head, trying to clear my thoughts. "No, I just... didn't expect to see you all fancy and dressed up when I woke up. I was expecting boxers, not a suit." I smirk wryly.

135

He grins and holds a mug out to me, and I know it's filled with coffee and a touch of his blood. I go to his side and take it gratefully, enjoying the scent of coffee that is distinctly him.

"Uh, where are the others?" I ask after the first sip of heavenly goodness.

He reaches over to the counter where a bouquet of flowers rests. I follow his movements as he holds them to his chest.

"What are those?"

He holds out the bouquet of pale purple roses in his hands and bows his head slightly towards the floor, but his eyes never leave mine. I take them, unsure what's going on.

He raises his head and speaks in a strong voice, making me wonder if he rehearsed this.

"Emerald, will you go on a date with me?"

I'm taken aback by how formal the request is. Why the flowers? Why all the formality when we already live together and sleep in each other's beds?

"Uh, sure. I'd love to."

Nik looks ecstatic at my response. His eyes are filled with happiness and his smile is contagious. He grabs my arm and pulls me after him, back in our bedroom, and flicks the lights on. "We're leaving in an hour. That's how long you have to get dressed and ready to go."

When I get to my still unpacked bags, he lets go of me and heads for the bedroom door. Before he leaves, he pauses and turns back with a grin.

"Oh, and make sure it's something you can dance in," he commands with a flirty wink before closing the door behind him.

Well, that was weird. He gave me no notice, and then tells me we're going dancing? *Oh, kill me now. I suck at dancing.*

I start to dig through my clothes frantically, freaking the fuck out over what to wear, when a knock sounds at my door.

I hesitate, wondering who it could be, when Britt barges in. She sees me frozen midway through digging through my clothes and grins brightly.

"I thought you might be needing this," she says, holding out a beautiful blue dress.

My arms wrap around her, and I could cry, I'm so relieved. I have no date-worthy clothes in my bags. I've never even been on a frigging date, except when the guys took me to the monument, but that was a group date. This is a one-on-one date! Pathetic I know, but when your pack ostracizes you, you don't exactly have men lining up at your door to take you out.

"Oh, thank God, Britt. I was freaking the fuck out!" I exclaim as I step back and take the dress gratefully.

She chuckles, guiding me to the closest bed where she makes me sit down. "Do you need some fairy godmother magic? Because I can help," she offers, and my shoulders slump in relief.

"Yes! Thank you so much. I owe you for this."

"Nah, that's what friends are for. Now, take a deep breath and calm down." I do as she instructs, my heart beginning to slow, but the butterflies in my stomach continue to churn sickeningly. "Good, now get dressed and then we'll work some magic."

I nod, taking the dress into the bathroom, pleased to see I won't have to wear a bra with it. My tank top goes flying as I hurry to get dressed, and when I am fully clothed, I can't help but stare. The dress, while long in the back, is split down the middle like an upside down V, revealing my legs. It's a dress made to move in and I actually find myself excited for the chance to dance with Nik.

On me, the dress looks dressy, yet still somewhat casual. I was right about not needing a bra, finding the built-in one holds my breasts up nicely and seems to draw attention to the markings on my pale skin.

My hair is in disarray, and my eyes are bright with happiness. A date wasn't something I expected, especially not so soon after our group date, but I am excited to spend time one-on-one with Nik and find out more about him.

The idea of having a singular relationship with each of them, while all of us still being together, makes me happy. We all kind of just moved in together, skipping the dating and the getting to know each other phase entirely.

This may be just what we need.

When I come back out into the bedroom, it's to see Britt holding the bouquet of roses I had set down on the dresser near my bags when I began searching for an outfit.

She breathes in deeply, taking in their soft scent with a dreamy smile before holding them out to me. I take them back, the action a bit possessive, which only makes her grin even wider.

"Do you know what lilac roses mean, Mer?"

I frown, unsure about what she means. She smirks, a hidden knowledge in her eyes. "Lilac means love at first sight. He's also given you thirteen rather than the traditional twelve most men would. He's using his old customs to woo you."

The obvious glee in her voice makes me want to blush. I hadn't actually noticed anything special about the roses, or about how many there were.

Her smirk grows, but I still don't understand what she's trying to say. "He never did any of that for Felicia. He shared very little of his Russian heritage with her."

My eyebrows shoot up in surprise. "Seriously? Why not?"

"Nope," she says, her mouth popping on the sound. "It seems he is very, very determined to prove how much you mean to him. Whereas she didn't want to know about what made him who he was, she just wanted the power that would come with it. She always referred to his russian heritage as nothing more than his 'archaic customs.' All she wanted was for him to marry her and make her his Princess, soul-tie or not. She should have known you can't become a Princess just by wanting it. And no way in hell was Nik ever going to marry her. He may have let her treat him like crap out of loneliness, but it would have never gone further than that. Then in you walk, a real Princess without even knowing it. You captured Nikoli first with your soul-tie, this bond he couldn't deny, and then he got to see everything that makes you the kind and wonderful best friend I know." She smiles warmly at me, and I return the gesture.

"And then, he declares his love for you with those flowers. It's so sweet, and I've never been happier for you."

I scoff, rolling my eyes. "Or maybe he just couldn't find flowers in any other colors. Maybe he didn't have time to research what each flower means like you obviously did."

She smiles in amusement as she guides me to the bed, and gets to work, weaving her magic on my hair and face. "Think whatever you want, Mer, but Nikoli is meticulous. He knows exactly what those flowers mean, and he wanted you to know what they meant as well. Why else would he have asked me to get your dress?"

I look up at her, confused, and she blows out a puff of air. "I'm a witch, Mer. Flowers are used in many potions, and Nik knows that. He would have known I'd be well aware of what they meant. He's a bit cheeky, if you ask me." She hums as she starts to move my hair with her magic, and I feel it pulling tight into a high ponytail.

I go over her words in my head as she plays with my hair, and I wonder if she's right.

Did he really give those roses to me in order to tell me he loved me from the moment he first laid eyes on me? Or was it just coincidence? And why wouldn't he just come right out and say it if that were the case? There's no reason for him to use flowers to tell me. I would have preferred he just be straightforward with me, although I will admit I find it cute that he gave me flowers that hold a special meaning, other than just as a nice gesture.

Maybe if it comes up on our date, I can ask him, rather than be left in the dark wondering what if.

Once Britt has finished magically curling my hair, she beams down at me, and I feel the soft touches of her magic as she applies my makeup. A girl could get used to this.

She takes a step back and frowns, tapping her chin. "There's something missing," she muses as she looks me over, and I fight to hold still under her scrutiny.

"AH! I know!" She bounces on the balls of her feet excitedly. "Stand up, Mer. I have an idea."

I get to my feet and wait as she concentrates, her magic building.

She begins to speak as she waves her hands through the air, and I watch as my dress starts to light up.

"So, I know this isn't exactly orthodox, but I wanted to do something special to the dress. It will give us all a little reassurance and offer you a little protection," she says and I nod my assent.

I trust her with my life. If she says whatever she's doing will help protect me, then I believe her.

Her hands glow silver as magic builds in her palms and she coats my dress in little sparkles. They settle on my dress, a tingle running through me before it settles, returning to its normal blue hue, just with an otherworldly aura.

My body tingles from the rush of magic, and I breathe a little faster, trying to get my beast to settle after the sudden surge of power.

Britt wobbles to the bed and sits down before she drops, looking completely exhausted.

"Shit! Are you okay? What did you do?" I ask, concerned by her pallid complexion. She looks like Talon did after not having fed for days. Maybe when a witch uses their magic, it drains their power, making them weak much the same way it would if a vampire or wolf didn't feed.

She smiles at me softly. "Don't worry, I'll be okay." She sighs, lying back on the bed as I look down at her. "What I did is a kind of warning spell. It will zap you if you're in danger, and will alert me or one of my guys, whichever is closest. Then, we can transport right to you if something happens," she explains and I look down at her in wonder.

My best friend is fucking amazing! I can't believe she did that, knowing it would drain her to this point. "You are awesome. You know that, right?"

A man groans from the doorway, and I look over to see Torie standing there, looking defeated. "Great, you've told her she's awesome, and now she'll be boasting about it for days."

I laugh, knowing it's true. She may not be modest, but she's still my friend. "She is awesome, and you should all bow down to her awesomeness," I tease as he walks into the room, dropping beside the bed and scooping her up in his arms. Her eyes are closed, and she has a soft smile on her face, but I can't help but worry about her.

Torie goes to leave, but I stop him by placing my hand on his arm gently. I look down at her still form. "Is she gonna be okay?"

He smiles warmly at me and pulls her closer to his chest. "She'll be fine. She just has trouble finding the balance when using her powers. She just needs to rest, but I'm sure she'll be up and about within a few hours."

I sigh, relieved to hear it wasn't as serious as I thought. I would hate for her to use her magic on me and be down for days because of it.

He smiles broadly as we walk out into the front room. "Don't worry, Em. We'll be sure to restore her energy if she needs it." He gives me a wink before making his way out of the room.

I watch the door close behind him, noticing he didn't use his hands to open the door or to close it.

My gaze swings around to Nik, who is standing at the kitchen counter waiting for me to speak. "Did he mean what I think he did by that?" I ask, Torie's words replaying in my mind.

Nik grins appraisingly as his eyes roam over every inch of my body. "If you think he meant that they recharge their energy through sex, then yes, that's exactly what he meant. They each hold a natural reserve and she can draw on that without intercourse, but there's something special about the way they're tied together that's different than it is for most witches. When she has sex with one of them, it builds her natural reserve without depleting theirs. And if she has sex with all of them at once, well, apparently it supplies her with an influx of power that could rival the coven as a whole."

Wow. I guess there's still a lot more that Britt and I need to discuss. How could she not mention any of that during our talk about all the trouble she's been having in the coven? Wouldn't that ability show the coven she's unique and worthy of being treasured, not bullied into sharing her husbands?

"You ready, Em?" Nik asks, drawing me from my thoughts.

I nod excitedly and reach for the blue shawl he holds out for me, the color matching my dress perfectly. "Yep! Any hints on where we're going?"

He considers his answer for a moment and then gives a cheeky grin. "No hints. I want it to be a surprise, but I do need to ask if we can take your car tonight? Talon and Dev took mine," he explains with a pout.

I laugh and grab the keys from the counter. I hand them over to him, keeping them pressed into his hand as I meet his eyes. "If you hurt her, though, and I mean even a scratch, well, lets just say the consequences won't be anything pleasant," I tease, enjoying the way his eyes linger over my lips.

I relinquish the keys, and we step out into the hall together, heading straight for the elevators. As we step inside to go down I think about where he could be taking us. Wherever it is, he better drive carefully in my baby. I don't want her scratched up.

Chapter Nineteen

NIK'S TIME

EMERALD

We walk through the coven to try and make our escape, but are stopped by my mother as soon as we step out onto the garage level. She has a camera in her hand and my father trailing behind her. I sense what's coming, but I really don't want to stand around and pose for pictures.

Not that it really matters what I want because then she gives me this sad look, which makes me feel guilty for not letting her take them. So I give in, if for no other reason than to get us out of there faster. She is treating me like I'm a child, and that is when it dawns on me. She missed out on all of these moments with me when I was growing up.

To be fair, I didn't have too many of those big picture-worthy moments in my life, but she missed out on the few I did have.

My mood goes from sour to depressed in a nanosecond, and at that point, I let her take all the pictures she wants. I pose with Nik for several and then take some with my father as well. Nik even gets hold of the camera at one point and takes a few family pictures of my parents and I.

Finally, they let us go. We say our goodbyes, and then Nik walks me to the car, opening my door for me. I sit down and rest my head back against the seat with a sigh. *Who knew taking pictures could be so tiresome?*

When Nik climbs into the driver's side, he leans over and claims my lips in a soft kiss, surprising me. When he pulls away, it's with a massive smile on his face.

"What was that for?" I ask, feeling a little breathless.

He smirks and starts the car. "The whole time we were in there, I could feel your anxiety. You didn't want your picture taken, and I could see it in your eyes. But then there was a moment when Sie got upset and you just... changed. Like something clicked in your mind, and you sucked it up and let them take all those photos."

I blush and look down at my hands, twisting my fingers as I do, trying not to let him see the worry in my eyes.

"I got angry that she was treating me like a child, but then I realized she never got that time with me. She never got to see me grow up, or go on my first date, or anything like that. Not that I did any of those things anyway, but I knew she deserved the chance to do what they would have if I was a teenager going on a date, which was to take a billion pictures apparently."

He remains silent and the only sound is the purr of the engine. I glance up and see a look of awe in his eyes. "You know, sometimes you amaze me. Tonight, you gave them something they will always cherish."

He leans forward and kisses me again. This time, however, the kiss is deeper and filled with need. I moan into his mouth, enjoying the way he nips my bottom lip when he pulls away.

He starts the car as I sit there with my heart racing. It's totally not fair that he just did that. How am I supposed to survive a whole night on a date with him, when all I want to do is call the whole thing off and have him take me right here?

"Emerald, is this really your first date? As in first real date period?" Nik asks, breaking the silence between us.

I let my hair fall down to cover my face, and focus on the road. "Uh... yes, technically. The date with the three of you was officially my first date, but if you mean my first date with only one man? Then yes," I reply, keeping my voice neutral.

He doesn't respond right away, and I worry he may be upset by the news. After a minute, we turn down a little street lined with restaurants specializing in all sorts of foreign cuisines and he parks my baby. He turns the ignition off before shifting in his seat to study me intently. "Why didn't you tell us? If we had known, we would have made the night that much better for you. Though, I admit the idea of being the first to take you on a traditional date fills me with a possessive streak," he murmurs, running a finger down my cheek, then along the side of my neck until he meets my heaving cleavage. I gasp, my panties completely soaked through. If I didn't know any better, I'd think he was trying to turn me on before dinner.

Well, two can play at that game.

I lean forward, fluttering my eyelashes. "Hmm, maybe we should hurry up and have dinner, so I can get dessert after," I suggest wickedly, my heart pounding.

He growls and leans forward, leaving only an inch of space between us. "Oh, I'll definitely feed you dessert, Emerald."

I give a sexy smirk and pull away, climbing out of the car before he can react. When he gets out, he glares at me across the hood of the car, and I grin back at him. "I'm capable of getting my own dessert, you know. I have three options to choose from after all," I tease playfully.

He throws his head back with a laugh, causing my heart to skip a beat. He always acts so serious in the coven, like he can't be free. To see the pure happiness on his face makes my heart swell with joy.

Nik comes around the car and wipes away a stray tear that escaped. "What's wrong?" he asks, a look of worry in his eyes.

"I'm not sad, I'm happy."

"Happy?" he asks doubtfully.

"Yes, happy. I'm happy because you're happy," I explain, and he cocks his head in confusion. "It can be a lot of pressure being with the three of you. At first, it was all new and exciting, but now I have worries about keeping all three of you satisfied. It's also kind of hard for me because you three already have this unshakable bond. Where do I fit in? Do I even fit in at all?"

He opens his mouth to speak, but I push on. "I know it's going to take time, but I just worry. What if I don't connect with you guys in a group capacity? Individually, we all get along great, but there are moments where I try to pay attention to one of you, and I sense the jealousy, or disappointment from the others. It's just hard to find the balance, and not to be a whiny girl here, but you guys don't exactly convey your feelings well. Unless it's anger, that is. That I recognize, but whether or not you're all happy, I have no idea."

Nik remains quiet, gazing into my eyes as if trying to determine whether I held anything back. Then he sighs and pulls me into his arms, embracing me tightly.

"Emerald, I am so sorry. We didn't really think about how our actions would affect you, and we should have. When we get back to the coven, I promise we will all sit down and talk." He leans away to look down at me. "The reason for this date was kind of for the same reason you just brought up. I wanted to see if this would work, and figure out if you had interest in me outside of the group of us, I guess."

I shake my head and can't help the smile that comes to my face. "I guess we're both pretty insecure in this relationship, aren't we?"

"Come on, let's go have a fun date night and forget all about this for a bit. For now, you're all mine and I want you to have a good night."

He leads me along the sidewalk until we come to a small restaurant nestled in between two apartment buildings. While most of the buildings on this block look pretty fancy, this place looks like a homey little restaurant. I glance down at my dress, worried that I'm overdressed, but then I look at Nik in his suit. At least I won't be the only one who stands out.

As we climb the steps to the restaurant, foreign sounding music that I don't recognize slowly seeps out from under the doorway, and I find myself intrigued. Nik holds the door open for me, and I gasp in shock.

I no longer worry about my clothes as I take in my surroundings. While on the outside it looks rustic and unassuming, the inside is beautiful. There are just under twenty tables on the main floor, and a server dressed in a tux stands off to the side, smiling when he sees Nik.

A chandelier hangs in the middle of the room, and under it a small space has been left open for people to dance.

The server approaches us, his back ramrod straight, and I reluctantly pause in my perusal of this gorgeous restaurant. He bows deeply to Nik, before rising. "My Prince, your table is ready for you," he says with an accent. It sounds like the slight accent that is present in Nik's voice when he gets angry, but this man's is more prominent, like he's been speaking Russian most of his life.

The server walks us through the restaurant, and up a set of steps where a small balcony rests overlooking the dance floor. As we get closer, I notice a bouquet of roses on the table, pale purple like the ones he gave me earlier.

Nik pulls out a chair for me. After I sit, he pushes it in and I'm unable to control the smile on my face. The server leaves, and I watch Nik with new appreciation. He could have anyone he wants, but he chose me. He was the one who arranged this lovely date after all.

For the first time in a long time, I feel confident with our relationship.

He returns my gaze and gives me a small smile. "What are you so happy about?"

I debate how to answer, not quite sure how to articulate how I feel, so I choose to divert the attention to something else instead. "The roses. You did want me to know what they meant." I beam, enjoying the slight tinge of pink that spreads across his cheeks.

He clears his throat and looks around, sighing with relief when he sees the server coming back our way, holding two plates of food.

The waiter places both plates in front of me, and another server comes out carrying another table. He sets it down next to us, and I watch in awe as the first server goes back and forth from the kitchen to our table, setting out multiple plates on the table they placed beside me.

Why so much goddamn food?

"Uh, I think the server made a mistake," I whisper to Nik, who chuckles as he reaches for one of the bottles of wine that was already on the table. He pours us both a glass as he speaks. "Em, I can't eat. All this food is for you to try. I want you to experience some of the finer foods my people have to offer. It's also why he brought the spare table."

Oh, that makes sense. "I may have forgotten you couldn't eat food," I admit, feeling slightly embarrassed.

He chuckles and reaches for my hand, intertwining them. "It's okay, I wracked my brain for hours trying to figure out what to do tonight. The guys suggested taking you shopping, but I asked Sie and Britt what girls like to do. Britt wanted me to take you to a strip club," he says wryly, and I can't help the burst of laughter that escapes me.

Of course Britt wanted Nik to take me to a strip club, because then we'd both be awkward as fuck, and it would amuse the hell out of her to hear how badly it went.

The server comes back with one last plate laden with food, bowing once more towards Nik. "Do you need anything else, my Prince?"

Nik shoos him away while I stare, and he shifts in his seat uncomfortably. "What?"

"Are you really a Prince?" I ask, my voice laced with amusement. I mean, it wouldn't surprise me if Britt was pulling my leg about the whole Prince thing, too.

He sighs as if he knew it was only a matter of time before I asked him that question, and gives my hand a reassuring squeeze. "I was a Prince. One of the Romanov's bastard sons to be exact, but that still gave me the title of Prince. When my father's family was wiped out, I too, was targeted."

"You don't have to tell me this," I say, feeling the sadness, frustration, and anger warring within him through our tie.

"No, I want to." He sighs, his face forming a blank mask. "But I want you to eat some food while I talk. Talon told us you've been denying your wolf side." He frowns, and I look down at all the various dishes in front of me. I shift them around, putting a plate of crumbed chicken in front of me. It looks like the safest option to start with.

I cut into it, juices leaving from the center, and I realize it's just a chicken kiev in front of me.

I don't want to offend him by telling him I'm terrified of trying new foods. One thing that always annoyed the crap out of my dad was how fussy I am about food.

He tried to encourage me to try new foods, but I was very set in my ways. I would rather eat a simple steak than try any fancy dishes.

And all of these dishes before me have me feeling nervous.

When I take the second bite of chicken, Nik starts speaking in a monotone voice as if he's trying to shield his emotions from me, but I can still feel them through this connection we have.

"I never really knew my father. He met my mother a couple weeks before he was shipped off to the army. From what she told me, it had been nothing but a fling. They wrote to each other, but when she finally got the courage to mention she was pregnant with me, he stopped writing back."

He pauses, taking the chicken and putting another plate in its place in front of me. I look down at it, a little worried. All it is to me is a pile of ingredients covered in sauce. *I'll just pretend it's spaghetti. Yes, that's all it is, spaghetti,* I tell myself as I place the first bite in my mouth.

I hum in appreciation, pleasantly surprised by the taste. It's a bit fishy and has mayo, I think? Weird, but it kind of works. "What is this?" I ask when I finish the mouthful, eager to try something else now. If all the food is this interesting, then I will gladly try a few more dishes.

He chuckles and takes the plate from me with a grin. "That was herring under a fur coat."

My eyes widen, and I run my tongue around my mouth, trying not to freak out. "Fur?" I ask, my voice barely a whisper. "You fed me fur?"

The few people close enough to hear my whisper look up at me with annoyed looks as if I just spat on them, but I don't care! *Nik fucking fed me fur! What the hell? Who does something like that?*

His laughter echoes across the balcony we're on, and a few people close by chuckle, his laughter infectious. I narrow my eyes at him, and he finally gets his laughter under enough control to speak. "Did it taste bad?" he asks, his eyes shining with barely contained mirth.

I grumble under my breath about feeding him fur, making him chuckle as I look down at the dish before me with a dubious expression. "I'm not eating that. You have severely worsened my trust issues with food. Why would you do that?"

He laughs and pulls out his communicator to show me he's on a call with someone. I cock my head, confused when he presses the communicator into my hands. I put the device to my ear warily. It doesn't take long for me to figure out who it is based on the laughter alone.

"You're such a bitch!" I growl into the phone, even as she keeps laughing. *She thinks this shit is funny? Oh, I will make her pay!*

"Oh come on, Mer. That was priceless! You sounded like Nik had just fed you a puppy or some shit!"

I take a deep breath and meet Nik's laughing eyes across the table as I speak to Britt slowly, making the threat in my voice obvious to both of them. "You may think this was funny, but Britt, you at least know how sensitive I am with trying new foods. I promise you now, even if it kills me, I will make you suffer for this."

Nik's expression goes from happy and smug to wary in a split second. He finally seems to realize he made a mistake, and I can't help the grin that grows as he fidgets in his seat. I imagine right now, he's seeing a side of me he didn't know I had, but no one, and I mean no one, messes with my food and gets away with it.

"What you gonna do, Mer? Growl at me?" She laughs through the phone.

I laugh, too, and she goes quiet at just how evil it sounds.

"Oh, Britt, my dear friend. You made one crucial mistake. You brought Nik into it, which means I can enlist the help of a few husbands you have at your disposal," I reveal slowly, waiting for that to sink in.

"You wouldn't."

I chuckle and enjoy the shiver of fear that runs through Nik as he watches me with wide eyes. *Good. He should be afraid. No one messes with my food.* "I totally would."

I pause and listen to her fast breathing with an amused smile. "Tell me, Britt, how many times have you pulled shit like this with your men? I can imagine they would all probably be a little excited at the chance for revenge."

She doesn't respond, and a second later I'm hearing the dial tone. I hand the communicator back to Nik with a small smile. He takes it gingerly and watches me cautiously as if he thinks I'll attack at any moment.

He should be wary, though. No one plays with me regarding my food and gets away with it. I take a deep breath, closing my eyes to center myself. Then I re-open them, and focus back on Nik.

"So, where were we?"

"Uh..." He clears his throat and meets my eyes nervously. "You know there was no fur in the herring, right? It was just a salad."

I shrug nonchalantly, noticing that my lack of anger seems to frighten him. Oh well, that's what he gets for teaming up with Britt to prank me.

He gestures with his hands over to the server. Suddenly a group of people file out of a hidden room and come to take all the plates, most still filled with dishes I didn't have a chance to try yet. "I think maybe it's time for dessert," he suggests, and the server gives a quick nod of acknowledgement.

I sit back, sipping my glass of wine and watch Nik with narrowed eyes while we wait for them to bring out our dessert.

Once dessert is on the table, I gesture over at Nik. "You were telling me about your father?"

He shakes his head, watching as I tentatively put a bit of everything onto one plate, and start eating. I figure it's probably better if I don't know what any of the dishes are called, so I don't ask.

"Yeah, I was, wasn't I? So, my mother thought they had some secret forbidden romance, until he returned. He ignored her letters, and even went as far as to threaten my life when I was a mere four years old. Shortly after I turned six, he married his wife. My mother raged for days after their wedding. She claimed she never loved my father, but as I grew older, I realized she lied to me about that. She had been madly in love with him, and died the day he had his first child with his new wife. All the nurses told me it was from a heart attack, but I knew it was a broken heart she died from. She loved me dearly, but knowing my father had another child broke her. I think she honestly couldn't live her life knowing I would be nothing but a stain on his reputation, while his new child with the Princess was revered."

I pause in my eating to watch him, feeling his sadness through our tie, but knowing he doesn't want to be comforted.

"At eight years old, I was left alone in the world. They shipped me to an orphanage, which I ran away from not long after. Then two years before my father's death, when I was just shy of my twenty eighth birthday, someone from the royal family saw me. I looked so much like my father that he thought I was and when I denied having knowledge of who he was, he went back to the palace, telling all who would listen of my existence. Not long after, two of my father's guards tracked me down and tried to kill me, which was the night I was turned. The guards beat me within an inch of my life, and left me for dead out in the cold winter streets. Talon had been watching from nearby when they dragged me out. He came out and offered me the chance to move on from my mortal life and become something more, so I said yes. He turned me, and I haven't looked back since. This year, I'll be celebrating my one hundred and second year as a vampire."

I fight the shock I feel, and my eyes rake over him appreciatively. *For someone over a hundred, he sure doesn't look it.*

I remain quiet and return to picking at my food, which is actually all quite good. Suddenly, he pulls back from the table and stands over me, holding out a hand in invitation.

"Uh, Nik, what are you doing?"

He smiles down at me, but his eyes are filled with an underlying sadness. "This was supposed to be a date, and I ruined it. So, I'm making it right. Will you dance with me?"

Oh crap. "While I appreciate the thought, you didn't ruin our date. I know you were just playing with me, and I'm glad you are comfortable enough with me to do so. I can tell you like pranking people just as much as the wicked bitch does."

"Is that a no to dancing with me then?"

I can feel his disappointment and know I can't refuse now, especially since he's already feeling down. "Okay." I smile warmly and place my hand in his, taking a leap of faith that he won't let me fall on my face. But even if he does, I'll just take him down with me.

Chapter Twenty

SPECIAL PICNIC

EMERALD

Nik didn't disappoint, leading me around the dance floor like a professional. He twirled me around like a Princess, and I marveled at the way my dress flared out behind me. Although I'm still plotting my revenge against her, I will admit Britt did good picking this dress out.

Nik's now leading us out the back of the restaurant, and I can't help but wonder where he's taking me. He didn't even pay for the food. We danced for a bit, then he looked at his watch and took my hand, leading me back here.

We step through the back doors and into a tree-lined lot. He pulls me after him, his excitement contagious, which makes me all the more eager to see where he's taking me.

A few minutes later, we step into an open area with a picnic blanket set up, as well as a tray of strawberries, cheeses, crackers, and a bottle of champagne.

Cushions line the edges of the blanket, and off to the side is a thick folded blanket.

Nik turns to me with a grin. "I'm sorry I screwed up earlier, but if you'll let me, I would really like a take two?"

"When did you even have time to do this?" I ask, perplexed. He hasn't left my side all night. There's no way he could of snuck away to do something like this without me noticing. Unless he did it before we even left? But it sounded like he wanted to do this purely to make up for earlier, so that couldn't have been the case.

His cheeks tinge pink and he looks down to the ground, murmuring, "I paid the server to set everything up while we were dancing."

Oh, that's so sweet of him. I look back up at him, feeling guilty. *He really thought he screwed up our date? Shit, I'm no better than Felicia.*

"Nik, honey, our date was going fine. I'm sorry if you felt the need to do this, but you really didn't have to. I've been having a great time," I reassure him, pulling him closer and pressing my lips to his, hoping to show how grateful I feel for the night he's given me. He even got me to dance, and I actually had fun. That in itself, made the whole night worth it.

He breaks the kiss and meets my eyes, his blue eyes alight with a fierceness I wasn't expecting. "No, this is your first one-on-one date, and you deserve for it to be the best. Though, I'll never ask Britt for advice on what will make you laugh again. I'm starting to wonder if she set me up more than she did you," he muses, and I chuckle, pressing my head to his chest.

She most definitely set him up as much as she had me. That's just what she does. We used to be partners in crime, but I guess she decided to go solo. Well, I've become especially good at sneaking around since she left me, so, she has another thing coming if she thinks I will just lie down and take it when it comes to her tricks.

"Come on then, let's just sit down and relax. It's nice just to be out in the fresh air," I comment and he helps me sit down without messing up the lovely setup. It obviously took a bit of time to arrange, and it feels wrong to make a mess of something so beautiful. He takes a seat across from me on the blanket and moves the silver tray with all the food between us.

He grabs the bottle of champagne and then glances around, looking a little confused. "Uh, I may have forgotten to pack glasses," he admits sheepishly.

Then he shrugs and leans over the cushions, aiming the bottle away from us to pop the cork.

I just shake my head as he waits for the bubbles to die down. He chugs directly from the bottle before handing it to me. I laugh and take a swig before passing it back to him.

I reach down to grab a strawberry and pop it into my mouth, looking up at the night sky as I savor the berry's sweet juice. When I reach for another, Nik's hand stops me, and I suck in a breath as I meet his blazing eyes.

He pounces in the blink of an eye, pushing me to the ground, a growl echoing around us as he hovers above me with need in his eyes.

I lift my hand and run it through his hair before gripping tightly, bringing his lips to mine in a hungry kiss.

His lips taste of champagne, and I imagine mine must taste like the sweet flavor of strawberry.

His tongue darts out and runs along my lips, seeking invitation, and I open my mouth for him with a soft groan.

He grinds himself between my legs, and I gasp as a zap runs through my body. I realize it must be the spell Britt placed on my dress. Nik pauses, his eyes darkening in anger. I feel the blade he slips into my hand, and in the same second, he's up, meeting our attackers head on.

Fuck, why did I wear a dress?! I roll to my feet, which probably looks awkward as fuck, especially when I almost trip on a goddamn cushion. I kick the heels off to the side as the first zombie reaches me. I swing upwards with my knife, stabbing it through the heart, but it still comes at me.

Nik cuts down the zombie in front of him and spins, coming over to mine. A fucking sword appears from nowhere and he slices the creature's head from its body.

"Stab them in the back of the head where the spinal cord meets the brain."

I don't have a chance to ask him where the hell he was hiding that sword, because suddenly we're surrounded by at least two dozen zombies.

These ones are moving faster than the zombies we faced off with before, and I struggle to not get overwhelmed as Nik and I fight back

157

to back. He takes down two for each one I kill, but it's like they keep appearing from nowhere.

"Britt, wherever you fucking are right now, this dress is doing nothing!" I shout as I fight off two particularly large fucking zombies. One manages to grab a hold of me, his nails digging into the skin of my forearm, which causes me to cry out in pain.

"Son of a bitch!" I scream, using the small dagger to stab him through the chin. Then I kick him hard, which sends him flying back, the dagger sliding from his chin as I keep it gripped firmly in my hand. I swing back just as the other zombie's nails rake down my chest, splitting my dress like it's made of fucking tissue paper. I ignore the pain and I duck under his arm in time to stab him in the back of the head.

I stumble dizzily, heat washing over my skin.

I worry for a split second the zombie somehow infected me, but then I realize the heat's coming from the dress, which is glowing.

"Nikoli!"

He turns to me and sees the panic in my eyes as I look down at my dress, which is shining brighter by the second and he moves using his vampire speed to get to my side. He looks down at me confused and the heat explodes out of me in a wave of blue flames reaching ten feet away from us in a blazing circle of fire. Neither Nik nor I are harmed in the blast, and I breathe a sigh of relief that Britt had a built in fail safe on my weaponized dress. If Nik had of been burnt to a crisp, she'd be getting a fucking earful from me.

Five minutes later the fire dies out, and Nik is walking among the charred remains, stabbing any zombies who still twitch, making sure to hit the brain stem to ensure they're truly dead.

I move through the remains, heading for the nearest tree that isn't surrounded by body parts to get a little space from the situation. As I lean against it, I focus on the feeling of pain in my chest and my arm as they slowly heal.

Once Nik finishes with the zombies, he joins me at my side. He stabs his sword into the ground before cradling my face and lookings into my eyes. "Did you see the guy controlling them?"

I straighten, having completely forgotten that zombies require some kind of master. I scan the area around us, adrenaline pumping through my veins.

"Do you sense anyone?" I ask, still poised for attack as I take in our surroundings.

"No, I think we're safe. Is your dress still zapping you?"

I shake my head and sink back against the tree, feeling relieved. Britt's spell would still be active if we were in danger. "Nope, it's all calm now. I think that means we're out of harm's way, for now at least."

"Good," he growls. I have no time to move before his lips are claiming mine in a fire-filled kiss as he presses against me.

I feel the pure desperation in his kiss and know exactly how he feels. For a second when I felt the fire coming from the dress, I thought he would burn to a crisp, and I wouldn't be able to save him.

I'm tired of waiting for the perfect time. I want him now.

He pulls back and we both pant heavily. His eyes meet mine, and are filled with such desire that I tremble. "I need you," he declares, his voice coming out as a thick growl.

I groan, watching as his gaze rakes over my exposed chest, his hand running over the almost healed wound. I watch as he leans forward to lick the blood from the cut with a sensual groan of his own.

He leans away and lowers himself to the ground, meeting my gaze as his hands slip under the dress. I watch him intently, waiting for the moment he realizes I'm going commando.

His eyes shoot up, and I grin wickedly. "I may have hoped we'd get some alone time together."

"Fuck me," he whispers, his eyes filled with heat. *Well, that was the point,* I think to myself smugly.

He stands back up, his hand going to his pants, and I watch as he unzips them, freeing his cock.

He reaches out and runs his thumb over my clit, making me clench, desperate for release.

When I moan, he meets my eyes, and I can see the struggle in his. "Are you sure, Em?"

"So fucking sure," I breathe, reaching for him and lifting my right leg to wrap around his waist. I ease him inside me, so slowly it feels like the most exquisite torture.

When he's fully sheathed inside me, I clench around him, drawing a groan from his lips.

He moves inside me slowly, increasing the pace once I get used to the size of him. I ignore the slight sting of pain that comes from not having had sex in a long, long time.

He must sense it, though, because he reaches down to rub my clit, making me instantly moan, and the pain eases.

I kiss him hungrily as he drives himself inside me, with me pinned to a tree in the middle of God knows where. We could be attacked again, and I wouldn't give two fucks as long as he's buried inside me.

My body tightens around him, and he loses his rhythm. "Em! Fuck! Honey, if you do that, I won't last," he pants, his eyes blazing in the moonlight.

I grin and clench again, glad I have awesome pelvic muscles. A feral look comes over his face and he thrusts hard inside me, burying himself deep enough that I cry out from the shock. "Two can play at that game," he says with a wicked grin.

He thrusts faster and faster, each of us teasing the other until we both come undone together.

His legs only just hold our weight, unsteady from the rush of adrenaline so I slowly unwrap myself from him, standing on my own two feet, even though they're also shaky. My back is uncomfortable, and I peel away from the tree with a grimace, knowing it's going to be bruised for a short time.

Nik gives me a gentle kiss after tucking away his length, and I respond by wrapping my arms around his neck. Gone is the ferocious lover, and back is the soft, tender man I've come to know.

He sighs and separates from me, guilt in his expression. "Sorry, Em, I have to call this attack in. I should have the moment we had it under control, but I just got carried away."

"Hey, are you feeling guilty about what just happened between us?" I ask, trying to get him to look at me. His gaze remains fixed on the communicator in his hand, though, so I pinch his arm.

"Nikoli! You answer me right now. Do you feel bad about having sex with me?" I demand, trying not to let the idea of that bother me, but it does. *Why fuck me against a tree if he's just going to feel guilty about it after?*

"I didn't want our first time to be like this; I wanted it to be special. You deserved so much more," he says sadly, regret in his eyes.

"Oh, Nik. Please don't feel bad about it. We were both running on adrenaline, and I loved every goddamn moment of it. If I hadn't wanted it, I would have told you. And if we had the chance to do it all over again, I absolutely would," I tell him, pushing the truth of my words through our connection.

He smiles and gives me a kiss, his eyes looking less burdened. "You're right. I think I was just a bit nervous." He looks down at the communicator and presses a few numbers while I look at the destruction around us.

"Though it doesn't help Tal and Dev are going to smell it on you the moment we get within a mile of them," he mutters under his breath as he walks away, but loud enough for me to still catch it.

Too bad for them. I'm not going to apologize for what happened between Nik and I.

I watch as Nik paces back and forth, gazing at our surroundings as he waits for an answer. He freezes when someone picks up, and I see the dread on his face before he speaks. "Hey, Tal." He clears his throat, and I can feel his anxiety from here. "Uh, yeah, she's fine. I called because, there was a bit of an incident..." he trails off. I feel a spike of anger go through our tie, and I know Talon is not happy.

"What? No! She's fine, I swear. Do you really not think I can handle looking after my soul-tie as well as you?" The derision in his voice has me worried. I don't want them fighting over me.

"I know. I care for her just as much as you do, and I'd die before I let anyone hurt her. Look, can you just send a team to clean up this mess? I'll hide the bodies as best I can, but I want to bring Emerald back as soon as possible. She's supposed to be coming on patrol with us later tonight, and I don't want her in a ripped dress when we leave. Not to mention that I want her to grab some weapons first."

He sighs as he ends the call, and we wait for a team to arrive. Within a matter of a few minutes, a group of witches and vampires show up to clean up what remains of the zombies, and Nik takes that as our cue to leave.

Chapter Twenty-One

CLEANING UP

EMERALD

By the time we're back in our room, I'm feeling gross, sweaty, and a little awkward in my blood-stained dress. We were lucky enough only to come across a few people on our way up, but from the looks of horror they gave me, it was pretty clear I'm not looking my best right now.

Our room is abandoned, and I sigh in relief, not quite ready to deal with the onslaught of questions from Talon or Devin.

Nik pauses at the door to our bedroom and looks back at me with concerned eyes. "You okay, Em?"

"Yeah, just tired and dirty." I walk over to him, enjoying the way he wraps his arm around me.

"Do you want to join me in the shower?" Nik asks, the usual carefree light coming back into his eyes.

I smirk, grateful nothing has changed between us. I worried that sex would alter the way he acted around me, but he's still the same guy he was before.

"Sure, but I may need help with this dress," I tell him honestly, thinking of the zip in the back.

He grins, stripping out of his clothes in a flash and stands before me, naked as the day he was born.

My gaze is drawn to his chest where my name is scrawled over his right pec. I reach out and trace the letters with my fingers, meeting his eyes when he shivers under my touch.

It's changed, becoming darker and more pronounced. I still can't believe how the marks seem to grow and evolve the closer we get. It's fascinating.

Nik grips my hand to stop me from going over it anymore, and I meet his steel blue eyes as they flare with desire. He doesn't say a word as he leads me into the bathroom, reaching into the shower to turn the water on, all the while freezing me in place with his gaze.

His eyes roam over my chest, going to the spot where it's ripped, and smirks. "Did you want to keep this dress, Emerald?" I look down at it, wondering what he's getting at, when suddenly he grips the seams. A drawn-out rip sounds in the room, and I finally get his intentions.

I shake my head no, but in a split-second he tugs harder, and the dress drops onto the floor, nothing more than a bundle of fabric at my feet, and I'm left a little surprised at the suddenness of his action.

He chuckles and runs a hand up my side and over my ribs, caressing the edge of my breast until he gets to where his name is scrawled on the right side of my collarbone. He traces it slowly, the same way I did his, but drawing it out even more.

My breath hitches as he gets to the 'I,' feeling the soft caress over what happens to be a very sensitive spot. He growls at my reaction, leaning forward to press his lips to mine. I sigh into the kiss, enjoying the feel of our naked flesh against each other. He grips my ass, grinding against me, and I feel his length hardening as he picks me up and carries me into the shower.

I wrap my legs around him, and he walks directly under the spray of water, not breaking our kiss as he does so. I nip his lip, enjoying the jerk of surprise from him.

He places me on my feet, and I let the water run over me, washing away the last remnants of dirt and blood staining my skin, and am glad to see my wounds seem to have healed. I only have three small narrow cuts remaining on the left side of my chest where the zombie scratched me, but they barely sting.

Nik moves over to the second shower head and watches me with lust-filled eyes as the water draining turns pink from all the blood on him. I have no idea where he was hurt, but it's healed by now, with no fresh marks remaining, and trust me, I am definitely looking.

We wash ourselves off in silence, our gazes locked on the other, and a tension builds between us. I close my eyes as I stick my head under the water to wash out the shampoo I lathered through my hair. When I'm done, I step forward and open my eyes to see that Nik is standing directly in front of me.

He cups my face, placing a gentle kiss on my lips. I sigh into his lips, and we stand under the spray of the water for who knows how long, just slowly kissing, running our hands over one other, exploring each other's bodies.

We finally pull apart, and I look down at the blood, which is still slowly coming off his back, and I feel the urge to take care of him.

"Turn around."

He doesn't need telling twice, immediately doing as I demand. When he turns, I gasp, seeing the horror that is his back. Scars upon scars cover every inch of skin, and I can see the remnants of the still healing wounds from tonight. *How the fuck did I not notice he was hurt that badly?*

Not once did he mention being injured or move like he was in any kind of pain.

I lather my hands with soap, using it to clear off the blood so I can get a good look at the new wounds. Based on the placement of the wounds, it looks like a zombie tried to rip his heart out through his back!

My breathing is ragged as my beast and I fight for control. She wants to attack anyone who would dare hurt what's ours, and I'm of the same mind, which is making it harder to fight the shift.

Nik notices my lack of attention and turns, the spray of water washing the soap down his back. "Hey, what's wrong?" he murmurs, looking in my eyes, which I imagine are red as I fight for control.

"My beast... is angry... you got hurt," I grit out, fighting for breath as my chest tightens. I hunch over, grabbing my chest as the pain rips through me, the force of the change being denied.

It's never been this strong before, but she seems to think Nik is hers now that he's claimed us, which is making everything harder to fight.

I look up and meet his eyes. "Run! Get out of here before I shift!"

He scoffs, and instead grips me by the hair, slamming his lips down on mine and the taste of his blood enters my mouth from where he's bitten his tongue to entice me. He strokes my tongue with his, and my beast immediately retreats to the back of my mind. I straighten with a groan, my vampire side now desperate, needing more from him. His cock hardens between us, making me crave more than just his blood.

He lifts me up and slams me against the wall, thrusting inside me with one smooth movement, making me cry out.

He moves his head to the side, offering his neck to me, and I bite down, sucking on the delicate vein as he fucks me hard against the shower wall.

I can feel a mix of emotions coming through the tie between the four of us, and I hesitate, feeling overwhelmed by the feelings rushing through me. But before I can overthink it, Nik explodes inside me with a growl, sending me over the edge of pleasure and into a new fucking realm!

When we're both steady enough, he helps me wash off again, taking his time to run his hands over my body, being especially gentle with my now thoroughly pounded pussy. He smirks when I twitch as his hand runs over my sensitive flesh.

When I'm all clean, he runs his finger along my collarbone, and under my chin, tilting it back to give him access to my lips. He gives me one last lingering kiss before turning the shower off and climbing out. He wraps a towel around his body, and offers one to me as well. I use it to wrap my hair, and he holds out a second one as if he knew what I would do with the first, and wraps me in it.

We walk out of the shower together, and despite feeling the others through our tie, I see the bedroom is still empty.

We each move to grab our clothes for patrol. I hurriedly get dressed, pulling on black leather pants and a skin-tight black long-sleeved shirt, adding my jacket to complete the badass look I'm going for.

I watch as Nik strips off the towel, and bends down to grab jeans from his bottom drawer. I wait, expecting for him to pull boxers on when I remember he went commando earlier. Maybe he likes it just as much as I do.

I re-think my no bra choice as I watch him pull on the jeans, and watch as he straps his sword to his waist. In the blink of an eye, it disappears and I realize he must have used his unique ability to camouflage it when we were out tonight.

Tonight will be my first time out on active patrol with the guys, and I'm a bit worried I'll disappoint them.

After all, I barely held my own tonight, and Nik was hurt because of it. True, he healed, but I still feel I should have been able to better protect him from harm.

"Nik?"

"Yeah?'"

"Uh, what exactly are we looking for on patrol? Is it just more zombies?"

He bends down to pull out a shirt, and I see his lips moving, but my gaze is distracted by the way his ass looks in those blue jeans. When I look up, it's to see his smile.

"Sorry? What was that?"

He chuckles, shaking his head in amusement. "I said, we're on the lookout for a team of witches. The coven has heard that there are a few rogue witches in town, which explains the the sudden rise of zombies. The wolves haven't really had much luck at finding them, but they seem to be the target of the zombie attacks at the moment."

"But, why aren't the witches trying to find their rogue members? Why are they making us do it?"

He sighs as he pulls on his shirt and moves towards me. "Because witches are capable of pretty much anything as long as it's for the right price. That leaves the good witches in danger of being hunted to take their powers for spells. And we do not want that. So yeah, it's left up to us."

I frown, not quite understanding all of what he's talking about, but I have too many other things going through my mind to bother asking any more questions right now. It might be easier to ask Britt about that kind of thing anyway.

Instead, I focus on putting on my boots, ready for a night of patrol. I only hope we don't run into any more zombies.

Chapter Twenty-Two

Patrolling Together

Emerald

*W*e've been walking around the city for over an hour and I'm getting bored. I thought this would be my chance to prove that I could take care of myself, but I haven't had the opportunity to do much of anything.

I sigh for what feels like the hundredth time, and Talon finally snaps.

"What on earth is wrong with you, Emerald?! You keep bloody sighing as if you have something to say, but you won't speak up. And I swear to whatever afterlife there is, if you sigh one more time..."

I hide the grin on my face, because now I am really tempted to sigh again just to poke the bear. My gaze shifts to Nik and his eyes sparkle with mischief as he mouths 'do it.'

Against my better judgement, I sigh dramatically, and Talon freezes. I wait to see what he does, but he just turns on his heel and stomps away, grumbling under his breath. Nik and Dev burst into laughter and high five each other, then I watch as Nik runs to catch up with Talon.

"I guess we're splitting up," he calls over his shoulder at us as he keeps pace with Tal. They turn the corner, and Dev shakes his head in amusement.

"I don't know how you do it, but if anyone else were to push his buttons like that, they would be on the ground, lying in a pool of their own blood. How in the hell he reins himself in for you, I have no idea."

"It's because I have boobs. No man can fight the power of the boobs. They have their own magic, almost as powerful as that of a witch."

Dev watches me perplexed as I push my boobs up for emphasis, then lets loose a laugh that echoes down the street. "Magic boobs."

I grin and wink at him. Now he's getting it. These babies are indeed, a magic of their own.

When his laughter subsides, I kick my toe against the ground. "I'm sorry, I'm just so bored. I thought we'd be out here slaying evil witches, and watching you guys do what you do best. Not just wandering the streets aimlessly." I pout in disappointment.

Dev grabs my arm, forcing me to turn and meet his gaze. "Em, you sound as if you're actually looking for danger. That's the absolute last thing we want. If our night remains uneventful, you should be glad of it. We don't wish trouble upon ourselves."

His voice, while sounding matter-of-fact, is filled with a sense of judgement. I look down, thinking his words over.

"I'm sorry," I say quietly. He smiles and moves his hand from my arm, intertwining his fingers with my own.

We continue walking along the path in silence until we pass a warehouse, and we hear the sound of moaning coming from within. Dev and I smirk, our minds reaching the same conclusion. Someone is getting some action in there.

As we pass the next alley, Dev pulls me to a stop and gives me a quick kiss. It takes me by surprise, and I don't even have the chance to respond before it's over.

I reach up, touching my lips gently. "What was that for?"

He smiles at me and opens his mouth to speak, but then his eyes focus on something behind me, going wide in fear.

Something bowls me over, and I take Dev down with me. As I hit the ground, I feel claws rip across my back. *Son of a motherfucking bitch!*

Dev flips me over before climbing to his feet, and I watch as he pulls two daggers from the sheaths at his hips. Before he can rise up against one of the attackers, though, one of his daggers is sent flying in my direction. I pick it up, and pull out the other dagger I had stashed in my boot. Then I get to my feet, ignoring the pain in my back.

A huge fucking man is on me, and it's then I realize we weren't attacked by zombies, but by fucking wolves!

The stranger hesitates for a fraction of a second when he meets my eyes, but I don't. My leg shoots out, sweeping his legs out from under him. Then I stab him through the kneecap to incapacitate him. I would kill him, but Dev seems to be having some trouble, and I know he needs help.

I feel a knife in my back just as I sense the presence behind me. I turn slowly, pulling the knife out and flinging it to the side as my beast pushes forward, my hands shifting into claws. I grin at the female vampire who dared to attack me from behind.

"Wrong fucking move, bitch," I growl as my energy builds, waiting for the right moment to shift.

She sneers at me before pulling a stake from her back. "I will rid the earth of you, abomination!"

She lunges at me, and I throw her off me using her own momentum against her. I watch as she flips, quickly righting herself.

She can die. She must die! My master needs her dead!

I cock my head in confusion. Did she just speak into my mind? What the hell?

I don't get a second more to wonder, because then she attacks. I feel arms grab me from behind as she lunges, stake at the ready.

RIP!

My beast tears from my skin in a split-second, and pushes the female away from us, the stake barely grazing our arm as she flies back, hitting the alley wall. I turn on the witch holding me, ripping into his arm, and my beast is enjoying that I've let go of all control.

The man flings me away with magic, and I hit the side of a dumpster. Shaking myself off, I climb to my feet, just as someone else lands on my back. A stake is pierced through my back.

I can tell they were aiming for my heart, but they must be fucking stupid, or maybe just have no idea where the heart moves during a shift. I encourage my beast to drop to the ground and play dead, and wait patiently for them to pull the offending item back out.

Three people are gathered around me: a vampire and two witches. I hear the unmistakable sound of footsteps, just as the stake that pierced through me is pulled out. Two wolves suddenly appear, each of them crying out in disbelief as they watch the stake get pulled from me. The wolf standing closest to me is the first to die. My beast lunges at him, ripping his head from his body and flinging it at the others who are staring at me, petrified by my ferociousness.

My beast gets immense satisfaction from the fear that radiates from them. I sense help coming, but my beast is too far gone to pull back now. I lunge at one of the witches, seeing him as the bigger threat, and rip out his throat. His blood still coats my lips and tongue as I land on the vampire, her eyes wide as she begs for her life.

I hear Talon calling my name and look up at him for a moment, before ripping the vampire's head from her body, which sends blood spraying over our faces.

I lick my lips, enjoying the metallic taste of the red liquid. As I look around, I notice the other wolf has disappeared, and I let loose a menacing growl. I'm about to leave in search of him, when I see Britt and her husbands running towards us. But before they make it to us, a witch appears from nowhere. A massive fireball forms in his hands, which he aims straight at my chest.

I close my eyes, waiting for the pain, but when I open them, it's to see myself unaffected. Everyone has frozen, and I watch as the witch meets my eyes, awed and equally afraid. "Impossible," he breathes, just as Britt flings her hands out, binding him.

He drops to the ground, not even trying to fight Britt or her guys as they summon magical bindings, instead his gaze remains squarely fixed on me. If I were human, I'm sure I'd fidget under the intensity of his stare, but my beast remains unconcerned, perfectly happy to kill him if he tries to attack us again.

Once he's contained, Britt comes over to me while her husbands walk among my guys, checking to be sure no one is hurt. She gestures for me to follow her, and we stroll down the alley together.

"You can shift back, I'll clothe you."

My beast evaluates the scene to ensure the threat is gone before receding enough to let me take control of my body once again. Britt waves her hands, using her magic to cover me in a simple black tee and a pair of black sweats.

She glances to the side over at her husbands, and I can tell she's mentally communicating with them because they cast quick glances my way, and then get to work keeping my guys distracted.

Britt waits until she's sure they aren't looking our way before she materializes a magic bubble around us just large enough to encase us. I reach out to touch the bubble, and my hand gliding over the edge of the magic sends tingles through me. Suddenly Britt mutters a curse. "Shit!"

My gaze swings back to her, and I can see her eyes are filled with fear. Britt is one of the strongest people I know and very little scares her, so to see her looking frightened has me worried.

"Britt, what's wrong?" I ask, afraid to know the answer.

"Emerald, I need to ask you..." She pauses, taking a deep breath as if trying to calm me, or maybe herself, but either way I'm already freaking out. She called me Emerald. She never does that. "Did you... drink a witch's blood?"

I pause, considering the question, before nodding slowly. "I guess. I mean I may have swallowed a bit when I ripped out the witch's throat. Why?"

Her expression goes from worried to one of full-blown panic. "Motherfucker!" She throws her hands up, before running them through her hair, gripping tightly as if she just wants to scream. She takes a deep breath before grabbing my shoulders, the intensity in her grip scaring me as she stares deep into my eyes. "I need you to listen to me, Mer. You can't tell anyone about this. If you start feeling strange at all, you come find me, or one of my husbands. Promise me, Mer!"

"Jeez! I promise! But why is it such a big deal? Surely I'm not the first vampire to drink a witch's blood," I remark, resisting the urge to roll my eyes.

"It's not the vampire side of you I'm worried about, Mer. If a wolf ingests our blood, it can make them go mad, unless they are cured with a potion made of the attacking witch's blood. But the witch has to be alive for that to work, and you unfortunately killed him while ingesting his blood."

My face pales and I turn, looking back at the scene of the attack as they pack up what remains of the bodies littered along the ground.

Taking a deep breath, I swallow the saliva that's building in my mouth and I turn back to Britt with eyes wide, not believing it. "But... I feel fine, not like I'm crazy or anything. Well, I mean if you don't count my beast, that is, but I think she's just crazy in general," I ramble.

Britt looks at me sadly and points up to the bubble around us. "Mer, this is magic. You shouldn't be able to see it. Only witches can."

Well, fuck. "What else is a sign of this madness? What should I be watching for?" I ask, feeling truly afraid. Sure, I can die and come back to life, but what happens if I go mad?

She glances around and sees Talon's gaze fixed on us. He knows we're talking, but I guess this bubble must be some kind of sound barrier that blocks even his sensitive hearing.

"Look, we'll talk about it later. Talon suspects something is going on, and if he knew just what had happened he would freak the fuck out. You're going to have to lie to him if he asks what we've talked about. At least until I know the extent of the effects it will have on you. So, if they ask you, just say I needed sex advice or something. Maybe you can claim it's PMS? You know how men get with anything related to your period; they really don't want to know about it."

I feel guilty for lying to my soul-ties but Britt's fear is enough to persuade me that it's for the best. At least for now. I won't keep it from them forever. Just a day or so while Britt figures out exactly what the witch's blood will do to me.

The moment I nod, she releases the bubble around us. Noise suddenly bombards me, and I flinch as I readjust. It's like the sound from the outside world had been muted for us, just as the inside was for everyone outside of the bubble.

Britt and I return to the group, and the moment I'm within touching distance of him, Talon grabs me. He begins running his hands over me, looking for any injuries. "Are you okay? Dev said you were stabbed multiple times. Where are you hurt?" he demands, the concern in his voice overriding all my thoughts of lying to them.

Before I even get the chance to speak, he turns me around and lifts the black tee that Britt magically dressed me in, running his hand over my bare back as he looks for signs of injury, either from the knife or the stake being plunged into my back.

"I'm fine, just tired."

He drops my shirt back down, and turns me back towards him so he can look into my eyes. I wait patiently, giving him time to reassure himself that I am indeed fine. Then he pulls me to his chest, his grip iron-tight as he clings to me.

I wrap my arms around him, breathing in his scent, offering comfort the only way I know how. He just wants to know I'm safe, which I can understand.

"Let's get out of here," he murmurs against my hair, and I nod in agreement. I just want to go home, take a nice long hot shower and curl up in bed with the men I'm falling in love with.

Chapter Twenty-Three

BONDED WITH WITCH BLOOD

EMERALD

I open my eyes a crack and listen carefully, trying to figure out if the guys are still asleep. I found a note from Britt on my bathroom mirror after my shower, telling me to wait until the guys were asleep before sneaking out to meet her.

It took a while for them to actually fall asleep. Talon was wound up tight when we came to bed, but he refused to talk about it. When I asked Nik or Dev to explain what was going on, they both clammed up and avoided eye contact.

I started to wonder if they already knew about the witch's blood. I mean, they watched me rip the witch's throat out, so surely they would have seen it, right?

It wasn't until we all went to bed together that I realized they were just concerned about me. Each of them was touching me reverently, their hands pretty much encasing me in a cocoon of safety.

My internal alarm woke me up after only two hours of sleep, and now here I am, trying to delicately maneuver my way out of the bed to go meet with Britt without waking any of the guys, but in sleep they seem to have shifted closer.

I finally manage to squeeze out from between Nik and Talon, and start to slowly step over Dev, who somehow ended up squished at our feet.

When I clear his still form, I sigh in relief, only for a hand to reach out and grab me. I muffle my sudden scream by slamming my hand over my mouth, and see those hazel eyes narrowed at me.

Dev looks between me and the bed. 'Going out with Britt,' I mouth, and he relaxes, sinking back in the bed.

I hurry to my bags, grabbing a change of clothes before heading to the door. I turn back and meet his eyes before leaving the bedroom.

His eyes watch me, and he mouths 'be careful.' I nod and blow him a kiss before closing the door softly behind me.

I get dressed quickly, throwing on a pair of shorts and a tank. I grab Nik's black zip-up hoodie and breathe in his coffee scent as I put it on. He won't miss it while I'm gone.

The moment I open the door, I'm greeted by Britt's smiling face. I take in her clothes and immediately want to go back inside and change. How is it we're dressed pretty much the same, but her tan-colored skin glows, while my pale skin just looks drab? *She must use magic!*

As I open my mouth to greet her, she places a finger over my mouth to keep me quiet, before miming we should walk down the hall.

My shoulders shake as I chuckle silently, but still I follow her as she moves down the hall, waiting until we're safely closed behind the elevator doors before letting my laughter escape.

I wipe a tear from my cheek and meet her narrowed eyes and pursed lips with a smile. "So, where are we going?"

She sighs at me, and I can tell she hasn't slept recently. "We're just going to a little café down the road. After what happened last night, I don't want us to go too far from the boys in case you're attacked again. If that happened, Talon will kill me. It's bad enough he heard what I did to you on your date with Nik. He stormed right down to our room. I swear, there was murder in his eyes, Mer," she whispers, real fear in her voice.

I fight to hold back the grin that's wanting to surface, using my hand to cover my mouth, while trying not to make it look obvious. It's not my fault she tried to prank me, and it's now backfiring on her.

Huh, I had thought using Blaine or Meron would be my key to

revenge, but maybe Talon will be my secret weapon? Hmmm, that's something to think about later.

The elevator opens, and we walk down the empty hall, straight out the massive church doors and into the early morning sun. I pause as the heat hits my skin and close my eyes. I tilt my head up to the sky, basking in the warmth.

It's nice to be out during the day again. Living with vampires doesn't exactly give you that much time in the daylight. And while the underground forest simulates sunlight, it's nothing compared to the real thing.

I have no idea how long I stand here with my eyes closed before Britt flicks her fingers in my ear, startling me.

"Mer, stop daydreaming."

I open my eyes to see her glowering at me, and I blush as we walk side by side down the street, past a few little boutiques.

We come to a little pale blue building, with a sign proclaiming it to be the Bluebird Café. We step inside and Britt goes to the counter to order for both of us. As she does that, I stand back with my hands wrapped around my waist, hating the fact I'm inside when the sun is out and shining.

Britt comes back towards me, holding a number. Then she heads out the door to a table outside, placing the number down as she sits. I hurry after, thankful she chose a seat that would benefit me.

I take the seat opposite her and smile gratefully. "Thanks for sitting out here."

"You obviously need it. Your aura is lit up like a firework show right now."

I look down at my skin, trying to see what she's talking about, and begin to laugh hysterically. *I fucking sparkle!* It looks like someone has spilled gold glitter on me. As I watch, the sparkle disappears completely, and Britt sucks in a gasp.

She reaches out, running her hand over my skin, before looking up at me with wide eyes. "Did you just do that?"

"Uh, do what?"

She's look at me as if I just did something remarkable, but I really didn't do anything.

"When you saw your aura, what did you think? What were the exact thoughts that went through your mind?"

I think back, considering what exactly had been going through my mind at the time. "I was surprised there were glitter flakes on my skin, and wanted them to be gone. 'I stand out enough already, I don't need gold glitter,' I think were the exact words going through my head at the time. Why? What does it matter?"

Britt looks around to make sure no one is paying any attention to us, and places a small dagger on the table between us. I frown when I recognize the knife, and my eyes widen. "You want me to make a blood oath? Why? What's so bad that we need to blood oath each other?"

A blood oath is a witch's most powerful way of ensuring secrecy, invoking loyalty, or even offering protection depending on the intention. I only know that because of the guys. One night when we were lying in bed, they explained that a blood oath is how the covens are controlled under one leader without all of them trying to make a grab for power.

A blood oath is a binding promise that can't be broken by anyone but the initiator. It can be broken willingly, but that rarely happens, so in most cases it won't end until the caster's death nullifies the oath. The fact Britt wants me to do one right now has me terrified.

Britt laughs, shaking her head in amusement. "No, Mer, I don't need a blood oath. I just need a drop of your blood," she states, but I look down at the dagger with apprehension.

"Mer, I promise, I only need one drop. In order to figure out exactly what happened, I'll need to mix it with this." She pulls a vial from her pocket and sets it on the table between us. Inside is a clear liquid, and I frown, unsure what's going on.

I look at the vial warily before glancing back up at Britt. I'm a bit concerned about doing this, but if this will give me the answers I need, then I will.

"Okay." I use the dagger to prick my finger while Britt removes the stopper from the vial. I move my hand closer, letting a few drops of my blood drip into the vial.

We both watch as my blood mixes with the clear liquid, which then turns a pale gold with glitter flakes in it. What the fuck?! Why did my blood turn to glitter?

Britt, however, seems relieved by the change, but if anything, I'm even more confused than I was when we got started. "Uh, Britt, I know that made sense to you, but I have no idea what that means."

She smiles as the server brings our coffees to our table, and I beam at the smell of hazelnuts radiating from my mug. When I first started drinking coffee, I made sure to dose it with any syrup that I could get my hands on, in order to sweeten the flavor. My step-mother was partial to hazelnut, and I would sneak bits at a time until she finally realized I was the reason her supply kept dwindling.

Britt was a key instigator when she stayed with us. Always going on about the missing syrup like she was innocent, when she was well aware we had both taken from the bottle. Ah, to be sixteen again. I have to admit that being here with her right now makes it feel like I've gone back in time.

The moment the server disappears, Britt leans forward, adding sugar to her latte, and stirring it as she thinks over her words.

"As I said earlier, when a wolf ingests our blood, they tend to go, uh, a little mad. They'll attack any who cross their path. The only cure is the blood of the witch who infected them, but the catch is they have to be alive for it to work. Vampires, however, get a power boost when they drink from a witch."

I sip my coffee as she speaks, and my eyes widen at the power boost part. *What kind of power boost are we talking about?*

"Don't worry, it's not anything to be too concerned with, just a little extra strength. Anyway, it wears out for vampires once their body has fully absorbed the blood. You are neither vampire or wolf, but a crossing of the two species, so if anything, I'd say you'll get a bit of both."

She pauses to take a drink of her coffee, and I just want to lean forward and shake her for more answers. Thankfully, though, the moment her mug is back on the table, she picks back up where she left off. "When my husbands and I battled the witch who cursed my mother, Dastian, we found a book hidden away among his things. In it, he was talking about crossing different species. He wanted to create some kind of super soldier. A combination of vampire, werewolf, and witch, each balanced precisely enough so as not to risk the soldier going mad, but strong enough to handle anything that was thrown at them. He tried forcing wolves to turn into vampires, then injected them with witch blood while they were in the midst of their change. When that didn't work, he tried to have witches turned into vampires and then fed them wolf blood in the hopes it would be successful and he'd get the super soldier he desired. According to his journal, he tried every goddamn combination possible, but nothing ever worked."

"Okay, Britt, this is confusing me. What the hell does this have to do with me ingesting that witch's blood? Am I going to get some power boost or go stark raving mad on everyone? Just give me a yes or a no!" I grind out, tired of this story and desperate for real answers.

She sits back and smirks. "Both. My Mer wouldn't have normally gotten that frustrated so quickly, beast or not."

I freeze and realize she's right. My anger had skyrocketed in a split second. I went from patient to annoyed faster than you could say 'beast.'

As I sit in shock at the realization, she leans forward and grips my hand. "Mer, I don't know how, but I think the witch whose blood you consumed was a grade five. I think that's what Dastian may have been missing in his experiments. All the witches he used were grade one or two. The potion I just mixed your blood with was a test. If the potion split, it would mean the blood would affect you like a wolf. If it sank to the bottom of the vial, that would indicate the witch's blood would give you the same power boost it would a normal vampire. However, if the potion changed to the same color as your aura," she pauses and squeezes my hand reassuringly. "If it mimicked your aura, that would mean the blood you ingested had bound to your own."

I sit in shock, with my heart racing. The phrase 'bound to your own' is echoing in my mind, and despite the worry I feel, I just have to

182

know. "What does that mean for me?" I whisper, barely able to hear my own words over the pounding of my heart.

"It means I may have to teach you magic." She laughs, only to pull up short at the glare I direct at her.

She lets go of my hand and leans back in the chair, her expression wary. "Look, Mer, I don't honestly know. Dastian's books talked about a hybrid of all species, but that was just talk. He never achieved it. You could develop powers, or maybe you'll just be able to see the magic around you. Who knows? It's going to be a bit of trial and error figuring it out, but I'm here for you. Blaine, Kellan, Torie, and Meron have also pledged to take you under their wings and teach you magic if anything arises."

"Couldn't I just go to the coven?"

Britt looks like she's about to answer, but then her eyes widen in fear as she looks over my shoulder. Her voice sounds in my mind. *Don't say anything.*

A shadow falls over me, and I look up to see an older man hovering over us, a warm smile on his face. "Hello, Brittany. What are you doing down here today?"

The man doesn't look much older than my father, but his green eyes shine with a wealth of knowledge far beyond forty years. His red hair and matching beard add years to his face, so he could actually be younger than forty, but it's probably rude to ask.

"Oh, hi, Malcolm. I'm just taking my friend out for a coffee. We needed a little break from the coven," she explains while fluttering her eyelashes, and I fight not to gag.

Sure, my men are older than me, almost a hundred years in some cases, but they still don't look any older than thirty.

Malcolm holds out a hand for me to shake, and I grasp it, feeling a pulse of electricity run up my arm. Before the energy can reach my heart, something happens to make him stumble away from me, and he drops his hand in the process.

Malcolm looks from me to Britt, who has a cocky smile on her face, but I know better. That magic wasn't from her; it was from my beast, or at least that place inside me where my beast rests.

He frowns at Britt and lifts his finger in warning. "There's only so much I will tolerate, Brittany. You'd best remember that if you want to keep your marriage intact."

With that, he walks away, without another word or even a wave of farewell. I turn to Britt with wide eyes. "Who was that prick?"

She smiles grimly, tears welling in her eyes. "That's the leader of my coven, Malcolm. He's the one who's pushing for my husbands to find other wives."

Oh. "What an ass! Do you want me to go bite him? I will do it!"

She giggles and leans back in her chair with a smile. "God, I've missed this, Mer. I've missed having someone around who has my back, with no hidden agenda or ulterior motives, just friends talking. We were only together for a few months, but it just felt like we were meant to be friends forever and it was all ripped away too soon." She sighs sadly. "I guess the world works in funny ways, and I'm just really glad I found you again."

"I missed you, too." I grin at her. "Though, don't think this means I won't still get even over that fur in my food incident."

She bursts out laughing, and we relax in our seats, shifting to more light-hearted conversation as we drink our coffee. Before we know it, an hour has passed, and we decide to head back to the coven.

As I stand up, a feeling of cold rushes through me. I stiffen, my heart beating rapidly, and my beast tries to push forth. She can sense someone watching us, and I look around, taking in our surroundings and trying to zero in on the direction of the stare, but all I see are people going about their day shopping and sightseeing. Nobody seems suspicious or out of place, but the feeling still persists.

"What is it, Mer?"

I scan the area around me one more time with careful precision, and still see no one watching us. My beast is still convinced of it, though, so I tell Britt.

"I could have sworn someone was watching me. My beast is reacting to it and won't calm down, even though I don't see anyone," I explain quietly.

She nods slowly and stands, ready to leave. "Let's get out of here, just in case. Besides, Talon is probably going to kill me for bringing you out, so I would like the chance to put magical locks on my room before he finds out. At least then I will sleep easy knowing he can't get in."

I hold back a laugh. "Yeah, he probably will. Lucky you can't die for real."

She smirks. "You know, he's gonna be pissed at you, too, for not waking him up in the first place. What are you going to say to that?"

I grin wickedly. "I'm gonna blame Dev." I flutter my eyes and will tears into them. "But Tal, Dev said I could go."

She throws her head back with a laugh as we stroll back to the coven. "I would pay to see that. It's a good thing Dev's wicked fast."

"Exactly! He can run away from Talon; I can't. Although, I could use my magic boobs," I muse.

"Magic boobs?" she asks with a snort.

I'm about to answer when she holds up a hand, stopping me. "On second thought, I don't wanna know."

I laugh and link my arm through hers as we walk back in through the church doors. As they close behind us, my beast rattles the cage in my mind and I feel the shiver of cold again. Someone is definitely watching me.

JEREMY

THIS IS IT. THE MOMENT I'VE BEEN WAITING DAYS FOR. I WAIT WITH bated breath as I listen to my partner breathe through the phone.

We've been in position all morning, waiting for Malcolm to test the abomination.

I press the phone to my ear, waiting for an answer. This is the only chance we had, and I knew that I had to get her alone.

I watch the boys training out in the front yard and smile at how much improvement Brendan has made. He accepted the news about Emerald a lot easier than I thought he would, and it seems to have freed up his conscience. I still see the sliver of doubt in his eyes about our missions, but I believe if it comes down to it, he'll do what needs to be done.

He hasn't confronted me about being his father. After I told him, he seemed to accept it with a blasé attitude, and while I'll admit I had hoped for a little more enthusiasm, I'm glad he's compartmentalized his emotions. We'll have all the time in the world to explore our bond after we get rid of the main threat to our way of life.

I hear shuffling on the other end of the line and focus back on the silence, waiting for answers.

"Has she met the witch yet?" I ask, growing impatient.

My associate's voice comes through loud and clear, and I can hear the smile in their tone. "Yes, they've just shaken hands." The voice pauses before drawing a small gasp. "He just stumbled away from her. He looks scared."

Good. He needs to know how much of a threat she poses to us.

"How come you didn't just tell him she was a hybrid? Why all these games?" my associate asks with curiosity.

"I did," I growl down the line. One negative of having a vampire as an accomplice is that they are full of themselves. "He didn't believe she was a threat, though, so this meeting was planned for him to discover the truth for himself."

"Or you could just kill her yourself?"

Feeling frustrated, I run a hand down my face and blow out a breath of air. "We've tried that! It obviously didn't work. We need a witch's help to figure out how to destroy her."

My contact understands what we're doing is for the good of both our kinds, but the endless questions are getting tiresome.

"Malcolm just left. Crap!"

I hear cursing and heavy panting as if my associate is running.

"What's going on?" I whisper into the phone.

The line is quiet for a moment before the voice starts up again. "Never mind, I thought she saw me. But she didn't."

"You need to be more careful. If she finds out you and I are working together, all our plans will be ruined."

"Pffft, I'm not stupid, Jeremy, and I would appreciate if you didn't treat me as such. I'll do what needs to be done, for the good of both our races. Even if it means I have to kill her myself."

Chapter Twenty-Four

SILVER SWORDS

EMERALD

Britt abandoned me on our way back to our rooms. She left, claiming her men were on another floor, and she was going to spend time with them. Honestly though, I think she was just afraid of telling Talon she took me outside the coven after what happened last night.

The elevator doors open, and I step out onto my floor, freezing when I sense someone's presence.

I quickly turn to the right and see my grandfather standing there, with his arms crossed and his eyes narrowed.

"Uh, hi!" I greet with fake cheer, unsure why he's lurking outside the elevator.

He frowns, brows furrowing as he looks me over as if I'm hiding something. "I don't know what you're doing outside during the day, but I'm watching you."

I cock my head in confusion. He's watching me? Has my life become some weird soap opera that everyone has to know about? To watch my every move for what happens next?

"I just went out for a coffee with my friend!" I reply indignantly.

I don't like that he's treating me like I'm some kind of criminal who should be locked away for all hours of the day. I've done nothing to deserve this kind of treatment from him.

He smirks as he takes a step closer, trying to use his height to intimidate me. "Then, why do you smell like witch?"

"Uh, because Britt is a witch! Why, is there something wrong with a vampire hanging out with a witch?" I demand, crossing my arms over my chest to mirror his stance.

"You can have any friends you wish. What I don't approve of, however, is you sneaking around our coven. You're supposedly my granddaughter, a Princess of this coven, yet you're acting like nothing more than an errant child."

He flicks his gaze up and down dismissively, and I feel the hate radiating off him in waves as he walks around me to press the button for the elevator. We stand in silence as the doors open, and then he steps inside, pressing the button for whatever floor he's going to. I turn to watch as the doors begin to close, glad this unpleasant encounter is over.

"I suggest you don't leave the coven during the day anymore. You may not be able to protect yourself." The doors close before I have a chance to reply to his threat and I shake my head, flabbergasted by the way my grandparents are treating me.

The threat in his voice has me going over things in my mind as I make my way back to our bedroom. I freeze at our door, wondering if the presence I felt watching me was him. *Was he spying on me the whole day?*

I take a deep breath, trying to rein in my anger. Where does he get off treating me like that?

I open the door to our rooms and frown at sight of the empty outer room, whispering a small prayer that the guys may still be sleeping.

Thankfully when I open the door, the guys are in fact, asleep. Talon and Nik are still sharing Tal's bed, whereas Dev has moved over to his own and has a pillow clutched between his arms.

I lean against the door jamb and just look between the two beds, my anger immediately dissolving. I used to never believe that a person could fall in love so quickly. That our matings were based on pheromones rather than actual love, but standing here right now, I can't help but feel a warm swell of emotion that threatens tears.

I think I love them. I'm not certain because I've never been in love before, but I imagine this is what it would feel like.

Butterflies in my stomach when they offer a small touch or glance. The way my heart races when they kiss me. And this, the pure happiness I feel at seeing them after a bad day.

I know Britt wants me to keep what I've learned to myself, but I believe that they truly only want what's best for me, and it feels like too big a secret to keep from them. Our relationship is complicated enough with the four of us, without adding lies into it.

Yes, I resolve myself to tell them as soon as we get time. It won't matter if I wait a few days, though.

A whimper from Dev's direction draws my gaze. I see him clutching the pillow tight, his knuckles white.

I take soft steps into the room, closing the door as quietly as I can before making my way to his bed. I strip down to my underwear and climb in next to him, peeling one of his hands away from the pillow to rest it on my hip instead.

Instantly, he relaxes, and I smile, happy that I can ease his nightmares.

As I settle back in to get a bit more sleep, I become more than certain that I love all three of these wonderful men.

"SUCH A GOOD DREAM," I MURMUR, FEELING THE TOUCH INTENSIFY AND move along my leg as he feathers me with kisses on the inside of my thigh. Another moan escapes my lips as his teeth graze my skin.

I arch up on the bed just as reality starts to seep into my hazy mind. My eyes snap open at the realization I'm no longer dreaming. Dev is indeed placing kisses along the inside of each thigh and nipping my flesh before kissing the place where he bit to ease the sting.

When did I take my underwear off? I'm absolutely bare in the bed before him, and he grins up at me from between my legs. "I see you chose my bed when you came back."

His voice is husky, and his breath caresses my skin, causing me to shiver with need.

"Yes, I climbed into your bed. Is that okay?" I pant the words, trying to control my rapidly beating heart.

He runs a hand up the inside of my leg, torturously slow, as he watches me intently. I expect him to tease me, but he taps my clit quickly, laughing at the sudden involuntary jerk my body gives in response. *Why the hell did that feel so good? Oh, who cares.*

He moves until his thumb hovers over my clit, gently circling it, my orgasm rising up within me.

"You are more than welcome in my bed anytime, Em. Especially when I wake up to you, naked and grinding against my leg."

Despite the movements he's doing, I still flush. My dream must have been more intense than I thought if I stripped off my underwear in my sleep.

Before I can respond with a smart-ass comment, he slips a finger inside me, groaning as my walls clench around him. He continues the slow circling while moving his finger inside me in a slow pace, and in the blink of an eye, my orgasm hits me.

As I come down from the aftershocks that have my body spasming, he lays down beside me and buries his head in my hair, inhaling deeply. When I finally regain enough control to speak, I ask, "Would you like me to reciprocate?"

I try for flirty and playful, but it comes out sounding off.

He chuckles into my hair, placing a kiss on my collarbone. "No, Em, I'm fine. That was all for you."

Oh.

We lay here nestled together until I can't take it anymore. I roll over to face him, gazing down at his body. There are small scars that litter his body, and the tattoo on his chest shines like a beacon.

"What does your tattoo mean?"

It looks like those Celtic designs you see on people who want to appear tough, but I have a feeling Dev isn't the type of person to get his body permanently branded without a good reason.

He freezes, and his face completely shuts down. The light that usually shines in his hazel eyes has been extinguished by my question, and I immediately feel guilty for asking.

I reach out and stroke my hand down his arm soothingly. "Devin honey, I'm sorry if I crossed a line. I was only curious. You really don't have to tell me."

He shakes his head, a sadness in his eyes. "It's not that I don't want to share my past with you, it's just that it's pretty dark, and I don't know if I'm ready to tell you yet. Nikoli and Talon know my story, but only because they were there for the worst of it." He sighs and meets my eyes. "While I'm not ready to tell you everything, I promise that I will in time. For now, I will explain that my tattoo was not one that I chose. It was branded onto me."

"Oh, Dev, I'm so sorry."

He shrugs and slides further up the bed to rest his chin on my head, and I snuggle against his chest. He pulls a blanket up over my naked body, and I sigh against him at the sweet gesture.

"It's okay, Em. It's just something I don't like talking about. Out of the three of us, I'm the youngest and at the end of the day, my issues feel like nothing compared to what Talon and Nik had to go through. And before you ask, I won't tell you about their pasts. That's up to them."

I laugh, playfully swatting him on the chest. "You know me so well." I would have jumped at the chance to ask, and while Nik shared some of his history with me, I'm not about to go and force Dev to offer something he's not ready for. No, I won't push him to reveal his secrets. We have years ahead of us to learn these things, but it means a lot to me that he told me a bit about his tattoo, even though I know it hurt him to talk about it.

I roll out of his arms and climb to my feet, ready to start the day. That's when I notice the others are gone. "Where did Tal and Nik go?"

My surprise must be obvious, and I bet he thinks it's more about the fact that they disappeared without waking me, but that's not it. I totally forgot Dev and I weren't the only ones in the room when he was pleasuring me. That should have been a thought that occurred to me when he was touching me, but not once did it enter my mind that they could have been watching. And I think what bothers me most is the fact that I'm not bothered by that. Shouldn't our relationships be separate from each other? I should work to try to get more alone time with each of them, but at the same time, it feels better when we're all together.

"They went out to check the patrol logs to see if there have been any more attacks. They should be back any minute, though."

I nod before moving to my clothes, picking something nice and comfortable to wear when Dev's voice stops me. "Ah, Em? Shouldn't you get changed into training clothes?"

I narrow my eyes in confusion. Why would I do that when there's no training today? "I don't have training today, unless there's something you aren't telling me?"

"Well, with everything that happened with your beast, and you almost getting killed again, we decided you need a permanent weapon. One that could be taken out with you when you leave the coven. A dagger won't help you if you end up getting attacked by multiple people again." He pauses before delivering the bad news. "Talon is taking you once he gets back."

Fuck! I knew he was building up to something awful. It will be his way to punish me while also helping me. He'll give me my new weapon then demand I use it against him, which is just code for kicking my ass.

I hold back a groan as I dig through my clothes.

"What's wrong?" Dev asks as I release a defeated sigh.

"I've been too busy to really do any washing, and since the amount of clothes I have is limited, I don't really have anything left to wear."

He chuckles, climbing out of the bed, and I marvel over his naked body, wondering when he stripped out of his boxers. The way his muscles move as he strides towards me holds me captivated. After a moment, he reaches out and waves a hand in front of my face, catching my gaze.

"Huh? What'd you say?"

He frowns at me, looking concerned. "Are you okay? You got this kind of glazed look. I was worried you were going to faint."

My cheeks heat up with embarrassment, and I avoid meeting his eyes. "Yeah, no, I'm fine. Just wondering what to wear."

He buys my excuse, but I swear he smirks as he moves me away from my bags, and over to a dresser that I assumed was Nik or Talon's, seeing as it's between their beds.

"Now, I don't want you to freak out, but Talon asked Britt to get you some more clothes because we know you only had the basics. He worried you might be upset if we got you clothes that either didn't fit or were the wrong color, so he gave the task to Britt. She took care of everything while you were on your date with Nik," he adds, as if he senses my confusion.

Damn Britt and her sneaky tactics.

He slaps a hand on the top of the dresser affectionately. "Everything in here is all yours."

I don't argue, since I know it would do no good for me to complain. It's why I suspect Dev made sure I knew Talon was the key person responsible for this surprise. Because at the end of the day, I'd rather not start an argument with him over both of us being stubborn. It would just end in me giving in, or him stomping out of the room.

My hands reach out, gripping the metal handles of the top drawer. I pull it open to reveal an assortment of bras and underwear, as well as crop tops that seem to be designed specifically for training.

I pull out a simple black pair of cotton boy shorts and a matching black crop top, pulling them on as Dev watches. While the bra is a perfect fit, the underwear is a little tight, but it will have to do for now. Who knows how much time I have before Talon barges in here, demanding for me to join him at training?

The second drawer contains a bunch of sweats and men's shirts. Basically, a lazy day drawer. I smile, glad that Britt remembered I like to wear loose fitting clothes. I hope they're the right size, though, because I swear this underwear is killing me.

When I open the third drawer, I let out a sigh of relief. A ton of yoga pants and light breathable shirts are folded neatly inside. I reach in and pull out a pair of dark blue pants with pale blue stripes up the sides, and set them on the top of the dresser as I go to peel the underwear back off. These pants look like they'll be tight enough to show an underwear line anyway, so may as well go without rather than be even more uncomfortable than I already am.

As I bend down to peel my underwear off, I see a flash of gold and see a price tag peeking out from the pants. I reach in and turn the tag over, gasping when I see the price. "Five hundred dollars?! Are you frigging kidding me, Dev?! For pants that price, I'd expect them to be made of gold!" I throw my hands up, acutely aware that I'm still wearing only my sports bra. "Who pays five hundred dollars for pants that will just get drenched in sweat?!"

Dev just laughs, ripping the tag off before I can object, and I almost faint. "Better get used to high-priced items, Em. We're all pretty wealthy, and your parents are too for that matter. Being a Princess has its perks." He winks, holding out the pants I had set aside. "You may want to hurry and put these on. Talon is almost here."

I growl, but snatch the pants from his hands and pull them on.

Sure enough, as soon as I pull the pants up over my hips, I hear Talon's voice from the outer room. I sigh and give Dev a quick kiss, before going out to meet my fate.

Nik is absent from the front room, and Talon doesn't say a word as he approaches, just intertwines our fingers and leads me from the room. I look back in time to see Dev mouth 'good luck,' which I respond to by flipping him off. He grins and closes the door after us.

The whole way down to the forest is filled with silence, and I don't break it by speaking, not wanting to upset him. There's an unusual energy around him, not quite anger, but it's certainly not happiness either. My beast wants us to soothe him, but right now, I have no idea how to do that.

When we step out onto the forest floor, he finally speaks. "After what happened last night, we decided it was time you got your own weapon."

"I think I handled myself exceptionally well, thank you very much."

He pulls up short, and I hold back a smile. This was the only way I could think of for him to get his issues out, by baiting him. I'd rather he yell and scream at me than hold back how he really felt, leaving me to wonder what the exact issue was.

"You... did... not... handle... yourself!" he growls out, the anger in his eyes growing with each word he says. "You were reckless and almost died!'

"I killed a few of them on my own! If I remember correctly, I also helped Dev! If I hadn't, he would've died!" I shoot back with just as much venom. "I know what I did was reckless, I'm not completely stupid, but I did it for a good reason! I couldn't lose Dev!"

Talon sighs, and I see his anger deflate. He reaches out and cups my cheek, forcing me to look into his eyes. "Devin would gladly die to protect you. That's his job."

Fuck that misogynistic shit! Men aren't supposed to have to protect women! Women are more than capable of protecting themselves! "Well then, he's fired. Actually, you're all fired."

He smiles patiently at me like I'm nothing more than a naïve child. "You can't fire us, Em. Only your mother can do that, and I'm pretty sure she feels just as strongly about your safety as I do."

Shit! I clearly didn't think that through. I'm sure I could convince my mother or father to reassign them, though. Maybe if I...

Talon watches me as I consider all my options. He smirks, obviously thinking he won this argument. "Come on, I have some new weapons to show you."

I follow him, my mind still going over ways to get a little more freedom. Despite the recent attacks, I don't want to be coddled for the rest of my life. Maybe we can come to some kind of arrangement that works for everyone. They seem to be willing to let me spend time with Britt alone, so maybe that's the key.

Talon stops, and I focus back on my surroundings, letting out a soft gasp at what I see on the table before us. It's covered with swords of varying styles and lengths, as well as an axe and a few other weapons I've never seen before. But that's not all. The blades I saw downstairs at the market the other day also reside on the table.

"What is this?" I ask in awe. I've never seen so many blades in one place before. I am so tempted to reach out and grab a few of the prettier ones, but I hold back, unsure what I'm supposed to do.

Talon chuckles, and grips me by the shoulders, moving me, so I'm standing near the center of the table. He goes to stand behind me, and his breath brushes against my ear as we look over the weapons in front of us. "All vampires who fight with a weapon believe that their weapon is chosen with their own energy. That energy binds with the metal creating an unbreakable bond. Or you may come across a weapon that has already been imbued with another's energy or even a witch's magic. Those weapons are the ones that are meant for the more powerful of us. If you read through that hefty book Jeannie gave you, you would already know all of this."

Damn those stupid books! When I finished training, I put them on the kitchen counter in our room and never looked at them again. I should really read them so I learn some of this.

Talon continues speaking oblivious to my internal thoughts. "One of these will be yours. You just have to find the right one."

When I reach out to pick up the blades I was staring at, he grips my arms tightly. "Now, don't go picking the first one you see, just because it looks pretty. I want you to look at every weapon carefully, while letting your instincts guide you."

I do as he says, but my gaze is still drawn to the first weapons that caught my eye, the twin swords from back in the marketplace. I take a closer look and see each blade has foreign markings etched along the length of them.

No matter how hard I try to shift my focus over to the other weapons on the table, I keep finding myself drawn back to the twin swords. Finally, I give up trying to resist and step out of Talon's space to reach for them.

When I pick them up, I see a small glow that starts in my hand and extends into my arms, and the swords thrum in response. The blades are no longer than my forearms, but still feel powerful enough to cut down my enemies.

Talon sucks in a sharp breath as I twirl them happily. It feels like

I've been reunited with a lost limb, and pure joy radiates from me. I turn to meet Talon's gaze with a hint of challenge in my eyes.

I feel like I could take on the world, and it would surrender to my power. Huh, that's a weird thought to have.

Talon just stares at me, with both shock and fear in his eyes. He seems to shake himself free of his thoughts and then pride fills his eyes, replacing all traces of fear.

"What's the matter? Did I do it wrong?" I ask, disappointed that I may be told to choose a different weapon.

"It's nothing, Em. Those swords are special is all."

"Hmm," I murmur absently, twirling them in each hand. Talon watches me appreciatively, and I fight not to give myself away. If he thought training me with swords would make for an easy win, then he was wrong. My dad made sure I trained with every weapon that I showed an interest in. Swords, however, were a personal favorite of mine.

At the time I would complain, saying all my sword training would never come in handy, but with everything that has happened over the past few days, I'm glad I am capable of defending myself with a weapon.

"So, what's special about these swords?" I ask, taking a few steps away from the table towards the open field. Talon grabs a sword in its scabbard that's hanging from a tree branch on the edge of the area, as if he knew I would find a sword to train with.

His sword is the same one I've seen him attach to his hip every time he leaves on patrol, whereas I know Dev carries a few daggers, but seems to prefer guns. Maybe it's because of the age difference between them?

"Those swords," he says as he faces me, unsheathing his sword. A shiver runs through me at the ringing of steel that echoes through the large forested room, and he grins wickedly. *Shit, maybe even my training won't be enough this time.*

"They're silver, and were infused with witch's blood when they were forged."

I frown, and start circling Talon. "So, silver really doesn't affect us then?" I think back to my mother's explanations and feel silly for still being fearful of silver.

"No it doesn't." He smirks and continues to move in a circle, and I mimic his steps, waiting for the inevitable attack. "What surprises me is that when I was given those swords to try, my hands were torched with witch fire. The witch who made them laughed at me and told me that one day I would get to see their true power, but it wouldn't be that day. He told me I would know when it was time to bring them out again. The thing is, I didn't put them on the table today. I sold them to a vendor a few weeks ago because I was tired of being their guardian."

"Why were they at the market then? And, why was I able to pick them up if they burned you? Or am I the first to pick them up besides you?"

"No, you weren't the first. A number of vampires and wolves have tried to steal them over the years, but no matter what, the blades always return to me. There have been whispers about so and so that stole the swords only for their hands to erupt in flames before the swords magically disappeared. But when I go to check, the swords are always back in my house, locked in their cabinet, with no evidence of having been taken. This is the first time I've seen them since I sold them." He shrugs, and I look down at the swords in my hands with a new appreciation.

"I have magic swords? Cool!" I exclaim, becoming even more excited. *Let's see what these babies can do.*

He nods, seeming amused by my eagerness. He gives a cocky smirk and looks at me in challenge. "Are you ready to begin?'

I smile coyly. "Yeah, just take it easy on me."

I position myself in a stance similar to his, and a small frown appears on his face before he springs forward.

I let go of my control, my movements coming automatically as he attacks me. The sound of steel hitting silver can be heard, echoing through the room. He keeps trying to get a hit in, but he can't get through my defense. That was one thing I was always good at.

He pauses and takes a wary step away from me. "This isn't your first time with a sword, is it?"

I grin at him. "Nope." I lunge forward, going on the offensive, enjoying the fact that he's forced to defend against me.

We get closer to the forest area as we fight until we're surrounded by trees. He smirks and leaps away from me, but by the time I follow the movement, he's gone.

Son of a bitch!

I move through the forest, trying to track him by scent, but the pine smell of the trees becomes all I can sense. Then it hits me; he's using his special ability to try and cheat! I close my eyes like he taught me, feeling the light breeze moving around me, and I begin to sway with it.

The wind shifts to my right, and I open my eyes just as Talon appears. I drop to the ground, meeting his attack from behind.

His eyes are filled with pride as I fight back, and I can't help but smile. "Truce?" I ask playfully.

His eyes narrow. "Never." He grins, twisting out of my attack.

He starts pushing me harder, and at one point I trip over a loose branch, having lost my footing during one of his ferocious attacks. He uses one of his swords to disarm me, first of one sword, then the other, until I'm left completely defenseless.

He raises his sword as if to strike, and I move my arms to shield my face. But then my hands open of their own accord and the twin swords suddenly appear in them, the magic of them coming up to block his downward thrust.

He looks down at my hands in wonder as I hold his sword away from my face, wondering why he was going to strike me. Then I notice his gaze is locked on the swords. He wasn't just testing me. He knew these swords contained some kind of otherworldly magic and was testing their ability to come to my aid.

I breathe heavily and meet his eyes.

"Did the swords just...?"

"Yeah, they appeared in your hands in the blink of an eye," he breathes out. "I think that's enough training for today."

Chapter Six

DATE NIGHT

JEREMY

The phone on the table taunts me as I wait for the call. My spy was unable to capture Emerald, but there is still hope the witch Malcolm will come through.

I slam my hand on the table in front of me, the crack of wood echoing through my small cabin, just before the phone begins to ring shrilly.

I pick it up on the third ring, trying to sound calm. "Yes?"

It's quiet on the other end, but I wait, outwardly showing patience when I really just want to shout into the phone.

Finally, he speaks. "I met the girl. I will do what you ask, but none of this comes back on me. Understood?"

The first genuine smile I've had in days crosses my face. "Of course. We will trick her into believing it is her witch friend, Brittany. I believe that you've been having issues with that particular witch?"

Malcolm laughs, and I can hear voices in the background as he goes quiet. "See that it's done."

The line goes quiet, and I close my phone, feeling more optimistic than I have in days. This whole business might be over within a few days. Now time to make sure my spy plants the seeds to divide Emerald from her witch friend. Only then will I be able to make my move.

Emerald

WE'RE OUT ON PATROL, AND I'M FEELING MORE BADASS THAN EVER WITH my new swords attached to my hips. It helped that Britt had brought me a kickass wardrobe. She had included a ton of leather pants, leather jackets and shirts, with phrases that made me believe she had them custom made. Like the tank I'm wearing under this jacket that says 'I'm immortal, you idiot!' When I saw it, I couldn't help but laugh at the obvious reference to the fact I can't actually be killed. There were a few others tops I wanted to read before we went out, but we ran out of time.

We had been asked to come out on patrol and keep an eye on the local pack lands, seeing as tonight was a full moon and the pack had a scheduled run. It was supposed to be a simple run for a few hours then we could go back home.

We had only been on patrol for forty minutes when we heard a howl of pain. We all take off at a run to find two vampires trying to attack a wolf who looks to be just a teenager. He whimpers and curls into a ball, letting the vampires continue to attack him. The guys exchange glances before apparently deciding to offer me up as proverbial bait. They quickly disappear before the vamps have a chance to see them.

I see how it is. If they need me to be bait, they're happy to put me into the line of fire, but if I jump into the fray of my own free will, then I'm just being reckless!

"Hey! What do you think you're doing? Get the fuck away from him!"

The vampires whip around, their eyes narrowing on me, and I freeze in shock. One of them looks exactly like Xander, from the brown hair falling in his eyes to the narrowed gaze he's giving me. The only difference is those blood red eyes that show his vampire is in complete control.

My beast rattles in her cage, and I can't fight it when she takes control. My feet move of my own accord and I run at the vampire, rage fuelling me as my beast demands retribution for everything Xander has done to us. He turned our own brother against us!

The vampire's eyes go wide as I leap on him, my fists swinging. I hear my name being called, sounding strange as though coming through a tunnel, but nothing matters anymore. I will make him pay for all the hurt he's caused me.

Arms wrap around me as I continue to deliver punch after punch, and they pull me off him with no effort. Dev and Nik are there looking over the Xander look-alike, and I turn my head to see Talon restraining the second vampire who had been attacking the wolf. The wolf in question has disappeared in the middle of all the chaos, which leaves me to wonder who the hell is holding me and why my beast isn't going psycho killer on his ass?

I tilt my head up to see a handsome man grinning down at me with vaguely familiar sky blue eyes.

"Easy, girl. The pup is safe with my pack now, and I think the young idiot has suffered enough already. Wouldn't you agree?"

It's debatable, but I relax in his arms anyway, which leads to him loosening his hold enough for me to drop to my feet, just as half a dozen vampires appear from nowhere. Four of them restrain the vampire in Talon's arms before carrying him off. The other two move over to the one whose face has been reduced to nothing but a bloody pulp. It's already starting to heal, but I still look away as they pick him up and take him away.

When my gaze swings back to the guys, it's to see Talon, Nik, and Dev looking at me like they've never seen me before, and I fight not to fidget under their gazes.

The newcomer, however, smiles warmly at me and bows formally. "Well, seeing as you're here now, I would say this is the perfect time to invite you all to my house for tea."

I watch him carefully, trying to assess if he's a threat, but I'm having trouble being rational when my beast feels so drawn to him. "Uh, sure," I agree, watching as each of my guys frown at me like I'm nuts. I shrug, wondering what the big deal is, but don't get a chance to ask before the wolf in question throws an arm over my shoulder possessively. "Excellent!" He starts guiding me through the trees, and I let him lead me along, all the while feeling a huge mixture of emotions coming off of the guys behind me.

What is their problem? He just saved me in the middle of a semi-breakdown. Shouldn't they be happy?!

As we walk, the wolf at my side continues to talk. "I'm so excited to see you again, Emerald." *Again? When have we met before?*

"Ever since I heard you were in my city, I have been waiting for the chance to see you again. Do you remember when we first met?"

"Uh, no..." I don't think I've ever seen this man before, but I could be wrong. We used to have wolves from other packs come to the pack all the time, so it's possible he visited at some point, and I just don't remember.

He smiles down at me. "I remember it as clearly as if it happened yesterday. I visited your pack about six years ago. You would have been fourteen or fifteen then. You were out in a field by yourself, training with a punching bag speared through a pole with a picture on the front of it so it would resemble a human. I watched as a girl appeared from nowhere and attacked you. Even though she obviously meant you harm, I could see that you pulled your punches, so as to not hurt her. Then when you finally knocked her out, you did so quickly and to minimize any pain."

I blush, remembering the day he's talking about. My father had told me of a visiting Alpha and his son. The Alpha was there in the hopes of finding a mate for his son, because while men don't need mates to rule, it is preferred.

The girl he saw me fighting was none other than Sophie, one of my frequent tormentors. She had come out of nowhere, like he said, attacking me while screaming obscenities at me. We fought, and I remember having sensed someone watching us, but at the time I just assumed it was my father.

No matter how much I tried to reason with Sophie, nothing got through to her. She was convinced Joel and I were in some kind of secret relationship, which we weren't, but no matter how much I denied such preposterous accusations, she still came at me.

Instead of sticking around to deal with the consequences of my actions after I knocked her out, I had run off. I didn't stop until I reached just outside my house where I sank to my ass and leaned against the house, letting the tears fall. That's when a stranger happened upon me and just sat with me while I cried. He didn't say anything, instead just offering me comfort. While I had no idea who he was, I really appreciated his kind gesture.

Back then, I assumed the boy who sat beside me was just a quiet pack member who preferred their privacy, so I had never really gone out of my way to find him.

"You sat with me while I cried," I murmur quietly, but it still draws the others' attention. My gaze remains fixed on the stranger beside me, and I wonder why he did that back then. I was just a stranger to him.

"Do you mind me asking your name? I never learned it," I explain when he raises an eyebrow in question.

"My name's Lincoln, though you can call me Linc." He winks with a cheeky smile, and I can't help the giggle that escapes me. *What the hell is wrong with me? Am I really flirting with him?*

We arrive at a small row of cottages, the area lined with narrow lamp posts and filled with silence, giving off the feeling of being abandoned. *Where is everybody?*

As if hearing my unasked question, Lincoln breaks the silence. "Everyone is still out enjoying the shift. They'll start to slowly trickle back once the sun begins to rise."

He grins over his shoulder at the guys, who are following silently. "Don't worry, guys, it won't be for a while yet. You've got plenty of time before sunrise."

He leads me over to a pretty unassuming cottage before letting go over my shoulder. He walks up the steps ahead of me and opens the door, flicking on light switches inside. I follow after him, with Talon, Nik, and Dev trailing after me warily.

With all the guys in one room, there's a tension that has me worried. Surely, they wouldn't attack the Alpha's son? If he was a threat, why would they have let him lead me here?

I choose the only single seat available, leaving Nik and Dev to share a loveseat. Talon remains standing close to me, while Lincoln sits directly opposite me in the other two-seater in the room.

"Forgive me, Emerald, but I'm going to be completely blunt with you because I imagine your soul-ties are feeling a little uncomfortable right now." He pauses and I glance at each of my guys to see them all with their eyes narrowed.

I return my gaze to Linc, who rolls his eyes. Then his expression turns to one of interest as he asks, "Do you have a mate?"

"Well yeah, that's what the guys are," I respond automatically.

He shakes his head with an amused smile. "No, hun, you have soul-ties. I know what you are, and I know that your wolf side won't be truly happy unless you take a wolf as a mate. I propose myself," he says, puffing out his chest with pride. "I'm financially stable, respected among my pack, and a great defender. Any pups we had would be cared for by the pack and you would be treated like the gem you are."

My mouth opens and closes as I try to comprehend the meaning of his words. That's when it comes clear that this isn't the Alpha's son, he is the Alpha, the very one who told the guys he wanted to meet me. I look for help from one of the guys, but they stay quiet. How the hell do I turn down the Alpha of a pack without causing some kind of diplomatic faux pas? I beg Talon with my eyes for some kind of clue, and he sighs in annoyance. "Emerald, we can't make this choice for you. It's your wolf, your body, your life."

I tear up at Talon's blatant dismissal, and I look back at Linc, replaying his words in my mind.

While my beast is practically purring inside me at his offer, my heart is torn. Do I turn him down and risk my beast being alone for the rest of our lives? I have to, though, because I'm already tied to three men. I won't add in any more complications.

"Look, Lincoln. I have already three soul-ties. My beast is more than happy with them," I lie, hoping no one sees through it. "I don't need a mate right now. But, thank you for the offer."

He smiles softly at me. "It's okay, I understand completely." With that, he gets up and walks to the front door before opening it for us. "You must leave now. The sun will be rising soon, and my pack is starting to come back from their shift."

I frown as the guys make their exit, and I follow after them, feeling like we've been kicked out because I turned Linc down. Where was the tea he offered?

I start to walk down the stairs, and Talon pulls me close when Linc calls out my name. "Emerald!"

I whip back around, starting to get annoyed by this guy's attitude.

"What?" I ask, cocking a hip in irritation. Talon, Dev, and Nik press closer, crowding my personal space.

Linc smirks as he looks down at my soul-ties gathered around me. "I'm certain I'm your mate. I knew it when I met you all those years ago, but your father insisted I was wrong. But I felt the same thing the moment I saw you protecting the pup out there. You are definitely my mate. My wolf felt it. Don't lie and tell me yours didn't."

I remain silent, not sure what to say. My beast does enjoy being around him, but I don't know whether that is the mate bond, or just curiosity.

He smirks as if he's won. "That's what I thought. Your vampire side and the soul-ties that come with it must be muffling our connection. That's why you don't feel it as strongly as I do."

I turn away, refusing to listen anymore, but he calls out to me one last time. "I'll be here, Emerald. When you're ready to accept me and what I am to you, I'll be here."

Chapter Twenty-Six

It's all Over

EMERALD

WE DRIVE BACK TO THE COVEN IN UNEASY SILENCE, THE GUYS HAVING not said a word since we left the pack. I try not to let it bother me, but it does. What did I do wrong? Why are they treating me like the bad guy?

By the time we get back to our room, my anxiety has turned to anger. I step through the doorway first and wait for the others to follow after me. When I hear the distinct sound of the door clicking shut, I turn my anger on them. "What the hell is wrong with you three? Why are you treating me like some kind of criminal? The whole ride back I was a nervous wreck because of the way you've been acting!"

Talons advances, reaching me in two quick steps, making me back up.

"What do you want us to say, Emerald?! You fucking attacked a newbie! A goddamn newly turned vampire! He could have ripped you to shreds before you even knew what hit you."

I open my mouth to speak, but he holds up a hand to silence me. "No, that's not the worst part. No matter how much we tried to call you off, you ignored us. It took the Alpha of the local pack tearing you off him before you finally stopped. What the fuck was going through your mind?!"

Dev comes up behind him and gives his shoulder a reassuring squeeze. "Tal, calm down, man," he murmurs, but Talon shakes off his touch.

"Don't, Devin. We all know she's been acting more and more reckless the past few days, and we're all sick of it. I won't let her walk all over us as if our concerns mean nothing."

Tears well in my eyes and I turn my gaze towards Dev and Nik, but their eyes hold only disappointment, and I can't help but feel I've screwed everything up.

How did we go from love, to this?

"I don't know what happened. I saw him, and he looked so much like Xander in that moment that I snapped! Okay? You happy now, Talon? A man I thought I once loved tried to kill me, and I lost it when I saw someone who looked like him!" I laugh harshly as he glares at me and then turn away, trying to fight the anger that's rising within me.

How dare he? I had a fucking breakdown out there, and he's judging me for it! I didn't get hurt, and the vampire will heal. Yes, my beast and I kind of blacked out and turned into a rage monster for a bit, but we're in control again now. Whatever Lincoln did to me back there calmed us both down.

"You hesitated."

I spin around at his whispered words. "What was that?"

He meets my eyes defiantly. "You didn't say no! When the Alpha asked you to be his mate, you looked at us like you needed us to make the decision for you! You should have just said no!" His tone, while angry, also has an underlying note of sadness, which gives me pause. No, I won't let them make me feel guilty for trusting them to help me in a political situation, because at the end of the day, it's a major move for the Alpha to proposition me, the Princess of the vampire coven.

I throw my hands up in frustration. "Well fuck, Talon, what the hell did you expect?! I was taken off guard. Hell, I'd been wondering about my wolf side having a mate for a few days, so of course when I was faced with someone who might have answers, I was curious." I glare down at the ground in frustration, knowing this isn't how I want to live. We take one step forward, but then five steps back. It's just not worth this much pain.

I narrow my gaze and straighten my back, feeling resolved. "I'm done."

Nik's eyes go wide, and Dev takes a step towards me, but Talon remains impassive.

I look to each of them, the tears falling silently as I speak. "I'm tired of being treated like some child to be told what to do and when to do it. Either you trust me to make my own choices, or you don't." I shake my head sadly when Dev opens his mouth to speak. I know if he says anything right now, I'll lose my resolve. "At first, I was ecstatic with our soul-ties, knowing they meant I could love you all, not having to choose between you, but I can't do this. What if another wolf propositions me like Linc did? Then what? Are you going to react the same way?" I look down at the ground, unable to meet their eyes. "No, I can't do that." I keep my head down as I walk past them, unsure where I intend to go, only knowing that I need to be away from them.

"Em, don't," Nik begs, and I pause to meet his gaze sadly.

"I can't do this with him anymore. First he's nice, then he's jealous, then nice again. I won't spend the rest of my life walking on eggshells, afraid of what mood I'll be faced with."

I open the door and hurry to leave before I can second guess myself. I make it all the way to the elevator before I collapse to the floor, sobs wracking my body.

The doors open, but I ignore it, too lost in my thoughts. But then suddenly arms are cradling me, and I'm looking up into cerulean blue eyes.

Blaine is holding me, while Meron, Torie, and Kellan all stand above me with furious expressions on their faces.

I cry in the safe hold of Blaine's arms, unsure why everyone else is angry, and just huddle in on myself, hoping Britt will come up too. I could use my friend right now.

After God knows how long, my cries finally ease. Blaine uses his finger to lift my chin so I'm looking him in the eyes. "You ready to tell us what happened?"

I shake my head. "No, it's okay. It doesn't matter."

Kellan laughs, running his hands through his long blond hair before crouching down to look at me with sympathetic pale brown eyes. "Emerald, do you want to know a secret?"

I nod, wiping away my tears as I sit up, but Blaine refuses to let me leave his arms, pulling me back into his lap when I try to stand up. I don't bother fighting him on it right now. I'm more curious about what Kellan has to say.

When he's sure he has my full attention, Kellan sits down on the floor beside me and crosses his legs. "When Britt found out you were here at the coven, she made us do something. Do you know what a blood oath is?"

My eyes widen at the mention of a blood oath. It feels too weird after having thought about it earlier for him to be mentioning it now. "Yes, I know what they are, and I know that each oath is different based on the intentions of the people who make them."

He nods with a smile. "Yes, very good. Well, Britt loves you and wanted to make sure you were safe, so we all blood oathed to protect you as we would her. She was very adamant about that, and if she was here right now, I know you'd tell her what happened. So, I'm asking you to please tell us what happened. We just want to help."

She blood oathed them into protecting me? And what did he mean by the part 'as we would her?' It felt like there was some hidden meaning behind those words.

After a minute of thinking things through, I nod and start talking. "I left them. My soul-ties. Lately, Talon and I have both been so angry at each other that I just couldn't see any hope for a real future between us. He would go from angry to nice in a second, and I would get irritated over small insignificant things. You don't do that kind of thing if you love someone."

Blaine frowns down at me before turning to look up at the others. They exchange glances, and I wonder if they're communicating telepathically.

In a swift movement, I'm transferred from Blaine's arms to Kellan's lap, and he takes me with a smile. "Why hello there." He grins down at me, and I can't help the small smile that crosses my face.

I look back and see that Blaine has taken off towards my former room with a determined stride, and Meron and Torie follow after him. Kellan climbs to his feet while keeping me cradled in his arms and carries me after them.

I tap his shoulder nervously. "Uh, I can walk."

"I know you can, but for the sake of making Tal feel guilty, just stay in my arms and look all cute. Not that you need to try too hard." He winks, and I find myself feeling a little stunned. Is he hitting on me?

He carries me into to the room, the door having been flung open by Blaine as he wields his magic like an oncoming storm, wild and dangerous.

I take in the room, but my gaze immediately focuses on Blaine, who is standing facing off with Talon. Blaine's hands are glowing the same vibrant blue of his eyes, obviously his aura, as he uses his magic to hold Talon against the wall.

Rage, pure rage, comes off Talon in waves, and Meron beckons me over to where he is standing by Blaine's side. Kellan walks me over to them, and I watch in shock as Blaine's left hand suddenly snaps out when I'm within touching distance. He grasps mine in vice-like grasp, not quite painful but not exactly pleasant either.

Cold runs through my veins before it's replaced with a boiling-hot pain that feels strong enough to burn me from the inside out. Before I can beg for it to stop, the pain eases. Blaine lets Talon drop and reaches out to cup my cheeks, his eyes running over me.

"Sorry, Emerald, I didn't have much of a chance to warn you." Blaine turns his gaze to Nik and Dev, who are standing off to the side, a mixture of wariness and fear coming from them. "You two need to pick up your third and take a seat. We need to talk."

Kellan sits down, with me still in his lap, and Dev, Nik, and Tal keep throwing longing glances my way. Blaine stares at my guys with fury in his eyes, and when he speaks, you can hear the underlying violence ready to spill over.

"We came up here after finishing our duties for a night with our friends, but when we stepped out of the elevator, we found your soul-tie, huddled on the floor crying."

Talon's gaze whips around to me so fast, but I can't meet his eyes. Right now, I feel more vulnerable than I ever have.

Dev and Nik look down at the floor in shame as Blaine continues. "She told us what the problem was, and before any of you get annoyed that she told us, you should know it's lucky she did. Talon was spelled, as was Emerald."

Talon frowns and leans forward, his eyes narrowing. "What do you mean?"

Meron's gaze lands on me. "Have you noticed a change in Emerald lately? A willingness to be more extreme or do things that are a lot riskier than normal?"

I blush at his question, and he smiles softly. "Don't worry, Emerald. it's nothing to be embarrassed about. In fact, you wouldn't have been spelled if you hadn't been drinking from Talon in the first place. He was the one spelled initially, and you were affected because you fed from him."

Nik frowns and looks between Talon and I, before a light goes off in his eyes. "Wait, so that's why they were so agitated with each other? Because of the spell?"

Torie nods from behind Blaine. "Yep. Whoever cast it didn't have much knowledge of how a hex works because it should have only affected their intended victim. However, there's the chance someone infected Talon because they knew he fed Emerald, but I think we're leaning towards our first theory. Only those closest to you would know that you feed her, after all."

"And you've fixed him? I mean, us? There's not going to be any more issues, right?"

Knowing there was a spell affecting us both eases my mind, and scares me at the same time. I almost walked away. If Blaine and the others hadn't found me in the hall, who knows what I would've done?

Kellan smiles down at me. "No more than any other normal couple, or triple couple or whatever it is you call multiple partners. Britt likes to call us her harem of slaves," he says. His eyes are sparkling with laughter, and I find myself getting lost in their depths.

I shake my head, clearing it from the thoughts that were trying to surface, all the while wondering what the hell is wrong with me. *Maybe they didn't fix this hex or whatever it is?*

Dev gets to his feet, clapping his hands together to grab everyone's attention. "Right! You four," he gestures around at each of Britt's husbands individually, "Out. We need to talk and see where this leaves us."

Each of the guys get up and leaves, including Kellan, but he takes me with him as he goes. It's not until we get to the door that Nik stops him. "Kel, I think you're forgetting something."

Kellan gives an exaggerated sigh, setting me on my feet with a disappointed smile. "It was worth a shot." He winks, and I giggle at the same moment Torie slaps him upside the head.

Torie grabs Kellan by the arm and leads him out of the room after Blaine and Meron, all the while chiding him for his behavior, saying he's going to tell Britt about it when they get back.

Once the door closes behind them, I turn back around to meet the stares of Talon, Devin, and Nikoli, waiting for some kind of... reassurance or something? I don't know. Anything that will make me feel like this has just been a bad dream, and that we can move past this.

"I'm sorry."

My gaze jerks to Talon, not sure if I heard him right. It sounded like he just apologized.

"Are you seriously apologizing to me right now?" At his wary nod, I sigh and move closer, looking up at him with a determined expression. "You do not need to apologize because someone messed with us. That's on them. All I want is for us to be in an equal relationship, not to feel like I matter less or have to be sheltered because I'm a girl, a Princess, or a hybrid."

Nik moves closer, his gaze softening. "That's all we want, too, Em. You just have to understand that even though Talon was spelled, he wasn't the only one who was upset by your actions. We already lost you once, and while some person on the other side claims you're immortal, it doesn't necessarily make it true. We'd just rather not risk it."

"We can't lose you," Dev whispers, his voice filled with heartbreak.

Sadness radiates through our tie as I step away from Talon, making sure they can all see me when I speak. I want to be able to see them and make them understand just how serious I am about this.

"Look, I get it, I really do. I know this is hard on you guys, but it's hard on me, too. Did you not think I was scared shitless the whole time you were gone when you went to the pack meeting without me? I was terrified that because of me, you might be executed, or at the very least punished in some way. Then there's each night you go on patrol without me, and I'm stuck laying here, worrying when you'll come back, if you will at all."

I take a shaky breath and meet each of their eyes, determined. "Even when I was spelled, I knew I was being reckless. Having it lifted makes me a little more aware of the stupidity that's happened, but I'm only going to tell you this once. I'm not glass, and I won't break. Sure, I will be a little more careful in the future, but I'm still learning what I'm capable of, and I can't do that if you put me in a little plastic bubble to keep me safe. If you want to do more training with me to ease your worries, then great. You want to make sure one of you comes with me when I leave the coven, then that's okay, too, but I won't let myself feel like a prisoner because you're all scared of what might happen."

Nik, Dev, and Talon each remain silent as they ponder my words, but I'm not done just yet.

"But," I add when I see Talon open his mouth to speak. "That means I want honesty from you about things. If for some reason you are worried, just be upfront about it."

"Are you finished?" Talon asks with a wry smile.

I nod my head with a grin. "I think so."

"Good. Because that's—"

"Wait," I interrupt, knowing he might be annoyed, but wanting to be straight with them. "In the interest of honesty, I feel you should all know when we were attacked in that alleyway, I swallowed a bit of witch's blood, and apparently, it's bonded to me, rather than making me crazy like it would a normal wolf," I blurt out in a quick rush, deciding it was easier just to rip the Band-Aid off.

Talon shakes his head, his eyes filled with confusion. "Okay, well we'll deal with the witch blood stuff in a minute. As for the relationship stuff, I just have one condition."

"Okay..." I say, filled with apprehension. I wait for Nik or Dev to say something, but they remain silent, letting Talon continue.

"We want more one-on-one dates. Nik told us how much he enjoyed his evening with you, and we all want the chance to build a separate relationship with you. We will still have a group date every week to help strengthen our bond as a unit, but for now, I think we need to start working on setting aside some alone time for all of us.

"As for patrol, if you want to join us when we go, then that's okay. We just ask that you be careful. It makes our job harder when we're trying to keep rogue witches under control if you end up getting hurt."

I nod, more than happy to agree to everything he just said, when Nik speaks, reminding me he and Dev are still here. My gaze was so fixed on Talon in that moment that for a split second, I forgot.

"Sorry, guys. I have something else I would like to add." He looks apologetically at Tal and Dev. Then his gaze swings to mine and he gives me a small smile. "This may seem crazy, but I want you to think about spending time with Lincoln, too. I know, I know," he says, his voice rising over Dev and Tal's immediate grumbling. "But, Emerald's beast is a part of her. If by some twist of fate she really is his mate, then we would be doing more harm than good by denying her that. What if Emerald had met him before us? He's the type of guy who would have encouraged her to explore her ties with us, so I say we offer him the same chance. As long as you want to, that is," Nik adds, as if it just occurred to him I may not be interested.

Before I can reply, however, the door to our room flies open, hitting the other side of the wall. Britt comes storming in, her eyes glowing with immeasurable power as she narrows her gaze dangerously at Talon. "You're a dead man."

Chapter Twenty-Seven

A Witch's Wrath

EMERALD

With a small wave of Britt's hand, Nik and Dev are sent flying to opposite sides of the room, then she begins to advance on Talon.

Her guys lazily wander into the room through the now broken door, and look between Britt and I with amused smiles. Why are they not more concerned by this? If she kills Talon, she may just take Dev, Nik, and I down with him!

"I don't care that you were hexed! You are a fucking monster! Why would you say those things to her?" she screams at Talon. He just stands there, taking the full force of her anger without a word.

"Aren't you going to do something?" I whisper to Blaine and Kellan, who have come to stand on either side of me, while Torie and Meron go grab beers from the fridge.

Seriously though, why aren't they freaking out right now? They're acting like this is a normal everyday occurrence.

Kellan laughs and wraps an arm around my shoulder, and Blaine presses against me from my other side. "If there's one thing we've each learned since meeting Brittany, it's that you do not get in her way when she's pissed. You just ride out the storm and hope for the best."

"Seriously? So basically, you're all just a bunch of wimps." I roll my eyes and shake them off of me. If they won't calm Britt down, then I will.

My footsteps echo across the wooden floor as I approach her, and

I can hear her husbands taking whispered bets on which of us will get the last word.

Men!

"Britt, can you please let my soul-tie go?" I ask softly, able to see the way her magic is wrapped around Talon, which explains why he's just standing there taking whatever she says. I would bet he can't actually speak right now either.

His gaze meets mine, and he gives an infinitesimal shake of his head as if he knows I'm going to intervene and doesn't want me to. I roll my eyes at him. This is exactly what I was talking about! Britt may be a witch, but she's also my friend. She won't hurt me. She's just trying to protect me in her own misguided way.

I wait for Britt to acknowledge my presence, and sigh when she remains focused on Talon, her shoulders hard with tension. I reach out to touch her, and all the guys behind me cry out in warning.

The moment my hand touches her shoulder, my body seizes up, and a crack rings through the room like a lightning strike. Britt and I are both flung back. Someone catches me, breaking my fall. I look up into Kellan's brown eyes gratefully. "Thanks."

He gets up and helps me to my feet. I can see Meron and Torie are holding Nik and Dev away from me and I can see the magic in their auras as they use it to enhance their strength. No way would they be able to hold back my guys otherwise. Talon is watching, but I think if he really wanted to get close to me, he would have found a way. Instead, he stands off to the side, watching my interactions with Britt's husbands with contemplative eyes as if he's seen the change in them.

But to be honest, it's hard not to. It's like a switch has been flipped, and they are all suddenly much more concerned about me than ever. I guess that has to do with the blood oath.

Shit, I should probably tell the guys about that, too, but I don't know whether Britt or I should be the one to explain things. She knows what the blood oath actually entails; all I know is that it's there to protect me.

Blaine and Britt walk towards me, and I notice how pale Britt is.

This is becoming a bit too hard to ignore. I know her magic drains her, but for her to look this bad? Something isn't adding up.

Britt frowns at me when she's within arm's reach. "Sorry, Mer. Are you alright?"

"Of course, just a little surprised is all. How about you? Are you okay?"

She smiles at me sadly, and her eyes seem to cloud with an emotion I know all too well. Defeat.

"What's going on?" I ask her, crossing my arms over my chest and glaring at her insistently. I know she's holding something back.

In a minute, she whispers into my mind. *Your magic seemed to react to mine. You actually managed to absorb a little of it.*

After whispering to me telepathically, she speaks out loud to the room and I wonder why she's not wanting the others to know everything. Something is clearly wrong. "Since Mer and I are both fine, I'm going to steal her for a bit, while you guys do whatever it is that you do on your boys' nights. We're going down to the forest to talk and train."

She slides her arm into mine and pulls me away from the guys towards our broken door. Then she stops, turning back to the guys.

"Oh, and make sure you fix this door before we get back. And, Talon," she smirks as she meets his eyes across the room, "if you ever hurt Emerald again, this will look like a walk in the park compared to what will happen then. Got it?"

He nods silently, looking guilty, but Britt turns us back around without another word and leads us out of the room and down the hall to the elevator. She remains quiet until the doors open on the forest level, then she turns to me. "I know everything that happened tonight."

I frown in confusion, before realizing she must be joking. "Ha! Ha! Very funny, Britt," I say, shoving her playfully. She stumbles, and I quickly reach out to grab her.

My brows furrow with concern as she grips onto me tightly for support. "Britt, what is going on? You're clearly not doing too good. Why didn't you tell the others?"

She's supposed to be immortal. How the hell can she be sick?

"It's a long story, but my husbands know. I told them everything after I blood oathed them into protecting you."

I guide her to a bench hidden among the trees that I remembered seeing the last time I was down here. I help her sit before taking a seat beside her, facing her with a stern expression.

"You tell me everything right now. Something is going on, and don't tell me it's nothing. You look like you're on your deathbed right now."

She looks away, unable to meet my eyes. I feel my face pale. "Britt, you're not really dying, are you?" I ask in a hushed tone.

She slowly lifts her head and gives me a sad smile. "Yeah, Mer. I am. But before I tell you everything, I need you to swear you won't tell anyone, apart from your guys, although they will probably already know by now," she muses.

It occurs to me that she separated us so that she can tell me everything that's going on privately, and at the same time her guys can tell mine as well.

"The only people who know are Aunty Macy, my guys, and now you. Though I imagine Kel will tell your guys sooner or later. But, you can't tell your mom," she insists, staring at me intently.

"Britt, I promise not to say anything to anyone else, but if Kellan hasn't said anything to the guys, then I'll have to. I made them promise honesty, and I won't be a hypocrite by not offering them the same in return. It's why I told them about the blood I accidently drank from the witch."

She smiles, looking glad, and reaches out to hold my hand. "I've known for two years that I'm dying. Despite being tied to the guys, my body is still continuing to weaken. I've been to multiple powerful witches but found no answers. We've used spell after spell until last week we finally figured it out. Dastian cursed me. One of his old associates said he cursed me before our bond was formed, and that the hex would only take effect if he died. And even though our bond is now strong and intact, each time I die, I come back less. My soul rips apart each time, until eventually, I won't come back at all; I'll be stuck in the in between place."

I sit here in silence, my heart breaking for her. I can't even imagine what she's going through right now. To know you're going to die would be a burden I don't think I could handle.

"Do you know when?" I ask, needing to know how much time we have left. I will make sure that she lives her life to the fullest for as long possible and do everything we ever dreamed of.

"Two, maybe three months. The more I use magic, the sooner it will be. Dastian cursed me so that any time I use magic, it eats away at my soul, one piece at a time until nothing's left. Even though we killed that bastard, he's still going to win." She gives a defeated sigh, and I can sense she's lost hope.

"No! Don't you sit there and give up! You need to fight this!"

"Mer, I have been. Do you really think I haven't spent the last year fighting this? I have. The only thing that can end this curse is Dastian's blood, but his body is well and truly gone. Aunt Macy and I officially ran out of options, which is why I pushed the guys to get married. I wanted to at least show my guys how much I loved each of them by being tied to them in an official way. There's nothing to do now but to make the most of my life and finalize my affairs, which is the other reason I brought you here."

Tears start to fall, knowing she's given up on her life, and I feel absolutely helpless to do anything. *What good is having magic if you can't fix everything?*

"My husbands are now blood oathed to protect you. With that, feelings may begin to develop, and I want to apologize for that."

I wipe away the tears, and give her a look of confusion. "What do you mean feelings? Like how they were all protective with me back there?" I ask with a sniffle, wishing I had a box of tissues.

She gives me a watery smile. "Yes, that's what I mean. I oathed you to them after you arrived and I started to sense you might be in danger. And if that witch's blood hadn't bound to yours, then it wouldn't be a problem. But, it happened, and now we're here. Blaine already felt a curiosity about you when he met you, and the others were nervous because I had talked about you a lot. I think they wanted your approval, but now everything has changed. You'll find yourself more attracted to them, maybe even doing things you wouldn't normally. But I want you to know, if anything happens between you all, it's okay with me. I just want them to be happy and if you can give them that when I'm gone, then there's no one better I'd rather see them with."

I frown, wondering why this sounds like she's gifting me her husbands. Surely that can't be what she means? Or maybe she's saying because of the magic, I'm going to start crushing on them?

"Britt, what's really going on? I feel like you're trying to tell me something, but I'm obviously not getting the memo, because now I am just straight up confused."

She chuckles and releases my hand. "Okay, so witches who decide to commit themselves to each other share their magic during a wedding ceremony. When we were alone after our ceremony, I made a blood oath with each of them, making them promise if something happened to us, we would find a way to move on. We wouldn't be stupid and waste our lives mourning. That was before we found out about being immortal, not that it really seems to be true after all," she adds bitterly.

"Anyway, the thing I'm trying to explain is that because of the shared blood, you will begin to crave sexual attention from them. It may not happen straight away, because the oath is so new, but I have a feeling, and if earlier was anything to go by, it's only a matter of time before you become territorial over them. Hopefully I'm wrong about all of this, but I highly doubt it. I've been wondering if they were even meant to be mine in the first place."

"Wait, shared blood? Britt, I haven't shared blood with you or any of your husbands," I point out, feeling a wash of relief go through me.

She flushes, and normally I wouldn't be able to see the blush stain her cheeks, but with how pale she currently is, it shows up easily. "Uh, about that. Remember when you got that really bad cut on your hand when I stayed with you guys? Well, I kept the cloth you used to wipe your hand. I've kept it preserved, just in case I ever needed your blood."

She did what? Stole the frigging cloth I used to clean the blood from my hand? "You... stole the cloth with the intent to use my blood at one point or another?" I ask, trying to make sense of this. Now I understand why my grandmother warned me about sharing blood. Britt nods, and I reach up, rubbing my temples in agitation.

Do not kill your best friend. Do not kill her. She stole your blood for an oath and used it to mystically tie you to her husbands. She did it to protect you, that's all.

No matter what I tell myself, though, my heart is hammering in my chest with fear. My best friend is dying. Does she just expect me to sit idly by without trying to save her? Or worse, does she want me to look after her husbands after she dies? And another thing I don't understand is why she told me she was trying for a baby if she's dying?

"Mer, if you knew you were going to die, would you not want to leave a part of yourself behind? Something for those you care for to love and hold on to? That's what I wanted with a child. I wanted to leave behind someone that my husbands could cherish, so they wouldn't truly be alone. Although, it's too late for that now. So, I am doing the next best thing. I am asking you to care for them when I'm gone."

"Britt–"

She holds a hand up, stopping me. "No, I'm not asking you to love them. Love is complicated, and you already have enough on your plate in that department, but I need to know that someone will help them. My death is going to challenge them in ways they've never dealt with before. Each one of my men has their own issues and without me, there's going to be blame, frustration, and anger among them. So, basically chaos. I need to know that you will be there for them and help them get through the hard times ahead."

I blow out a puff of air and meet her eyes, determined. "If, and I mean that as a really big if, anything happens to you, I will ensure they are taken care of. I will even vet any new girls that enter their lives if you'd like," I tell her, ignoring the fact she implied she wants me with her guys. "But, I want you to know right now, Britt, I won't just lie down and let you die. I will search the world over for something that will help you, and you will just smile and nod and accept it. Do I make myself clear?"

She gives a small smile, but her eyes are filled with sadness and defeat, which only makes me even more determined. *I won't let her die! I will find something, anything that will help her. Even if it means selling my soul to the devil.*

She lets out a breath and plasters a fake smile on her face. "Okay, no more depressing thoughts. There was another reason for bringing you down here. I doubt you meant to, but you projected everything that has happened over the past twenty-four hours straight into my mind, and into my husbands' by extension, which leads me to believe you have telepathy as your ability."

She stands up from the bench, looking more stable then she had when we got down here. "So, we're going to do some mind training for you so you can get a handle on things. Because I do not want to be hearing about your dirty thoughts when you have a wolf or vampire in front of you." She smirks playfully, and I roll my eyes at her. There were no dirty thoughts about the wolf, and she damn well knows it. Well, okay maybe a kind of mild curiosity, but that's completely different.

"Okay, first off, there were no dirty thoughts." I glare as I get to my feet, following after her as she wanders off through the trees. "And secondly, what is mind training?" I ask, feeling completely out of the loop.

"Mind training is pretty much just that. We train your mind to keep up a barrier to stop others from hearing your thoughts, and you from projecting them. It just ensures you don't cross a witch on the street, or another vamp with telepathy and unwittingly reveal who and what you are."

I give her a sarcastic smile. "Yeah, because I totally just walk around thinking 'My name's Emerald. I'm a vampire-werewolf hybrid shifter. Come at me, bro.'"

She laughs, her eyes sparkling rather than filled sadness like they had been earlier. "Okay, maybe you don't go around thinking that, but your beast is a part of your mind. For example, when you met with

Lincoln, while you were confused and upset by the turn of events, your beast was projecting a desire to shift and rub herself all over him like a cat marking its territory."

"She was not!" I exclaim, completely shocked.

Britt smirks and nods her head slowly. "Oh, yes she was. It's why I want to help you build these walls. You were lucky that none of your guys got spill over from her. Can you imagine?"

My face pales, and I think back to Nik's add on thoughts earlier about spending time with Lincoln. Is there a chance he heard my beast in my mind? If Britt has issues controlling her thoughts with her guys, then it stands to reason my guys would be able to hear mine too sometimes. *Oh no!*

"Okay, let's do this." I don't want to hurt my guys any more than I already have. I want this relationship to work, and if shielding my thoughts helps to keep me from hurting them, then I'll do it.

Chapter Twenty-Eight

TELEPATHY

EMERALD

"Come on, Mer. You need to concentrate."

I grit my teeth in frustration. We've been down here for an hour now, and I still haven't been able to block her from hearing my thoughts.

Once she assured me she wouldn't use any magic during our training, I let her teach me how to build a wall in my mind, but it's flimsy at best. No matter how much I try, I can't get the hang of blocking her from my thoughts.

"Alright, obviously this isn't working, so let's try something else." She sits down on the ground across from me, crossing her legs and holding out her hands. "I'm going to tap into your magic in order to get a feel for what you're doing wrong."

I narrow my eyes and pull my hands out of reach. "No, no magic for you."

She rolls her eyes, clearly annoyed, but I don't give a damn. If she weakens more every time she uses magic, then clearly the only real option is for her to stop using magic altogether.

"Mer, I am going to use your magic, not mine. I'll be fine, unless I use my own magic. I just need to peek into your mind as you build your wall so I can see exactly what's going wrong."

I sigh and give in, placing my hands in hers. A jolt of energy runs through me as soon as her mind connects to mine. Mine feels light and carefree, filled with bright colors, while Britt's is clouded in darkness. There are sparks of color here and there, but they fade quickly.

A tear falls, and I'm glad my eyes are closed, so Britt can't see the heartbreak I feel for her. She's all but given up on any chance of ridding herself of this hex.

"It's okay, Mer. I've accepted my fate. There's no need to be sad," she whispers, and I stifle a sob. How can she be okay with this?

"Concentrate on your wall, so I can see it," she murmurs, and I bring my focus back on the task at hand.

I summon a vision of a giant silver wall protecting anyone from entering my thoughts, and she appears, standing before the wall. She knocks on it once, and it shatters, raining down around us like pieces of glass.

"Gotcha." She winks teasingly.

"Seriously?! Stop messing with me and teach me how to control my thoughts."

Stupid best friend trying to play me. I need to learn this!

She laughs, and I open my eyes to meet hers. "I wasn't playing you."

I roll my eyes in frustration. "Ugh! Stop reading my thoughts."

"Make me." The challenge in her voice makes me more determined than ever. I close my eyes despite her chuckles and concentrate on shutting her out. Instead of a wall, though, I imagine a blanket going over my mind, darkness shrouding me from any who would want to peek into my private thoughts.

Did it work? I focus on projecting my mental voice, hoping not to let too much through.

Yeah! You did it! I can't hear your endless thoughts any more. Only your voice when you're speaking telepathically.

My eyes snap open, and my mouth gapes like a fish out of water. I honestly didn't think that would work.

Britt's eyes shine with pride. "Just as I thought, you're a telepath," she breathes. "That's... so... COOL!"

I almost fall backwards at her sudden exclamation and hold a hand over my heart, which is racing from the shock of her outburst. "Jeez, Britt. Don't fucking scare me like that."

"Sorry, sorry. It's just, do you realize how awesome this is?! We can talk to each other in our minds now. You don't even have to try to send secret messages. Oh, I so can't wait to try it when the guys are around. Come on, let's practice a little more and then go have a little fun."

Two hours later, and I'm absolutely exhausted while Britt is brimming with energy. Little does she know, though, I tried something while she was tapped into my mind. I fed her a bit of my own energy to see if it would help, and seeing her bounce around like this leads me to think it has. Maybe there is hope after all.

I smile to myself as I open the door to our room, and Britt skips in after me, causing her husbands to look up in surprise. I imagine they haven't really seen her bounce around like this lately.

The coffee pot is still sitting on the bench, and I place my hand close enough to the glass to see if it's still permeating heat. It is, so I go about pouring myself a cup, while Britt leans against the counter, bubbling with excitement. I can see the giddiness in her eyes.

Kellan approaches us, and Britt jumps into his arms, catching him off guard. He fumbles to catch her weight, and she presses her lips to his quickly before sliding down his body, landing on her feet with a wide smile. He looks between Britt and I, seeming confused. "You girls okay?"

I nod with a small smile, but Britt just ignores the question completely, gesturing silently towards Talon. On our way back to the room, we had talked about showing them that I had a handle on my telepathy. I'm nowhere near a pro yet but at least I can project thoughts easily enough.

My mind goes empty and I focus on Talon, feeling the blanket over my mind peel back, giving me a peek into his mind.

She's so amazing. I can't believe I almost screwed this up because of stupid jealousy. When I find that witch, I'm going to rip him to shreds and feed on his heart.

I smirk at the viciousness he has in his mind and know he won't be the only one going after the witch who hexed him. *You didn't screw it up. The witch did, and I can guarantee if I beat you to him, I'm going to do a lot worse than eat his heart.*

Talon's gaze swings around to mine, and his brows furrow in confusion. *What the fuck? Did Britt just project my thoughts? She promised she wouldn't invade our thoughts anymore. Blatantly listening in and projecting those thoughts to someone else, that's crossing a line right there.*

I smirk, winking at him. *It wasn't Britt.*

Talon shoots up from his seat at the table, his eyes wide in shock. His chair falls back, drawing everyone's gaze as it clatters to the floor.

I turn my gaze to Nik with a grin. *The night you fucked me against the tree was one of the best nights I've ever had. I love you, Nikoli.*

His eyes widen, mimicking Talon's shock, and he looks away as his cheeks tinge with a faint blush.

Dev is looking around, seeming confused and frustrated. "What's going on? Why are you two acting like you've just seen a ghost?" He eyes Tal and Nik for a few seconds, so I try the trick Britt showed me.

I push an image into his mind, the thought of the shower when he gently washed me, taking care of me both emotionally and sexually as he did so. I push the feelings that went through me and watch as a slow grin curves his lips. He looks up to meet my eyes, his own filled with lust. "You're a telepath."

I smile, proud of my efforts, and he shakes his head with a small laugh. "Just when we thought you couldn't get any more interesting, you go and discover your ability. Your parents are going to be ecstatic. There hasn't been a vamp with telepathic abilities in hundreds of years."

My heart sinks at the realization it's just another thing that sets me apart from the others. I thought I had found my place among the vampires but this is going to be yet another reason for them to fear and hate me. I look to Britt, wondering if she knew, but she just shrugs. Clearly, she had no idea, otherwise she would have told me.

My body sways, and I blink to clear my vision, but then I feel myself dropping to the ground. Britt tries to catch me, but my dead weight is too much for her. We end up tangled together in a heap on the floor, and Blaine has to pull her off me, so Nik can get me out.

"Is she okay?" I hear Nik ask.

Britt replies, but her voice sounds far away. "She's just exhausted. She's still new to using her ability and witch magic in one. We'll have to teach her how to separate the two, so she doesn't drain herself. Even I haven't gotten a handle on my ability. At least, she won't go through it alone. We'll be there with her every step of the way."

I listen as she talks and remain silent, knowing the real reason I'm feeling faint has nothing to do with my telepathy. I'm still feeding small bits of magic through to Britt. I have no idea how I'm managing it, but I'm glad it seems to be working. She looks the healthiest I've seen her in days.

Meron frowns down at us, giving me a long scrutinizing look and I fight not to fidget. "Guys, how 'bout we take Brittany up to bed? She needs to rest."

Each of the guys agree hastily and I smile. I can only hope my relationship with the guys stays that strong that they will want to spend every second with me, even years from now. Britt leans forward to give me a hug before Kellan, Torie, and Blaine lead her out of our room, waving farewell as they go.

Meron lingers, though, offering up an excuse that he needs to ask Talon something. He waits until the door is shut before crouching down beside me, pressing a hand against my forehead, and closing his eyes in concentration.

"What are you–?"

"Quiet!" he commands, interrupting Dev. He does as he's told, sitting down and keeping his mouth shut while Meron does whatever the hell he's doing. I feel magic suddenly run through me and gasp. His eyes fly open, and I find myself staring into eyes as black as the night sky. The whites are encased by the black, and it takes a second for them to fade back to their regular deep gray color.

"Emerald, I know you want to help Britt, but if you keep feeding her energy, you will die and possibly take your soul-ties with you."

"No, I'm only feeding her my energy. The guys will be fine, and I'll come back if I die," I tell him stubbornly.

He shakes his head sadly. "Sweetie, that's not how it works. Your soul-tie is designed to give you energy when you get low, which means it will drain from each of the guys, killing them one by one until you are all that's left, and it will eventually kill you, too."

I look around at my guys helplessly before settling my gaze on Meron. "I can't just let her die."

"And we won't, but we'll find another way. If you die, Britt may go dark again just to raise your body from the dead so she can throttle you."

I bark out a laugh, knowing she would do it, too. I can just imagine her stomping around, mumbling under her breath about her plans to raise me just to kill me again.

"I don't know how else to help her. Magic is a novel concept to me. I have no idea what else I can do," I admit, feeling tired beyond belief.

"I know. I promise if there's a way to stop this, we will. We're happy to show you everything we've been looking into if that helps. Britt likes to think we'll just accept her wishes and let her die in peace, but that won't ever happen," he insists vehemently.

I have no real idea how to shut my magic off, but I nod and close my eyes, imagining a cord between Britt and I, which I snip with an imaginary pair of scissors.

The effects overwhelm me immediately, and I feel less drained. Which means Britt must be feeling tired again. I frown, worried. *She shouldn't feel like that.*

"Good girl," Meron whispers, before pressing a kiss to my lips. "Get some rest, and we'll talk when you're up for it."

He gets up, and Talon leads him to the door, while I sit here in Nik's lap, wondering what the fuck just happened.

Meron kissed me, and none of the guys felt any jealousy? Is it some kind of cultural thing maybe, and I'm just reading into it? Like how the French kiss on both cheeks?

After a moment, Talon comes back over to us and helps Nik and I to stand. "Come on, we're all going to bed to get some rest. It's safe to say today has been a little much for all of us."

Dev goes ahead of us, remaining uncharacteristically quiet as he opens the bedroom door, and then goes to the bed to pull back the covers for us. Nik and Talon stop by the bed, helping me strip down to my underwear and letting me crawl into the center. I snuggle into the pillow, closing my eyes with a deep sigh, and the sounds of them getting ready for bed around me lulls me to sleep.

Chapter Twenty~Nine

OVERPROTECTIVE FATHER

EMERALD

I roll out of bed, the need to pee driving me. It's not until after I've relieved myself that I realize I woke up in bed alone.

That's when I remember the whispered goodbyes as the guys left a couple of hours ago. They had to go on patrol and I'd been too tired to join them. They left me to get some more sleep, but now that I'm awake for the day, I decide to have a quick shower and then go talk with my parents.

As I shower, I go over everything in my mind. I have to tell them about my ability, that I know. I have no idea whether to tell them about the magic from the witch, though, or about the fact that I seem to have magic swords that come back to me when called. Then there's also the matter of the Alpha wolf who thinks I'm his mate.

There's so much I wish I could talk to them about, but I know I can't. There's only one person I want to talk to right now, and without him here, I feel so lost.

I get dried off and dressed before taking a seat on the bed I woke up in, playing with the burner phone in my hand. I dial and delete the number a few times before I finally press the call button.

It answers on the first ring, and my dad's voice comes through the phone. "Brent here."

Tears well, and I let out a little laugh. "Hi, Dad."

"Emmy? Oh, thank God! All Axel would tell me was that you were

239

fine. You are okay, aren't you?" he asks, a thread of concern in his voice.

"Yeah, Dad," I breathe in a hushed tone. I know there's no one here, but I can't help but feel like I have to keep this to myself. "I miss you," I tell him, just as a tear falls.

"Oh, Emmy. I miss you, too, darling, but it's not safe for us to be talking."

"I know, I just needed to hear your voice. So much has happened, and I feel like my world has been tipped completely upside down. I don't know what to do anymore, Dad," I admit, my voice filled with fear and uncertainty. I feel so out of my depths right now.

I came here knowing only I was some kind of cross between two species, but then I died and came back to life. Now, I also have witch's blood running through my veins, making me a mix of three supernatural races. *Is there even a word for that? Or does hybrid still apply?*

Then there's the curse Britt is dealing with. My best friend is dying, and she has practically gifted her husbands to me. It doesn't help that feelings are beginning to surface that I didn't believe were even possible. How long before I can no longer ignore them?

And then, there's Lincoln. What do I do about him? Should I do as Nik suggested and get to know him, or just leave the matter it be?

"A couple of weeks away, and you've already forgotten everything I taught you." He chuckles through the phone. "You follow your heart, Emmy. No matter where it guides you. Love is the key to happiness, and if you aren't happy, then you aren't in a position to help anyone else. Do you remember our exercises we used to do when we felt a panic attack coming? Well, I want you to take ten minutes right now and do your exercises."

I hear Brendan's voice in the background before the sound becomes muffled. My father comes back a second later. "I'm sorry, Emmy. I have to go, but just do what I said. Listen to your instincts. And if that doesn't work, talk to Axel. I love you, baby girl," he whispers into the phone, before his voice is replaced by the dial tone.

I throw the phone across the room, watching as it smashes to pieces. Then I put my head in my hands, taking deep ragged breaths.

My heart hurts from all this crap! Why does there have to be so much animosity between vampires and wolves? Why can't we all just get along?

Instead of getting myself down, though, I focus on my breathing exercises, clearing my mind and asking myself what to do next. When I used to struggle with keeping myself calm, this is what I would do to regain focus.

After a moment, it all becomes clearer. I need to tell my parents about the magic. I will respect Britt's wishes for now, but soon, I know I will have no choice but to tell them about her situation. They may know of another way to help, and it will feel so much better to get some of this burden off my chest.

With my mind made up, I leave my room, heading straight to my parents' quarters.

As I approach their room, I hear the sound of voices and slow my steps to listen.

"Please, I know you haven't found another advisor yet. I can guarantee I won't let my feelings get in the way this time. Just give me another chance to prove myself."

The familiar sound of Heather's grating voice makes me cringe, and I hang back around the corner, wanting to hear more. Like why the hell is she back?

"I've been with you for five years, my Queen. Where else will you be able to find someone with my knowledge?"

My mother's voice comes out stern, but with a slight edge of sympathy, and I can just imagine the pity in her eyes. "Heather, I understand you want another chance, but there are many things that have to be considered before I would give you your job back. If my daughter is around, are you going to let that it affect your job? What about Talon? He's happy with Emerald, and I can imagine that doesn't exactly sit well with you. What if Emerald gets pregnant someday? Could you handle seeing Talon fawn over her and the child they share?"

My face blanches, and I have to calm my racing heart. Pregnant? Why the hell is she so keen on me having kids? Who would want to be tied down this early in a relationship? I want to have time to explore with each of them. I think we deserve that time to get to know each other. I don't want kids in general, but even if I did, it wouldn't be until I'd known the guys for at least a few years.

I shake my head at how easily I got distracted and focus back on Heather as I poke my head around the corner. She's down on one knee bowing, while my mother looks down at her.

Heather, of course, continues to speak. "Am I upset that I lost him? Yes, of course I am. But do I want him back? No." She sighs with a shake of her head. "At the end of the day, she's his soul-tie, the one he's destined to be with. I hoped that my love was enough, and over time he'd eventually love me back. At least, that's what I thought until I found my own soul-tie. But, fate seems to be playing with me because it turns out he's not satisfied with just me. So, the only options I have are to stay there and get treated like a sex slave along with three other women, or come back here and live, where at least I had a purpose and my life held some meaning. That's all I ask."

My mother's gaze softens, and I know she's going to give in and let Heather work for her again. That's when she catches sight of me, and I step out from behind the corner.

"Sorry, I didn't mean to interrupt. I'll come back later." I don't wait for a reply, instead just turning back to leave.

Whore.

I freeze as the word is whispered through my mind, and it takes everything in me not to spin around and destroy this bitch!

I know for a fact that it was Heather because her mental voice sounds just like her speaking one.

Whether or not she knows I could hear her is a whole other problem, and not one I can handle right now.

I straighten my shoulders and keep on walking, right back to my room. Once inside, I press my back against the door and close my eyes, letting a sigh escape me.

As much as I try not to let her being back worry me, the feeling seeps into my bones nonetheless, radiating out of me in waves. Is she really back just for her job?

"Em! Where the hell did you go? We came back to check on you and make sure you were fed, but you were gone!" Dev's voice has me snapping open my eyes. All three of them are there watching me with concerned expressions.

My gaze lingers over Talon for a split second as I decide whether to tell him or not, and I know I have to be one hundred percent honest. I don't want lies to become a natural part of our relationship.

"I'm sorry," I say quietly, stepping into Dev's arms to reassure him that I'm fine. "When I woke up, you were all still gone. I wasn't sure how much longer your patrol would be, so I decided to go talk to my parents, and tell them all about my telepathy and witch powers. But," I put up an emotional barrier around my heart as I meet Talon's gaze, "instead I ran into Heather, who was there begging for her old job back."

Talon goes still, and his gaze hardens as stares at me. "Do you think just because she's back, I'm going to leave you for her?" he asks through clenched teeth.

I have to admit the thought did cross my mind. She clearly loves him. He admitted that it was just out of loyalty to a friend that he stayed with her, but I can't help but wonder if there wasn't something more between them. Why else would she have held on so tightly?

I shrug my shoulders, focusing my gaze on his neck and refusing to meet his gaze. "Maybe. I mean, she would probably be better for you than a vampire Princess who has no idea what she's doing. She was obviously nice enough if you stayed with her for five years before I came into the picture. And let's be honest, I've been nothing but a disappointment lately."

As I bare all my insecurities, Dev runs a hand up and down my back soothingly, while Nik just remains silent, standing a few feet away.

After I finish, Talon stalks towards me, determined. I can feel his frustration build with every stride he takes until he's right in front of me, his eyes burning into mine.

"I want you to listen carefully, Emerald, because if I have to tell you more than once, I am going to throw you over my shoulder and lock us away in a room for days until it really sinks in." I shiver at the heat in his voice, while Dev continues to rub his hands gently over my back.

"You are the only woman I want. There is absolutely no one else." Talon's lips slam down on mine, and I gasp, allowing him to slip his tongue inside to brush against my own, the desperation in his actions causing me to moan.

He ends the kiss, pulling away to where I can see his eyes, which are flaring a bright red with his vampire. "I'm sorry about the past few days, and if it gave you reason to doubt me, Emerald. But I promise from this moment forth, I'll do everything I can to prove to you how much I love you and show you that you are the most important person in my life."

I smile brightly as he bends down for one more chaste kiss. My heart swells at his words, and I wrap my arms around his neck, still feeling the way Dev presses against me. I love the fact neither he nor Nik seem bothered in the slightest by their friend kissing me.

Talon sighs, pulling away and rests his head against mine. "Do you want me to come with you to tell your parents about everything? They really do need to hear it from you before someone else has the chance to tell them."

"That would be great. I know it's cowardly, but I don't want to be there when she is. Not without some kind of buffer at least," I admit, relieved by his offer.

"All you had to do, sweetheart, was ask. I'd destroy the world for you."

My cheeks flush at such a corny sentiment, but when I look up into his eyes, I know he meant every word of it.

Nik takes a few steps closer and looks me over. "Are you sure? You can just wait until she's gone if you'd prefer."

I shake my head, feeling resolved. "No, I want her to see Talon and I, together and stronger than ever. It will hopefully drive home the fact she isn't ever getting him back.

Nik smirks and Talon hides his chuckles behind his hand, but I heard it anyway. I don't see what's so funny, though. If that bitch tries to pull some kind of childish bullshit in order to tear us apart, I may let my beast loose on her crazy ass.

"Okay, off you go then," Nik encourages. Talon intertwines our hands, before leading us back to the place I just left.

I sigh in relief as we get closer and I don't hear Heather's voice, but I'm not completely lucky. Felicia walks out of my parents' room as we approach, closing the door behind her with a soft click.

When she sees Talon and I, she offers us a polite smile. "I was just thinking about you, Emerald. I wanted to let you know that just because Heather is back doesn't mean I was lying before. I want to be friends, and I've told Heather there's no room for her in my life anymore."

"Oh."

She smiles brightly at me. "Maybe we could go get coffee or have lunch together someday? I would love to get to know you more."

"Uh, sure," I lie, faking a cheery smile. I doubt we could ever be friends. There are just some things you don't do with your boyfriend's ex. It creates drama where there doesn't need to be any.

She grins with happiness and leans in for a hug. I freeze, staying immobile until she lets go, offering Talon and I a quick goodbye before leaving with a spring in her step.

"That was weird, right?"

He frowns deeply, looking down the hall in the direction she went. "Very."

I shake off my concerns and knock on my parents' door, waiting for them to answer.

After a moment, my father answers with a smile, moving aside to let us in. The moment my mother sees me, she jumps up from her seat and crosses to me, encasing me in a bone-crushing hug.

"Emerald! What a wonderful surprise." Her fake cheeriness makes me sad. She's pretending that Heather wasn't here and that I didn't see them talking. I hide my disappointment, though, knowing it's not my place to tell her what to do.

Talon shakes my father's hand, and my mother lets go of me and moves over to Talon, offering a kiss on the cheek, while my father embraces me.

When he lets go, he throws an arm over my shoulder, the same way my dad had many times over the years. My mother grabs Talon and leads him to the couch. "Come, sit."

Talon and I take the offered seats, pressing close to each other. He reaches out to grip my hand, giving me strength I didn't know I needed.

I smile to myself, glad of the change between us in the past twenty-four hours since the curse was broken. To think we went from fighting to happy, it's amazing. If anything, I thought we'd be weaker together now than we were before the curse, but our tie seems to have strengthened instead. Even now as I sit here, I feel a sense of satisfaction and protectiveness from Talon directed at me. I'm actually able to determine each of their individual ties to me, which makes everything feel like it's finally coming together. Like now, our life together can truly begin.

The worst is over, and we can finally just focus on being together.

I take a deep breath and look over at my parents, watching their happy expressions disappear as they take in my worried gaze. "I, uh, did actually come here for something in particular," I apologize. They exchange glances and nod for me to continue.

"What is it?" my mother asks, her voice filled with fear.

"Well, it's three things really. Last night, I, uh, found out what my ability is."

My mother's eyes widen in surprise, and she leans forward eagerly. "Oh, that's great, honey! We were a little worried that your wolf side might cancel out any chance you had of getting one."

My father beams at me, filled with pride. "So, what is it?"

I open my mouth, feeling hesitant to answer, knowing that once it's revealed, more pressure will be put on my shoulders. The rarity of my ability and the dangerousness of it, will have more people fearing me and everyone will most likely try and use it as yet another reason to coddle me.

My gaze swings to Talon, beseeching him with my eyes. He gives my hand a reassuring squeeze before turning to my parents, taking the spotlight off me.

"Em's power is telepathy. She can project words, emotions, and images straight into our minds."

Just as expected, a series of expressions quickly cross their faces, like a movie on fast forward. Fear, awe, sympathy, wonder, and curiosity. Each expression goes by, until they finally get enough control to meet my eyes, with only curiosity left in their own.

"Can you show us?" my father asks, his voice filled with intrigue.

I smile shyly and close my eyes, bringing an image to my mind. The moment I first saw them and realized who they were to me. Wonder, joy, and sadness filled me. I had missed out on getting to know them, and they had missed out on my entire life.

That moment is one I will always carry with me. I project the memory out to the room, and Talon grips my hand harder as sadness runs through his bond, followed by wonder and joy, before sadness returns again.

When I open my eyes, my mother is crying openly with a bright smile on her face. My father is trying to be stoic, but his eyes are glassy with the threat of unshed tears.

"Beautiful," my mother whispers in awe.

My father stands abruptly and moves over to the side table. He pulls out a potion similar to the ones I remember seeing down at the market and opens it, throwing it at the door. A pale blue liquid coats the door, which turns to a mist that spreads out from the point of impact until we're in a room that is completely shielded by blue mist. It seems to have sealed off the cracks under the doors as well.

My father turns his intense green eyes to Talon. "We've got an hour before the spell wears off."

Then his gaze swings to mine, and I blanch at the fear I see in his eyes. "What do you know about vampire telepaths, Emerald?"

"Uh, only that there hasn't been one in hundreds of years. Why? You're acting like this is a horrible thing? I thought you would be more excited."

My mother gets up from her seat and squeezes herself next to me, reaching out to hold my free hand between hers. "It is good. But, some others may not see it that way. The last known vampire telepath was killed because he went mad with power. He could push images into people's minds like a form of torture, and eventually he grew too dangerous and had to be stopped. Some of our kind still remember him and the madness he instilled in people. We are just worried what people will think of your ability, especially when combined with the fact you are not completely a vampire."

My father hovers near the door, concern evident in his gaze. "What your mother is trying to say is your gift is powerful. Many people would kill to be able to do what you can, and would stop at nothing to get their hands on someone who had such a power."

Well, fuck. Not exactly the news I wanted to hear. I glance to Talon and know that now more than ever, I need to tell my parents about my magic. "Okay, so then you should also know that I, uh, accidentally drank a witch's blood when we were attacked, and now I seem to have witch powers on top of everything else."

The heavy silence in the room makes me fidget, and I wish Dev or Nik were here to crack a joke to lighten the mood.

My father's gaze swings to Talon, a menacing growl slipping from his lips. He dives across the couch, landing on Talon, who pushes me out of the way before my father can accidently hurt me. My mother grabs me and pulls me out of the fray, just as the couch tumbles backwards.

I watch in horror as my father throws a punch at Talon's face. My soul-tie just lays there and lets the blow connect. "Hell fucking no!" I spit out, feeling enraged. *Father or not, no one hits my soul-ties!*

My mother tries to keep me by her side, but I shake her off and march over to where my father is sitting over Talon, beating into him like he's done something unforgivable. I grab my father by the hair, lifting his head sharply so he can see the fury in my eyes as my beast pushes to the forefront. Her anger is nothing compared to my own.

My father growls as I use my grip on his hair to pull him off of Talon. When I know we're a safe distance from Talon, I fling him away, letting go of his hair as I do so. He takes a step towards Talon

248

again, but I move to block him. "I fucking dare you to try that shit again!"

"He was supposed to protect you!" He growls out each word slowly as if that will excuse his behavior.

"No, it was never his job to protect me. As a matter of fact, I recently fired all of them from their positions as my guards." I smirk, enjoying the dumbfounded look that crosses my father's face.

My mother takes a step forward to my father's side, wringing her hands nervously. "Emerald, you need guards. You could get hurt."

And that's exactly why they were fired. "I know I can be hurt, but what kind of life is it for any of us if the men I love are being ordered to protect me? We've come up with our own arrangement, but if you aren't happy with that, I can leave."

"Leave?" My mother's face pales at my words. I know it seems childish to be threatening to leave, but I just want to live a normal life. Sure, I was picked on in the pack for being an outcast, but here I am under a constant spotlight, and I'm not sure if that's any better. I would much rather find my own place, get a job like humans do, and support myself, instead of relying on them and feeling locked away from the world.

I could live on my own, and I think if I found a good outlet for my beast, then I'd be fine.

"You'd let her leave, knowing the danger she's in?" my father spits at Talon like this is all his fault.

Talon gets to his feet slowly, his face already showing bruises, which just amps up my anger. "Emerald is an adult. I know that's hard for you to hear, Ax, but the sooner you and Sie see her for the capable young woman she is, the sooner you'll realize just how amazing she is becoming and that she's able to care of herself. But if she wants to leave, Dev, Nik, and I will follow her wherever she chooses to go."

My heart melts, and I feel him wrap his arms around my waist from behind me. He rests his chin on my shoulder, meeting my father's eyes.

"I think it's best if we leave you guys alone now, so you can think over some things," I tell them, my own anger still needing an outlet. If I stay here much longer, who knows what I'll do?

Talon uncurls from behind me and laces our fingers together, sensing my boiling point rising through our tie. He leads us to the door, but then I turn, having one last thing to say.

My mother is watching us nervously, while my father's wolf is still clearly pressing close to the edge. As someone who has to deal with a wild beast on a daily basis, I can understand his struggle, but I need him to understand this.

"If you ever lay a hand on one of my soul-ties again, we're done. I lived without you for twenty-one years, so there's no reason to stick around if you don't respect either me or my soul-ties."

My father nods in understanding, and I let Talon guide me out of the room. I watch in interest as the pale blue mist starts to dissolve as soon as the door opens. It must automatically lose its power when the room's seal is broken.

We close the door behind us, and Talon hurries us into the elevator, pride oozing from him along the tie. As the elevator doors close behind us, he meets my eyes with an intense expression, before claiming my lips in a hungry kiss. The elevator beeps when we reach our floor. We break apart, panting, and walk back to our room in silence.

As I reach out to open the door, Talon stops me. "You didn't have to stand up for me in there, although I appreciate it. And if you truly do want to leave, Nik, Dev, and I each have houses of our own, so we would have plenty of places to stay. But I need to know, did you say that just to get a reaction from them, or did you actually mean it?"

I smile fondly and reach up to cup his cheek with my hand, running my thumb over the small line of stubble that's growing, taking in the small bruise that is slowly fading. "I meant every word I said. I want you three. My life has been so lonely, and if I have to leave behind the supernatural world to have a real life with you, I will do so willingly. You three are my future, and as much as I want to have a good relationship with my biological parents, we barely know each other. Besides, even if I left, I would still visit and try to build a bond with them, but I won't force it either way."

"Good," he says, pressing a light kiss to my cheek. "Now we have to tell the others what happened."

I grimace as he opens the door. Damn, I didn't think that far ahead. I hope they're okay with my decision.

Dev is the first to see me. He smiles brightly and moves towards me, pausing when he sees the state of Talon's face. "Jeez, Em, I know Talon is prettier than you, but did you really have to make his face that grotesque just to try and compensate?"

Laughter bubbles up in me. I know Dev is joking, but with everything that's happened in the last hour, I'm now in a state of hysteria, giggling like mad until my laughter dissolves into tears.

Nik appears suddenly, pulling me into his arms as tears continue to trail down my face. "I take it a lot more than just an explanation of Em's powers occured," he says over my head, looking at Talon.

"Yeah," he replies sadly.

Dev looks at me worriedly. "I'll make some coffee. It looks like she's going to need it."

I don't even care right now that they're talking about me like I'm not here. I just want a moment to get control of myself.

Chapter Thirty

IT'S A TRAP

Talon explained to the guys about everything that went down in my parents' suite. Their eyes went wide with shock when he told them about me threatening to leave.

I offered a nervous smile to try and reassure them, but I could tell they were still worried. Now, we're waiting for Nik to rearrange our schedule. We were supposed to be on patrol in a few hours, but the guys didn't think I was up to it emotionally, and for once, I agreed.

When Nik returns, he slams the door closed behind him, fuming as he enters. "Jasper is refusing to reschedule our patrol. We have to leave in an hour."

They each frown and their gazes swing to me. "It's okay, we can go."

Talon opens his mouth to object, and I place a hand on his knee. "Talon, the world doesn't stop because we're dealing with shit. Just give me a moment to myself, and then I'll be good to go."

"Em... We don't have to, we'll just go out somewhere and pretend we're on patrol. No one has to know," Dev suggestions with a look of concern.

"That's sweet, but if we're not on patrol because I was feeling emotional and someone ended up getting hurt, I'd never forgive myself. So, let's just get ready and go. Maybe we can grab me another coffee before we leave. Coffee always helps."

"Fine, but only one. I don't want you bouncing off the walls." Talon frowns, and I can see his worry. Even though he knows we're doing the right thing by leaving, he's worried about my emotional state.

I do agree, though, the last thing we want is for me to be hyper and distractible when I need to be concentrating on the task at hand.

AN HOUR LATER AND I'M STRAPPED WITH MY WEAPONS IN THE FRONT seat of the car, while Nik goes to grab us all coffee. I wanted to go in with him, but they pointed out it wasn't exactly easy to conceal the two short swords at my hips, whereas Nik's could easily be hidden with his ability.

After Nik returns with our coffee, we get back on the road. Talon sits in the passenger seat, giving me directions, and I think the further out of town we go, the more nervous he's getting. Not because of where we're heading, but because of my driving.

"Take a right up here," he directs, pointing up ahead. "Gently," he emphasizes when I press on the accelerator with a grin. His warning doesn't stop me from taking the corner at a sharp turn, and I let loose a carefree laugh when one of the guys squeaks.

God, Britt would love to hear about this. I send the image through to her mind, and let her feel my joy and happiness, hoping it will help brighten her mood. Sure enough, I feel the light trickle of her laughter in return, and it boosts my mood immensely. Anything to make her happy.

The place we've been assigned to for patrol is on the opposite side of the city, in a small housing district. According to the note Jasper left the guys, there was recently a reported incident of a vampire feeding on some humans in the neighborhood.

We finally reach our destination, and as I climb out of the car, I have to wonder if we're in the wrong place. There are only five houses on the street we're parked down, and they all appear abandoned. Either that, or everyone in this neighborhood goes to bed before the sun is down, which I doubt.

"Uh, guys? I have a bad feeling about this," I say, looking up at a flickering lamp post nearby. Like why the hell would a lamp post be flickering in the middle of a seemingly deserted street? *If that's not a bad omen, I don't know what is.*

Nik comes to my side and looks over at Talon and Dev with concern. "As soon as we find this vampire, we should leave."

I shrug and pull my jacket out through the open car window, putting it on to protect my bare arms from the night chill.

"Okay, but if you want to keep an eye on me, how about we all just stick together? Something tells me if we split up, things will go badly."

Dev reaches out and links our hands together, squeezing comfortingly. "We'll stay close, don't worry."

We make our way down the street, and the feeling of dread grows with each darkened house we pass. I let go of Dev's hand a minute ago, reaching down to grip my magic swords for comfort.

Britt thinks the man who made them knew I was meant to carry them one day, which is why no one has ever been able to access their power. They were specifically designed for me. They hear me when I'm in need and will come to my aid. What we don't know is what their limitations are as far as distance, or if they'll be able to appear no matter where I am.

During our mind training, Britt made sure to reiterate that she thinks I'm a lot more important than I give myself credit for, saying that if a witch had the foresight to craft such unique and powerful swords for me, then they must have seen a reason I would need them one day. Foresight is a very rare gift, and the visions are guided by the spirits to help keep the world running on its proper course.

As we walk down the sidewalk, the guys are on alert, while I'm lost in my thoughts. A shiver runs through me when I hear rustling from a nearby garbage can.

I freeze, sending my mental voice to Nik, who is closest to me. *Nik, did you hear that?*

He pauses mid-step, cocking his head to the side as he turns to me. "Hey, babe, are you okay? Is the dark frightening you?"

Talon and Dev turn at his mention of me being frightened, which I knew would give them some kind of signal. Me being frightened is not something that happens often.

Nik starts to takes a step back to me, and I frown as a sudden pain blossoms in my chest.

Talon and Dev pale, their eyes darting to my chest. I reach up, touching the source of the pain, and coming away with blood-soaked fingers.

My heart pounds, and I feel everything going fuzzy as I fall to the ground. Nik manages to catch me just before I hit the pavement.

My eyes close on the world around me, only to open in a new one. I see a hand in front of me, extended in invitation. I reach up and take the proffered hand and stand. I see a woman before me, and the last time I was here suddenly comes rushing back to me.

"Seriously? I'm dead again?! What the fuck?"

She smiles serenely. "I know it sucks, but the spirits choose when you die and when you don't. The day will come when you die, and you won't come back. That will be the day when the world is at peace again."

I frown, shaking my head in annoyance. "No, I don't want to keep coming back. I want you to make sure Britt has my gift. Fix what's broken with her, stop worrying about me," I plead, hoping she may give me answers about what is wrong with Britt, or may know of some way to fix her.

"My daughter is going to die. She messed with things she shouldn't have in her crusade for revenge, and the spirits are now taking what is owed to them, to ensure the balance is restored. She will join them when she dies, so do not fear. She won't be lost forever. She was always destined to become your guardian in the spirit realm."

My mouth gapes open in shock. The reason Britt's dying is because she made a few messed-up choices? Hell, I've made a shit-ton of bad decisions these past few weeks, but I don't see her saying, 'Oh, the spirits will rain hell down on you.' And what is this nonsense about Britt being fated to be my guardian? Why didn't she tell me this last time?

"I know you must have so many questions, Emerald, but you

were brought here for a reason. I have a message," she says ominously, and I roll my eyes. Because it can't get any fucking worse, right?

"Your soul-ties aren't the only bonds you will form. If you're going to survive, you need to be open to what happens with all your bonds, both current and new. You have many challenges to face, and I promise, it's all meant to play out like this. There will be tests meant to bring you to your knees, but you will emerge from the ashes so much stronger than before." Her gaze looks down at my hips, where the swords have started to emit a soft golden glow. "You better go now, your men need some help." She winks, and in a flash, I'm waking up on the ground, as fighting rages all around me.

I get to my feet, feeling a little shaky, and the swords at my hips are still glowing. I remember more of what happened than last time I died, but there's no time to think about that now.

Dev is being tackled to the ground by two wolves and a zombie, losing the battle against the overwhelming forces who seem to have appeared from nowhere. I take three steps, unsheathing my still glowing swords as I do. I feel the rush of pure power run up my arms as I kick the first wolf off Dev. Then I swing out, decapitating the remaining wolf and zombie in one swift movement.

Dev smiles up at me, looking relieved and grateful, but we don't have a chance to say anything before a witch's fireball goes flying past, narrowly missing us. I turn, my body vibrating with anger. "I've had enough of this shit!" I shout and stalk towards a bunch of witches who are displaying nothing but cockiness as they hide behind a shield of magic.

Dev reaches out to stop me, just as a fireball comes straight at us. I don't feel any fear, only the surety it won't hurt me. I lift the sword in my free hand and block the fireball, enjoying the gasps from the witches who are watching me.

I give Dev a smile. "Don't worry, Dev, I've got this. You help the others." I gesture over to Talon and Nik, who are still fighting off at least a dozen enemies.

He gives me a quick kiss before running over to the others, obviously trusting me to handle myself, for which I'm grateful. As he leaves, I wonder why the guys haven't called for reinforcements?

I turn my attention back to the witches. "Who do you work for?" I ask, hoping for some kind of explanation to this craziness. I'm not stupid to think it's coincidence that we've been ambushed every night I'm out with the guys. Especially when I know that no one else has been attacked while out on patrol. Hell, even when we went on our dates, we were attacked. The only time we weren't was when Britt and I snuck out during the day.

Hey, Britt? If you're still in range, do you think you could send some backup? We've run into a bit of trouble.

I don't get any response from either Britt or the witches in front of me, and I sigh, feeling annoyed. "Fine, don't tell me who sent you, but I feel I should warn you, no matter how many times you kill me, I will come back angrier and more vicious than before. So if you value your lives, now is the time to surrender."

An aged man steps between the witches coming front and center, and I cock my head in confusion. I've seen him before. He'd visited the pack a few times when I was growing up.

"We'll die before we surrender to you, abomination," he spits, raising his hands and flinging power at me. Before I have a chance to react, someone appears in front of me in a pop. The magic disperses and his head swings around, those cerulean blue eyes twinkling with mischief. "You called for backup?"

I smile at him and move forward so we're side by side. I'm glad Britt sent Blaine. He seems like the most ruthless of the bunch, and I could use that right now. "Why yes, I did. These idiots don't seem to want to tell me who they're working for." I pout playfully.

Blaine's gaze swings to the man who attacked me. "Jerry, how about you tell us who sent you here, and I won't tell Malcolm you're attacking someone under his protection."

I watch as the man named Jerry pales and the four women around him fidget nervously.

Jerry hardens his eyes, just as I hear Talon shout for Dev to watch out. I swing my gaze behind me and see that my men are overrun by

258

the remaining vampires and wolves. "Shit! Have you got this?" I ask Blaine, gesturing to the witches. "The guys need help."

He nods sympathetically, and aims a wicked grin at the witches before him. "Go, I can handle these pussies."

I splutter out a laugh and turn back to the mayhem behind me, realizing the guys are holding off twenty supernaturals to keep them from swarming us. They were so busy protecting me that they let themselves get overrun.

As I get closer, a wolf breaks through the guys' line of defense and dives for me. I twirl the swords in my hands as his body soars over mine, and drag them up along his belly. His insides spill out over me and he drops to the ground behind me dead.

The rest of the wolves who've been trying to break through start to become more ferocious. I smirk at them, licking the still warm blood from my lips as my beast presses forth, my eyes turning red with her influence.

I rush forward to help my men, attacking any who dare get in my way. The two wolves closest to me go down without a fight, my swords cutting through their throats like butter. Nik catches sight of me, and it's as if seeing me alive brings him a renewed determination, and he wields his sword like a fucking maniac. He cuts down three vampires and another witch who throws fire at him, which singes his skin.

In a matter of minutes, the attackers' numbers have been cut in half, and I watch as the vampires and witches take off at a run just as our reinforcements arrive. The wolves, however, don't know a lost cause when they see one.

They become more vicious in their attacks, fighting recklessly until only one of them is left. But instead of attacking any of us, the wolf goes straight for Blaine, who's behind me.

Seeing the wolf land on him sets my beast off in a rage, and we move faster than we ever have before. Before I can peel the wolf off of him, however, Blaine sends him flying back. I pause, watching in anger as the wolf runs off into the night with Blaine's blood coating its fur.

My beast wants nothing more than to follow, and I take a step in its direction when a hand lands on my shoulder. "Don't even think about it."

I sigh at the serious tone of Talon's voice and drop my hands. I watch as the swords disappear from them, only to reappear in the scabbards at my hip. That's so cool.

Talon looks me over, and once he's satisfied I'm unhurt, he takes charge of leading the reinforcements who showed up to help with the cleanup.

I turn my attention to Blaine, who is laying on the ground, with his eyes squinted shut in pain. The witches he had been dealing with lay dead a few feet away.

I drop to my knees beside him, furrowing my brow in concern. If that wolf did any fucking damage, I will hunt his ass down, and make him pay. My heart hammers at the sudden possessive turn of my thoughts, and I choose to pretend I didn't just think of Blaine as one of mine. It's just the magic affecting me, that's all.

"Blaine, are you okay?" I ask, looking him over to see where the wolf drew blood.

He opens his eyes, and I can see the pain within them. "Yeah, he bit my fucking neck," he mutters out angrily.

I bend over his body, unable to see the wound from my current vantage. I gasp when I see the full extent of it. *Son of a motherfucking bitch!* I pull my jacket off and press the fabric to his neck, ignoring the hiss of pain from him. Blood is seeping from the wound, making him go paler by the minute.

"Dev! Grab a healer!" I call out urgently, knowing even if Dev isn't close by, one of the others will be.

"Em, I don't need a healer," Blaine claims, his voice sounding tired.

I look down at him in horror. "I am not going to let you die, asswipe! You have a big gaping hole in your neck, so just stay quiet until the healer gets here," I command, pressing my other hand to his chest to stop him from moving.

He chuckles and reaches up to lay his hand on mine. "I meant, I just need some energy to speed up my natural healing," he says, raising an eyebrow as I flush in embarrassment.

Why am I acting this way? It's like I know what I'm doing, but I can't seem to stop myself.

"Oh, whose energy do you need? You can use mine," I say quickly, volunteering myself before I have any idea what I'm even offering myself for. *Shit, I really need to snap out of this.*

Blaine smiles up at me as if he can sense the internal dilemma I'm having. "If you really don't mind offering your energy, you just need to place your hand over my heart and will the magic to me. You'll feel it flow through you like a cold wave as it leaves your body. You may also feel like your core temperature is down for a few hours after," he explains, and I can't help but stare at the lucidity in his eyes. Shouldn't he be gasping for breath, approaching death even as we speak?

I place my hand over his heart, deciding to ask him after he's healed just why he's acting so calm and collected. I let whatever the hell magic is in me flow up through my body, and into my hand. Instead of a cold wave like he described, all I feel is heat. Not a bad heat, though, the type of heat you get when you're embarrassed, like a warm flush.

I watch the light flow from me through to Blaine and notice the way he's beginning to perk up. "It's so warm," I murmur, my body lighting up with need.

I avert my gaze from Blaine when he meets my eyes, his own filled with the same need I feel. Instead, I move the jacket away from his neck with my other hand and smile, relieved to see the wound is completely healed.

"Are you sure it's warm?" Blaine asks, his voice husky.

I turn my gaze back to him and nod. "I'm sure." Then I focus on slowing the flow of magic, cutting myself off as I fall back away from him, needing to stop touching him. It seems that touch is making these feelings worse.

Talon appears by my side to help me up as I sway a little, and I sink into his embrace. Blaine stands up, looking better than ever. "Thanks, Em. You okay?"

"Yeah, but how were you still lucid during that? You were bleeding out. Shouldn't there have been gasping or more dramatics? Something," I press, feeling frustrated, not with him, but myself for letting myself get this worked up over my best friend's husband.

I need to find a way to control these impulses. I should talk to Macy and see if there's something I can do to suppress the desire that I feel.

"I was using magic to stem the bleeding. That's why I said I didn't need a healer. I could have walked back to the coven like that, and I still wouldn't have died," Blaine explains with a shrug.

Well, fuck. So, I didn't need to share energy with him after all? Why didn't just he say that then? Ugh, men.

Instead of asking more questions, I turn to look at Dev, Talon, and Nik, who all seem bloody, but no more worse for wear. If it wasn't for the fact I can't smell their blood, then I would be freaking out, but I know they're only doused in the blood of their enemies, just as I am.

"Sie is gonna be pissed when she hears about this," Talon mutters.

I glare at him. "They attacked us first! They shot me! I had to go to that bloody abyss place before I came back. If anyone should be pissed, it's me!"

"Shot you?" Talon exclaims, his eyes widening in fear. He exchanges glances with Nik, Dev, and Blaine, and they all converge around me in a protective circle.

Talon's back is pressed to mine, while Nik's back is pressed to my right side, and Dev's to my left side. Blaine moved to press his back against my chest, effectively stopping me from moving.

"Um, guys? You realize everyone here is dead right?" I ask, unsure why they're acting like a bunch of cavemen.

Nik moves his head slightly to respond. "Em, we didn't find anyone among the dead who had a gun on them. That means the person who shot you is probably still out there, watching us," he whispers, and my eyes go wide.

The person who shot me is still out there? My beast rattles in its cage in my mind, wanting to shift and track the son of a bitch down right now.

It's quiet between the five of us as the guys listen for some hidden threat. Suddenly, I feel a pulling at my mind. I concentrate on the mental voice, hoping to find the source, when I hear the thoughts, as loud as if she was standing next to me.

Just fucking die already, you whore!

Fucking Heather! I should've known she'd be part of this bullshit!

Guys? I question, hoping to project to all four of them. Fingers crossed it works. *She's close by, I can hear her thoughts.*

She? Dev questions loudly into my mind, and I fight not to jump at the sound.

"Yeah, she," I breathe loud enough for them all to hear as my gaze swings back and forth over our surroundings, trying to figure out where she could be hiding.

We're in the middle of a residential street, and all the houses are still blacked out. Then again, she could be hiding inside one of them.

I twist around, looking at each house carefully and see the shine of a reflection up in a window.

If I can't have him, neither can you.

I don't think, pushing Talon down to the ground just as the bullet that was meant for him grazes my shoulder.

Dev and Nik move as one to the house the shot came from, and Blaine crouches down over Talon and I, erecting a magical barrier around us. The people who arrived to clean up and offer us assistance now swarm around us, with half of the group breaking off and heading towards the house, like Nik and Dev did.

A few minutes later they return, with Nik dragging an unconscious, or possibly dead, Heather behind him by the hair.

My father appears from nowhere, and Blaine lets me up. He grabs me by the shoulders, looking me over carefully before helping Talon to his feet. When my father's gaze crosses to Heather, he smirks cruelly and looks back at me. "How do you feel about me laying a hand on this one?" he asks, jerking his head towards Heather.

I smile wickedly, and I imagine it looks scary as hell to see me covered in blood while wearing a grin so vindictive. "Oh, you can do whatever you want to her. In fact, let me know when the interrogation starts," I smile sweetly, and he nods once.

"You heard her, boys. Take her to my fun room."

At his command, a few of the vampires come forward and pick her up, carrying her limp body between them.

My father looks back at me with a proud smile. "It seems I underestimated your strength, Emerald, and for that I am sorry. Now, you really should head back to the coven and feed."

I nod, feeling ravenous. The energy used in the fighting, my death, along with the energy I gave Blaine has weakened me immensely.

On top of that, it's been a few days since I've actually eaten anything or consumed any proper amount of blood.

I need to set some kind of alarm or something to remind me to feed. If I don't, I'm going to end up starving myself.

Chapter Thirty-One

LITTLE KILLER

EMERALD

The moment the door locks and we're safely back in our room, Talon growls and advances on me. "When was the last time you fed?"

"Ahhhhhh..." I delay answering, knowing he won't like the truth. "It may have been a couple of days ago, or..."

His eyes harden at my words, and Dev and Nik take a step forward, as if ready to intervene. "Have neither of you fed her in the past few days?"

They glance each other, before all three turn to me, their gazes pinning me to the spot. I go on the defensive. "What? I told you my body hasn't exactly been telling me I need to feed. What do you expect me to do? Set some kind of alarm every day to make sure I remember to feed?"

I don't bother to tell them that is exactly what I was thinking of doing. If they want me to feed regularly, they're going to have to help remind me, because I already have enough going on in my life. I can barely keep track of normal stuff, let alone when to eat or drink blood.

Talon sighs, shaking his head sadly. "You're right. There are still so many changes going on in your life, and I didn't think to remind you of the little things we view as simple, or take for granted. Whatever it is about your dual natures, or triple natures as the case may be, it seems to block out some of your basic instincts. I will help remind you to feed, or maybe we'll make up a schedule, so we'll all be able to

265

stay on top of it. If your bloodlust is satiated, you should be able to go without food for longer period of time."

I sigh, relieved that he didn't get angry. This must be the reasonable Talon who isn't under a hex. "For what it's worth, I'm sorry, too. I should have kept better track of when I last ate or fed, but I just forgot."

He smiles and takes a hesitant step closer. I meet him halfway and he wraps his arms around me, giving me the hug I really need right now.

Dev and Nik stare at Talon's back with dumbfounded expressions at his behavior, and I smirk, poking my tongue out at them, not caring how childish I seem.

Talon breaks the hug after a long moment, pressing a gentle kiss to my lips, and I sigh. One kiss from him I think would be enough to wake me from a spelled sleep. He gives so much of himself in just one little kiss.

When the kiss is over, he turns so he's facing the guys and looks down at me with an amused grin. "So, who's feeding our girl?"

Dev fidgets as if he's about to deliver some bad news, and I glare at him, growing frustrated. "Just spit it out, Dev."

"Uh, well, it's just that we have to leave to go meet up with Linc now. We're supposed to inform him if there are any new attacks, and we need to let him know there are wolves running around. Not that one wolf can really do too much damage against the pack, but still, as part of our agreement we have to tell him if anything like this ever happens," he says with a touch of annoyance in his tone.

Nik frowns. "I still think he only did that so he could demand updates on Em any time we go. I mean, why can't it just be one of us? Why did he stipulate all three of us have to go?"

Talon growls and rubs his temples in annoyance. "Okay, we'll go deal with this, and then we can come back and feed you right after. Is that okay? Do you think you can last that long?" Talon asks, his voice thick with concern.

"Why don't I come with you, though? I could always feed from you in the car," I suggest hopefully.

The door to the room opens, and my mother storms in, her eyes blazing. "You're not going, Emerald. Every time you leave the coven, you end up getting attacked. That tells me someone is hunting you, and I won't let you get hurt again."

I go to open my mouth to argue, but I see my father coming in behind her, shaking his head with a look of concern, and decide to let it go. For now. Besides, without all the guys here, it might give me the chance to do what my beast is dying to do: hunt.

She looks at my guys with hard eyes. "We're leaving now. Lincoln has agreed to loan us more wolf guards to stay here and protect Emerald while we are gone, but we must hurry before whoever is behind these attacks figures out our next move. Macy and Britt have already left for their coven in the hopes they too, can get extra wards around the church. We've also cancelled any markets until this mess is all sorted. We don't want to risk the chance someone will try sneak in."

She turns to leave without another word, and my father gives me a sympathetic smile. "Sorry, Em. She gets pretty protective when someone she loves is threatened. Something I've heard you have in common." He winks, and I blush under his scrutiny.

Nik and Dev each offer me a quick kiss, before following my mother, and my father trails after them. Talon lingers behind and pulls me close. "Listen, Em, I know you want revenge for the wolf almost killing Blaine, but please, don't do anything stupid while we're gone. Just stay here, and we'll be back before you know it."

I don't say anything, knowing I can't keep that promise. The moment they leave, I'm going to hunt that wolf down and make him regret ever coming near me or mine. My beast growls her agreement in my mind, and Talon hesitates, as if he knows what we're thinking.

He goes somewhat reluctantly, as if he's afraid to leave me, but he should know by now I am more than capable of protecting myself.

I wait for ten minutes after they leave before I go and change into a different set of clothes, a pair I can easily throw away. I'm already thinking about the cleanup of his body, and ensuring no one will ever find out what I did.

The scent of the wolf who escaped after ripping a hole in Blaine's neck is still burned into my mind, and I am more determined to find him than anyone could understand. He hurt my guys. Then had the audacity to try and kill my friend's husband, someone I've grown to like. No, he doesn't get to run.

I will hunt him down like the dirty animal he is.

My backpack is just big enough to stash a spare set of clothes and a small dagger. I don't bother packing anything else, knowing when I shift, I won't need it.

I tread slowly through the halls, doing my best not to sneak, knowing if I look suspicious, I'll be more likely to be pulled to the side and questioned.

When the elevator opens up on the ground floor, I step out, freezing at the sight before me. Felicia is chatting with my grandparents, her eyes sparkling as she laughs at whatever they just said. She notices me, taking note of the bag on my shoulder, and works to keep my grandparents distracted as I turn and walk in the opposite direction to the back door.

When I reach the other end, I smile at her gratefully and mouth 'thank you' before sneaking out into the cool night air, determined to get rid of this vermin.

I don't know how long I walk before I come across a park lined with benches and trees surrounding the path.

My nose twitches as I breathe in the scent of the wolf I'm tracking. I drop the bag to the ground, looking for a place to hide it and get undressed.

Along the beginning of the path, near the first bench is a shrub with red berries, and I decide it's probably the best I'm going to get for a hiding place. I strip down, letting my beast push forward, the shift taking me in seconds.

My beast utters a growl from behind the bushes, our senses tenfold now we're free. I let her have more of the reins and take a back seat as she hunts for our prey.

As I prowl through the trees, I notice the scent of humans has pretty much been overwhelmed by that of the wolf we're hunting. He must have frightened off the humans and ran out here to hide. What surprises me is the fact he hasn't come out and attacked me yet. If he's walking through the trees, he would have scented me by now.

I turn a corner and see an old maintenance shed, most likely used to store the park workers' tools and such.

I take a step towards it, just as the wolf leaps out from the darkened trees beside the shed. He lands on me, but I throw him off in one quick movement, my beast filled with rage. *He is nothing! We will crush him!*

A growl rumbles in my chest as he takes a step forward, and I push power out at him. *I am an Alpha! How dare he defy my orders?*

The human part of him wars with his wolf, and he ends up attacking. My beast is thrilled by this, though. She knows I want to kill him, not in cold blood, but in the heat of combat.

We roll around on the ground, his jaws snapping precariously close to my neck as we fight to gain the upper ground, until he slips up, leaving himself exposed for my attack. I bite into his chest, the part concealing his heart, and clamp down, enjoying the spray of blood that fills my mouth as his heart beats frantically, trying to heal his wounds. My beast smiles triumphantly in my mind as she tugs out part of his rib cage, his heart coming along with it.

The light in his eyes dies out like the insignificant ant he is, and I sit on my haunches, my beast receding to the back of my mind now that the threat is gone. I lap at the blood that flows freely from his wound.

When I finally feel satiated, I sit up, stretching out lazily. I hear a twig snap from behind me, and I spin with a ferocious growl, protecting my kill. I take in a quick sniff, scenting the wolf and know he wants my meal.

The wolf in front of me is someone I know, though.

"Well, look what we have here. I have to say, Emerald, I thought you'd be too soft for such carnage."

My beast instantly calms at his presence, and I feel the shift collapse back inside me as if she was never free to begin with.

I stand naked before Lincoln and look down at the dead wolf at my feet, not feeling an ounce of guilt. All I feel is hungry. While my wolf side has just been fed, my vampire nature still requires sustenance.

"Go ahead, little killer. Drink your fill."

I frown, wondering if he's disgusted by the thought and decide maybe he's just testing me to see if I will. I move around behind the dead wolf, pulling his lifeless body into my lap and latching onto his neck.

While I feed, I look up at Lincoln, expecting him to have left or be observing with revulsion, but instead he watches me with lust-filled eyes.

When I'm done, I drop the wolf's lifeless, drained body and stand, not caring that I'm now covered in even more blood.

Lincoln's eyes run over my naked body. Despite the blood, his eyes are burning with desire. He takes a step towards me, and my beast purrs in eagerness. My nipples harden as he gets closer, until he's right in front of me.

He reaches out, running a hand down my ribs, caressing the edge of my breast as he does so, and smirks cockily when I let out a sharp gasp.

"Don't," I breathe out as he lowers his mouth to hover over mine.

"Just a taste. That's all I want," he murmurs. My heart hammers wildly in my chest, moisture pooling between my legs.

He takes my silence as a yes and presses his lips to mine. I respond eagerly as his hands slide down to my waist, holding me pressed against him, so I can feel his growing arousal.

Before I know it, he ends the kiss, backing away with a grin. "Told you, killer. Just wanted a taste."

My heart is pounding loudly as I try to process what happened, and I realize what I just did. I let him kiss me!

"Stop... calling... me... killer!" I growl between clenched teeth as I glare at him, blaming him for everything that just happened, when deep down, I know it's my fault. There's something wrong with me. Hell, I'm attracted to my best friend's husbands for God's sake! That's not normal!

He leans against the tree nearest him and smirks as his eyes flick from me to the body on the ground. "But it suits you so well. I thought you were going to be some weak little mate who needed protection from others, but you, you don't need anyone to protect you, do you?"

He watches me intently, but I remain quiet, not wanting to admit that if anyone needs protection, it's the people who mean me harm.

"That's your secret, isn't it? Those three soul-ties want to protect you, but at the end of the day, I bet you'd be the one better equipped to protect them, than the other way around. Hell, I bet with proper training you could take on an army by yourself." He laughs and takes a step away from the tree to look down at the lifeless body.

I follow his gaze, worried about what to do. Lincoln is surely going to inform my parents about this kill, which is just going to lead to me getting in shit. It's not like I can call one of the guys and say, 'Oh yeah, sorry, guys, but I may have left the coven to hunt down this piece of shit who hurt Blaine. Now I need help disposing of the body.'

I doubt they'll ever trust me again, but I needed to do this. I know it's stupid when Blaine isn't really mine, but I couldn't stand the thought of the wolf returning to finish the job.

"Don't worry about the mess, killer. I'll take care of it for you."

I let a sigh of relief cross my lips and relax a little, but then a thought occurs to me. "Wait, why would you do that?"

He opens his mouth, when I remember the guys and my parents had been going to meet Linc earlier. "Shit, if you're here, the others must have already headed back to the coven. I need to go."

He grabs my arm, preventing me from running off. His sky blue eyes stare deeply into mine, offering reassurance. "Relax, killer. I left them with my Beta so I could come take care of this little problem, but you just beat me to it. And as for why I would do that for you, it's because you're my mate. Even if you killed an entire pack, I would cover for you."

The sincerity in his tone has me confused as to how to respond. On the one hand, it's sweet that he would go to such lengths to protect me, but hiding the fact I killed a whole pack? I don't know whether to go 'Awww, that's sweet' or 'You're a fucking psychopath.'

"Why did you come here, though? You could have just sent your Beta," I ask in confusion. To have an Alpha doing the pack's dirty work is rare to say the least.

He reaches a hand out, trailing it down my cheek, which sends goose bumps all over my body. "I'm an Alpha, my little killer. That means protecting what's mine, not letting others do it for me."

He takes a step closer, pressing his body against my naked one. "My Beta can handle all the political bullshit the coven likes to go through. But when someone threatens my mate, I will burn down the world if I have to in order to destroy them."

My heart picks up pace at his declaration, and I find myself asking, "How do you know I'm your mate?"

He smirks, catching my bottom lip between his teeth. He pulls on it gently before letting go. "I know the same way you do, even though you're trying to ignore it. The racing of your heart, the way your eyes dilate when I'm staring at you, then there's the feelings that ignite when I kiss you. You may not feel it as strongly as I do, but when I touch your skin, my body feels like it's being electrified, in a good way."

I pant softly as he speaks, feeling the truth of his words. "Can't you feel it, even a little bit? The pull when we're around each other?" he asks, running a finger down my collarbone, and I fight the sudden shiver, blaming it on the cold.

I take a step back out of reach. "No, I have three soul-ties. Whatever this is, it's not real. It's just hormones. I feel nothing for you."

"Fine, if you want to live in denial, then have it your way. But there's gonna come a time when you can't fight it anymore. Your wolf already craves me, and the longer you deny the mating, the stronger the need will get."

He walks around me and over to the little shed, pausing to look back. "Well, come on, I gotta hose you down if you don't want to drag wolf blood through the coven. I'm assuming you don't want your soul-ties to know you were out on this little run?"

"Oh, thank you," I say gratefully. I hadn't even thought about hosing off the worst of it before going back. I hadn't really thought much beyond killing the wolf, to be honest. It's a very smart idea, though.

He brings over the hose and I shiver in the cold, waiting for the spray of water to hit me. He aims the cold stream at the worst of the blood-soaked areas before slowly running the water over my chest, taking great care like I'm some kind of plant that needs watering. I glare at him, and he chuckles wickedly, gesturing for me to come closer. "I need to do your hair. It's gone from strawberry-blonde to a pale pink."

I sigh and bend down so he can run the water over my hair, rinsing out as much of the blood out as he can manage. Hopefully, I'll be able to sneak back in without anyone catching sight of me, so I can shower it off more thoroughly before the guys return.

He turns the tap off with a sigh. "There, all done. Better get some clothes on, though. I doubt the people of St. Louis are prepared to see you roaming the streets in the buff."

I shake my head and walk away to find the bush where I hid my clothes. Lincoln follows after me, talking as he does. "You know I don't want you to give up your soul-ties, right? I understand they're just as important to you as I am. I just want you to give me a chance."

"Look, Linc, I don't know what to do with that information. One of my soul-ties is already encouraging me to date you, and I just... I want to do what I want without everyone telling me what they think is best. I want the chance to figure shit out on my own without constantly fearing a reprimand for my actions."

"I can understand that. I just want you to know that if you ever need me for anything, you can call on me and my pack. I'll drop everything for you."

With that last statement, he turns and strolls back to the dead wolf, hiking it up over his shoulder like a hunter carrying its trophy. "See you around, killer." He winks and takes off quickly in the opposite direction I came from.

The moment he's gone from sight, I resume my walk through the trees to where my bag is. I throw the same clothes back on, not bothering with a bra or underwear, knowing I'm just going to destroy these clothes anyway.

I rush back to the coven, and manage to sneak in the front door and up the elevator without being seen. Thankfully, the guys aren't back yet, so I hurriedly climb into the shower, keeping my clothes on as I do. I scrub the clothes down using the scented body wash I find so overpowering. If it worked to hide my arousal around my parents, I'm hoping it'll do the trick this time, too.

Once I'm sure there's no scent of the outside left on them, I strip off the wet clothes, throwing them in the corner. Then I get to work, washing my body and hair at least five times to ensure there's no chance of someone picking up the scent of the wolf I killed.

When I'm finally satisfied, I get out of the shower and quickly dry myself off before wrapping myself in a towel. Then I move over to the vanity and proceed to brush my teeth, my tongue, the inside of my cheeks, and even the roof of my mouth, trying to be as thorough as possible.

After I'm done and dressed, I look around, trying to decide where I can take them to be destroyed. I'll just stash them away in the hamper for now. Who knows, maybe a maid or something will take care of them? Then again, I haven't seen a maid in here before. Well, if the guys ask why they're wet, I'll just say I wasn't feeling well and went into the shower to vomit. The majority of the blood is gone, as is the scent of wolf so the likelihood of them figuring out what I've done is pretty slim, but it still doesn't calm my racing heart.

Shit! I am so goddamn stupid. What if the wolf's blood comes back up? What am I going to say? Maybe that I decided to try a bag of the cloned blood because I got hungry waiting for them?

I pause as I step out of the bedroom, feeling a sliver of guilt sneaking in. I hate that I'm going to lie to them, but I don't think they'll understand why I did what I did. Even I'm having trouble comprehending it and I'm starting to wonder more about Britt's words about being territorial of her guys. My desire to kill that wolf didn't come from just worrying about him being out there, but the fear of him hurting Blaine again.

The cabinet under the TV is open, so I pull out one of the guys' video games, knowing then my high emotions can be explained away by the violence and fast-paced movements.

About an hour later they come home. I'm just lazily sitting there, beating the guys' high scores when they fan out behind the couch, looking down at me.

"How'd the meeting go?" I ask on the end of a yawn. My car crashes into the wall of the track when my eyes drift closed, and I concentrate to get myself back on track.

Talon sighs, sounding frustrated. "It was horrible. The Alpha decided to skip out on the meeting, instead running off to go do something reckless. He didn't come back until we were just leaving, and was carrying the body of the wolf who attacked Blaine. He threw the wolf at our feet, as if he were boasting about killing him. Lincoln was covered in blood, cuts, and scratches, and he seemed far too proud of his stupidity."

I concentrate on the game in front of me, trying not to react in any way.

"Was he okay?" I ask nonchalantly.

"Who knows?" Nik shrugs, sitting down opposite me. "All I know is what he did was stupid and reckless. There are people who rely on him, a whole pack of them, and he just up and left to go hunt down a rogue without any assistance."

And that's exactly why I won't ever admit the truth about this to them. If they are this upset thinking about Lincoln doing that, imagine how much worse they'd react knowing it was really me.

Dev groans, stretching his neck and sits on the floor in front of me, grabbing the controller from my hand. "I don't know, I kinda think it was pretty awesome. He knew he was strong enough to handle the threat and went to take care of it. In some ways, I admire the strength he showed and his drive to protect those he cares about," he muses. I look down to see him giving me a cheeky grin, and that's when I realize.

He knows I killed the wolf.

Chapter Thirty-Two
SAFE HOUSE

EMERALD

I roll over, snuggling into the warm body next to me in bed, feeling a hardness pressed against me. I reach my hand between us, stroking his length. A hiss escapes him, and I open my eyes to meet Talon's green ones.

He smirks at me, and my breath stops at the realization we're alone. For the first time since we got together, there is no one to stop us. I see in his eyes that he had the same thought, and he thrusts his hips upward, causing me to stroke his length.

"I knew it was only a matter of time before I'd get you all to myself."

Talon rolls on top of me, and I can't help but reach up, wrapping my arms around his neck and pulling him to me with a moan.

He kisses me slowly, his tongue gently brushing against mine. Then he breaks the kiss, peppering light kisses along my jaw, moving down to my neck. His tongue traces over his name on my skin, and I shiver in anticipation.

I watch as he slowly moves down to my breasts, trailing his tongue over my hypersensitive flesh.

He circles my right nipple before gently sucking it into his mouth. His fangs scrape the edge of my breast when he releases me.

I pant with need, wanting him to hurry up, but loving every second of his touch.

He moves to my other breast, sucking my nipple into his mouth with care so his fangs don't scrape the sensitive nub, and I can't tell if I'm relieved or annoyed by that.

He continues his exploration, moving down to the top of my panties and pressing a gentle kiss to my waist. Then he sits up, peeling my panties off and throwing them across the room somewhere.

A banging sounds in my ears, and at first I can't believe just how hard my heart is beating, but then Talon dives from the bed and I realize the sound came from the door. Talon spins and comes to stand with his sword raised, just as the bedroom door flies opens.

I prop myself on my elbows, wondering who the hell would just barge into our room like that. I squeak in surprise, hurrying to pull a blanket over my naked body when I see my father standing in the doorway, his chest heaving.

Talon relaxes, lowering his sword, and my gaze is drawn to his other 'sword,' which is still standing at attention. He sees the direction of my gaze and curses, tucking himself back in his boxers before facing my father.

"What's going on?" I demand, giving Talon a moment to compose himself. When he turns back around, my father glances between us with a frown, and I fight not to laugh. He looks somehow both embarrassed and angry by what he just walked in on, but I'm just annoyed my father caught me naked. Sex is natural, especially between soul-ties, but there are some things you don't ever want your father to see.

His gaze settles on me, seemingly unable to look at Talon. "Your mother and grandparents have called an emergency meeting. You're to get dressed and come down to the hall immediately."

He turns to leave, but then glances back. "No lingering. It's urgent and all our safety depends on this."

We both nod in understanding, and he leaves the room in a rush, not even bothering to close the door behind him.

Talon rushes over to the dresser, pulling out clothes. Then he goes through my drawers, grabbing out a a t-shirt and pants and throwing them at me. I hurriedly get dressed, knowing when someone says it's urgent, it could mean the difference between life and death.

We make our way out of our room, and down the hall to the elevators. For the first time since I arrived here, it's packed. We squeeze inside, heading for the ground floor. I notice that most of the vamps in the elevator are carrying bags over their shoulders, as if planning to leave.

We arrive on the ground floor, and head straight to the sanctuary, where the pews have been moved up against the walls so everyone can stand assembled as they wait to be addressed.

Talon sees my parents at the front of the room, and grips my hand. As we approach them, I can see my mother arguing with my grandparents, and their voices carry over the chatter enough for me to hear.

"She will be fine with her ties. That's the reason the spirits gave her three," I hear my grandfather say in his gravelly voice, and I roll my eyes at the faked concern in his tone.

My grandmother chimes in. "Exactly! Really, Sierra, you need to stop treating her like a child and let her learn how to protect herself. If you coddle her, she'll just become a self-entitled brat."

"Jeez, I can feel the love all the way from over here, granny," I mock, taking pride in the nickname, because I'm sure she'll hate it.

She cringes as if I just called her old. Which, technically, she is. Just because she looks like she's in her twenties doesn't change her actual age, which is over six hundred years old.

Dev and Nik spot us from across the room and stride straight to us, while my parents and grandparents remain silent.

"What's going on?" Talon asks from my side as Nik and Dev come to flank us.

Before either of them can answer, a drum sounds in the room, drawing everyone's attention to the front steps of the altar, where five vampires walk up and stand to face the room. I feel each of my guys straighten in a show of respect, and I have to wonder who exactly these people are.

The older-looking man in the middle steps forward. His black hair shines in the light, but you can see slight streaks of gray on the side, which makes him appear more mature than the others. The men surrounding him seem like nothing but teenagers when compared to the power of the first man.

He waits for the room to go quiet before addressing all the assembled vampires. "You have all been summoned because of a breach in our security.

"Last night, one of our own was attacked, and this was not the first time, either. We have to believe it's safe to assume this individual is being targeted, and for everyone's safety, we are evacuating the coven until further notice."

Voices rise throughout the room, and I shrink in on myself, knowing I'm the individual he was referring to.

"QUIET!" the man booms into the room, and all sound immediately ceases. "We had an intruder infiltrate our walls twenty minutes ago. For that reason, we have deemed the coven unsafe and will be evacuating everyone to the safe houses. You each know the evacuation procedure for reaching the safe houses. One guard will be assigned to take ten of you. Split into groups, unless otherwise instructed, and move to your assigned safe houses. Once there, the guards will be kept up to date on the threat and you will be advised when it's safe to return."

He steps back and gestures to my mother, who climbs the steps and faces the coven with a grim expression. "I know this is a trying time, and hopefully we'll soon discover who is orchestrating these attacks and be back before you know it. Until then, stay safe."

She steps down, effectively dismissing everyone, and I watch in fascination as the assembled crowd immediately walks in an orderly fashion to each of their guards. It's like they've done this before. Maybe they have drills to prepare for these kinds of situations?

Then my mother approaches me, her heart in her eyes as she does so. I can see fear, worry, and anger flashing in her eyes one after the other, before they finally settle on fear. She obviously doesn't want to leave me, but her position in the coven would require more protection than mine, even if I am her daughter.

"Emerald, you'll be going with Talon, Nikoli, and Devin. They will make sure you're protected. We have no idea who to trust right now, and Nikoli is one of the guards who has a safe house assigned to him. Only he knows its location, so you should be safe while we think of what to do next." She sighs heavily and pulls me into her arms, hugging me tightly. "Please stay safe."

"Mom, it's okay. I can protect myself just fine, and each of these guys would die before letting anything bad happen to me," I reassure her, gesturing at Dev, Nik, and Tal who stand to the side, with pride in their eyes that I trust them enough to keep me safe.

A sudden bright smile lights up my mother's face, and tears glisten in her eyes. "You called me 'Mom,'" she murmurs as a tear falls. I fidget, feeling uncomfortable. It was nothing but a slip of the tongue, but it obviously meant more to her than I could imagine.

"Uh, yeah, I did." My cheeks flame at the admission.

"Fine, I'll pretend it didn't happen, this time," she says with a smirk, pulling me in for another hug. "But you did call me Mom," she gloats happily before backing away.

Before I can respond, my father steps into my personal space, wrapping me in a bone-crushing hug. "I know I screwed up, but I really don't want you to leave. I want to know my daughter. After this, I promise I will do better," he whispers into my hair, and I feel my eyes watering. I blink furiously to hide any trace of tears.

"Be safe, sweetheart," he urges as he steps back, grabbing hold of my mother's hand. He tries to remain stoic as they walk away, but I see the sheen in his eyes, giving him away.

My grandmother looks over at me with a harsh expression, while my grandfather follows after my parents without a word. "I heard about your weapon of choice."

I nod, waiting for some kind of remark about how I'm not worthy, but what she says next surprises me.

"You've made me proud, and one day soon, we will train together. I will show you exactly how to wield your weapons." At that, she gives the guys a nod of respect and turns to catch up with her husband and my parents.

"Well, that was kind of nice, I think." I mean, she did also imply I have no idea how to wield them, but I suppose I'd better just take what I can get for now.

"Okay, we'll go upstairs and pack the bags. You guys head to the garage, and we'll meet you there in ten," Nik declares, and then he and Dev take off at a run.

Sure enough, ten minutes later, they meet us in the garage, each carrying a massive duffle bag. They walk straight to my car, and I climb in the back, knowing that if Nik is the only one who knows our location, it would make the most sense for him to drive.

"Why are we going to separate safe houses? Why not just one main one?" I ask as Talon gets in beside me.

Nik and Dev throw the bags in the trunk before climbing in. Dev turns to me, having heard my question. "Because, if someone is being targeted, in this case you, then it makes no sense to send you to the same place as everyone else. That way, on the off chance we're attacked, then no one else will be harmed."

"So, we're being used as bait to see if I am the reason for all the attacks?" I ask, feeling slightly annoyed. *Why not just throw me outside on the street and see what happens if that's the case?*

Nik shakes his head as he starts the car. He drives out of the garage, and onto the streets of St. Louis.

"It's not just that, we have to be careful because Sie may actually be the intended target. Someone could have been trying to target you, so they could use you to get to her. We have to be prepared for any and every possible scenario. Besides, it won't be that bad. I made sure to tell Torie the location of my safe house and blood oathed him not to tell anyone else. So, Britt and the guys will be there when we arrive. They left as soon as the call for the meeting was put out," he says, smiling at me through the rear view mirror.

"Well there's that at least. So, how long will we be at this safe house then?"

The car becomes dead silent, and I know the answer isn't going to be one I want to hear. "Well," Dev says nervously after a moment, glancing over at Talon who remains stoic. Dev rolls his eyes before turning to me.

"We could be there anywhere from a few days, weeks, or maybe even months. It all just depends on when we find the person responsible. We may even have to move around if we find out it really is you they are targeting," he adds on, sounding matter-of-fact, like he didn't just tell me we could be in hiding for months.

I sit back in the seat, feeling completely defeated, and I turn to stare out the window as we drive. Hopefully, we get to this safe house soon because I want nothing more than to just sit under a nice warm shower and recharge. It seriously feels like this day will never end.

Chapter Thirty-Three

BROKEN

EMERALD

We've been driving for a little over an hour when I start to get worried. I know they said the safe house is on the outskirts of the city, but as to how far it is, I have no idea, and the longer we drive, the lighter the sky becomes as dawn quickly approaches.

I look out at the pale purple light, my heart hammering in fear. If we don't get there soon, the sun is going to come out.

"Guys? You do know the sun's almost up, right?"

Talon turns to me with a grin. "Sun won't kill us, Em, it just weakens us. We'll be fine. We should just get–"

I jolt forward suddenly, my head hitting Nik's seat as my baby is rammed into from behind. Talon grabs me just as the car is struck again on side, the screech of metal on metal hurting my ears.

The last hit sends my car spiraling out of control, and we end up slamming into a tree on my side. The windows are smashed on impact, and glass flies all over the seat. I smell blood and frantically look at each of the guys to see who's bleeding. Talon is still conscious, but his eyes are dazed, and a line of blood runs from his forehead to the bottom of his chin.

I reach back, unclipping my seatbelt and slide closer to Talon. "Talon, baby. I need to know if you're okay? I have to check on the others."

His eyes meet mine, and he looks me over to make sure I'm not

285

hurt. Then he lifts his hand slowly, waving me away. "Fine. Check them." The words come out slurred, and I know he needs a moment to heal.

Instead of waiting for him to heal so he can help, I climb through the middle, and try to shake Devin awake. He remains unconscious, so I give his face a light slap. I watch as he seems to gather consciousness for a brief moment before closing his eyes again.

"Dev, honey, you need to look at me," I plead, ready to slap him again.

He blinks his eyes a few times, seeming to become more aware. When he realizes where he is, his eyes shoot up to mine.

"Shit, Em, you okay?"

"I'm fine, Talon took the brunt of the damage. I just need to make sure you're alright before I check on Nik."

The sound of a car door slamming reminds me it wasn't an ordinary accident we were just in. I look out the rear view mirror, seeing the two cars who hit us, both with damaged front ends, and four people striding towards us.

I debate in my mind over what to do, but I know there's no real option. The sun is only minutes away from being fully up. If I wait any longer, the people who hit us will be able to use the daylight to their advantage. I need to get rid of them myself.

Talon sees the look of resolve in my eyes as I stare out the window, and reaches forward to grip my arm. "Em, don't."

"I'm sorry, I have to. You guys can't protect me this time. Please, trust me to keep you guys safe," I say, before opening the door on Dev's side and crawling over his lap, Talon's grip too weak to really keep me contained.

Dev struggles to climb out of the car after me, but his seat belt keeps him locked in place. I look back at Nik, who hasn't woken up yet. "Look after Nikoli, and I'll get rid of these idiots."

I tune out their protests and make my way to the back of the car, wishing I was wearing something more badass than just sweats and a tee. My body heats for a moment and when I look down, I see myself dressed in a white tank, sheer enough to show my black bra, and a pair of matching black leather pants. Even my shoes have changed from slip on ones I had when we left the coven to a pair of steel-toed boots. It must have been my magic. Normally, I'd take a second to appreciate my newfound power, but I have more important things to take care of right now.

I prowl around the back of the car and shake my head at the man standing before me. My heart pounds in my chest, a sliver of fear running through me before I lock it away in my cage along with my beast. He can't hurt me anymore.

Brendan and Xander stand beside him, looking smug as hell, while Sophie is off to the side, looking bored out of her mind. Movement behind me has me flicking my gaze back, and I see Joel and Brian strolling out of the tree cover beside the highway, as if they had been waiting there all along.

"I don't know what you want, Jeremy, but I'm only going to give you this one chance. Leave here now, and no one has to die," I offer, holding my palms out peacefully.

Talon and Dev try to climb out of the car, but I push magic at them, keeping them locked inside where they're safer. Jeremy doesn't want them, only me.

"The only one who will die here today is you, you filthy abomination," Jeremy spits angrily, the vein in his temple bulging.

I crack my neck to each side, concentrating on my swords, and wishing them into my presence. My hands grow warm and a second later, my swords appear in my hands, giving me a sense of being reunited with a lost piece of my soul. I watch in satisfaction as everyone takes a step back.

"What's wrong, Jeremy? Your spies didn't tell you about the new powers I have?" I boast with a smirk, twirling the blades in my hands.

"I suppose it's you I have to thank for that, though. After all, you're the one behind the attacks, aren't you?"

His face reddens, just as I hear a twig snap behind me. I spin, sword poised at the throat of the newcomer. When I recognize who it is, however, I lower my sword and smile.

"Who the fuck is that?" Xander growls, and I roll my eyes. Of course he would be intimidated by Lincoln. He's a monster of a man after all, and his wolf shows in every move he makes. The sign of a true Alpha.

"I'm her mate. And I take it you're the idiot who fucked her over," Lincoln says, his voice lowering dangerously and his gaze remaining fixed on Xander. Lincoln must have made the connection based on how similar Xander looks to the vamp I nearly beat to death, because it's not love and rainbows he's projecting right now. No, it's death and darkness.

"Whoever the hell you are, this is none of your business," Jeremy spits out, his voice filled with rage.

Rather than answer Jeremy, Linc instead turns to me. "What do you say, killer? We take three each? That would be fair," he suggests, appealing to me with a wicked smile.

I give a grin in return. "How about you take one, and I'll take the rest?" I suggest, just as I feel the wind shift behind me.

I leap out of the way just as Joel and Brian's wolves land on Linc. Trusting him to handle his attackers, I turn to face my former trainer, my brother, my ex-lover, and one of my biggest bullies. "Brendan, I beg you to reconsider this. There's another way we can handle this. The vampires, witches, and wolves here have all accepted me, why can't you?"

My brother lets out a war cry, running towards me, and I sigh in defeat. It's like he's been brainwashed. The second he gets within touching distance, I kick out and send him flying across the road, wincing as his arm is grazed on the broken glass that litters the ground from the crash. I don't want to hurt him if I can avoid it, but he's not giving me much choice.

Xander and Sophie are in front of me in the next instant, coming at me with their fists. I use my swords, swinging around and cutting them along their arms deep enough to do some damage.

Sophie lunges for me, and I stab her straight through the heart, watching as the girl who bullied me for years drops to the ground in a heap, her lifeless bloody looking no different than when she was alive, other than the blood of course.

Arms wrap around me from behind in a death grip. I smell Xander's disgusting pine scent on me, which makes me want to hurl.

Jeremy takes a step towards me, ripping the swords from my hands and throwing them on the side of the road with a smirk. "You forget, Emerald, that I trained you. There is no move you can do that I won't know how to counter."

I burst out laughing, feeling my smirk grow as wariness enters his expression. "You trained me during normal class lessons. After a year of your training," I spit out, emphasizing just how much I hated his stupid class, "I went to my dad and asked him to teach me. Every day, morning and night, he trained me."

My head flies back, headbutting Xander. I ignore the pain in my skull and stamp on his foot, following it up with an elbow to the solar plexus, before summoning my swords.

Jeremy's eyes widen in surprise, but he doesn't have time to stop me. My swords descend in an arc from each side, decapitating him in one smooth motion.

I look down at the severed head at my feet, before kicking it over at Brendan, who has just gotten up. His eyes fill with hatred and he glares daggers at me

"Leave, or suffer the same fate," I warn him coldly. I'd rather not fight my brother, but I won't back down if he decides to continue on this path.

Linc joins me, wrapping an arm around my shoulders, and the scent of fresh blood comes off him in waves. We stand side by side and watch as Brendan grabs Xander by the shoulder and takes off, climbing back into one of the cars.

I wait until they're out of sight before rushing back to my car, letting my magic shielding drop. I peek in and see that Talon and Dev both look remarkably better, at least if their anger is anything to go by. "You can be angry later. How's Nik? Is he awake yet?"

Dev's gaze goes from angry to worried. "No, and I don't think he will. He's lost too much blood, and we didn't think to bring any with us."

Linc and I walk around the other side of my baby, and he peels the car door off. Looking at Nik slumped in the driver's seat, I can see just how much blood he's lost.

Holy shit! The whole floor is soaked in blood and more keeps dripping down from where a piece of metal is jammed into his leg.

"Shit, that looks fucking gross!" Linc exclaims, looking down at the metal in fascination. "You know, one of us is going to have to pull that out if we want him to heal."

Talon nods grimly, still looking at me, refusing to acknowledge Lincoln's presence. I sigh heavily. There is no way I can pull that out.

"Linc, can you do it? Just give me a second? I have a feeling Nik isn't going to react well to having a huge chunk of metal being ripped from him."

He nods, and crouches down beside the car, looking over the metal as I try to concentrate my thoughts. *Nik? Can you hear me? I need you to wake up.*

Tired. His mental voice alone is filled with exhaustion, and I realize we don't have much time.

I lift my arm, and hold it in front of his mouth, but then Talon grabs me from the back, stopping me. "Em, you haven't fed in days. If you feed him now, you'll pass out."

I meet Dev's eyes, and we share a look of understanding. He pries Talon's hand from my wrist. "She has fed recently, don't worry. Just let her do this."

Lincoln grins up at me, the secret between us thickening the tension in the air. After this, I'm going to have to tell Talon and Nik, because keeping this from them is killing me. I also think it may help if they know I was able to drink another's blood without throwing it back up like some scene from a horror movie.

I nod down at Linc, signaling I'm ready. Then I turn my gaze back to Nik, waiting for the vampire side of him to lash out.

As if there's not enough tension already, Linc starts counting. "One, two–"

"Son of a bitch!" I cry out as Nik's mouth latches onto my wrist, ripping skin away as he feeds desperately.

He feeds for a good few minutes before letting go with a gasp, his eyes red as his vampire pushes forward to the edge of control.

"Get in the car," he growls at me, and I nod, quickly climbing over his lap to squeeze into the back. Linc smiles at me through the broken back window. "I'll follow in my wolf form and make sure no one else tries an attack," he murmurs softly. Then he turns, shifting into a white wolf, with black markings similar to a panda. I chuckle and remind myself to bring it up at a later point.

Nik starts up my all but demolished car and speeds down the road without a word, Lincoln's wolf following after us. The wind rushes in through the side of the car where the door has been ripped off, but luckily, we're only on the road for a short time before Nik turns down a long drive off the highway. The safe house was literally only ten minutes away from where we were ambushed.

We come to a stop and Dev quickly climbs out of the car. I worry though, that there's no other cars around. Britt should have been here by now.

Talon and I climb out from the passenger side of the car and go around to help Nik out. Just then Lincoln shows up in his wolf form, loping towards me. Nik places an arm over Talon and my shoulders, and his head lolls to the side, breathing in the scent of my neck with a moan.

"If you're still hungry, Nik, you can feed. I have plenty left to give," I reassure him, moments before his fangs sink into the tender flesh of my neck.

I groan as he takes his fill, Talon standing there keeping him propped until he is able to stand a little steadier on his own.

Nik finally lets go, licking the spot once, which makes me shiver. Linc's wolf rushes over, rubbing his body along mine as I waver, my vision blurring. Nik must have taken a lot more than I realized for me to be feeling this faint.

We walk up the cobblestone path to the two-story brick house just as Dev opens the door for us. Dev takes my spot, leading Nik to the couch. I frown, feeling an odd tingling in my chest and over my soul-tie marks.

"Have you contacted the coven?" Talon asks Dev as they help Nik sit down. Then Dev hands him half a dozen blood bags he found in the fridge.

"Yeah, I called Axel and Sierra, and told them what happened. No one has heard from Brittany or the guys, though. Sierra is leaning towards the possibility that Britt may be the mole," Dev reveals, sounding disappointed.

I shake my head, trying to clear the ringing sound in my ears. "That's impossible. Britt is my best friend. She would die before betraying us."

Dev opens his mouth to say something else when I suddenly sway, almost falling over Lincoln.

Talon grabs me at the last second, looking down at me with concerned eyes. "Emerald, you alright?"

"Yeah, I just don't feel good. My body is all fuzzy..." I mumble, having to swallow my saliva multiple times after I speak. It's like that feeling you get when you haven't had enough to drink. "It must just be blood–"

I drop to the floor, crying out in pain, with my heart pounding loudly in my ears. Pins and needles break out all over my skin, and a ringing builds in my ears, growing ever louder until with a final snap, I scream.

Time ceases to exist as I'm overwhelmed with the agony that consumes my soul.

The sound of whimpering is the first sign I'm back with the world of the living, but the echo of pain I feel within my soul makes me wish I was dead.

Gray wolf eyes look down at me as Lincoln nudges me gently with his nose.

My head lolls to the side as I look for the others, no longer able to feel their presence. When I catch sight of them, they all wear the same traumatized look I imagine is on my own face.

The door bursts open, and some sort of commotion ensues, but I really don't care. *Just kill me and get it over with. Life isn't worth living without them.*

Britt's face suddenly appears above me, looking down at me with the same grave concern as Linc, but I close my eyes, unable to meet her gaze.

Her best friend is gone, and the only thing left is a broken shell.

"Em, what's going on?" she asks in a whisper. I open my eyes, and a rush of tears spills out.

"My soul-ties are broken."

EPILOGUE

BRENDAN

THE DOOR SLAMS OPENS AND I PUSH FORWARD, MY ANGER FUELING ME as I make my way further into the witches' coven.

Jeremy, my real father, is dead and I don't know how to handle all this rage inside me. All I want is to kill that piece of shit who calls herself my sister. For one tiny moment, I thought she cared about me, by letting me live, but it turns out she was just gloating. She wanted me to see Jeremy dead and bring me to my knees.

"Where is he?" I demand of the witches who are gathered around a formal dining table, eating their breakfast.

Just then, the witch in question walks through the double doors leading to the kitchen, carrying a plate of pancakes. He places them on the table before walking towards me.

My wolf is pushing at the seams of my sanity, demanding I make that bitch pay for the death of my father.

"I want her killed. She killed my father! I demand justice for that!"

He smirks at me and reaches out to grab a drink from the table.

"Don't worry, young wolf. It's been taken care of. This very second, the abomination will be wishing she was dead."

"Wishing she was dead, and being dead are not the same thing!" I growl out, craving vengeance.

"All in due time. Now, if you please," he mutters, gesturing at the people gathered, "I have guests."

He moves around me, effectively dismissing me. I turn on my heels and make my way back through the house. When I get to the entryway, I stop at the sight before me. A vampire stands there, blocking my exit from the house.

"What do you want?" I growl, my wolf looking for any reason to attack.

She smirks at me, and takes a step forward, handing me a card. "Don't worry, young pup. I kept your father well informed, and I'll be sure to keep you in the loop, too. The time will come when she's all alone, and then you can take her out. She won't have her soul-ties to keep her alive anymore."

The woman turns around and opens the door, and I can't help but watch her, mesmerized. "Why are you helping us?"

She shrugs, looking over her shoulder at me. "Because I, too, believe she is an affront to nature."

She takes another step from me, ready to leave. I call out, because I have to know. "What's your name?"

"Felicia." She winks and steps out of the house, into the midday sun. It doesn't appear to bother her one bit, in fact she seems to bask in its glow.

I look down at the number on the card, intrigued by this vamp. She might very well be of use to me.

I'll bide my time. Sooner or later, Emerald will finally be alone, and I'll make her pay for everything. She took my father, and killed my biological father. I won't let her take the pack too. When I'm done with her, she'll regret ever being born.

NOTE FROM AUTHOR

Ah! I hope you guys don't hate me for leaving you all on a cliffhanger like that but I promise I am working my fastest to get book three out. I also wanted to leave a note for the people who might be confused by some parts. I tend to be a seed planter author, meaning I like to leave little clues throughout each of the books so when the ending finally rolls around, its like that 'OH!' moment.

Thank you guys so much for reading book two and I will keep you all updated by my page or in my group. Thank you to everyone who gave this book a chance.

Printed in Great Britain
by Amazon